THE WILD BREED

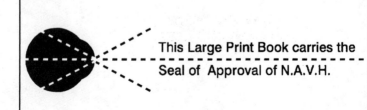

This Large Print Book carries the
Seal of Approval of N.A.V.H.

THE WILD BREED

FRANK LESLIE

WHEELER PUBLISHING
A part of Gale, Cengage Learning

GALE
CENGAGE Learning

Detroit • New York • San Francisco • New Haven, Conn • Waterville, Maine • London

GALE
CENGAGE Learning

LIBRARY OF CONGRESS CATALOGING-IN-PUBLICATION DATA

Leslie, Frank, 1963–
    The wild breed / by Frank Leslie.
        p. cm. — (Wheeler Publishing large print western)
    ISBN-13: 978-1-59722-799-5 (pbk. : alk. paper)
    ISBN-10: 1-59722-799-4 (pbk. : alk. paper)
    1. Gunfights — Fiction. 2. Rescues — Fiction. 3. Mexico — Fiction. 4. Large type books. I. Title.
PS3552.R3236W55 2008
813'.54—dc22   2008016840

Published in 2008 by arrangement with NAL Signet, a member of Penguin Group (USA) Inc.

Printed in the United States of America
1 2 3 4 5 6 7 12 11 10 09 08

To Dad and Betty

CHAPTER 1

Looking around cautiously, jaws set grimly, Yakima Henry climbed a low rise stippled with crumbling volcanic rock and paloverde shrubs, and reined in his sweaty, dusty mustang — a blaze-faced, coal black stallion with the fire of the chase in its eyes.

Brush snapped and rustled ahead and to the left, and the half-breed touched his pistol grips. A mangy brush wolf bounded up a nearby knoll, a charcoal-colored jack hanging limp from its jaws. The coyote turned its head to give an owly, proprietary glance over its shoulder, then dashed over the rise and disappeared in a mesquite-choked arroyo.

Yakima Henry was tall and broad shouldered, his muscular frame sheathed in a sweat-stained buckskin tunic, blue denims, and brush-scarred chaps. A leather thong strung with large, curved grizzly teeth hung around his neck. He wore undershot boots, and a flat-brimmed, dust-caked plainsman was angled low on his forehead. Dropping his hand from the stag-horn grips of his .44, he shifted his gaze again to the horse tracks dropping down the rise and disappearing in the chaparral.

The tracks were those of four horseback riders herding four unshod mustangs toward the town, which lay a good half mile away. The town consisted of a handful of log and adobe dwellings and cow pens clustered in the vast, rolling desert, bordered distantly on all sides by the bald crags of isolated mountain ranges.

Beyond Saber Creek, the ridges rippled away like ocean waves, foreshortening into the misty, blue-green reaches of Old Mexico.

Yakima shucked his Winchester Yellowboy from the saddle boot under his right thigh. The mustangs belonged to him. The rustlers had taken them out of his corral when he'd been off hunting more wild horses to break and sell to the army. They'd hazed them through the slopes and arroyos, dropping down and away from his small shotgun ranch nestled at the base of Bailey Peak, no doubt intending to sell them south of the border.

Out here, if the Apaches didn't burn you

out, the rustlers and border bandits would steal you blind. On the upside, he had no near neighbors, for the trouble this country bred was damned discouraging to most.

Yakima levered a fresh shell into the Yellowboy's chamber, off-cocked the hammer, set the barrel across his saddle bows, and booted the horse off the ridge, his shoulder-length black hair winnowing out behind him in the hot breeze.

A few minutes later, horse and rider gained the stage road, followed it past the first cow pens and horse corrals of Saber Creek, then across the dry creek bed that the town was named for, and into the sun-baked little village, somnolent and sweltering in the late-afternoon heat.

Buildings of whip-sawed cottonwood, sandstone blocks, and adobe brick lined the narrow main street over which a lone ranch wagon clattered, heading toward the opposite end of town. Chickens pecked along the boardwalks. Dogs lazed in shade patches. Few people were about, but Yakima noticed a couple of silhouettes peering at him through sashed windows.

Cicadas whined, a goat bleated unseen in the distance, and the faint tinkling of a piano rode the breeze, drowned by the occasional screech of a shingle chain.

At a fork in the street, Yakima turned the stallion right, angled around the town's cobbled square surrounded by old Mexican adobes and a sandstone church with a frayed rope hanging from the boxlike bell tower, and drew rein before a stout, log blacksmith shop.

He stared at the eight horses tied to the hitch rail fronting the Saguaro Inn Saloon and Hotel on the right side of the street, just ahead. The horses stood hang-headed in the shade of the brush arbor — all eight dust streaked and sweat foamed. Only four were saddled. The rifle boots tied to the saddles were empty.

Yakima booted the black up to the hitch rail, dismounted, and dropped the reins in the ankle-deep dust and manure. "Stay here and don't start no fights."

Patting the horse's slick neck and resting his rifle on his shoulder, he stepped onto the boardwalk. He raked his jade green eyes — which to some seemed startlingly incongruent in his otherwise dark, Indian-featured face — across the four barebacked, unshod mustangs. Then, chaps flapping about his legs, sweat streaking the broad, flat plains of his dust-caked face, he wheeled from the street and pushed through the batwings.

He paused in the cool shadows just inside the door, letting his eyes adjust as he took in the room — the ornate mahogany bar and back-bar mirror running along the wall to his right, the dozen or so tables to his left, the stairs at the back. A little man with spats and close-cropped gray hair played a piano — a slow, Southern ballad that might have been recognizable had it been played in the right key — against the far wall, below the stairs. Near him, four hard-faced hombres in ratty, dusty trail garb played cards, Winchester and Sharps rifles leaning against their table or resting across empty chairs nearby.

One of the two men facing him wore a couple big pistols in shoulder holsters revealed by the thrown-back flaps of his spruce green duster.

To Yakima's left, a girl's voice said, "Well, look what the cat dragged in! Did Mr. Henry get tired of taming horses and come to town to see what *else* needs tamin'?"

Yakima turned to see a small, pale-skinned brunette, clad in a low-cut, knee-length red dress, sitting alone at a table, her bare knees crossed. The dress was so sheer he could see her small, pear-shaped breasts through it, and nearly all other aspects of the pretty girl's delicate anatomy, including a mole on the inside of her right thigh. A strap hung off her skinny shoulder.

She smiled up at him, showing a missing eyetooth and wagging a dirty, slender foot, the red paint on her toenails as chipped and scaled as the siding on an old barn.

An empty shot glass and a half-empty beer mug sat on the table before her. Her admiring gaze ranged across Yakima's broad chest and yokelike shoulders before climbing back to his face.

She twirled a finger in a lock of her curled hair.

He nodded. "Rose."

"Yakima?" The bartender suddenly rose from behind the bar — a string bean with wide-set eyes, thick pomaded hair, and a pronounced overbite. Floyd Sanchez scowled savagely. "What the hell are *you* doin' here? I thought the sheriff done banned you from town for breakin' up my place and every *other* place in Saber Creek!"

"Go back to work, Floyd," Yakima growled, barely favoring the man with a glance.

He sauntered forward, his spurs chinging on the rough puncheons, the barrel of his Yellowboy repeater still resting on his shoulder as he approached the table before which the four saddle tramps played cards.

One of the men facing him — the man with the duster and the double-rigged holster filled with matched Smith & Wessons — glanced up at him, a stogie in his teeth, five cards fanned out in his left hand.

He was a hulking hellion with a freckled, sunburned face and a thick, red beard still slick with sweat and coated with seeds and trail dust. He smelled like horses, mesquite smoke, piss, and stale tobacco.

"Hey, lookee here," he sneered around the stogie, elbowing the round-faced Mexican beside him. "We got us a newcomer."

The Mexican looked up, black eyes rheumy from drink. He, like all the others, had looked toward Yakima when he'd first pushed through the batwings, but he, like the red-bearded, double-rigged gent, feigned surprise at seeing him at their table. He grinned, showing chipped, crooked teeth, including one of gold, inside his thin black beard. "You want in, amigo? Always room for one more if you got money. We don't play for trade beads!"

He elbowed the red-bearded gent and laughed through his teeth.

One of the two with his back to Yakima glanced behind him, running his slit-eyed gaze up and down Yakima's tall, rugged frame. He turned back to the table and

13

tossed some coins into the pile before him. "I don't care if he's packin' gold ingots fresh from El Dorado. I don't play with half-breeds."

The red-bearded gent leaned toward him, canting his head toward the round-faced Mexican. "You play with greasers, but you don't play with half-breeds? Where the hell's the logic in that?"

Suddenly the piano fell silent, and the little, gray-haired piano player swung his head toward the room.

The Mexican grinned, chuckling again through his teeth, as he stared glassy-eyed at Yakima. A corn-husk cigarette smoldered in the ashtray beside him, near a big Colt Navy, its brass chasing glistening in a shaft of sunlight from a window behind him.

Yakima's voice betrayed a hard note of irritation, matter-of-fact contempt for losing two days' work by having to chase stolen horses — horses he'd worked damn hard for the past three weeks to break and ready for the remount sergeant at Fort Huachuca. "You seem like a right tight group, so you boys can just keep playin' with yourselves. I'm here for those green-broke mustangs you stole outta my corral. And I'm here to make sure it don't happen again. Get my drift?"

"Ah, shit," the bartender complained behind Yakima. "Charlie, fetch Speares!"

The little man rose from the piano bench, adjusted his spats, and slowly walked across the room as though skirting an uncaged lion, shuttling his fearful blue-eyed gaze between the cardplayers and Yakima. When he was past the table, he broke into a run and bolted through the batwings like a bull calf who'd just been steered, his running footfalls fading into the distance.

"Breed," said the big hombre with the shaggy red beard, a dirty black Stetson tipped back on his red curls, "you ain't callin' us *horse thieves,* now, are ya?"

"Since you spoke English, I naturally assumed you could understand it."

"Them horses — they are not branded," said the Mexican, canting his head toward the batwings. He had a BB-sized white spot just left of his left, inky-black pupil, and it seemed to expand and contract at random. "How can you prove they're yours, huh?" He shrugged his shoulders, as if deeply perplexed by his own question.

"I didn't brand 'em because the U.S. Cavalry generally likes to do that themselves. But I don't need to prove anything to you coulee-doggin' sons o' bitches. I tracked *them* and *you* here, and I'm takin'

15

those horses back with me. But I'm willing to wait for the sheriff, so we can all sit down and discuss it, civilized-like, over a drink." Yakima quirked a challenging grin. "That is, if you are."

The red-bearded hombre cut his eyes around the table. The Mexican poked his tongue between his teeth and hissed a chuckle. One of the men with his back to Yakima half turned his thick neck and long-nosed face and grumbled, "Me, I personally don't like bein' accused of long-loopin. Not by no half-breed, 'specially."

The gent next to him — square-built and wearing a fancily stitched doeskin vest with a rabbit-fur collar, said in quickly rising octaves, "Especially one that smells as bad and looks as *ugly* as fresh dog shit on a parson's *porch!*"

He hadn't gotten that last utterance out before he slid sideways in his chair, a silver-chased revolver maw appearing under his right armpit, angled up toward Yakima. Yakima stepped quickly to the left, snapped his rifle down, back, and forward, smashing the octagonal maw against the side of the man's head, just above his ear.

The man screamed and jerked sideways as the pistol under his right arm popped, stabbing smoke and fire, and drilling a slug into the ceiling above Yakima's head.

The report hadn't stopped echoing around the narrow room before the half-breed swung the Yellowboy back in the other direction. The other hardcase was halfway out of his chair, reaching for his own holstered pistol, when the Yellowboy's barrel caught him in the same place it caught the first gent, throwing him sideways with a coyote-like yelp.

He hit the floor with the report of a hundred-pound sack of parched corn dropped on a flatbed railcar.

"Half-breed son of a bitch!" shouted the red-bearded gunnie as he bounded straight up, lifting the table and thrusting it forward with one hand while reaching for one of his big pistols with the other. As the table tumbled toward Yakima, shedding bottles, glasses, playing cards, and coins, the red-head aimed a Smith & Wesson .44 straight out from his shoulder.

Stepping straight back from the table, Yakima snapped up the Yellowboy, aimed quickly, and squeezed the trigger.

"Ahhshhh!" the red-bearded gent yelled as the thundering rifle punched a slug through his left shoulder, jerking his exploding pistol enough that the slug sheered past Yakima's head to shatter the window at the other end of the room, causing the whore, Rose, to break into an unladylike stream of epithets.

"Goddamnit!" Sanchez shouted, ducking down behind the bar. "Take it the *hell* outside, you sons o' bitches!"

As the red-bearded gent twisted back, stumbling and raging, the Mexican, on one knee, extended his Colt Navy at Yakima; he chuckled drunkenly, spittle bubbling on his lips.

He snapped off one wayward shot before Yakima, quickly ejecting the spent brass from the Yellowboy and seating fresh, sent him tumbling straight back off his heels with a dollar-sized hole in his chest. The Mexican threw the pistol straight up toward the ceiling, where it knocked out a hanging lamp with a wicked crash and rain of shattered glass.

Pistols popped around the wheeling half-breed, one searing a shallow trough along his right cheek. Crouching and levering the Winchester mechanically, he sent the two shooters on both sides of him spinning, rolling, and dying against opposite walls, blood painting the floor and the square-hewn ceiling joists around them.

Another pistol popped in the shadows at the room's rear, the slug tearing across the top of the half-breed's left arm before spanging off an iron pot somewhere behind the bar and evoking another outraged shout from Sanchez. Wafting powder smoke churned so thickly that Yakima could see only a shadowy glimpse of the red-bearded gent about fifteen feet away.

But in the silence following the gunfire he could clearly hear the click of a hammer being cocked.

Ignoring the fiery sting in his arm, Yakima snugged the Yellowboy's butt against his gun belt and, crouching, fired three quick rounds, the empty shell casings clinking onto the floor behind him like the last dying notes of a player piano.

A shout rose from the smoky shadows. "Son of a *bitch!*"

A pistol flashed and barked. Yakima rolled right and came up firing at the bulky shadow bounding toward the stairs. He'd fired only two shots, hearing the slugs bark into wood and plaster, before the rifle clicked empty.

He blinked through the wafting powder smoke. The red-bearded gent, holding a long-barreled revolver in each hand, stumbled up the stairs. His spurs chinged raucously, his boots hammering the steps. He paused, extended a pistol out over the railing, and shouted, "Dog-eatin' son of a bitch!" and fired.

The slug careened past Yakima's right ear and thumped into the floor.

The half-breed dropped his rifle, gained a knee, and grabbed his .44 from the holster on his right hip. He fired twice, one shot gouging the adobe wall behind the fleeing redhead, the other clipping the railing near his right-hand gun, evoking a startled yelp.

The redhead fired twice more at Yakima as he gained the top of the stairs. Yakima triggered his .44. The man lurched forward and dropped to a knee, grabbing his right shoulder. He poked the pistol through the rail pillars, showing his teeth as he glared down the revolver's shivering barrel.

The pistol flashed and popped, the slug chewing into the floor and throwing slivers across Yakima's boots. The half-breed sprinted to the bottom of the stairs, grabbed the newel post, and sprang up the steps two at a time as the redhead scrambled to his feet and bolted off down the hall, bellowing like an ox in an abattoir.

The half-breed had just gained the top of the stairs and lined up his gun sights on the redhead's back, halfway down the hall, when the man lunged to his right and pulled a girl out of an open doorway. Screaming, curly brown hair and pink night ribbons flying around her head, the tall, half-dressed dove — Stella was her name — twirled around in front of the man, who snaked a hand around Stella's neck, pulling her taut against him.

Aiming his pistol over her shoulder, he marched her down the hall toward Yakima, a savage grin stretching his lips.

His guffaws echoing off the walls with the girl's screams, he triggered his six-shooter. Yakima flinched as the slug sliced over him and barked into the railing.

He aimed as the man and whore drew near, but he couldn't risk hitting Stella. As another bullet sizzled past his face and over the main saloon hall behind him, he scrambled back to his feet, dropped two steps down the stairs, and pressed his back to the wall.

The redhead bounded out from behind the wall, glaring savagely over the girl's shoulder. "Die, ya mangy half-breed son of a bitch!"

Yakima snapped up his Colt, but before he could fire, the redhead thrust the horrified girl toward him, his six-shooter roaring and blossoming flames over Stella's tangled, sleep-mussed hair. The slug tore across the top of Yakima's shoulder, missing his chest only because Yakima's boot slipped off the step as he threw his hand out for the whore.

21

The gun roared again.

Stella screamed as she flew forward into Yakima. The girl's head buried in his throat, he fell straight back to hit the stairs hard, one hand flailing for the rail beside him.

Missing the handhold, Yakima flew sideways, and then the stairs were pitching and rising and falling around him as he and the girl, limbs entangled, rolled together like a single human wheel down the steps.

The redhead howled and triggered several more shots in their direction before Yakima and the girl piled up together at the base of the stairs, the half-breed half reclining against the wall, the girl sprawled on top of him, her wrapper coiled around her waist, bare breasts pressed against his chest.

She moaned and lifted her head slightly.

Yakima blew her hair from his lips and peered up the stairs through the wafting powder smoke. The redhead was gone, heels thundering down the hall above.

Yakima gentled the girl to one side, scrambled out from under her, surprised to find his right hand still wrapped around his Colt's stag-horn grips. "You all right?"

She muttered incoherently as she flopped onto her back, bare breasts jostling. She didn't appear to have taken a bullet.

Shaking the cobwebs from his brain,

Yakima bounded back up the steps, cursing under his breath as he turned left down the hall, stopped, and extended his Colt.

"Hold it there or take it in the back, you long-loopin' son of a bitch!"

At the far end of the hall, silhouetted by the window behind him, the redhead wheeled, thrusting his long-barreled S&W straight out from his shoulder.

The Colt in Yakima's hand leaped and roared, stabbing flames.

The redhead triggered his own revolver into a half-open door on the left side of the hall as Yakima's slug tore through his chest and punched him back through the window. The glass crunched and shattered loudly, and the flour-sack curtains billowed outward under the weight of the man's falling bulk.

His upper body dropped below the level of the window while his knees hooked over the sill. He ground his heels into the wall, trying to hold himself. His head shot up, and Yakima caught a glimpse of his red hair and beard as he flailed for the sill with his left hand.

Then the head and hand dropped out of sight, his legs fell slack as the life left him, and the weight of his upper body pulled his dusty, high-topped boots up the wall to the sill and out the window.

A second later, a wooden, thumping clatter rose from the street, and Yakima winced.

Apparently, the redhead had landed on a woodpile.

Someone cleared his throat loudly in the saloon below. Yakima turned. Three big men wearing deputy sheriff's stars were spread out in a triangle before the bar, cradling shotguns or rifles in their thick arms, staring up at him like schoolmasters who'd found the culprit who'd hidden the snake in the girls' privy.

CHAPTER 2

Staring down at the three lawmen scowling up at him from the saloon hall, their eyes openly hostile, Yakima Henry opened the loading gate of his Colt .44. He shook the spent brass onto the floor, where the shells clattered and danced around his boots.

Goddamnit, he couldn't win for losing.

"How many times you boys gonna let that son of a bitch wreck my place?" complained the apron, Floyd Sanchez, who came out from behind his bar to inspect the damage. "Good Lord — just look at this mess!"

Yakima replaced the spent brass with fresh shells from his cartridge belt. He flicked the loading gate closed and spun the cylinder.

"Don't worry, Floyd," one of the deputies said, cradling his sawed-off gut shredder in his arms and staring like an eager fight-dog up at Yakima. "We'll put it all to right for ya."

Dropping the Colt into its holster thonged

on his right thigh, Yakima sighed heavily and, boots thumping, spurs ringing, started down the stairs, glancing into the saloon hall to his left.

The little man who'd fetched the lawman stood by the batwings, fingering one of the doors as if deciding whether he should stay or leave.

Sanchez pointed at him. "Speares done banned him from town for a good three weeks, but here he is, tearin' up my place just like he done *twice* before!"

"Once before," Yakima corrected as he reached the bottom of the stairs. "And I didn't start that one any more than I started this one."

He reached down, scooped his Winchester Yellowboy off the floor, and scrubbed sawdust and tobacco from the brass-chased barrel. When he came up again, he was facing all three sheriff's deputies, lined out before him as though for inspection, except their heavy brows were bunched and their little eyes were hard.

Yakima wondered where the sheriff had found this bunch; they didn't look all that more housebroken than the four he'd just turned toe-down.

"You boys look real good," Yakima said with a taut smile. "Speares should be proud he hired such able-bodied lawmen. You look reasonable, too, which means, I hope, you're gonna let me walk out those doors and fetch my horses without trying to stop me."

He started forward between the one on the right and the one in the middle, but they stepped together quickly, closing the gap. He didn't know their names but, like Sheriff Speares himself, they all had the look of former outlaws, which they no doubt were. One or two probably even had some paper on him.

Yakima knew that Speares preferred hiring outlaws because they were more honest than most folks, and they weren't skittish about killing. Besides, deputies were hard to find in this backside of dusty hell. Speares had even offered a badge to Yakima, who'd turned it down as much because he couldn't stand the thought of living in town as anything else.

"The Mex is right," said the one on the left — a hard-bodied, snaggle-toothed hombre holding a Henry carbine across his chest, his funnel-brimmed hat pulled low over his tiny eyes. "Sheriff Speares done barred you from town, breed."

"For a month," smiled the tall, dark man in the middle, who rested the sawed-off barrels of his double-bore shotgun casually on his shoulder. "It ain't been near a month since you broke up the mercantile and broke the jaws of the mercantiler's two boys."

"I feel real bad about that," Yakima said. "But they were cheating on my freight bill, and called me a liar. True, they added a diamondback to my wagon box for free, but that still don't make us even." He glanced at the dead men around him and continued in a reasonable tone. "I didn't intend to come in here. I followed them long-loopers in. I didn't break any laws, either — Mr. Sanchez and Rose will tell you those boys made the first moves — so I'll be gathering my stock and heading out."

The man across from Yakima — pimple-faced and with a patch over one eye, a long, corded rope scar around his neck — took one step straight back and leveled his Winchester at Yakima's chest. He grinned. Like the others, he enjoyed the power of the tin star on his chest. And, like the others, he enjoyed using it, even when he had no call to.

"You're comin' to jail, breed. When Speares gets back from Tombstone, we'll discuss what to do with you. Meantime, you can clean up the jailhouse. Me an' the boys let it get really *bad* in there!"

"Hope he can work with his feet shackled," mused the dark deputy in the middle, mouth corners quirking in a sardonic grin.

Yakima chuckled as though at a joke between them all. "I can't even keep my own cabin clean."

"Well, you're gonna have some practice, now, ain't ya?" said the deputy on the far left, who stepped wide around him, aiming the barrel of his Henry carbine at Yakima's chest. "Now, suppose you set that rifle on the table there, then lift that .44 up slow, just two fingers."

"We all know how you can fight," said the man ahead of Yakima. "You so much as twitch one of your damn feet, I'll be paintin' that wall back there with your savage Injun blood."

The one-eyed deputy hadn't finished the sentence before Yakima bounded straight up in the air, flinging his right boot viciously up and out, the toe slamming against the underside of the deputy's rifle stock. As the man screamed, watching the rifle fly straight up over his head, Yakima bounded off his right foot, twisted in midair, and slammed the heel of his left boot against the head of the deputy behind him.

Yakima had moved so quickly — a blur of arms, legs, and buffeting hair — that the deputy had time to blink only once before he was flying sideways, triggering a round into a ceiling joist before tumbling over a table and a chair and falling to the floor in a groaning heap. At the same time, Yakima ducked a punch thrown by the one-eyed deputy, then straightened, rammed both his fists into the man's midsection, and followed them up with a savage haymaker to the man's cheek.

"Crazy bastard!" the tall deputy shouted as, about ten feet to Yakima's left, he spread his boots and extended the double-bore greener straight out from his belly.

Yakima was still holding his Yellowboy, but he knew that without Speares around to dampen the town's rage, a half-breed killing a deputy would only inspire a hang party. Holding the rifle straight up and down before him, he stepped behind a stout ceiling joist from which the piano player's small tip bucket hung.

The shotgun's explosion filled the room like a cannon blast. The bulk of the double-ought buck carved a barrel-sized hole in the far wall while several on the grouping's periphery blew the empty bucket off its hail and against the far wall with a clamoring clang. Several more tore through the slack of Yakima's tunic, peppering his left side just above his cartridge belt.

They felt like a dozen simultaneous bee stings.

Ignoring the pain, he stepped out from behind the post, grabbed a chair by its back, and flung it across the room, catching the deputy, who'd flung the empty barn-blaster aside and was reaching, across the head and shoulders, for a sidearm. The deputy cursed loudly as the chair, breaking apart, flung him sideways against the piano. Bent forward and groaning and holding his bloody head, he remained there for a few seconds before sagging down, overturning the piano bench, and falling over it. He lolled from side to side and moaned.

Thumbing cartridges from his cartridge belt into the Winchester's loading gate, Yakima stood inspecting the damage — two deputies unconscious, one incapacitated, all three looking at stitches, maybe some dental work, wired jaws, and painful days ahead.

The barman, Floyd Sanchez, sat against the wall near the end of the bar, knees and arms raised defensively, his eyes bright with fear and rage. Though his mouth was halfway open, he didn't say anything as the halfbreed racked a fresh shell in the Winchester's breech and backed toward the front of the room, kicking a chair out of his way.

"You all right, Yakima?" Rose asked.

The little brunette sat where she'd been sitting before, wincing as she glanced at Yakima's bloody side. Crouched over the table, Stella sat beside her, sobbing into her arms as she wagged her head of disheveled hair and night ribbons from side to side.

"I'll live. How's Stella?"

Rose glanced at the sobbing whore and ran a hand through Stella's hair. "She's just got the jitters . . . all this on top of what happened last night."

"What happened last night?"

"She got the giggles when some freighter couldn't get it up, and he chased her around the whole place with a hatchet, threatenin' to cut her head off and mount it on his wagon. Took four girls and three of the other customers to wrestle him down."

Yakima continued backing toward the door. "I reckon I'll be seein' ya."

"I reckon it won't be anytime soon."

"No, I reckon not."

He turned out through the batwings, planted his rifle butt on his hip and, keeping an eye on the saloon door, cautiously scrutinized the street. A couple of shopkeepers watched him from open doorways, and a barn-swamper regarded him uncertainly from between the open doors of the livery barn as he moved up to his four mustangs at the hitch rail, a shovelful of straw and dung in his arms.

Spying no imminent danger, Yakima began untying his four horses from the hitch rail — a feisty buckskin, a short-legged coyote dun, a hammerheaded blue roan, and a steeldust with a shredded left ear. None of the four — scarred from rocks, cacti, and tussles over in-season mares — would have won a beauty prize, but the soldiers at Fort Huachucha would be lucky to have such desert-hardy mounts beneath their ball-busting McClellan saddles.

With the ends of the four lead ropes in his left hand, Yakima swung up onto Wolf's back. He turned the black stallion into the street and, the four mustangs snorting with habitual peevishness and kicking up dust behind him, reined eastward, galloping through the Mexican part of town with its crumbling, sun-bleached adobes, brush corrals, wailing children, bleating goats, and the supper smells of spicy meat and roasting chili peppers wafting on the warm, dry wind.

He jogged through the rocky, saguaro-stippled hills at the east side of town, picked up a ragged two-track trail, and headed southwest into even more broken country.

Pausing on a butte crest to make sure he

wasn't being followed, he dropped down the other side into a broad, shallow canyon choked with mesquite and ironwood shrubs. To his right, a tan adobe casa with a red tile roof perched against the bluff's steep, rocky shoulder, sheathed in saguaros and flanked by goat pens and a stone chicken coop.

On a sandy flat before the casa lay a log barn and brush corral in which one fat mule stood, chewing its evening hay and corn husks.

Yakima put the black down the slope, twisting amidst the cacti and boulders, then reined up in front of the barn. Still mounted, he opened the brush corral's peeled log gate, hazed the four snorting mustangs inside, then gigged the black in, as well, and unsaddled him. With his saddle-bags draped over his shoulder, the rifle in his right hand, he pushed through the gate and headed toward the casa, which glowed salmon in the west-angling sunlight on the shoulder of the hill before him.

Hearing a baby's jabber, he paused at the base of the stone steps rising to the casa's second story. At the top of the steps, just inside the open door, a young Mexican woman, holding a diapered toddler on her hip, stood peering down the steps at him.

Sabina Flores's pretty, round face was

expressionless; her thick, auburn hair, which was burnished by the sun, was piled in rich swirls atop her head. She wore a sleeveless, low-cut blouse stitched with red and green thread that showed off the swell of her full breasts. A coarsely woven skirt fell to her ankles, her hips round beneath it. Her slender, bare feet shone below, as well as a leather ankle bracelet bearing a single bear's tooth.

Sabina was the best pleasure girl in southern Arizona, though she was mostly patronized by well-mannered banditos slipping across the border on horse raids, and by wealthy dons traveling between their haciendas and business interests in Arizona.

Yakima had stumbled onto her place a few months ago, when he'd been returning from a horse-selling trip to northern Sonora, and had spent several blissful days in the girl's company — enjoying the delights of her body as well as her mother's cooking. He'd never asked her how she afforded such a large house, but he surmised it had been bequeathed to her by a wealthy satisfied customer, probably from Mexico.

Yakima didn't regularly frequent whores, but he'd found himself returning to Sabina's place twice since that first visit, when his depleted larder had required a freight run to Saber Creek. He usually brought coffee, tea, sugar, or tobacco, and he felt bad that he bore none of those gifts today — just a buckshot-peppered side and sundry other scrapes and burns, and five horses requiring feed and water.

As Yakima climbed the steps, the young woman's eyes swept him, taking in his bloodstained tunic and buckskins. She chuckled huskily, reprovingly. "What have you gotten yourself into now, you crazy halfbreed?"

The little boy on her hip extended a damp hand, and Yakima closed his fingers around it gently. "The usual."

She clucked and shook her head. "Upstairs. I will bring my kit."

She turned away.

He said, "I have only a few coins in my pocket."

She glanced back at him, frowned derisively, as if he'd offended her, then walked away, bare feet slapping on the cracked flags, the baby fingering her hair. Ten feet down the hall, she disappeared through an open doorway from which emanated the smell of burning mesquite and spicy chicken stew, and the halfhearted cries of another child.

Yakima ducked under the low door and

moved down the hall, pausing to glance into the room where Sabina had disappeared — a large kitchen in which a stout old woman in a sackcloth dress stirred a pot over a broad, smoky hearth. The woman held a tiny, red-faced baby on her barrel-sized hip. A corn-husk cigarette smoldered between her thin, cracked lips.

She turned to Yakima, her eyes sweeping him, and grinned conspiratorially, showing a single, discolored tooth in her wizened jaws.

Yakima pinched his hat brim. "Dona Valentina, how are you and the little ones?"

The old woman rattled off some Spanish too quickly for Yakima to follow before shaking her broad head capped with a taut, gray hair bun, and returned her attention to the bubbling stew pot. Ashes fell from her cigarette onto the floor around her plump, bare feet.

Yakima adjusted the saddlebags on his shoulder and continued down the hall, up a short flight of stairs to the second story, and pushed through a door into Sabina's large room. There were a fireplace and a washstand, a few sticks of rough furniture, and a brass bed with a corn-husk mattress covered with a bobcat hide. A wooden crucifix hung over the bed, and a half-dozen candles were arranged about the room, none of them lit.

The single window looked out on a narrow balcony and the corrals in the canyon below, which was quickly filling now with purple shadows as the sun sank behind the western hills. A lone coyote yammered atop the opposite, saffron-bathed ridge — a slight gray smudge beside a single, gnarled pinion, the brush wolf's slender snout canted skyward.

Yakima dropped his saddlebags on a chair and leaned his rifle against the wall beside the window. The pad of bare feet sounded in the hall, and he turned as Sabina entered, a beaded leather pouch in one hand, a basin of water in the other. A narrow-bladed, bone-handled knife rested across the basin, and the up-curved tip reflecting the salmon light from the window made Yakima wince involuntarily.

"Out of your shirt," Sabina ordered, setting the pouch and basin on the washstand.

Yakima gingerly pulled his shirttails out of his pants and, making a face as the buckskin pulled away from the congealed blood on his lower right side, slowly lifted the garment up over his head. He sighed at the burn of the pellet wounds, dropped the shirt on the floor, then sat slowly down on the bed, propping a pillow against the frame and sagging back against it.

Sabina struck a match and walked around the room, lighting the candles. When all were lit, the light flickering and dancing across the cracked adobe walls, she retrieved a bottle from a shelf, doused the knife blade with tequila, then walked over to the bed with the basin, the knife, and the bottle, and sat down beside Yakima, hiking up one long, well-turned leg.

She gave him the bottle. He took a long drink, the tequila burning pleasantly as it slid down his throat, instantly soothing and partially numbing the pain in his side.

Glancing at the half-dried blood smeared about his ribs, Sabina sucked a sharp breath through her teeth. "It hurts?"

"What gave you that idea?"

She plucked a sponge from the water, wrung it out, then began wiping the congealed blood away from the pellet wounds. It took a good ten minutes of swabbing before about twelve small, BB-sized holes shone clearly against the ripples of his hard, corded belly, above and below his rib cage.

Blood bubbled up from a few, like perfect, crimson beads.

"What did you do for someone to come after you with a shotgun?" she asked, plucking long-handled, sharp-edged tweezers out of the water.

"Took back some stolen stock."

"How many men?"

"Four."

"Next time, let the horses go and count your blessings." Crouching low over his belly, she pressed the tweezers into one of the small holes. "You are only one man. A strong man." She shook her head slowly, and her rich, auburn hair partially fell from its bun to spill about her slender shoulders. She ignored it. "But only one man."

As the tip of the tweezers touched the tender flesh, Yakima stiffened, the veins standing out in his neck.

"There won't be a next time," he grunted, taking another pull from the bottle. "Not for those four, anyway. Besides, it was one of Speares's men who loosed the buckshot."

She dug around for a while, then, using the sharp knife tip to hold the wound open, pulled the tweezers out of the hole, a small, blood-coated pellet wedged between the tines. She held the BB up for inspection, then dropped it in the water with a tinny splash. "You have too many enemies. Badmen and lawmen."

Yakima chuckled and winced at the same time, as she dug around in another hole. "You got that right."

"*Putas* are loved by all. Except wives."

Sabina snorted, and the skin above the bridge of her nose wrinkled as she scrutinized the hole she was prodding. "That is why I live alone out here."

Her voice slowed, acquiring a meditative air as she began withdrawing the tweezers from the hole, nibbling her lower lip. "Just me, *Mamá,* the bambinos . . . some goats . . ." She lifted the tweezers, another bloody BB held between the tines, and dropped it in the water. "And the chickens and the mule."

She sighed. "Better have another drink," she said. "There are many more." As Yakima lifted the bottle, she grabbed it from him suddenly, threw back a drink, then, smiling devilishly, wiped her mouth with the back of her hand. "The doctor drinks first."

She gave him back the bottle, then threw one leg over his waist, straddling him, and, tossing her hair back from her eyes, crouched low over his belly, squinting her eyes and frowning. Her dress drew back from her knees, revealing her smooth, tan thighs. She lowered the tweezers to another hole, and Yakima braced himself, squeezing the bottle in his right hand, clenching his left fist.

Her blouse fell away from her chest,

41

revealing brown breasts angling down toward his belt buckle.

When she straightened, lifting another BB from another hole, she caught him staring at her bosom. Her eyebrows and the corners of her mouth rose. "Like the view from down there, huh?"

"What's not to like?"

She laughed huskily and leaned down, letting the blouse drop from her breasts once more but making him wince when, with a devilish chuckle, she poked the tweezers into another hole. "Take a good look. Then another drink. You're going to need both for this one. Very deep!"

When she finished, and a dozen BB's rolled around in the bloody basin, she cleaned the wounds with the tequila-soaked sponge. She rubbed a salve made from peppermint and aloe into the holes, and wrapped his waist with several thick lengths of bleached, tequila-dampened burlap.

Yakima lay back against the headboard, half-drunk, sore, his loins aching with lust.

She rose from the bed, set the roll of burlap on the washstand, beside the basin and the knife. Then she turned back to him, the candlelight flickering in the sunburnished highlights of her hair — the entire auburn mass now spilling across her shoulders, framing her round face with its pug nose and the light birthmark on the nub of her right cheek.

Her brown eyes danced; her lips stretched back from her teeth. In a single motion, she lifted the blouse up over her head and flung it across the room. She unbuttoned the skirt, let it drop to her ankles, and kicked it away.

Out the open window, the night was silent but for the cry of a single nighthawk.

"Now," she whispered, "to finish the procedure."

CHAPTER 3

A voice called from far away.

A weight rose from Yakima's chest, and he opened his eyes. Sabina, her naked body sprawled across his, stared up at him. Her sleepy brown eyes, veiled with swirls of auburn hair, seemed to search his, as though looking for the origin of the yell.

It came again — a woman shouting in Spanish.

"Mamá!" Sabina jerked her head toward the window, her hair brushing Yakima's chest.

"What'd she say?"

"A rider approaches."

She climbed out of bed and walked nude to the window. Yakima began to lower his legs over the edge of the bed, froze when his side grieved him, feeling as though an enraged dog were chomping down on him hard, then eased his feet to the floor. Rising gingerly and throwing his hair back from his eyes, he moved to the window and stood looking out beside Sabina.

The sun had not yet risen, but the sky was bright green and the orange of dying embers silhouetted the saw-toothed, eastern ridges. Below the house, the mule, Yakima's black stallion, Wolf, and the four green-broke mustangs had their heads lowered, eating from the several small clumps of hay someone had forked there recently. When the woman's voice rose again, Wolf lifted his head and, chewing the hay protruding from his grinding jaws, turned eastward.

Following the horse's gaze, Yakima saw a bulky, brown shape moving through the rocks and chaparral about a hundred yards southeast of the barn and ambling toward the house. It was Dona Valentina, a baby riding her hip, an apron buffeting about her stout legs, and a walking stick prodding the ground by her side.

Behind and east of the old woman, the slender shadow of a horseback rider descended a rocky slope toward the canyon floor, moving along the trail from Saber Creek. When the rider turned slightly sideways, something on his chest flashed in a stray shaft of orange sunlight bending around the peaks behind him.

A badge.

Yakima grunted, "Speares."

"I will go down and tell him to keep riding," Sabina said, her voice pinched with indignation. "That outlaw lawman *no es agradable aquí.*"

"I can handle Speares." Yakima walked over to the washstand and filled the cracked porcelain basin from a wooden pitcher, then splashed water on his face and the back of his neck.

"How you handle Speares, *hombre salvaje?*" Sabina asked behind him. "You kill him, uh? That would be nice, to have him gone. He drives the banditos away. My livelihood."

Toweling his face with a swatch of frayed burlap, Yakima turned to her. She reclined naked amidst the bed's twisted sheets, her head propped on an elbow, her rich hair spilling across her wrist. A smoky smile lit her eyes, which the sun discovered as it rose now behind the eastern ridges and slanted through the window.

"Might not have to." Yakima turned back to the basin and washed his privates. "He and I have a history down in Mexico."

"You save his life?"

"Something like that."

"Shame on you. I should pop him through the window!" She smiled lustily, savagely, showing her teeth. "Then you can stay here with me, and we will make the bed groan like it did last night." She paused, raking her eyes up and down his dark, scarred frame, lean as chewed rawhide but strapped with muscles hewn from a lifetime of hard riding and even harder toil. "You make me feel like a woman."

Stepping into his jeans, the muscular half-breed moved to the bed and sat down beside her. He placed his hand on the back of her neck, drew her to him, and kissed her hard. Keeping his hand on the back of her neck, he smoothed her hair back from her face with the other and caressed her smooth cheek with his knuckles. When he started to rise, she jerked up and wrapped her arms around his neck, kissing him hungrily.

"Stay with me, wild man. I'll put you up, huh? You can break your horses here. When they break you, I'll set your bones."

Holding him firmly around the neck, she stared into his eyes for a time, squinting slightly as though trying to puzzle him out. He cupped her chin between his thumb and index finger, and held her gaze. If she only knew how much he wanted a life with someone else, and how much, because he was who he was — a half-breed drifter who couldn't stand the company of anyone but horses for more than a few hours — he couldn't have it.

He decided to make a joke out of it. "Jesus, woman, don't scare me like that."

Slowly, as if reading his mind, she drew away, a sardonic smile curling her upper lip, and settled back onto her elbow. "A man gives me a good tumble, and I get sentimental on him. I wouldn't blame you if you never came back."

Yakima kissed her forehead, rose, went over to the chair, and dug around in his saddlebags for a spare buckskin tunic with whang strings, and pulled it over his head. He followed it up with the necklace of bear teeth, a good-luck talisman he'd fashioned from the rogue grizzly who'd tried to make a meal of him and Wolf when they were tracking a black-tail buck up a long, deep draw near Yakima's cabin.

When he'd stomped into his boots, knotted a bandanna around his forehead, and donned his broad-brimmed hat and chaps, he grabbed his saddlebags and Winchester, and headed for the door. "I'll bring some sugar next time."

He pinched his hat brim to Sabina as she watched him from the bed, that same sad, sardonic smile on her face, and went out. He stood there for a moment, his back to the door — finding it damn hard to leave the expert loving of a woman like Sabina Flores, because he never knew when he'd get it again — then shifted the saddlebags on his shoulder, and descended the stairs.

He paused at the top of the stone steps rising from the canyon floor, which was bathed in soft pink light and purple shadows.

Hearing the clomps of the oncoming horse, the occasional ring of a shod hoof clipping a stone, Yakima descended the steps and tramped over to the corral. The black mustang trotted toward him, snorting, regarding his rider expectantly, twitching his ears, ready to go.

"Soon, boy." Yakima draped his saddlebags over the fence, then rammed a fresh shell in his Winchester's breech, off-cocked the hammer, and leaned the rifle against a fence post.

As the hoof clomps grew louder in the brush to his left, and he could hear the squawk of unoiled tack, he rested his forearms over the corral gate, dug in his shirt pocket for his makings sack, and began building a quirley. Wolf looked toward the chaparral and nickered loudly. The approaching horse whinnied a reply.

In the corner of his right eye, Yakima saw the horse and rider emerge from the scrub. He continued rolling the quirley, then stuck the taut cylinder between his lips, licking it closed.

Wolf pricked his ears and lifted his head sharply, but the ensuing whinny died stillborn on the black's lips as Yakima growled, "Easy."

As Yakima snapped a lucifer to life on his thumbnail, Speares stopped the grulla about ten yards away and leaned forward, resting his forearms on his saddle horn. "Nice-lookin' broncs you got there."

Yakima turned his eyes to the four mustangs clumped at the other side of the corral, eyes wild, tails swishing. "Hope the army thinks so."

"You oughta keep 'em to home."

Yakima turned, blowing smoke through his nostrils. The sheriff sat the horse easily — a big, rangy man with thick, silver-blond hair curling onto his collar, his bangs combed low across his right eye, beneath the curled brim of his battered Stetson with a diamondback band. He wore two long-barreled Remingtons in cross-draw positions, a faded yellow duster, and shotgun chaps trimmed with hammered tin, his stovepipe boots adorned with large-roweled

California spurs. A perpetual, sneering half smile twisted the sheriff's lips beneath his soup-strainer mustache.

Yakima spat a tobacco fleck from his lips. "I try."

"I got three deputies back in town. They been caterwaulin' like trapped bobcats all night. One's got him a dislocated shoulder that took two men to locate. Another's got a broken jaw and won't be eatin' much but gruel and raw eggs for about three months. *None* of the three'll be any good to *me* again for about three weeks."

Leaning on his dinner-plate, Mexican-style saddle horn, the sheriff chuckled. "But I reckon they're luckier'n the four the undertaker's plantin' on Boot Hill later to-day."

Yakima took another deep drag from his cigarette, turned, and rested his forearms once more atop the corral gate. He spoke slowly, with a speculative air. "If you're here to make trouble, Speares, then make it so we can have it over with. I gotta get these horses to Fort Huachuca."

"I reckon you're callin' your note due, the one I gave you for saving my hide in Mexico, you half-breed son of a bitch!" Speares straightened, sighed heavily, and squinted down at Yakima. "Why don't you move your

51

ranch over closer to Tucson? Break up someone else's town for a change."

Yakima ran his hand down Wolf's long, sleek snout. "I like it where I am. I got a nice tight cabin and an old coyote that comes around to keep me company."

"Then how about you pin a deputy sheriff's star to your shirt? Like I said, I done lost three deputies because of you, and they ain't easy to come by in this neck of the godforsaken desert. If I can't kill the damn bobcat, I'm thinkin' maybe I can at least put him to work."

Yakima turned toward the sheriff, shaking his head and smiling stubbornly.

Speares turned toward the casa on the hill's shoulder. Yakima turned then, too.

Sabina descended the last few steps to the canyon floor, her legs bare, holding a wine red, velvet shawl about her shoulders. She padded barefoot toward the corral, loose hair blowing out behind her. Sidling up to Yakima, she favored the sheriff with a sneering, insolent smile.

"If you're looking for banditos, Sheriff, they've slipped back across the river."

Speares let his gray, snakelike eyes slide across the young whore's shapely body before returning his gaze to Yakima. "They'll be back, Senorita Flores. And so will I.

Maybe close you down one of these days, huh?"

"Keep the profits in town, eh, Sheriff — for the whores and gamblers who pay you to discourage competition?" Sabina squinted hatefully. "You can try."

Speares flushed, eyes narrowing.

He turned to Yakima, leaning forward and slitting one eye for emphasis. "If you won't work for me, I don't want to see your half-breed hide anywhere near Saber Creek for two months. You need supplies, take an extra day and ride to Benson or Tucson." He glanced at Sabina, who stood beside Yakima, holding her cape closed with one hand. "The whores in Tucson are a whole lot better than the mouthy peon scrubs you find out this way."

Speares pinched his hat brim and sneered, his scraggly mustache hiding his mouth. "Damn near forgot. I was about to turn in last night when a pretty little blonde with a small party of hardcases paid me a visit. She said she was headin' for Mexico, and she was wondering if I could tell her where she could find you. I told her I was damn sorry that I could. Makin' a long story short, she and her boys're waitin' for you out at Yaqui Springs." Speares neck-reined the grulla around and said over his shoulder,

"Name's Faith, if I recall. Do me a favor. On your way back to your cabin, swing wide of Saber Creek!"

The sheriff galloped off into the chaparral, hoof falls dwindling behind him. Yakima stood scowling, astonished at the name the sheriff had mentioned.

Faith.

It was like a cold slap to Yakima's cheek. He wasn't quite sure he'd really heard it. Maybe he was hearing things.

When Speares's jouncing, broad-backed figure was gone, Yakima turned to Sabina.

She was staring up at him, strands of hair sliding around her eyes.

He must have looked as shocked as he felt. He opened his mouth to speak, but before he could draw the words up from his thudding chest and suddenly parched throat, she slid her hair back from her face with one hand, and turned away.

She began walking back toward the house.

"It's a long ride to Yaqui Springs," she said softly. "I'll pack some food."

CHAPTER 4

Faith . . .

The name rolled around in Yakima's brain as he rode west through an ancient, steep-walled river canyon, leading the four feisty broncs. The burlap food sack that Sabina had packed for him flopped from his saddle horn.

He was badly torn. He wanted to ride west as badly as he wanted to have his fingernails removed slowly by howling Apache squaws. He needed to get home and ready the horses for the sale to Fort Huachuca. They needed another good month of sound training and gentling and mountain riding loaded with gear before they'd be fit cavalry mounts.

But the name Faith kept clanging around in his head like a cathedral bell, setting the back of his neck to burning and his loins to pricking.

Had Speares been playing a trick on him

— bringing up a name from Yakima's past that prodded his heart like the tip of a sharp stiletto? But Speares didn't know about Faith, which meant he couldn't have known what the young, blond whore whom Yakima had left in the mountains of Colorado had meant to him. Nor how hard it had been for him to leave her in the cold, wintery mining camp of Gold Cache.

She had worked for the notorious pimp and roadhouse hustler, Bill Thornton, who had mistakenly thought Yakima and Faith were lovers. He'd tried to cut her face with a razor — the traditional punishment for a two-timing whore — but Faith had wounded the man with a small-caliber pistol and tried to flee.

Yakima had saved her, nearly leveling Thornton's roadhouse in the process. It was following that debacle that Thornton had sicced his men on them, chasing them into the peaks and canyons of the Rocky Mountain Front Range.

Stalked together, she and Yakima had fought together and, ironically, become lovers as Thornton had feared. A bond grew between them, which, strong as it was, couldn't have lasted any more than a bond with Sabina could last, they both being what they were — renegade drifters of one type or another.

That didn't mean he didn't love her, though. He hadn't really known how much until after he'd left her. He loved her enough that even Sabina had noticed his reaction at the mention of her name.

What was Faith doing out here with a party of hardcases? Yakima couldn't fathom a reason she'd be this far from her brothel in Gold Cache.

Jesus, was he really going to see her again?

He pulled up out of the canyon and picked up a faint, two-track trail that had once been used by the Spanish on gold-seeking and soul-saving forays into Arizona a hundred years ago and more. Later, it had also been used by smuggling trains out of Mexico until increased cavalry patrols had caused the smugglers to abandon the trails for those farther west. Nowadays, since the smugglers had left and the gold and silver mines had pinched out, the ancient village of Yaqui Springs was seldom frequented by anyone but brush wolves, outlaws, and roaming bands of Apaches.

It was late in the morning, the shadows drawing taut against the saguaros and boulders, when Yakima rode into the rugged foothills of the Yaqui Range — sun-burnished knobs of bald granite and heaps of cracked boulders rising on both sides of the narrowing, winding trail.

Yaqui Springs was only a few miles farther on.

He halted the horse suddenly, brows ridged. To his right, just beyond the shadow of a low rock wall ahead and to the left, another shadow had moved. He'd picked it up out of the corner of his eye, and while it could have been the shadow of an armadillo or a chaparral cock or some other harmless desert creature, warning bells tolled in his head.

He crouched over Wolf's ear. "Down!"

Instantly, the horse dropped to its knees. As a rifle cracked above and behind him, Yakima flung himself out of the saddle, and rolled. As the bullet blew up dust near his right shoulder, the rifle report still echoing around the ridges, Yakima palmed his Colt and fired three quick rounds.

The stocky figure wearing a steeple-brimmed sombrero atop the rock behind him stumbled straight back, knees buckling. He groaned. The man's Remington rifle sagged in his hands, then fell, bounced off the rock near his high-topped, high-heeled boots, and tumbled to the ground.

The man followed a second later, turning one complete somersault before falling atop the rifle with a loud thump and a fart.

As the horse rose onto its forelegs and, snorting, trotted up trail past Yakima, the half-breed gained his feet, looking around, keeping the cocked Colt extended before him. Not detecting any more bushwackers, he strode forward and looked down at the man he'd killed — a stocky, buzzard-faced Mexican in a striped serape and patched, baggy denims.

Soaking the poncho, blood welled from the man's long, thin nose and from the three bullet holes in his chest. The man's eyes were squeezed shut, his two front teeth — cracked and yellow — visible between his slightly parted lips. A big knife handle jutted up on the outside of his poncho, from a beaded deerskin sheath.

A border bandit.

Yakima looked around again, apprehension gnawing at him. He was beginning to wonder if Speares had sent him into an ambush to get rid of him once and for all. He wouldn't have put it past the man.

But how would Speares have known to use Faith's name?

Yakima climbed a jumble of rocks and scouted the corduroy, cactus-studded slopes two or three miles away. In the middle distance between two scarps, the sun winked off something — either metal or glass. Where there was one bandito, it was safe to assume there were more.

Yakima leaped off the rocks and, keeping his eyes and ears skinned, moved up the trail to where the black stood in the shade beneath a tall mesquite cropping of galetta grass. He grabbed the horse's reins and shucked the Yellowboy from the saddle sheath, then swung up into the hurricane deck.

Booting the horse ahead, he said, "Nice and easy, boy."

Riding slowly, holding the rifle across his saddle bows, he swung his gaze from left to right across the trail, picking up the fresh prints of six shod horses swerving onto the trail from the direction of Saber Creek. They probably belonged to Faith's group riding out from Saber Creek.

Yakima booted the horse ahead, until the old pueblito of Yaqui Springs rose up from the saguaro and greasewood — a motley collection of white adobes spread across the scrub and cacti, with here and there a sun-blistered, wood-frame building hailing from more recent years, when there'd been a small gold boom in the nearby canyons.

He swung the mustangs into a ravine sheathed in mesquite and gnarled sycamores, tied the horses to shrubs, then climbed the ravine wall and stole through the scrub brush toward the pueblito. He inspected the village carefully, spying no movement amongst the cracked, sun-bleached ruins, except wind-tossed tumbleweeds and occasional, hunting hawks.

There didn't appear to be anyone here.

Anxiety nibbled at his gut, and he wasn't sure if it was caused by the possibility that he was being lured into a trap, or by the prospect of seeing Faith again. He'd done his best to forget her, for the thought of her often caused him misery akin to a hot knife laid to the loins. But he hadn't forgotten her at all. In fact, he was willing to risk getting shot for the possibility of seeing her again.

Approaching the village a few minutes later, he bolted out from a thick brush patch, and pressed his back to the wall of a brick adobe chinked with mud-packed straw. He looked to his right and left, seeing nothing but the irregular line of abandoned hovel walls, with here and there the remnants of a woodpile, chicken coop, brush stable, or goat pen. A dust devil rose briefly to twist on a sudden breeze, then died against a post oak.

He crept along the backsides of the crumbling adobes, the oldest and most dilapidated of which were half buried in sand, cacti, and bunches of wiry, brown grass. Peering through a narrow alley toward the main street, he saw nothing but swirling dust and the sun-splashed adobes on the street's other side.

He turned into the shaded alley abutted by cracked walls and, holding the Yellowboy straight up and down in his arms, moved toward the tall rectangle of bright sunlight at the other end.

A horse whinnied. Yakima stopped.

The sound had come from the building on his left.

Ahead was a stout wooden door. He moved toward it, wrapped his gloved right hand around the rusty handle hanging by a single nail, and pulled. The door opened only about two feet before ramming against upheaved cobbles; he turned sideways and forced his way through the crack.

He found himself in a stable with several stall partitions — musty straw on the floor, tack moldering from ceiling joists. Shafts of washed-out sunlight angled through ragged holes in the ceiling. Pigeons cooed in the rafters. Peering through the shadows, Yakima saw a horse standing outside, between the open front doors. It was a clean-lined, broad-chested claybank with a golden mane.

It tossed its head, rattling its bridle and bit chains.

Someone placatingly muttered to the horse. There were low scraping and ticking sounds.

Yakima moved forward slowly, setting his feet down carefully, and peered around a stall. A snuff brown hat with a snakeskin band shone before the horse's right fore-quarter, the crown dipped toward the horse, bobbing slightly as the person worked.

Yakima moved forward, keeping posts or hanging tack between him and the open doors. He pressed his left shoulder against a post, listening to the dull rasp of a hoof file about twenty feet away. He tightened his finger on the rifle's trigger, turned around the post, leveled the Yellowboy straight out from his right hip, and rammed a fresh shell into the breech.

The metallic rasp sounded inordinately loud in the close quarters. The man stand-ing beside the horse bent forward at the waist and, running a file across the hoof clamped between his long, slender legs, gave a surprised, "Oh!" and straightened.

He stumbled back — *she* did, rather — the hat's broad brim tipping back to reveal a young woman's smooth, oval face. Two wide-set blue eyes glinted shock and fear between framing wings of gold-blond hair swirling about her narrow shoulders. Full, pointed breasts pushed up from behind her man's pin-striped shirt and doeskin vest, a leather cord hanging down her neck and disappearing down her deep, suntanned cleavage.

Faith.

The horse beside her skitter-hopped sideways, startled, and raised another, shriller whinny.

Ignoring the horse, Faith stared at Yakima, the startled look in her eyes softening — a hundred memories washing through her gaze at once. The rich lips parted as she began to form a smile. Then the smile faded, and the eyes sharpened. "Yakima Henry, you damn near gave me a *heart* stroke!"

Yakima blinked. It really was Faith standing before him. Her clothes were rough and dusty, and dust and seeds clung to her hair, but she was still the most beautiful woman he'd ever seen. He blinked again. It was like a dream in which people appeared in improbable places.

Numbly, he depressed the Winchester's hammer. He tipped the rifle barrel up as she moved toward him, taking long, confident strides, brown leather chaps flapping against her legs clad in black denim; then she was in his arms, wrapping her own slender arms around his neck and pressing her face against his shoulder, knocking her hat off her head to hang by a horsehair thong behind her back.

"I wasn't sure you'd come," she whispered.

"Crazy place to meet." He would have braved the fires of hell to see her again, but he had to keep his wits about him. "This is bandito country. Why the hell — ?"

"Shh," she said, grinding her face against his buckskin tunic and taking a deep breath, as if savoring his smell. "We don't have much time. . . ."

She let her voice trail off as running footsteps rose from behind the adobes to Yakima's left. A man's voice called, "Faith? Darlin', are you all right?"

She drew away from Yakima, glancing up at him, a flush rising in her high, tan cheeks. She took his hand in hers, and glanced to her left as a man ran out from the front of a pink adobe, aiming an ivory-butted Smith & Wesson straight out from his belly, the hammer cocked.

He was a rakishly handsome, blue-eyed gent in his early thirties. At least, he would have been handsome without the long, red, jagged scar running down from beneath the brim of his leather slouch hat. The scar stopped at his right eye before continuing on below it and stopping in a twisted knot near his right nostril. The eye didn't appear blind, but it wobbled slightly off center and was a tad lighter blue than the other.

Slim-waisted and broad-shouldered, long-ish blond hair hanging beneath the brim of his brown slouch hat, the handsome scar-face wore corduroy trousers with two holsters, both positioned for the cross-draw, and a green shirt under a dusty pinto vest. A garish, lemon yellow neckerchief hung like a streamer down the right side of the vest, the end brushing his flat belly.

When the man's eyes found Yakima, they raked him quickly, and he frowned warily, deep lines forming across his broad, tan forehead and around his eyes.

"Ace, meet Yakima Henry," Faith said, letting Yakima's hand slip from her fingers and half turning to shuttle her gaze between the men on either side of her. "Yakima, meet Ace Cavanaugh, my husband. . . ."

CHAPTER 5

My husband.

The phrase was a horse kick to Yakima's gut.

He kept his face expressionless, however — at least he thought he did, though his green eyes might have sunk a little deeper into their sockets and a slight flush might have burned in his broad, russet cheeks — as he held Ace Cavanaugh's flinty, blue gaze with his own. His stomach felt like a dried gourd. He let the Yellowboy sag against his right leg as he resisted the urge to grab Faith by her slender shoulders and yell, *"Why?"* at the top of his lungs.

Why him?

Yakima didn't often make snap judgments based on a person's looks, but Cavanaugh was obviously a lowlife and hardcase, a professional confidence man or cardsharp. He hadn't gotten that grisly scar delivering free milk and Bibles to homebound Methodist widows.

"Oh," Cavanaugh muttered, lifting his Colt's barrel as he eased the hammer down against the firing pin. Annoyed, he let his cautious gaze rake Yakima once more before glancing at Faith curiously, then back at Yakima. "Faith didn't tell me you was a breed."

Before any of the three could say anything else, more footsteps rose from the front of the pink adobe, and then four more men appeared — all wearing dusty trail garb not quite as stylish as Cavanaugh's, three wielding pistols, while the fourth held a Winchester carbine straight out from his hip. One was a good twenty years older than the other — gray-bearded and wearing an old, wool suit coat that had seen better days.

"Step down, fellas," Cavanaugh said, keeping his eyes on Yakima. He held up his right hand, on which he wore a soft doeskin glove. On the outside of the glove, around his middle finger, he wore a square-cut ruby ring set in gold. "Looks like Faith's friend has done arrived."

"Yakima," Faith said in her husky, sexy pleasure girl's drawl, "these are friends of Ace's. Pop Longley, Jim Taylor, Cliff Schickel, and young Willie Stiles. Lou Brahma's tending the other horses and keeping watch. Smiley Burnside's around here somewhere, but Ace —"

"I got Smiley prowlin' the perimeter, keepin' an eye skinned for trouble," Cavanaugh cut in, dropping the ivory-gripped S&W into the empty holster on his left hip and giving his ring a quick polish. "We cut Apache sign on our way out from Saber Creek."

"You sure it wasn't bandito sign?" Yakima said. "A Mex tried to give me a backache about three miles down trail."

"I told you I spied dust on our trail," said the gray-bearded Pop Longley. He spat a wad of chew in the dirt. "It was just a devil, you said. Like hell, Ace."

"*Mexican* dust devil, more like," said the youngest of the group, a scrawny, wild-looking rannie named Willie Stiles. He wore a low-crowned opera hat and two big bowie knives on his waist, with the worn, walnut grips of an old-model Colt Army angled over his belly. He grinned, revealing a chipped front tooth.

Cavanaugh cast a quick, sharp look at both men. "Shut up, both of you. Apaches, bean-eating bandits — what the hell difference does it make?"

Faith's eyes were still on Yakima. "Why don't we go on over to the cantina and have a drink? It's the only place in town still open. We can talk there."

"Yeah, why don't we do that?" the man named Taylor said. "This heat's damn near —" He palmed his revolver suddenly, and wheeled, crouching.

At the same time, a rifle blasted from a roof on the other side of the street. The bullet punched through the crown of Taylor's hat, knocking him back instantly while blood and bone spewed from the back of his head.

Faith gave a startled, *"Oh!"*

The horse screamed.

Yakima had seen the shadow on the roof at the same time Taylor had. He grabbed Faith's arm, jerked her back behind him, and bounded forward. Raising the Yellowboy, he laid the sights on the silhouetted figure crouched beside a falling-down brick chimney, and fired two rounds — one after the other.

Boom-rasp-boom!

The banditos had trailed Faith's group for Faith herself. She had to be what they were after. There wasn't anything else of value left in Yaqui Springs.

Cursing her and her group's foolishness — this was far too dangerous a territory for a beautiful woman — Yakima rammed a fresh shell into the breech. Turning toward another shadow sliding out from a corner of a wood-and-batten structure with a broad front porch and faded letters announcing THE CRYSTAL PALACE SALOON AND DANCE HALL, he fired another round. The shadow jerked back, and a silver-plated revolver flashed in the sunlight as it fell, the gunman clapping both hands to his face and loosing a hideous shriek as he dropped to his knees.

Hooves thundered left, two horsemen galloping out of an alley on the other side of the street. Crouched low in their saddles, the Mexicans triggered revolvers as they swung their sleek Arabs toward Yakima's group. Before Yakima could bring the Yellowboy to bear, Ace Cavanaugh and Pop Longley dropped to their knees, palmed their revolvers — Cavanaugh had one in each hand — and blew both riders straight back off their horses.

A boot clipped a stone on Yakima's right flank and he whipped around, the Yellowboy leaping in his hands, the bullet plunking into the far front corner of a jailhouse, spraying rock shards. The man who'd just snaked a Spencer carbine around the corner, showing half his leather-brown face beneath the brim of a palm-leaf sombrero,

71

gave a clipped scream. Triggering a wayward shot, he disappeared back behind the stone wall, his spurs chinking, boots kicking up dust.

Gunfire popped on the other side of the street. Cavanaugh and Longley returned it, Cavanaugh diving behind a stock trough while Longley dropped behind an abandoned wagon chassis.

Vaguely noting that both men seemed right handy with their sidearms, Yakima whipped his head toward the stable behind him. Faith was on her knees, wincing, holding one hand to an ear while the other halfheartedly gripped a .36-caliber Colt.

"Get back inside the stable!" Yakima shouted, then bolted toward the jailhouse as a slug tore up dust about three inches off his right boot heel.

"The claybank!" she cried.

"Inside!" Yakima shouted once more as he turned around the jailhouse and sprinted along the building's west wall.

He ran down the wide gap between the buildings, leaping bricks and cactus, then pressed his back against the wall of the building on his left — a ramshackle little house whose roof had long since caved in. Spurs jingled behind the house, fading into the distance.

Yakima stepped out from the corner, dropped to a knee, and raised the rifle to his shoulder. He drew a bead on the left calf of the bandito sprinting away between the rear of the buildings and the chaparral encroaching on the other side. He fired.

The bandito grunted, fell, rolled in a fog of wafting dust and gravel, and came up with a pistol in his hand, eyes wide with pain and fury.

Levering a fresh shell into the Yellowboy's breech, Yakima squeezed the trigger.

Krr-boom!

The bullet punched through the bandito's left eye and into the ground behind him with a dust puff. The man's head snapped up. Blood welled from the eye socket. He dropped the pistol and slowly sagged backward, arms and legs thrashing madly as he gave up his ghost.

Ejecting the smoking shell, Yakima looked around and listened, then crept behind the building, passing the dead bandito in his final death spasms. He continued walking west until he came to the end of the town — only a faint trail through the scrub and saguaros beyond, rising to crenellated ridges colored saffron and green by the searing sun.

He paused, hearing a couple of guns crack

on the other end of the pueblo. Someone yelled in Spanish. Yakima sleeved sweat from his forehead, then, swinging the gun barrel back and forth in front of him, crossed to the other side of the street. He'd begun tramping down behind the buildings lining the main, cobbled thoroughfare, beginning to think all the attackers were either dead or fleeing, when, from behind a jumble of ruined pens and privies, horse thuds rose ahead.

He stepped behind a tall, narrow adobe. The hoof falls grew. A horse whinnied. A man breathed heavily. Yakima stepped out from behind the adobe and raised the Winchester. The rider was twenty-five yards away and closing, holding a hand to his chest as he looked back over his left shoulder, his large sombrero dancing around behind his back.

When he turned his balding head toward Yakima, his mouth opened suddenly. Yakima's bullet tore through his throat. He gagged and clapped both hands to his neck as he sagged down the other side of the galloping, buck-kicking mount.

As the horse passed, Yakima saw the man's head and shoulders hit the ground. His boot must have gotten caught in the stirrup, because the horse continued straight on past the half-breed, bouncing its rider along the ground beside it like a six-foot-long rag doll. Horse and rider disappeared in the grease-wood and cholla, hooves clomping, body thumping and smashing brush.

Yakima continued along the alley and stopped when he found a man slumped facedown across a rain barrel, a deep knife gash in the middle of his bloody back. Yakima grabbed the man's collar and drew him away from the barrel. As the stocky gent fell back on the ground — a *norteamericano* with a bushy mustache and light red hair — Yakima saw that his throat had been cut just above his knotted green neckerchief.

Leaving the man where he lay, Yakima stole forward, swinging his rifle between the brush on his right, the backsides of the business establishments on his left.

Cicadas whined in the brush and the sun lay like a hot, heavy blanket, searing his head through his scalp, runneling his broad, hard-chiseled cheeks with mud.

A boot crunched gravel in a gap between the buildings. He swung his Winchester around as a man stepped out of the gap, a long-barreled S&W extended before him, the ruby ring glowing brightly. Cavanaugh's good eye met Yakima's and both men froze at the same time, snapping their weapons up and away.

"Anything?" Cavanaugh said, his scarred eye floating slightly outward.

Pop Longley stole along behind him — a good five inches shorter and stoop-shouldered, lips stretched warily back from his tobacco-stained teeth.

"Only the man one of your boys shot. He's finished." Yakima squinted into the brush where a kangaroo rat scuttled amidst the caliche, disappearing over a rotten log. He turned back to Cavanaugh. "That man you posted to watch for banditos have red hair and a mustache?"

Longley nodded. "Smiley Burnside."

Yakima jerked his Winchester's barrel to indicate the direction in which he'd come. "He's not smiling anymore."

Pop Longley cursed and looked around, chewing his mustache, which was the same color as the hair curling down from his shapeless canvas hat. "Sons o' bitches musta spied us ridin' out from Saber Creek. Must've been after the horses." He gave Cavanaugh an accusatory stare. "Or that woman of yours."

Cavanaugh met the man's look with a flinty one of his own. "That woman o' mine is the reason we're out here, Pop."

Pop cursed under his breath and glanced

away, vaguely sheepish.

"Speaking of her," Yakima said, "you best go find her, pull her the hell out of here. Take her back to Colorado. This is no place for a woman."

Yakima shouldered his rifle and turned to walk away, when Cavanaugh grabbed his arm. "That's it? That's all you have to say?" He paused, his eyes studying Yakima's with vague suspicion. "She said you two were amigos."

"We were."

"She has a favor to ask you, *friend*. Now, whether you say yes is up to you, but why don't you hang around awhile, at least let her ask it."

Yakima glanced at Longley, then turned to see the man named Willie Stiles — round-faced, rangy, sandy-haired, and looking nothing like a Willie — sauntering toward them from behind, a corn-husk cigarette smoldering between his lips. He wore two big bowies on his hips; another was sheathed on the outside of his left boot. His low-crowned, leather sombrero shaded his young, mild, patch-bearded face.

Yakima cursed and turned to peer south. Extending an arm, he said, "You see that notch in the peak yonder?"

"I see it," Cavanaugh said testily.

"Gather your horses and meet me there. No telling who-all our gunfire has drawn to the village."

Yakima turned away to continue investigating the east end of the village. Spying no more banditos, he headed across the main street and tramped into the desert after his horses.

CHAPTER 6

Jaws set, Yakima hoofed it back to his mustangs, mounted Wolf, and, leading the fiddle-footing broncs by their single lead line, traced a wide arc around Yaqui Springs. He headed for the notch in the tallest craggy peak south of the village, remembering that at the base of the notch, which looked as though a giant knife had been driven deep into the ridge crest, a run-out spring trickled.

Damn those horse thieves. If it hadn't been for them, maybe he'd never have gotten word she was in the country. He'd never have known she'd gotten hitched to some sharpie named Ace Cavanaugh. He'd still be entertaining his fantasies of growing old with her, while fighting off the memory of their parting back in Colorado, in his cabin nestled at the base of Bailey Peak.

. . . my husband . . .

Why couldn't she have left him alone?

What the hell did she want?

He arrived at the base of the wall below the deep notch just before sundown, the desert behind him filled with green shadows and silence. Right of the notch, two finger-sized streams trickled out from the black rock of the ridge, filling several rock tanks below, which were sheathed in galetta and Mormon tea. The tanks tilted down an arroyo, creating several small waterfalls and lifting the quiet, peaceful rattle of flowing water.

Yakima watered the horses at the tanks, then wet some saddle blankets and rubbed each horse down thoroughly, parrying the nips and attempted head butts of the half-broke stock.

When he'd cleaned the gravel and cactus thorns from their hooves, he tied the mounts to a picket line strung between two mesquites. He laid out his saddle and bedroll, and built a small fire in the rocks near the base of the notch.

His pan of tea water was chugging and bubbling when he spied a line of five riders winding through the mesquites and chaparral about a half mile below the slope — brown shadows in the gathering dusk. Damn. He'd half-thought they wouldn't come. A gambler played the odds, and Cavanaugh had to have gotten the message that the odds were damn long out here on hell's back doorstep.

Faith rode second in the ragged procession; the gold-blond hair jostling about her slender shoulders glinted like copper. In the setting sun, the flashing hair recalled an image of her beneath him in the deep grass lining a stream bank in northern Colorado, that wheat-colored hair blending with the grass under and around her pale, naked shoulders.

Blinking away the memory while feeling foolish for having pined for her all this time during which she'd been hitching her star to Cavanaugh, he poured green tea into a tin cup. Ace Cavanaugh led the others up the slope through the saguaros and giant boulders, swaying easily with his horse's rhythm, the mount's hooves clacking on the scalelike upthrusts of rock.

He, Faith, the kid Willie Stiles, the graybeard Pop Longley, and another man whom Yakima hadn't seen before lined out in front of him, their sweaty horses blowing. Cavanaugh removed his hat and swabbed his forehead with his shirtsleeve.

"We had to bury our stiffs," he said, as if explaining what had kept him.

He glanced at the man to his left — a

broad-shouldered, heavy-gutted man with a square, dark, pockmarked face and heavy jaw, with deep-set blue eyes and a nose like a wedge. He was clean-shaven except for shaggy sideburns running down to his jawline. His furrowed black brows, small darting eyes, and pursed lips bespoke a bully. Yakima had an urge to slap the man silly, but he wasn't sure if it was because of Brahma himself, or the situation.

Faith pulled her clay up between Brahma and Cavanaugh. Her voice was cool. "Yakima Henry, meet Lou Brahma from Laramie."

Before Yakima could say anything, Cavanaugh gave Brahma a surreptitious glance before returning his gaze to the half-breed. "Lou, say hidy to Yakima here — my wife's friend she done told us so much about."

Lou Brahma dipped his head just enough that his eyes disappeared under the brim of his dusty, black hat, the brim of which was decorated with a colorfully beaded band. He grinned, his eyes retreating back into their sockets, his chapped lips spreading.

"Christ Almighty," Brahma chuckled, glancing around at the other men. "It's a damn heathen!"

"That's about the way of it," said Pop Longley, turning his head to dribble molasses-colored chaw into the orange dust near his horse's right front hoof.

Faith's blond brows ridged with annoyance. "Be civil, Lou. He came all the way out here to meet us."

"Came out here to meet you." Brahma shrugged and grinned again. "I was just statin' a fact. I was expectin' a white man, I reckon. Never took you to run with Injuns, Miss Faith."

Faith said, "Well, now you know."

Brahma chuckled again as he studied the half-breed sitting by his fire.

"Water yonder," Yakima said, blowing on the lip of his teacup. "You can picket your horses near mine, but keep 'em away from those four broncs unless you want patches of hide bit out."

The men glanced at each other conspiratorially, Brahma still chuckling with incredulity. As they began to rein away, Faith turned to her husband. "Ace," she said, swinging down from her saddle and tossing the reins to him, "take the clay, will you?"

Cavanaugh shuttled his dubious gaze from his wife to Yakima, that lighter-colored eye wandering slightly once again, then took the reins from her. "Of course, my queen."

As Cavanaugh led the claybank off down the slope to where the water rattled in and out of the tanks, Faith turned to Yakima, spread her feet, and hooked her thumbs in her cartridge belt — the .36 Colt jutting from the holster hanging low on her right thigh. "I met him in Gold Cache. He's a good man when he's sober and not too deep in debt. He's a professional gambler."

Yakima sipped his tea, his implacable expression belying the ache in his heart. "I never figured you for the marryin' type."

"You can't turn tricks forever . . . or expect to run a brothel without financial backing in a place like Gold Cache. Business booms in the summer, dribbles out in the winter." She moseyed over and sat down on a rock a ways back from the fire. "How've you been?"

"Can't complain." Yakima reached into a saddlebag behind him and tossed her a cup. "Tea?"

Faith scooped the cup out of the dust, blew it out, then used a charred leather swatch to lift the tin pot from the fire and pour the tea into the cup.

As if anticipating a question, Faith said with a frustrated edge, "He staked me when times were tough."

"A *good* gambler."

She glanced at him over the rim of her steaming cup. "You didn't need to leave, you know. We could have stayed together."

"For how long?"

"For as long as it lasted." When Yakima didn't say anything, she sipped from the cup again. "Still drinking tea . . ."

"Whenever I can get it."

"Just like Ralph," she said wistfully, referring to the old Chinaman with whom Yakima had laid railroad track and who'd taught him how to fight in the ancient Eastern style. His name, of course, hadn't been Ralph, but that's what he'd called himself in the States, because no one here could have pronounced his Chinese name.

Yakima saw no reason to mince words. "Why are you here, Faith?"

She set the teacup on a rock of the fire ring. She swiped her hat from her head and spun it in her gloved hands. "My brother — my youngest brother, the only one I've got left — is in jail in Mexico."

"That's lousy luck. I'm sorry to hear it." Yakima sipped his tea. "Thinkin' about breakin' him out, are ya? Count me out. It ain't hard to get into a Mexican prison, but getting out — that's a whole other thing."

"I don't intend to break him out. I intend to buy him out. I'm carrying two thousand dollars in gold coins. I hear that's the going rate for American prisoners in Mexico — at

85

least, in this particular Mexican prison."

"Those banditos must have gotten wind of the lucre," Yakima said, canting his head in the direction of Yaqui Springs. "Either that or they were after the *bonita gringa* in the group."

Not reacting to the compliment, she said, letting some bitterness enter her voice, "Ace was playing poker in Saber Creek. A high stakes game. I figure the Mexicans saw, decided to follow us out of town, see how much we were carrying."

She glanced in the direction of the rock tanks beyond the firelight, where the men's voices rose softly above the continuous clatter of the water. "It won't happen again."

"Forget it," Yakima advised. "You'll never make it. *Bonitas gringas,* especially blond *bonitas gringas,* don't last long in Mexico. Send the men on with the money to buy your brother out. You hightail it back to Colorado."

She dropped her chin to peer at the ground between her spread knees. She lifted the sides of her boots, then set them back down on the ground.

"Or," Yakima said wistfully, raising his cup to his lips, "don't you trust your husband, Mrs. Cavanaugh?"

She looked up angrily, a flush rising in her

face, a strand of gold-blond hair dropping down from beneath her hat to curl against her smooth, lightly tanned cheek. "It's not that. I mean — Ace, he's a gambler. He doesn't mean any harm, but . . ."

"He might blow it all in a poker game."

She shook her head quickly, as if trying to dismiss the thought. "I'm going, Yakima. Kelly needs me. That's that." She leveled a hard gaze at him. "None of us knows Mexico. Oh, Lou's been down there before, in his younger days, but that was Chihuahua, not Sonora. Will you guide us? I can pay you a thousand dollars — five hundred now, five when we finish."

"Where?"

"Tocando." She grabbed a stick from the pile beside the fire, then used the stick to scratch an outline of Sonora. She drew an X into the province's southern middle. "It's a small town with a rurale headquarters and a prison. Kelly's being held in the prison."

"Why?"

"He and a friend were prospecting in Mexico, thought they'd find their El Dorado in a year, and come back to the States wealthy men. Kelly's only eighteen, and he's never been one for using his head. The rurales raided a cantina Kelly and Rick were getting drunk in, and hauled all the customers to prison. Apparently they were throwing a broad loop, hoping to find revolutionaries. Somehow, Rick got away and sent a letter to me in Gold Cache, explaining what had happened."

Yakima looked at her ruefully.

"What?"

"Look, Faith . . ."

"You think he's dead."

Yakima sat back on his rock with a sigh. She broke the stick over her knee, rose, walked around the fire, and crossed her arms on her chest, staring out at the deepening dusk. Her hair fluttered in the chill night breeze.

"Kelly almost died as a baby, and he's never been strong. I've heard that rurales out of Tocando enslave their prisoners, putting them to work in mines and such." Faith shook her head gravely. "Kelly wouldn't last long in a hard-rock mine."

She turned to him as a lonely wolf howled, her eyes beseeching.

"It's Mexico," Yakima muttered, as if that said it all about her chances of getting her brother back.

"He's all I have left of my old life." She hugged herself as if chilled. "My other brothers are dead. Kelly's all I have. Don't tell me he's been taken from me, too. I won't believe it."

Footsteps and voices rose from Yakima's right. He turned to see Lou Brahma move toward him up the grade, carrying his saddle and blanket roll on his shoulder, his Winchester carbine and saddlebags in his other hand.

Approaching the fire, Brahma shuttled his gaze between Yakima and the girl. He gave a wry chuff as he continued forward and threw his saddle, bedroll, and saddlebags on the ground to Yakima's left.

The other three followed — Cavanaugh, the young string bean, Willie Stiles, then the grizzled Pop Longley, bringing up the rear, all carrying saddles, bags, and blanket rolls. Cavanaugh stopped before the fire, glancing between Yakima and Faith as Longley and Stiles tossed down their gear, puffing dust and fanning the fire's flames.

"So what's it gonna be?" Cavanaugh said, glancing at Faith. He canted his head toward Yakima but kept his eyes on his wife. "He gonna come or ain't he?"

Faith looked at Yakima, her eyes worried.

Yakima set his cup down, grabbed his rifle, and stood. He rammed a fresh shell into the Yellowboy's breech and off-cocked the hammer. "I'll think on it. In the meantime, we'll each take an hour's lookout. I'll take the first one."

He shouldered the rifle and turned left to glide off between the rocks, to take reconnaissance of the area and to get the hell away from Faith and Cavanaugh. Seeing the two of them together made his gut raw, caused him to feel like a moon-calf, and to wish he'd never met her. At least, until a few hours ago, he had pleasant, if regretful, memories. Now she was only an angry stitch in his chest, and he felt like hitting somebody.

Lou Brahma, lying on his side, propped on an elbow, gave another haughty chuff. "Who's givin' the orders around here?"

Yakima wheeled toward him, clenching a fist. Then he opened his hand and raked his glance around the others. "You boys better decide tonight if you can take orders from a heathen, because I'm givin' 'em. Any objections on this side of the border, you're on your own. Any objections *south* of the border, all bets are off."

He turned again and disappeared in the darkness.

CHAPTER 7

With the night breeze rustling the brush around him, Yakima traced a broad circle around the camp, moving silently, listening and watching, hearing little but the breeze, occasional wolf howls, bobcat whines, and the light padding of a jack or armadillo in the chaparral.

He stayed for a time with the horses, watching them closely from his haunches for the roll of an eye, the twitch of an ear, or the sudden lifting of a nose, to indicate the subtlest hint of danger.

Satisfied the horses had deemed the area free of interlopers, Yakima drank from the springs running out of the rock wall above the tanks, splashed water on his face, then stole up the grade to the bivouac. The fire was low. A coffeepot steamed on a flat rock near the glowing coals. The four men were spread out a distance from the fire ring, rolled up in their blankets. Cavanaugh lay with his head tipped back against his saddle, hat canted over his eyes. Faith lay curled up beside him, turned away from him, her blanket drawn up to her face. Her hair was fanned across her cheek.

Cavanaugh snored softly, pooching out his lips, his hat rising and falling slightly as he breathed.

Yakima kicked Lou Brahma's right leg, waking him. When the stocky man had cursed angrily and stumbled off into the darkness, hitching his cartridge belt around his waist, Yakima moved around the fire to his own gear spread out along the base of the cliff, a good fifteen feet from the glow.

Doing so, he glanced down to see the crude map, slightly scuffed, that Faith had sketched of Sonora, with the X marking the village of Tocando. He crossed over it, inspected the area around his gear for scorpions or snakes attracted by the fire, then lay down on his back and drew his blanket up to his chin.

Closing his eyes, he wasn't aware of Faith lifting her head to peer over her husband at him. After a time, she laid her head back down and tried to relax into a sleep that had so far eluded her.

The stars faded slowly.

A long, slender line of orange light grew in the east, as if the sun were being called up by the coyotes and cactus wrens.

Walking back to the camp after the last watch of the night, Yakima dropped a slender ironwood log on the glowing coals. The clacking thump jerked the other five sleepers awake, but only Brahma, Longley, Cavanaugh, and Faith lifted their heads.

"Come on, Willie," Longley said, tapping the youngster's shoulder. "Rise and —"

"Don't touch me, goddamnit!" Stiles hissed as he lay back against his saddle, eyes wide and unblinking as he stared at the sky. His tan, boyish face was pale.

"What the hell's the matter with him?" said Cavanaugh, blinking sleep from his eyes. Faith rolled away from him, groaning wearily, and rested her head on her arm.

Stiles's voice rose, thin and shrill as a girl's. "I — I think I got me a bed partner."

"What's that?" Lou Brahma growled, resting his forearms on his raised knees and smacking his lips.

Slowly, Stiles slid his left arm out from under his wool, moth-eaten army blanket. He reached across his chest, pinched the upper-right corner of the blanket between his thumb and index finger, and slowly lifted the blanket until his shoulder, belly, and right hip were revealed — as well as the diamondback rattler resting its head in the crease between the man's wide leather belt and his belly.

"Oh, shit," Longley whispered.

The others jolted with a start. Faith lifted her head sharply. "Shit!"

"Don't make any sudden moves, damnit!" Stiles beseeched, staring tensely down at the snake asleep in his lap.

"Hold on."

Yakima moved slowly around the fire, crouched, and took the corner of the blanket from between the younker's fingers. Even more slowly, he peeled the blanket up and away until the entire snake lay revealed. Bowing along the inside of the young man's crotch, it extended down along the inside of his left leg. The rattle protruded a few inches beyond his hole-riddled left sock, lying flat against the red sand, mesquite berries, and gravel.

Not moving his head, Stiles rolled his eyes up to Yakima. "Can ya . . . git a stick and . . . ?"

Cavanaugh had slipped his revolver from the holster snugged to the horn of his saddle. Now he raised the Smith & Wesson toward the snake. "Here," he said, ratcheting back the hammer.

The snake lifted its head instantly. Its long, scaled length became a taut, quivering coil against Stiles's crotch, rattle twitching, lifting a cicadalike, quivering hiss. Its head protruded above the man's belt, flicking its long, forked tongue.

"Ace, you son of a bitch!" the kid hissed, his jaws so taut that his cheeks dimpled. Sweat glistened on his brow and ran in rivulets through the fine, sandy whiskers on his cheeks.

"What're you gonna do?" Yakima said, lifting his eyes toward the gambler. "Geld the sprout to kill the snake?"

All eyes turned to Cavanaugh. His scarred eye twitched and his face flushed slightly. He shrugged and lowered the pistol. Keeping his voice low, he said, "Anybody got any better ideas? That snake bites him there . . ."

"He's gonna find out real fast which one of us likes him the most," Pop Longley quipped, wheezing a short laugh.

"Ah, Jesus," Stiles cried softly.

Yakima stepped slowly back away from the kid's right side. The snake's tongue followed him. The rattling had eased, but now it increased once more, rising to a veritable cacophony. The BB-like eyes shone with flat, expressionless menace.

Hitching his denims up his thighs, Yakima

dropped to his haunches and rested his elbows on his knees. The snake's head slid and bobbed. The eyes turned on Yakima, and the rattling grew louder, the body tightly coiled and quivering.

"Yakima," Faith warned.

Yakima stared at the snake. The snake stared back.

Yakima lifted his right hand from his thigh, opened his fingers, and turned his palm to the snake. With painstaking slowness, trying not to shake, he moved the hand forward, keeping it just below the level of the viper's head. Snakes saw poorly, and they saw below their line of vision even more poorly.

No one said anything, and no one moved.

Behind Yakima, the fire popped softly, and he jerked with a start. The snake's head shot forward and up, toward his face. Yakima thrust his arm out quickly, caught the snake in midstrike, and wrapped his hand around the neck, just below the head, and rose from his haunches.

Hanging down from Yakima's hand, the snake coiled maniacally, rattling horrifically.

Keeping his hand wrapped tightly around the neck, Yakima sidestepped the fire, half turned, and flung the slowly coiling and uncoiling viper into a gully cutting through the slope about twenty yards away.

"Jee-zuzzz!" Willie Stiles exclaimed, rising swiftly and swatting at his torn, faded denims as though the snake were still there, razor-sharp fangs digging into his balls. "For the love of God . . . *Jee-zuzzz!"*

The others stared after the snake with hushed awe.

Then Lou Brahma heaved a long sigh and chuckled.

Pop Longley whistled.

Her face drawn and pale, Faith cursed again.

"I'll finish him," Ace Cavanaugh said, turning toward the gully and raising his six-shooter.

"Leave him," Yakima said.

Cavanaugh turned toward him, scowling with disbelief. "Say what?"

"No harm done. Leave him."

He walked around Stiles, who stood in a half crouch, a revolted expression on his bleached face, and grabbed his saddle off the ground. With his other hand, he grabbed his blanket roll and, shouldering the saddle, headed off toward the water tanks and the horses.

"Hey!" Cavanaugh called behind him. "You going with us, or aren't ya?"

Yakima stopped. With his back to the

group, he glanced in the direction he'd thrown the snake. "I reckon I'd better."

He tramped off through the brush and slowed when he approached the horses — his four wild mustangs tied separately from Wolf and Faith and Cavanaugh's remuda of seven, which included the mounts of the two dead men they'd left in Yaqui Springs.

He slipped the oat sack off the black stallion's head, then bridled and saddled the horse. As he tied the four broncs together, tail-to-tail, he cursed his plight — heading to Mexico with an old flame and her husband. Foolish — and a sucker's game.

But, damnit, he'd never loved another woman. As she'd told him, he should have stayed in Gold Cache and mined out their vein. But he hadn't, and, in spite of her marriage to the cardsharp, she held a tender spot in his foolish, still-aching heart.

Tender spot, hell. He still loved her. Maybe more now than he had before.

Left alone with those men in Mexico, she'd end up in an unmarked grave.

When he had the four broncs ready for the trail, he walked over and inspected the mounts of his trail mates. He was running his hand down the right forequarters of Cavanaugh's steeldust when the others approached from the camp, their saddles on their shoulders — first Cavanaugh and Faith and then the other three men.

Lou Brahma was razzing young Stiles about the snake.

Cavanaugh stopped and studied Yakima suspiciously. "Hey, what're you doin' there?"

"Lookin' at your horse."

"What about him? Brought him all the way from Colorado. He's a good horse."

Yakima stood, nodding. "Yeah, they're all long-legged and clean-lined — fine-lookin' horse flesh — but you're gonna need hammerheaded desert mounts. Horses that are used to the dryness and the heat — with plenty of sand and bottom. We gotta figure we'll be running from Apaches, Yaqui, banditos or rurales a time or two. Maybe all four."

"Hey, wait a minute now!" Lou Brahma protested, puffing out his cheeks.

Yakima grabbed his reins and the four broncs' lead rope, and swung into his own saddle. "You can stable them in Nogales, and ride my four. They're only about half-broke, but the best way to ride the rough off a gelded bronc is to trail him." Yakima swung Wolf around and booted him between a couple of gnarled saguaros. "I'll scout ahead, meet you up trail."

When he'd disappeared in the chaparral,

the tail-tied broncs kicking up dust behind him, Cavanaugh and the others turned to Faith, scowling.

"He knows this country," she said, staring after the half-breed, wanting to smile but keeping her mouth straight, "so he's the boss."

As she hauled her gear over to her clay-bank, set her saddle down and draped the blanket over the horse's broad back, the other three men wandered up on either side of Cavanaugh. Lou Brahma removed the quirley from between his lips and scowled into the dust sifting behind Yakima's horses.

"You sure we really need that breed?"

Cavanaugh glanced at the lanky Stiles standing beside him, and chuckled. "Ask Willie." He moved forward and set to work saddling the steeldust.

Yakima led the procession through the rolling chaparral, along an old wagon road he picked up two hours after leaving the bivouac below the notch. He stayed a good fifty yards ahead of the others, so the dust from his five horses wouldn't choke and blind them.

He hated trailing this many mounts. To keep from sending up too much dust, and risk signaling his presence to banditos or

Apaches or the rough breed of *norteamericano* border tough haunting the stage lines and ranches populating this remote country, he had to hold Wolf to a slow jog. Even then, the dust of his own five mounts lifted a scaly, copper haze visible to most white men from at least a mile away.

An Apache could spot it from five.

At midday, he turned the horses off the trail, following a dry arroyo to a ridge of strewn rock and mesquites and a few cottonwoods drooping their sun-blistered leaves around a spring. The watering hole had been built up with adobe-chinked rock fifty to a hundred years ago, probably by nomadic Spanish goatherds. While the chinking had crumbled and several rocks had disintegrated, creating leaks that trickled like wind-jostled bone chimes, the trough still held a few gallons of water.

A cottonwood leaf lolled atop the trough, amidst a thin layer of desert dust, which meant no one had been here in at least a day. The unshod hoofprints, no doubt belonging to Apaches, and marking the mud around the spring, appeared that old, as well.

Yakima tied the horses to the cottonwood a ways back from the spring, loosened Wolf's saddle cinch, slipped his bit, then wandered about with his rifle in his arms, scouting the area carefully.

Returning to the horses, he filled his hat, watering each. The fourth bronc was drawing water from the hat when the other riders approached from the direction of the main trail, walking their horses and ducking under mesquite branches.

"We'll rest the horses here for a half hour," Yakima said.

Cavanaugh swung down from his saddle. "How much farther to Nogales?"

"Two, three more hours. We'll be there before sunset."

Faith and Cavanaugh's group milled around the spring, Brahma and Stiles rolling quirleys and Faith adjusting her stirrups while Cavanaugh bit the end off a square-cut cigar and Pop Longley, grabbing a wad of old newspapers from his saddlebags, ambled off into the brush.

Yakima took a long drink from his hat, then scrambled up the rocks behind the water hole. Hearing scuffs and laughter from below, he turned to glance down the rocks. Brahma and Stiles were wrestling while Cavanaugh popped the cork on a whiskey bottle, shaking his head.

"Kid, when will you ever learn?" The gambler chuckled. "Hell, Brahma broke ole

'Iron' Jake Nordstrom's neck in the Long Branch in Dodge City not five years ago!"

Sitting against a mesquite trunk, Cavanaugh stopped the bottle halfway to his lips, and looked up at Yakima. His laughter died as he continued staring, canting his head and squinting his scarred eye. Brahma and Stiles stopped wrestling to follow his gaze.

Faith turned from her claybank to stare up the ridge, as well.

Yakima continued on up the rocks, leaping cactus clumps and boulders with a pantherlike grace. When he'd disappeared over the shoulder of the ridge, Cavanaugh continued staring up the rocky slope, shading his eyes with his hand.

"Kind of a loner, ain't he?"

Faith didn't say anything. Her expression was pensive as she stared up the slope.

"Makes me nervous," Brahma said, his bearlike arms wrapped around Stiles from behind, pinning the kid's arms to his sides. "Them half-breeds always do. No tellin' what kinda hell he's gonna get us into down in Mexico."

"He got me *out* of hell, Lou," Faith said tightly, tugging on the stirrup's strap. "All kinds of it. So shut up about him, will you?"

Brahma glanced at Cavanaugh. "You

notice she tends to defend that breed an awful lot?"

"Yeah, I did notice that," Cavanaugh said, nodding, the brow over his good eye ridged as he studied his wife darkly.

CHAPTER 8

Perched on a slab-sided boulder just beneath the ridge crest so as not to outline
himself against the sky, Yakima scanned the
surrounding terrain, spying little except for
more knobby ridges like the one he was on,
separated by flat stretches of chaparral-
stippled caliche.

The sun was straight up and brassy. It
burned through his hat, seared his cheeks.
The air was so dry that his sweat evaporated
at nearly the same time it began dribbling
down from his hatband.

The only movement was the occasional
dust devil — lifting suddenly, dying just as
fast — and a lone eagle soaring high over a
distant western knoll. It loosed a shrill, cat-
like cry, which was quickly swallowed by
the moonlike vastness. At Yakima's boots, a
horned toad peeked out from a crack in the
rocks, then scuttled back into its niche
through sprigs of dried grama.

Yakima dropped onto his hands and knees and peered over the side of the slab-sided boulder, into the shaded, sandy niche below. Spying no snakes or spiders, he hoisted himself into the niche, dropped to his butt, and rested his back against the side of a relatively cool slab of rock. He crossed his boots, rested his rifle across his thighs, tipped his hat over his brows, and folded his hands on his chest.

In less than a minute, the sounds of the cicadas and the breeze faded as he eased into a nap, always rejuvenating despite its shallowness and brevity.

He'd been out maybe ten minutes when the ching of a spur rose from the rocks below the niche. Yakima opened his eyes, tipped his hat brim off his forehead, blinked, and waited. Boot heels scuffed the rocks, and then he could hear someone breathing.

"Yakima?" It was Faith.

He remained where he was, repressing his annoyance at having his nap interrupted. "Here."

The footsteps and spur chimes grew louder. A shadow slid across the edge of the niche, and then Faith leaned her head over a boulder to his right. Her face was flushed, hair dancing about her dusty cheeks. "Prowling around and napping like a mountain lion . . . as usual."

She lowered her slender legs — black denims sheathed in brush-scarred chaps — over the edge of the rock, then dropped into the niche. She doffed her hat, pulled a pouch up out of her low-cut blouse, and lifted its loop-thong from over her head. As her hair fell back into place, she set her hat back on her head and extended the pouch to Yakima.

"Five hundred dollars." She jerked her head sideways. "The same amount I gave the others, except for them I threw in ten percent of the brothel. I'd bring you in, but I figured you weren't interested."

Yakima glanced at the sack, and frowned. "Who are those rannies, anyway? I've heard of Brahma. Used to be a fairly notorious cattle rustler and stage robber in northern Colorado, southern Wyoming. Spent some time in prison."

"Ace used to run with him," Faith said, dropping her gaze to the money sack, which she fingered between her knees. "I didn't know it before we were married, but they spent time in prison together.

"As for Willie, he fancies himself a cardsharp like Ace. They met on the trail somewhere. He swamps the brothel for me, runs meals to the rooms. Pop Longley had a ranch south of Laramie, until the Cheyenne burned him out and killed his wife. He did some rustling with Brahma and Ace, then tried placer mining up around Gold Cache. He was our sheriff for a while, and a regular at the brothel. He might not look like it, but he's good with a gun and a horse, so I hired him to come along."

She shrugged a shoulder and tossed the money sack down beside Yakima. "There you have it, and there's your cut."

Yakima tossed it back. "Keep it. Take it home. Put it into your business. Buy yourself a nice steak in Tucson on the way back to Gold Cache."

She frowned and opened her mouth to speak, but Yakima grabbed her forearm and squeezed. "I know you love your brother, but this is dangerous country. Gringos don't live long down here. *Gringas* — especially beautiful *gringas* — fare even worse."

"That's why I've hired *them*," she said with strained patience, jerking her head again to indicate the men below. "And *you*."

"Cavanaugh's boys are most likely capable sorts by Colorado standards, but the odds are stacked against them down here. There's an old saying — first-time visitors to Mexico either get lucky or disappear. Cavanaugh and them others — good with guns, knives, and cards, and *overconfident* — are just the sort whose luck pinches out fast down here, where even the most civilized hombres are rough as shucked cobs."

Cavanaugh's voice rose from below. "Faith, what the hell you doin' up there, honeybunch? You don't come down soon, I'm like to get jealous."

Brahma and Longley chuckled.

Faith stared at Yakima. She held up the money pouch and arched a brow. Her lips were set firmly together, and there was steel in her blue eyes.

Yakima sighed with frustration. "I won't take your money."

"You'll go?"

"If you're going, I'm going." He chuckled dryly. "Just remember, it's never too late to change your mind."

"Thanks. I'll remember that," Faith said, looping the pouch around her neck, letting it fall back down her shirt. "I'll let you rest." She turned and climbed up out of the niche, then dropped her head down once more, regarding him curiously. "Why did you leave Gold Cache? We might've had a couple of months, at least."

He ran a hand through his long, sweat-damp hair. "Leaving wouldn't have gotten any easier." As if dismissing her, he tipped the hat low on his forehead, then poked it up abruptly.

"Hey?"

She turned back toward him, frowning.

"You love Cavanaugh?"

She glanced down for a moment, then returned her eyes to Yakima, and shook her head. "No."

He waited until he heard her boots on the rocks as she drifted down the slope, then once more lowered his hat brim over his eyes.

It took Yakima several minutes to fall into his usual doze after Faith left, and it was a lighter doze than usual. After about ten minutes, he pushed his hat back, dug into his shirt pocket for his makings sack, and rolled a cigarette.

He smoked the cigarette leisurely, keeping his ears pricked for sounds of danger and clearing his mind. It was a good five-day ride to Tocando — a dangerous ride through Indian and bandito country — and he had to keep sharp. Nothing like a woman to dull the senses. Sometimes he wondered why God had ever invented them.

When he'd finished the quirley, he picked up his rifle and scrambled back down the rocks to where the men rested in the shade of the mesquites with the horses. Wolf turned his head to Yakima, shook his head and blew, eager as always to hit the trail.

"Mount up," Yakima said to the others, slipping Wolf's bridle bit into his mouth and tightening his saddle cinch.

"Hey, that black of yours bit me," Lou Brahma said as he rose from under a mesquite and turned to show Yakima his right shoulder. "Look there." The shoulder seam was torn, the thread frayed. "I was waterin' my own horse, and he just leaned over and bit my shoulder. If them others are even rougher than he is, how in the hell do you expect us to ride 'em to Tocando?"

"Carefully," Yakima said, grabbing the rough string's lead line and swinging into the saddle. "Remember to stay behind me a good fifty yards or so, keep the dust down."

He booted the black into the chaparral, the rough string of snorting broncs thundering along behind. Yakima smacked Wolf's neck with the back of his gloved hand. "How many times do I have to tell you to mind your manners, you ornery son of a bitch?"

Wolf lifted his head and snorted defiantly as he lurched into a jog. Yakima swung him onto the main trail and booted him into a slow lope, glancing behind occasionally to make sure the others were behind him, settling in for a long, hot ride.

The trail passed in a blur. The sun hammered down. Cicadas whined. Occasionally, a roadrunner ran out onto the trail and sprinted ahead in a zigzagging red blur before disappearing back into the creosote and mesquite shrubs.

They passed over a low mountain range, then dropped into a broad, bowl-shaped valley surrounded by dun-colored barrancas shimmering in the heat haze. Yakima, walking his horses and riding casually with a leg hooked over his saddle horn, sat up suddenly and dropped his boot back into the stirrup.

He'd heard something, and now he heard it again — a girl's scream. He jerked his head to the right as a horse whinnied and gunfire snapped beyond a low rise in the northwest.

Yakima kept Wolf walking along the trail, but when he heard more gunfire punctuated by the jubilant whoops and yells of at least a half-dozen men, he cursed and turned the black to the right of the trail and booted him into a gallop toward the rise.

He'd ridden fifty yards when he checked Wolf down and leaped out of the saddle. He dallied the broncos' lead line around his saddle horn, then looped Wolf's reins over a paloverde branch. He shucked his Yellow-boy from its sheath, grabbed his spyglass from his saddlebags, and began heeling it toward the rise, beyond which more guns popped, men whooped, horses whinnied, and women screamed.

Near the crest of the rise he doffed his hat and crawled until he was able to lift his gaze over the lip and peer into the valley on the other side, exposing only the top of his head between two sage clumps. With his naked eyes, he could see several horseback riders galloping wildly through the chaparral, turning their horses back and forth, pistols and rifles popping in their hands. Brown figures ran amidst them, screaming and wailing, babies crying, riderless horses lifting shrill whinnies and galloping, buck-kicking west-ward.

Yakima raised the spyglass and adjusted the focus. The riders wore the dove gray uniforms of the Mexican rurale, complete with cartridge bandoliers crisscrossed on their chests, and steeple-peeked, broad-brimmed sombreros adorned with the customary silver eagle badges flashing in the sunlight. The Mexican rural policemen turned their horses tightly, triggering pistols toward the black-haired, brown-clad figures

— Apache women and children — running madly from the yowling Mexicans, horses, and bullets.

Yakima picked out one rurale wearing captain's bars and followed him galloping through the brush. The man threw his head back, howling with laughter as a young woman ran away from his galloping, iron gray Arabian. The young woman, long hair flying out behind her, swerved around a saguaro and continued sprinting toward a low rise in the north. Her short dress whipped about her light brown thighs, catching on the brambles and cholla.

The Arabian lunged forward, drawing abreast of the girl. With a victorious whoop, the rurale swung the barrel of his rifle against the girl's head. She gave a clipped scream as she stumbled forward, hit the ground, and rolled in a flurry of flying black hair and roiling brown dust.

The rurale drew back on the Arab's reins, white teeth flashing between spread lips. He shouldered his Sharps carbine as other women and children screamed in the brush around him, and as other rurales fired guns and galloped horses. The rurale captain swung his leg over his saddle horn and dropped straight down to the ground.

Running feet thudded behind Yakima. He

lowered the spyglass and turned. Ace Cavanaugh, Faith, and the other three men were running toward the rise, Brahma and Stiles holding rifles. Pop Longley jogged along, red-faced and cursing, throwing his arms out for balance, his old coat flapping around his lean hips. Yakima motioned for them to keep their heads down, then turned to peer once more through the spyglass.

The young Apache woman was scrambling to her feet and, holding her head with one hand, tried to run away from the captain, who laughed as he strode confidently toward her. The girl stumbled on rocks, then dropped to a knee. As she tried to push herself to her feet once more, the captain reached out and grabbed her long hair, whipping her head back. The girl's mouth opened, but her scream didn't reach Yakima's ears until the captain, pulling her hair savagely, had thrown her down in the gravel to his right.

The man then kicked her bottom, throwing her forward, then planted one high-topped boot against the back of her neck, holding her head down against the ground. She thrashed and kicked her bare legs to no avail; the captain kept her head pinned snug to the ground.

The man threw his head back on his

shoulders, laughing as though at an especially funny joke, then leaned his rifle against a saguaro and began unbuckling the cartridge belt wrapped around his waist.

"My god — what's happening?"

Yakima turned. Faith lay to his right, propped on her elbows, holding a pair of field glasses to her eyes.

"Rurales hunting Apache scalps," Yakima said as the guns popped, hooves thundered, and more — though not as many as before — screams tore on the hot breeze.

"Christ," Faith said. "What're they doing this far north?"

"Rurales on the Apache trail don't recognize the border."

"Isn't there something we can do?"

Ace Cavanaugh lay on the other side of Faith, sucking a weed stem. "Hell, they're Apaches."

"They're women and children," Faith said, handing the glasses to Cavanaugh. "I don't see a single Indian man amongst them."

Yakima raised his field glass again. The rurale captain had pulled his pants and underwear down to his knees and raised the Apache girl's dress above her flaring hips. Holding the thrashing girl around her waist, he thrust his hips against her naked buttocks, grinding against her savagely.

Yakima's blood boiled. He lowered the spyglass and grabbed his rifle. Lou Brahma reached over from the left and clamped his hand down on the Yellowboy's brass breech.

"Don't get your back up, breed. You count how many rurales are down there? Nineteen."

Yakima whipped his head toward the man, clenching his left fist. Brahma stared back at him, light brown cheeks framed by long, black sideburns. Pop Longley squinted a sage gray eye over Brahma's shoulder. The wind ruffled his silver beard and the silver hair falling from under his hat.

"Lou's right," the oldster wheezed.

Yakima unclenched his fist and pulled his rifle out of Brahma's grip. He'd like nothing better than to drill a round through the rurale captain's spine, but doing so would not only get himself killed, but the others in his party, as well, including Faith.

He set the rifle down beside him and took up the spyglass. The rurale captain pulled away from the Apache girl, who lay slumped on the ground before him. The girl stretched an arm in front of her head, as though feebly attempting to crawl away. Her bare bottom, heartbreakingly exposed and vulnerable, glistened dully in the blasting sunlight.

"Let her go, now," Yakima silently ordered the man. "Turn and mount your horse, ride away."

Looking down at the girl, the captain stood, pulled up his pants, buttoned them, and wrapped his cartridge belt around his waist. Two big knives jutted from sheathes on the wide, leather belt trimmed with brass cartridges.

Yakima gritted his teeth as his heart thumped in his chest.

The captain unsheathed one of the knives. His jaws moved as he stepped forward, crouched over the girl, and jerked her head up by her hair. As he reached down with the knife, Yakima lifted the glasses slightly, so that he could see only the top of the rurale's peaked hat.

Then the man straightened and turned toward Yakima. He held up the bloody scalp in his left hand, the long blue-black hair ruffling in the breeze.

Yakima tightened the focus until the man's face filled the vision sphere — two eyes set close beside a long, eaglelike nose, with a mole set at the outside base of each nostril. He wore an impeccably trimmed black beard, very short and cropped. A long earring — a small silver wolf's skull — hung from his right ear. His braided, silver-streaked hair hung down in front of his right shoulder.

Yakima let the man's visage seer itself into his retinas. If he saw the man again — and he hoped he would — he would kill him.

The captain's mouth opened. The victorious whoop didn't reach the rise where Yakima and Faith's group lay until the man had turned to his horse, hooking the fresh scalp over his cartridge belt.

Yakima slid the spyglass to the girl, then removed it quickly, oily fingers clawing at the back of his throat, nearly making him retch. The girl was dead, her throat cut, bare legs and bottom unmoving.

Around him, the others didn't say anything as they stared down the slope before them.

Yakima glanced at Faith. "What do you think?"

She swallowed as she turned to him. "I think I'm still going to Mexico."

There was a long silence as they all seemed to ponder what had just happened. Brahma laughed, breaking the tension.

"I don't know about you boys," the big man said, crawling straight back down the rise, "but I need a drink. Let's get to

Nogales while the cantinas are still open."

Pop Longley laughed. "Hell, Lou, the cantinas never close in Nogales." He rose from his knees and followed Brahma down the rise.

"I'm with them," Ace Cavanaugh said. He reached over and swatted the knee of Willie Stiles. "Come on, Diamondback." Rising, he grabbed Faith's hand and gave it a tug. "You, too, senorita. Too damn hot on this hill for me."

The others tramped down the rise, kicking dust up around their ankles, Cavanaugh's arm draped around Faith's shoulders. Yakima glanced once more into the valley. The gunfire had stopped and so had the screaming, but the dust and gun smoke still wafted. The babies, too, were silent.

The rurales milled around the brush, laughing and admiring their handiwork.

Yakima crawled several feet down the rise, grabbed his rifle, and, muttering a frustrated curse, heeled it after the others.

CHAPTER 9

Late in the afternoon, Yakima's party crossed Sonoita Canyon at the southern edge of Arizona Territory. They slogged across the Santa Cruz River — merely a muddy rivulet this time of year — and into Nogales.

The border town, nestled in dun brown, yucca-peppered hills, dozed in the late-afternoon heat, only a few dogs and goats out, a couple of horses slouching at hitch rails along the main street. The hot wind flapped laundry hanging from clotheslines, swirled the dust and manure, and tossed tumbleweeds this way and that, picking a couple straight up and throwing them back into the desert from where they'd been blown.

The last time Yakima had visited Nogales, on a horse-selling trip, he'd stabled Wolf on the southeast edge of town. He couldn't remember where the barn lay exactly, but, feeling his way, he swung the black stallion and the gelded broncs off the main drag, past a couple of brush-roofed, mud-brick hovels and a chicken coop, around a one-armed saguaro, and pulled up to a two-story, adobe-brick establo half buried in scrub and cactus at the base of a sandy butte.

A spidery old man in a ragged green serape and white canvas trousers sat in a chair before one of the barn's two open doors, shaping the stout chunk of ironwood on his lap into what appeared to be a leaping panther. A straw-basketed demijohn sat on the ground beneath his chair.

"Hola!" the old man intoned, his eyes brightening at the *norteamericanos* pulling up before him. "Welcome to Nogales, senores and" — his brown eyes sparkled as they landed on Faith — "senorita!"

"Buenas tardes," Yakima said. "We'd like to stable six horses for a week, maybe two, but we'd like to stable these four, the claybank, and my black just for overnight. How much is that gonna set us back, amigo?"

"Gringo money, senor?"

Yakima nodded.

The old man tugged at his goat beard. "One silver dollar a night for each horse, and that is the best buy in town, amigos.

That includes feed and water, of course."

Yakima jerked back on the lead rope when one of the broncs started at a buzzing black fly, but kept his eyes on the liveryman. "And a daily curry."

The man looked as though he'd been threatened with an ax handle. "Such hard work for such an old man! No, no. It is an impossibility!"

"That's all right," Yakima said, turning away. "We'll try Establo Robles. Saw the sign farther on down the main drag."

"Don't be so hasty, amigo," the old man grumbled, rising and placing the carving on the chair. "Now that I think about it, the exercise will do me good." As he reached for Yakima's lead rope, his rheumy brown eyes brashly removed every stitch of clothing on Faith's exquisite frame. He chuckled lustily. "I will stable two of your horses for free if you leave the senorita here with me, as well, hokay?"

Yakima turned to Faith sitting her horse between him and Cavanaugh. She chuckled and leaned forward on her saddle horn. "How kind of you, senor" — she glanced at the large shingle stretched across the barn, just below the open loft door — "Ramirez. But a night in the arms of such a man as yourself might make me decide to stay here in Nogales forever." She smiled her winning smile. "And that would make my husband most *sad!*"

Brahma, Stiles, and Longley chuckled while Ace Cavanaugh flushed and swung down from his saddle. "All right, all right," he growled. "Let's stable these beasts and find a tavern. My throat's as dry as that last arroyo we crossed."

They tended their horses, unsaddling them and rubbing them down themselves while the old man, assisted by a sullen, skinny boy, hauled water and oats and continued flirting with Faith. When the mounts had been fed and watered and turned into the corral, and the tack hung on creaky wooden trees in a lean-to shed, they shouldered their gear and headed out toward the town's main thoroughfare.

In the shade of a saddle shop, they gazed west along the dusty central drag over which the evening shadows were closing quickly. Siesta had ended, and the scantily clad, sleepy-eyed whores were pushing out shutters and lighting cigarillos on sagging balconies. Vaqueros and *charros* in sombreros and brightly colored shirts and neckerchiefs milled before the shops and cantinas, and the celebratory strains of a fiddle lifted over the tiled roofs from the northwest.

Above and beyond the village, the swollen, copper ball of the Sonoran sun dropped slowly over a distant range of black, jagged peaks, mares' tails of salmon and lime green fluttering broadly out behind it. A ray of light reflected off the bell in the church's stout brown tower and shone like gold.

"Good hotel over there," Yakima told the others clumped beside him as he nodded at the two-story hotel sitting kitty-corner across the street. From the second-story balcony, a couple of *putas* were beckoning to him and the other men, one teasingly pulling one side of her lace-edged purple wrapper back from a full, brown breast, revealing all but the nipple, and wagging her finger at Willie Stiles.

"Looks fine as frog hair to me," the kid said, grinning up at the women.

"Reckon I could handle it," said Brahma, doffing his hat and patting his curly black hair down against his head.

Pop Longley wheezed a laugh. "Shit, I'm fixin' to have a heart stroke just lookin' at them beauties!"

"How's the panther sweat?" Ace Cavanaugh asked, biting the end off a cigar. "Any gambling tables?"

"No gambling, Ace," Faith admonished

125

with a strained smile. "Remember the agreement?"

"No gambling tables," Yakima muttered, adjusting the saddlebags draped over a shoulder. "But the hooch is as good as anywhere in town. I'll meet you at the general store first thing in the morning. We'll stock up on trail supplies, then pick up the horses and push south."

As he began heading west under the brush arbors and along the boardwalks, Faith called behind him, "Where you goin'?"

"I'll see you tomorrow," he said, keeping his head forward and stepping over a campesino still taking siesta before a cantina, a three-legged, yellow cur stretched out between his legs.

Yakima couldn't have said exactly where he was going or what he was seeking. He knew only that a nettling need hounded him like a rabid dog at his heels, and the only place to satisfy such a need was on the west end of town, far from Faith.

The din grew louder ahead of him as he crossed the plaza between the statue of the Virgin Mary and Baby Jesus and the sandstone church before which a portly gent in a brown robe and frayed straw sombrero swabbed the stone tiles with a mop, kicking at stubborn horse turds with his sandaled feet. The padre deliberately kicked the shit toward the two-story, stone and wood building on the opposite corner, on the balcony of which a half-dozen scantily clad, heavily painted *putas* milled, smoking and laughing and chatting intimately with a couple of well-dressed Mexican businessmen on fainting couches shoved up against the wall.

"Come on up, Padre!" one of the girls called over the balcony, opening her powder blue wrapper to flash her heavy, pale breasts. "I'll give you a special rate as long as you aren't so hard on me at my next confession!"

The padre eyed the girl speculatively for a moment, the heavy breasts jostling as she swayed drunkenly from side to side. Then, catching himself, the robed gent waved his hand as though swatting a fly, and turned back to his mopping, a flush rising in his clean-shaven cheeks.

Yakima passed the padre, crossing the side street to the saloon from which the din of conversation and howls of laughter already emanated, and whose massive shingle on the front of the second story announced EL PALACIO DE NOGALES. No signs precluded Indian or half-breed customers, for nearly everyone in Mexico had some Indian blood. Ignoring the girls calling to him from the second-story balcony, smelling the sweet aroma of marijuana and the musky-sweet odor of opium, he mounted the broad front porch and passed through the batwings.

Though he couldn't afford either the girls or the hooch, Yakima had stopped here before, so he didn't need to take the place's measure long before he moved past a group of well-dressed vaqueros and businessmen — the Nogales House catered to the more moneyed on both sides of the border — and strode along the long, mahogany bar with its large, polished back bar and mirror.

He found what he was looking for midway along the bar — a beautiful young whore in a red, black-edged corset and gossamer black gown that resembled nothing so much as thin, black fog. He'd never seen her before, here or anywhere else, but she'd do.

The tight corset lifted the girl's full, creamy breasts. She wore red lipstick, a black choker and jade cameo around her neck, and purple feathers in her blue-black hair, which was piled in loose, glistening swirls atop her head. Her red skirt dropped to midthigh, and her long, well-turned legs were covered in black, fishnet hose. Her shoes were as black as her hair, the heels like stilettos.

Lounging back with her elbows on the

bar, legs crossed seductively, she glanced at Yakima, her eyes dropping down his lean, tall frame, then rising again to his green eyes. Her own eyes were soft, a little uncertain, the pupils wide as beads. She'd probably been smoking the good marijuana the place was known for.

"*Hola*, big man," she said in silky Spanish, probably taking him for Mexican. Most people in Mexico thought he was a half-breed Apache. "Welcome to the Nogales House. Prettiest putas and best liquor in Sonora."

"Let's go to your room, Senorita."

Her eyes widened slightly, taken aback by his boldness which one usually found only in the cantinas on the other side of the street. "Of course," she said uncertainly. "But . . ."

"Let's go," Yakima said, glancing at the broad, carpeted stairs at the back of the room.

A tall man in a black sombrero, leather charro jacket, and gold-embroidered chaparral slacks had been standing on her opposite side, facing the bar and speaking to another man to his left. Now he turned suddenly toward Yakima, pushing away from the bar to see around the *puta*. He had a round, pockmarked face and thick, curly sideburns. Judging by his attire, he fancied himself important. Two matched pistols hung on his hips, tied down at the thigh.

"Amigo," he said in English, having heard Yakima speak to the girl, his eyes flashing anger, "Dolores is with me this evening. You want your *indio* ass kicked up around your ears, huh? Please don't insult me further by standing this close to me." He poked his thin, black cheroot toward the door. "The cheaper girls are across the street."

He smiled, pleased with himself, then ran his hand up over the girl's naked shoulder, taking a lock of her hair between his thumb and index finger. The girl flinched a little, as if his fingers were snake tongues. The Mexican moved her head toward her neck, pooching out his lips before he stopped and glanced up at Yakima, as if surprised to find the half-breed still standing before him.

"What — my English is not clear enough for you?"

"It's clear enough," Yakima said tonelessly, dropping his saddlebags on the floor, leaning his rifle against the bar, and resting his right elbow on the mahogany with a near-casual air, like a cat sunning himself on a hillside.

He smiled, the hard planes in his face softening but his jade eyes remaining flinty, cold, and confident. He was being too reck-less, downright foolhardy, but a restlessness burned in him — a frustration he'd felt since he'd found out that Faith was mar-ried. He'd take what he wanted tonight, and God help anyone who stood in his way. Aware of the girl staring up at him, wary and bewildered, he kept his gaze on the Mexican, whose face colored slowly, as though exasperated by the half-breed's inso-lence.

"Just so happens I find my heart set on this girl right here." Yakima's voice was even, the ominous half smile frozen on his lips.

The Mexican's face turned the deep rus-set of a Sonoran sunset. Gritting his teeth, he grabbed the girl's arm, and she gave an indignant yelp as he jerked her back behind him so quickly that she tripped over her own high heels, and fell to her knees. She clamped one slender hand over the edge of the bar top to keep herself from falling all the way to the floor, and stared angrily up at the Mexican.

The conversations around Yakima and the angry Mexican stopped abruptly, and most of the faces within ten or fifteen feet turned toward them, a couple of the well-dressed, cigar-chewing gents elbowing others beside them to redirect their attention.

The Mexican stepped out away from the bar, brown eyes hard, and gritted his teeth, smiling savagely, as his right hand flicked to the ebony-handled stiletto on his left hip. He was already leaning forward to press the point of the razor-edged blade to the underside of Yakima's chin, when he screamed suddenly and jerked sharply right.

The watchers behind and around them saw only the Mexican's sudden movement, as though he'd been kicked by a mule, and then heard the stiletto clattering onto the floor and skidding off under a table before coming to rest against a fancily-stitched Chihuahua boot. The sudden slash of Yakima's left hand against the man's wrist had been too fast for the unprepared eye to follow.

So, too, was his sudden, violent manipulation of the man's arm. Then there was a sharp, anguished cry and a black and silver blur as the man turned a somersault in the air beside the bar, and hit the floor with a thunderous boom on his back. His large-rowled spurs followed a half second later with a raucous grinding of puncheon splinters.

Yakima stood beside the bar as though he'd never moved, staring down at the tall Mexican. The man groaned and grunted as he lifted his head and looked around. He winced sharply and, as his eyes rolled back into his head, his head sagged back down to the floor.

His head tipped to one side, and his eyes closed. His chest rose and fell slowly. His right wrist, lying on the floor beside him, bulged grotesquely with the dislocated bone.

Yakima cast a quick glance around, his right hand brushing the carved-bone grips of his .44. But seeing no one making a move against him — in fact, most of the eyes sliding between him and the unconscious Mexican owned a distinctly wary, half-admiring cast — he casually shouldered his saddlebags once more, and grabbed the Yellowboy.

He drew the girl up gently by her wrist. She stared at him, frowning a little worriedly, as he turned her around and began heeling it toward the carpeted stairs at the back of the room, drawing the girl along behind him.

Her high heels made a cleaverlike chopping sound, and she was tripping over her own feet before she stopped suddenly, jerking her hand from Yakima's grip, then kicked out of the high-heeled shoes — first one, then the other, sending both shoes flying under an occupied table in the shadows at the end of the bar.

"Okay," she said, and thrust her hand into his once more.

He led her so swiftly up the steps that her hair came loose from the bun atop her head, and fell in a pretty mess about her shoulders. She had to take a couple of steps at a time, fairly leaping, before they reached the top, and he stopped and glanced at her.

"Which way?"

She canted her head straight down the hall, and they continued forward, passing the hushed onlookers — the other *putas* with their bleary-eyed customers — on the balconies angling away to both sides. He slowed his spur-ringing steps to let her pass barefoot on the red and gold Turkish carpet glowing softly in the wan, fluttering light of the stout, colored candles hung in wrought-iron wall sconces.

Yakima guessed the girl wasn't yet twenty, though her eyes betrayed maturity beyond her years. As he followed her, he admired her rich hair billowing in large, disheveled rolls on her shoulders and down her slender back, and the delectable flare of her hips over the round bottom pushing out from beneath the tight red skirt. Her bare feet padded softly on the carpet's thick material, the gossamer black rapper flowing out behind her, the faint smell of cherry and lavender perfume lacing the air around her.

They went up a short flight of steps, turned down another hall, and paused before a door flamed by candles in glass-covered sconces. She withdrew a key from her cleavage, favored him with another pensive stare, her brown eyes sweeping his chest and shoulders before flicking toward his expressionless eyes framed by his dusty, black, sweat-damp hair, and poked the key in the lock. She cursed as she jerked the key in frustration.

Yakima closed his hand over her own, adjusted the key, and turned the key and her hand slowly to the right until he heard the bolt click back from the latch. She glanced up at him once more, then turned the knob. As the door opened, she stepped into the room lit as the hall by flickering candlelight, though the room was filled with enough candles for a Catholic shrine.

It was a big room by Mexican whorehouse standards, with a thick carpet and heavy wooden furniture including a broad marble washstand, a red brocade fainting couch, and a high, four-poster bed under a red velvet canopy. Drapes covered the long windows facing the street from which the strains of guitar music and occasional celebratory pistol pops and coyotelike whoops sounded.

The girl closed the door and stuck the key in the lock. Yakima set his rifle and saddlebags down, drew her to him, and kissed her. At first, she jerked back, afraid, tightening her shoulders and drawing her forearms together, but as the kiss continued, her body relaxed. She gave a groan, then, stepping into him, rose up on her toes and slowly wrapped her arms around his neck.

Yakima's loins warmed at the feel of the silky, slender body in his arms, her own body warming to his, the full breasts pushing against his chest, her hands pulling gently at his long hair falling down the back of his sweat-damp buckskin shirt.

After a time, his blood boiling, he eased her away from him. Her hair had come even farther down from its bun; he slid a thick wing of it from the side of her smooth, fine-boned cheek, the smooth skin darker than usual. Probably, like him, she carried some Indian blood. Probably Apache.

He stared into her eyes for a time, a fire burning in him, consumed by his own desire, at once giddy and amused by it, like a man in the middle of a three-day drunk. Had he really turned the tall Mexican downstairs inside out? He snorted at the recklessness. Liable to get himself shot and no use to Faith at all.

Faith . . .

He drew the beautiful *puta* toward him again, kissing her, running his hands up and down her back. She groaned and pressed her breasts against his chest, digging her fingers into his biceps. He began to move her back onto the bed, but stopped suddenly, sucking a breath.

No use rushing things. It would be a long evening.

Breathing heavily, she stared up at him, ridging her brows, puzzled.

Yakima turned and kicked out of a boot, the spur singing as he kicked the boot into a corner. He took another step, kicked out of the other boot, then continued to the washstand, yanking his shirttails out of his pants.

He pulled the shirt over his head, dropped it on the floor, and poured water from a stone pitcher into the washstand's porcelain bowl. Leaning over the bowl, he splashed the tepid but refreshing water over his face and across the back of his neck; then he lathered up with soap from the cake in a little wicker basket on the washstand.

When he'd scrubbed his face, neck, chest, and under his arms, he rinsed away the soap, fingered water through his hair, then toweled dry. He tossed the towel onto the stand, then, unbuckling his cartridge belt, turned to the bed.

He stopped abruptly, feeling as though a bee had just stung his loins. The girl lay on the bed, propped on an elbow and watching him bemusedly, her skimpy clothes piled on the floor. She was completely naked, one arm curved across her belly, just beneath the full, heavy breasts, pushing them up slightly. She'd taken her hair all the way down, and it spilled across her slender shoulder and down the arm on which her head was propped.

Her legs, one atop the other, were slightly bent and, letting her almond-shaped eyes rove across Yakima's muscular chest and hard, corded belly, she slowly flexed and unflexed her toes.

"*Muy hombre,*" she said softly, watching him as he dropped his cartridge belt on the floor around his boots and began shucking out of his pants. "I hope you will be kinder to me than you were to Senor Lopez."

"The gent downstairs?"

"The son of the alcalde who fancies himself a pistolero and, as you saw, an *estilete artiste.*"

"He can go back to bein' a stiletto artist

tomorrow." Naked, Yakima moved to the bed, the girl's eyes widening slightly as they dropped to his crotch. "As long as he stays out of my way tonight."

"*Sí,*" she said, scuttling sideways to give him room on the bed, her cheeks flushed, her heavy breasts rising and falling sharply.

Yakima sat down on the edge of the bed, lifted one leg, and started to roll toward her.

She held him back with a firm hand. "Wait."

She moved up beside him, rubbing her cheek against his shoulder for a time. She groaned sensuously as, running her hand up and down his thigh, she kissed his chest and belly before glancing up at him demurely, flinging her hair from her eyes.

She gave a coquettish half smile as she closed her hand over his stiffening member. She stared up at him, her lips parted, eyes bright, as though gauging his reaction as her hand worked on him gently. Scuttling closer, bringing her knees up toward her sloping breasts, curling her coffee-colored legs, she cleared her throat and lowered her head to his crotch.

He kept his left leg on the floor while the girl showed him why she had the best room in the house. As she worked slowly but relentlessly, with excruciating precision, his heart beat erratically, his temples pounded with desire, and his fists grabbed at the sheets.

He pulled her brusquely up. She gave a startled, laughing cry as he slid her hair back from her face, flung her back on the bed, and, kissing her with a frenzied passion, spread her legs apart with his own.

"Ay caramba!" she cried, reaching up and smoothing his long hair back from his scarred cheeks and throwing her head back on the pillow. *"Muy hombre!"*

CHAPTER 10

Yakima woke at first cock crow, opening his eyes in the room's semidarkness even before the bird's raucous yowl had dwindled into silence.

He stared up at the canopy over the bed, then turned to the girl lying facedown beside him. The sheets and single quilt were pulled down to her thighs, revealing her slender back, a breast bulging out from under a bent arm, hips flaring to the two firm globes of her bottom.

As he admired the girl's dusky, curving form beside him, he silently cursed his idiocy, the wildness in him that occasionally boiled to his otherwise stoic surface and had, a few times, resulted in his waking up on a jail cot with his face and knuckles bloody, head throbbing from fists, thrown furniture, and hooch. At least, this morning he had something more pleasant than a tin slop bucket and iron bars to look at.

He leaned down and lightly kissed Dolores's left buttock. Yawning, cursing inwardly as he remembered what he was doing here in Nogales, he began sliding his feet toward the edge of the bed.

The girl groaned, snaking a hand out from beneath her pillow to lay it flat atop his bandaged belly, splaying her fingers.

"It's early. Snuggle with me, *mi amor*."

Yakima lifted her hand and kissed it softly. "Gotta long ride ahead."

As she groaned in protest, he threw the covers back and dropped his feet to the floor. He yawned again and ran his hands through sleep-tangled hair. The girl squirmed around on the bed beside him and turned onto her side. "I don't know who you were making love to last night, amigo, but whoever she was, she was a very lucky lady!"

Yakima's head shot toward her. He must have had one hell of an angry look on his face, for the girl jerked back slightly, blanching, as though bracing herself for a slap. She canted her head to one side, narrowing one eye. "Maybe one you want to forget, no?"

"Maybe."

Yakima leaned forward on his knees, took a deep breath, as though preparing for a strenuous climb, then rose and strode over to the washbowl. He poured out last night's water into a slop bucket on the floor and refilled the bowl. He washed quickly but thoroughly, hearing Dolores snore softly into her pillow once more. As he dried his face with a heavy towel, he reached up and flipped the latch of the shutter before him, and drew one side back against the wall.

The cool morning air pushed against his face, refreshing in spite of the stench of dung it carried. A dog, which resembled a small coyote, walked along the cobbled street below, tongue hanging, as though it had had a busy night in the country and was looking forward to a long nap in the straw. As Yakima raised the towel again to his face, the dog turned to peer behind and quickened its pace along the cobbles.

Yakima lowered the towel once more to follow the dog's glance back along the street. As he did, the clomp of shod hooves rose, and horseback riders appeared, moving along the main drag from the west. The clomping rose to a near din echoing off the surrounding adobes. Little dawn light filtered into the street, but as the column drew near, Yakima saw the dove gray uniforms and straw sombreros with the silver eagle insignias of the Mexican rural police.

On the shoulders of the hawk-nosed lead rider, gold captain's bars flashed dully in the vagrant light. The man wore two big knives on his hips, and two long-barreled pistols. Several long, black scalps swung from his cartridge belt.

Yakima stood frozen, staring down at the column, his heart quickening slightly as the rurales drew to a halt before a small, yellow adobe on the other side of the street. Murmuring amongst themselves, yawning loudly or groaning, the men dismounted and, moving stiffly, obviously having ridden all night, looped their reins over the hitch racks in front of the yellow adobe, and mounted the boardwalk under the brush arbor.

A few milled amongst the horses, one rolling a cigarette. The captain, chuckling, slapped another man on the shoulder; then, standing at the edge of the boardwalk, he turned toward the street, tipping his bearded face up toward Yakima as he planted his hands on his hips and bent backward, stretching. The silver wolves dangled from his ears to his shoulders.

He said something, turned his head to both sides, continuing the stretch, then dropped his hands to his crotch and began unbuttoning his trousers. As he heaved a long, relieved sigh, Yakima heard water trickle into the street.

As the captain directed his piss flow back and forth along the cobbles, groaning and muttering, the scalps ruffled across his thighs and over the gun and knife sheaths . . . including an especially long, blue-black length of satiny Apache hair.

Without a doubt, it was the scalp of the pretty Apache girl Yakima had watched the captain butcher yesterday afternoon. As the captain continued pissing into the street, Yakima ground his heels into the floor and resisted the impulse to grab his Yellowboy and shoot the man's pecker off.

When the captain had shaken himself off and tucked himself back into his pants, he turned and strode onto the boardwalk, said a few more words to the men around him, then sauntered through the cantina's batwings, the other rurales following close at his heels. One stopped to flick a cigarette butt into the street, then disappeared through the doors, the batwings squawking behind him.

Yakima's hands quivered with suppressed rage. But what had he expected? This was Mexico. Life's value was weighed on a far different scale down here.

He pressed the towel to his face, finished

drying himself off, then dressed and picked up his gear. He planted a last kiss on the sleeping *puta*'s tender rump, and slipped quietly out the door.

He stole around the dark building until he found a door that let out to outside stairs to the back alley in which a couple of goats were cropping grass around the building's stone foundation. At the top of the stairs, he looked around cautiously; then, deciding no danger lurked, he dug in his tunic pocket for his makings sack, and rolled a smoke.

He should have been making better time than this, but then, hell, he wasn't sure why he was here in the first place. He was in no hurry to see Faith again in the company of her Colorado cohorts . . . and her husband. . . .

He'd have given a lot not to have received her message. He'd needed that like he needed an Apache war lance through both ears. Well, he'd take the job. He'd see it through, see her safely back to the States. And when he'd led Faith and the others — with or without her brother — back to Arizona, he'd make a beeline back to his Bailey Peak ranch, and he'd give careful consideration to ever leaving that mountain again.

Licking the quirley closed, he hiked his

146

saddlebags onto his shoulder and descended the stairs. The goats dashed away, bleating angrily, as he strode east along the alley, then swung through a gap between buildings toward the main drag.

He had a quick breakfast of fried goat burritos and beans, then rolled a second quirley as he made his way east of the central plaza, stepping over drunks passed out on the boardwalks. He stopped under the broad arbor of a *tortillería* to fire the quirley, and looked up quickly, the lucifer still burning between his fingers. In the periphery of his vision he'd spied an object projecting from an alley mouth about forty yards away. Now the object — he wasn't sure but he thought it had been a steepled sombrero crown — was gone.

Yakima glanced around, frowning, then lit the quirley. He dropped the match on the sun-blistered boards and continued walking. He passed a grocery store smelling of cured meat and peppers, and stopped, pressed his right shoulder against the adobe wall, and edged a look into the alley. At the same time that he heard a spur chime, he saw a boot disappear around the back of the same building he was sidled up against. Halfway down the alley, a corn-husk cigarette butt smoldered amidst rusty tin cans and goat dung.

Yakima took a deep drag on his own quirley as he stared down the alley, then continued on past the alley mouth, smoking, a pensive frown ridging his brows. A lone rider passed him, a vaquero heading out of town, riding low in his saddle, drunk and half asleep. From somewhere on the other side of the street there rose the clatter of an early-morning roulette wheel . . . or one from last night that hadn't yet been silenced.

Yakima stopped when, approaching a large dry goods shop, he spied the silhouette of a woman standing atop the shop's loading dock. The sun rising in the east shone like liquid gold in her blond hair hanging down from her man's broad-brimmed hat. She was smoking, one arm crossed beneath her breasts, staring over the roofs on the other side of the street.

Yakima crossed to the loading dock and mounted the steps. Faith turned toward him, and their eyes met as he continued to the top of the platform.

She looked him up and down with a faintly skeptical air and, keeping her arm crossed beneath her breasts, blew a plume of tobacco smoke. Her carbine and saddlebags were piled near her feet. She wore a checked, low-cut blouse, which revealed more cleavage than he would have liked, and a glimpse of a lace-edged camisole. It took a powerful woman to shake a man's soul after he'd spent the night with a beautiful, bronco senorita adept as any *puta* at man-pleasing, but Faith could do it, all right — right down to his spurs.

"There you are," she said, with a wry smile, narrowing a blue eye at him. "Sleep well?"

"Well enough. You?"

"Very well, in spite of the noise. After sundown, this side of town started hopping like Thornton's place on Saturday night." She canted her head toward the door of the shop. "Ace and the others are inside, trying to get the proprietor to understand their English."

"You weren't invited?"

She exhaled another smoke plume. "Too early for me. Remember? Back at Thornton's, I was the girl who rarely got started till noon."

Yakima didn't want to remember that or anything else about Thornton's, or his and Faith's long run from Thornton's to Gold Cache.

He pushed through the mercantile's door and stopped just inside. At the rear of the broad room, Cavanaugh, Brahma, Longley,

149

and Stiles stood facing the counter, saddle-bags on their shoulders, rifles resting across the countertop before them.

Cavanaugh and Brahma were trying to get the short, apron-clad Mexican behind the counter to understand their orders — Brahma thrusting his outstretched arm at a sack of coffee beans on the shelf behind the man while Cavanaugh, with strained patience, was loudly enunciating the letters C-O-F-F-E-E.

Stiles was chuckling and shaking his head. "Jesus Christ, Ace, how's spellin' the word gonna help?"

As Yakima sauntered toward the counter, Cavanaugh and the others turned toward him. "Hey, Henry, you know some *Mejicano*, don't you? I can't get this greaser to understand a damn word of what's on our supply list. I say coffee, and he tries to sell me wheel dope!"

The Mexican, red-faced with anger, opened up with a string of Spanish, most of which seemed to question Cavanaugh's breeding and manhood.

Stiles said with an air of exasperation, "Seems about the only English he knows is *greaser* and *bean-eater*, and they done piss-burn him good!"

Yakima set his saddlebags and rifle on the

counter, then walked around behind the bar. The Mexican halted his tirade against Cavanaugh and turned to Yakima with an incredulous expression, blinking behind his dusty spectacles, his coal black hair still showing the wet tracks from his morning comb.

Moving back and forth behind the counter, then back out and around the store, and spatting out his cow-pen Spanish, Yakima pointed out the flour, coffee, pinto beans, baking powder, salt, salt pork, and jerky, indicating with his fingers how many pounds he wanted of each. He also ordered six spare canteens, one for each of the riders in his cavvy, as there were damn few water holes this time of the year on the devil's dance floor of desert they were about to traverse.

As the man was scooping the dry goods into burlap sacks, Yakima shook a box of .44/40 shells in front of his face, and held up five fingers. *"Balas. Cinco."*

"I need .45's," said Cavanaugh.

"And what about some hard candy?" Stiles said, indicating a bin of sugary sweets behind him. "I always get a sweet tooth just before I turn in at night."

"Forty-five shells we'll pack, but no candy." Yakima tossed a sack of flour to Lou

Brahma and a sack of sugar to Pop Longley. "Nothin' but the essentials. Stuff those in your saddlebags. We want the weight divided equal. It's gonna be a long, hot pull, tough on the horses."

"How far did you say it was?" Stiles asked, leaning back against the counter, yawning.

"A good five days, maybe six," Yakima said, stuffing a couple of shell boxes into his saddlebags.

"Shit," Stiles growled. "My sweet Nova girl's gonna done forget my name before I get back to Gold Cache."

Pop Longley laughed as he organized his saddlebags. "Nova never could remember your handle in the first place." The gray-bearded gent winked at Yakima. "Nova's one of Miss Faith's special whores, and Willie here done tumbled for her despite the fact she insists on callin' him *Ernest!*"

Longley and the others laughed while Stiles popped a hunk of hard candy into his mouth and tossed a penny onto the counter. "You boys don't know shit from Cheyenne. We ain't even begun this tramp, and I'm already sick of your funnin'!"

Yakima shouldered his saddlebags as the mercantiler finished piling the dry goods onto the counter before Cavanaugh, who was counting out silver from a leather pouch. On his way to the door, Yakima glanced at Stiles. The younker seemed an unlikely choice for a dangerous trek to Mexico. He wore his big bowie knives as though he knew how to use them, but, wide-eyed, jug-eared, and flushing, he looked like a thirty-and-found saddle tramp to Yakima.

"What do you do in Gold Cache?" Yakima asked. He figured he must do more than just run errands for Faith.

"Me?" said Stiles with a complacent shrug. "Hell, I'm a bouncer at Miss Faith's place, and Ace there's teachin' me black-jack." He grinned, showing his big, white teeth, eyes slitted under a wing of sandy hair. "And a lover of women!"

"Sure ya are, Ernest!" jeered Brahma as Yakima moved back onto the loading dock, pulling the door closed behind him.

Faith sat on a bench at the edge of the dock, facing the store, a Winchester carbine laid across her slender thighs. Hands raised to tie her hair back, she looked up as Yakima passed her, heading toward the steps. "Give a Spanish lesson?"

"Border Spanish with a lot of finger point-ing." He started down the steps. "They'll be along in a minute."

"Yakima?"

He turned back to her. She stood now,

staring at him beseechingly, holding out a slender strip of rawhide. "Would you tie this around my hair? It keeps slipping loose on me."

Yakima slid his gaze to the mercantile door, then back to Faith. "That's your husband's territory." He continued down the stairs and eastward up the street, glancing around to make sure he wasn't being set up for an ambush.

At the livery barn, he found the hostler, Anselmo Ramirez, currying one of the broncs while Anselmo's grandson, Pedro, hauled water from a well. The other broncs and the black stallion were skirmishing in the rear corral, Wolf apparently trying to maintain his position as remuda ramrod. Yakima saddled the roughest of the half-wild broncs — a wild-eyed coyote dun — then took him for a hard ride in the rolling desert south of Nogales, neck-reining and backing, then neck-reining again, curbing the beast when it began to buck under the spur.

When he thought he'd taken some of the sand out of the gut-twister's craw, he rode back to the corral, where the rest of his crew had gathered, throwing their saddles on the other three broncs and on Faith's claybank — the strongest-looking of the Colorado horses. The clay wasn't a desert horse and it was too clean-lined for Yakima's taste, but, with its short legs and a broad barrel, it would weather the trip well enough. Besides, she obviously had a soft spot for the horse, and he wasn't about to force her to exchange it for a Mexican cayuse.

"Which one of you wants to ride this cyclone?" Yakima said, swinging his right leg over the saddle horn and dropping straight to the ground. He opened the corral gate and led the mount into the corral where the rising sun had found the dust and turned it copper. "I'd ride him myself, but I trained Wolf not to carry anyone but me."

"A cyclone, huh?" Lou Brahma shouldered his saddle and walked over to where Yakima was stripping his own gear from the coyote dun. The bronc blew and nickered, twitching its ears and taking swift, contentious glances at Wolf. "Long before I earned my reputation as a *woman*-tamer, I broke horses for Jalba Flynn in southwest Wyoming. Old Jalba caught the wildest damn horses in the whole damn country."

Brahma dropped his saddle and, swaggering and drawing on the quirley drooping from a corner of his thin-lipped mouth, plucked his bridle off the apple and eased it up toward the dun's head. "He gotta name?"

"I reckon Cyclone's as good as any," Faith said, glancing over her right shoulder as she adjusted her own saddle on the clay's back.

Carefully, Brahma slipped the bit through the dun's teeth and slid the straps up and over the horse's stiff ears. When the gelding just stood there, staring straight ahead, not fighting the bit, Brahma gave a satisfied chuckle.

He stooped to pluck his saddle out of the dirt. As he set the leather on the dun's back, he said around his cigarette, "Don't mean to contradict ya, there. Miss Faith . . . and I reckon we can call him Cyclone if you *want*. But I have a feelin' by the end of the day — after I rode the venom outta this bronc's nasty ole bones — we'll be callin' him somethin' more like Spring Breeze."

"Spring Breeze, huh?" chuckled Pop Longley, reaching under his buckskin's belly to tighten the latigo.

Watching the dun's eyes cautiously as he adjusted the saddle, Lou Brahma snorted, "That's what I said."

Seeing that the bulky man was taking his time and, in fact, seemed to know what he was doing, Yakima threw his own leather on Wolf. He'd just slid his Winchester into the

156

saddle boot when he turned to see Faith, Cavanaugh, Willie Stiles, and Pop Longley standing by their own saddled mounts, directing their skeptical, bemused attention to Yakima's left.

Yakima turned. The bulky Brahma had finished saddling the dun, adjusting his saddlebags, and attaching the rifle sheath. Now he eased up to the dun's left side and grabbed the horn. He whistled confidently as he turned out the stirrup and toed it.

"Easy," Yakima warned. "Let him get used to your weight."

"Me and him," Brahma said, resting his butt in the saddle, then squirming around, adjusting his position. "We had a little discussion. Man-to-man. Eye-to-eye."

"Shit," said Stiles tensely.

Cavanaugh winced. "Pop, you best run and fetch a sawbones. We'll no doubt need him shortly."

All eyes were on Brahma. The big man sat the saddle, stiff-backed, holding the reins high, sliding his eyes around as though he were listening for a distant train whistle. A half smile played across his lips, his broad, pitted cheeks bunching. The smile widened as his confidence grew, and his small, blue eyes slitted.

"Well, there, now." He looked around at

the others. "See?"

"Don't just sit there," Yakima warned, stepping forward quickly. "Get him —"

He hadn't set his foot down before the coyote-dun chuffed once, like a Baldwin locomotive preparing for a pull up a steep hill, then dropped his head nearly to the ground and kicked his back legs straight up in the air. His hindquarters whipped up and forward like a catapult.

Brahma grunted as he rose up off the saddle, one hand grabbing the apple before the bronc twisted in midair. The sudden jolt tore Brahma's gloved hand from the horn, his boot from the left stirrup, and threw him down the horse's right side like a big, dark sack of potatoes, hat flying, red neckerchief whipping in the wind.

The big man's head and shoulders hit the dirt while his right boot got hung up in the stirrup. The bronc dragged him a good fifteen feet, his broad butt carving a deep furrow through the ankle-deep dust and dung, before Brahma jerked his boot free, rolled once, and came to rest against a corral post.

A copper dust cloud wafted around the big man's supine form. His hat swirled down through the dust and landed a foot from Brahma's right knee.

The others held their breath collectively as the coyote-dun pranced and skitter-stepped off toward the corral gate, issuing victorious snorts and whinnies as it shook its head and rippled its withers.

"Son of a —," Brahma wheezed, grunting and rolling onto his shoulder, his slitted, fury-bright eyes trailing after the bronc. "That goddamn, hammerheaded son of a bitch!"

Seeing that only the man's pride appeared to have gotten injured in the violent tumble, Cavanaugh, Longley, and Stiles chuckled.

Pop Longley yelled through the sifting dust, "Ole Jalba Flynn ought to have taught you not to just sit a bronc, waitin' fer him to buck you off, Lou!"

"Yeah, Lou," Cavanaugh called. "I never even broke horses, and I coulda done *that!*"

"Son of a bitch!" Brahma shouted, climbing to his knees and elbows. As he heaved himself to his feet, dust still sifting around him, coating his face and hair, he grabbed his silver-plated, pearl-gripped, artillery-model Colt's pistol and thumbed the hammer back as he cursed and spat grit from his lips.

Standing beside Wolf, the black's reins hanging in the dust near his boots, Yakima plucked his own Colt from its holster, cocked it, and aimed it straight out from his belly. He didn't say anything, but let the ratcheting scrape of his gun hammer do the talking for him. The other men fell instantly quiet.

Brahma swung his belligerent face toward Yakima. He swung his cocked Colt around, as well. "That cayuse is gonna get a bullet through both lungs, then another through his goddamn *head!*"

Yakima opened his mouth to speak, but he stopped when hoof thuds rose on his right. Faith galloped her clay between him and Brahma, and jerked back on the reins. She palmed her ivory-gripped S&W .36 and aimed it at the big man, rising up in her stirrups as she shouted, "Goddamnit, Lou. Leather that iron or I'll drill one between your post-stupid eyes!"

Yakima could see Brahma's head sticking up beyond the clay's neck. The big man turned his steel eyes on the girl, and his jaw hardened. Faith raised the pistol higher and lowered her head to aim down the barrel.

"Do it!"

Brahma stared hard at her for stretched seconds. He glanced over the clay's neck at Yakima. Slowly, the flint leaving his eyes, he lowered his Colt, depressed the hammer, and rammed it angrily back into its holster.

"You try anything like that again," Faith warned, "you'll be sporting a third eye." She neck-reined the horse around sharply. "Open the gate, Ace. I'll be waiting for you *boys* in the street!"

When Cavanaugh had done as he'd been ordered, and Faith and the clay had disappeared, Yakima threw a loop over the dun's neck and led the snorting bronc over to where Brahma still stood, as mean-eyed and sour as a bulldog in the driving rain.

"Mount up," Yakima said, dropping the reins at the man's boots. "I reckon we got a trail to fog."

CHAPTER 11

When Lou Brahma, grumbling and cursing indignantly under his breath, had climbed back onto the coyote dun's hurricane deck, Yakima's party of six headed straight south of Nogales on an old Spanish trading trail scored by the horses of countless vaqueros and ranch wagons.

Yakima had traveled through Mexico enough to know that the safest way to avoid bandito and Indian attacks was to avoid well-traveled routes, so, five miles out of Nogales, he pulled right of the trace and headed the party cross-country, through the burnt-orange caliche tufted with saguaros, greasewood, mesquite, and catclaw.

"How the hell you know where we're going if you don't stick to the main trace?" Cavanaugh asked.

The gambler and Faith rode directly behind Yakima. They were flanked by Stiles and Lou Brahma, with Pop Longley riding

162

drag, his lean, old body swaying easily with his bronc's rough stride. Brahma and the coyote dun had come to a truce of sorts, though the bronc cast occasional, taunting glances up at its rider. Brahma answered the looks with gritted teeth and muttered curses.

Yakima turned Wolf wide of a deadfall saguaro, then lifted his gaze to a range of purple peaks hovering over several nearer ranges on the southwestern horizon. From this distance the cordillera resembled a massive storm front swollen with midsummer, gully-churning moisture.

"See that far mountain range?"

"I see it," Cavanaugh said.

"Those are the Sierra Olivadas. Tocando lies at their west edge, nestled amongst the foothills."

"Five days, you say?"

"Give or take."

"Those mountains look closer than that."

"Near sundown, they'll look farther away than the moon."

They rode for a time, the sun blasting down and reflecting blindingly off the caliche and boulders humped here and there along the trail. An occasional kangaroo rat or armadillo thrashed in the brush.

Faith called, "What does *Olivadas* mean

in English?"

"The Forgotten Mountains," Yakima said. "Riddled with all sorts of dark legends, not to mention Yaquis. We'll stay wide."

He took his reins in one hand, and hipped around in his saddle, swinging his gaze in a full three-sixty.

"Keep going," he ordered the others.

Reining Wolf left of the trail, he galloped up a low hill. He crested the rise quickly, not wanting to show his outline against the sky for more than a second, and rode halfway down the other side before pulling back on the reins. He sat the stallion near a nest of cracked boulders and spindly pinions, squinting northwest through his own sifting dust.

After a minute, his eyes picked out the same foxtail of rising, adobe-colored dust he'd spied a half hour earlier. It was angling around him to the west, tracing a wide semicircle.

Yakima sucked dry air through his front teeth, cursed his own stupidity, then neck-reined Wolf back up and over the hill, angling ahead of the others who walked their horses through a heavy copse of octotillo, the branches of which striped the ground with shade. On the trail only a few hours, the five in Yakima's charge already appeared dusty and sunburned as they eyed him curiously through the chaparral.

"See anything?" Brahma called.

"Nothing worth mentioning." Yakima galloped out ahead of Faith and Cavanaugh, then checked Wolf back down to a walk.

He kept his eye on the foxtail for the rest of the morning. At high noon, he led the group up a low rise upon which an ancient, hollowed-out casa sat amidst the creosote and saguaros.

Built of stone two hundred years ago or more, the house had no doubt once belonged to a wealthy hacendado. Sonora was pocked with these ghostly reminders of early, bygone settlers. The walls were a good two-feet thick, stout enough to repel Indian attacks, but the windows, doors, and ceiling had long since vanished. The desert had reclaimed everything except for the square stones of the walls, which had likely been carved from the overhanging basalt ridge, though they, too, were buckling and disintegrating from the ceaseless harassments of time.

Quickly inspecting the place from horseback and finding nothing inside the hollow house but sand, sagebrush, and the remnants of earlier campfires, Yakima turned Wolf toward the others. "We'll camp here till early evening, then start out again by moonlight. Tend the horses and stake them out in the galetta grass on the other side of this slope. Go easy on the water. If I remember right, we won't come upon more till midday tomorrow."

"Where you going?" Faith called as he touched spurs to the black's ribs.

"Gonna scout around," he said, galloping back the way they'd come. "Won't be gone long."

Ace Cavanaugh rode up beside Faith, who, sitting her clay with both hands on the horn, was looking back at Yakima riding off around a rocky knoll.

"Kind of a restless sort," Cavanaugh said with a wry air. He narrowed one eye at Faith. "But then, I gotta feelin' you already know that . . . and a whole lot more about that rock-worshipping half-breed." He lifted his chin and slitted both eyes accusingly. "Don't you?"

Faith's smooth cheeks colored, and her jaws hardened. "Don't ever call him that again, Ace. Do you understand me?"

"So, it's true." Cavanaugh chuckled without mirth. "What kind of a whore were you, anyway? Sleeping with a half-breed . . ."

Bringing her hand back and forward, Faith laid a blistering slap across Cavanaugh's left cheek. Cavanaugh's head whipped sideways. When he turned back to Faith, his teeth were gritted, eyes narrowed beneath his hat brim, and his cheek was cherry red. He opened his mouth to speak, but before he could get the words out, Faith cut him off.

"Remember, Ace. You need me as much as I need you. Your money is tied up in the house, and if *I'm* not in charge of the house, *neither* of us turns a profit. And you know *how much* you enjoy turning a profit."

Cavanaugh leaned out away from his horse, pushing his face to within a foot of Faith's, one hand on his reins while he clapped his free hand down on her knee. "And don't *you* forget, Missy, you're carrying a thousand dollars of *my* money for bailing your brother out of that Mexican hotbox." He blinked and gritted his teeth once more, his good eye blue as winter ice. "Do *you* understand *me?*"

Cavanaugh snorted as he swung down from his saddle and began leading the roan away behind the others.

Faith sat watching her husband and the other men disappear around a wall of the stone house, a thoughtful cast to her gaze. It didn't make sense that she hadn't told Ace about her and Yakima. She'd been a prostitute before taking over as a "non-entertaining" madam of her own brothel, and marrying Cavanaugh. Ace knew about most of her past. She'd had no reason for keeping quiet about any of the men she'd taken to bed.

But then, she hadn't been in love with any of the others.

Brows ridged pensively, she slid her eyes back in the direction in which Yakima had disappeared, his dust still sifting behind him.

Reining up beside a sprawling mesquite, Yakima rose in his stirrups to peer over the low, rocky ridge just ahead. Dust sifted above the ocotillo about a half mile away, skeining up like the gauzy smoke of an ironwood fire.

Three or four riders were heading directly toward him, in the direction of the ruined casa, following his own group's fresh horse prints. They were obviously trailing his party and, while there were any number of reasons you might be shadowed in Mexico — most of them deadly — he had a feeling he knew it was he himself who was being shadowed here, and he also knew why.

Senor Lopez, the man he'd assaulted in the fancy Nogales whorehouse, had sent them.

Yakima set his jaws. He had to be one of the dumbest bastards to have come across the border in a good, long while. Faith couldn't have found a bigger fool had she tried.

Yakima booted Wolf off to the left. Where the hills narrowed together to form a gully of sorts in which a couple of gnarled mesquites crouched, Yakima swung out of the saddle. He dropped the mustang's reins, and shucked his Yellowboy from the rifle boot.

"Stay, boy."

Wolf snorted and turned his head back to sniff his master's shoulder, as though trying to learn Yakima's intentions by his scent. Yakima rammed a fresh shell into the rifle's breech, off-cocked the hammer, then, giving the stallion's rump a reassuring pat, heeled it back the way he'd come. He climbed halfway up the low ridge, saw the dust growing before him, and hunkered down against the ridge's shoulder, tipping his hat against the blazing sun, waiting.

Five minutes later, the clomp of hooves and squawk of tack rose on the other side of the ridge. Yakima waited, listening, hearing the occasional clank of a hoof clipping a rock and the crunch of spindly branches.

He turned his head to the ridge and, lifting his chin and rising slightly on his knees, edged a glance over the crest. The riders were thirty yards from the ridge and closing, offering occasional glimpses through the creosote of leather vests and sombrero brims, tack trimmings flashing in the sunlight. Yakima waited a count, then stood, crested the ridge, and stared down the other side, thumbing the Yellowboy's hammer back to full cock.

The three riders, moving more or less side by side, continued toward the ridge for several more yards before the man on the far right looked up from beneath his sombrero brim. His eyes widened, and his lips stretched back from his teeth.

He drew sharply back on his steeldust's reins and barked in Spanish to the other two on his right, "*Madre Maria* . . . on the ridge, you idiots!"

The brims of the other two sombreros shot up to reveal dark beard stubble and startled, brown eyes rising to Yakima. He stood spread-legged atop the ridge, holding his Yellowboy down low across his thighs. The other two riders cursed and grunted as they jerked back on their reins and reached for the pistols on their hips — each man wearing two revolvers in oiled holsters.

"I wouldn't do that," Yakima said.

The men's hands froze on their pistol grips, their faces frozen in grimaces.

The three Mexicans — two stocky, round-faced hombres, one lean but short with the gaunt face and hook nose of a desert predator — stared up at Yakima, eyes hard. Yakima stared back, the furnacelike breeze whipping his hair back from his shoulders. Slowly, the lean, hook-nosed hombre removed his bony hand from his Schofield's grips and cracked a smile, brown eyes glinting in the sunlight.

"*Hola, amigo.* You startled us!"

"Better me startlin' you than you startlin' me with .44 slugs while I took siesta."

Hook-Nose manufactured a surprised look, as though he couldn't believe what he was hearing. "Amigo, you think that we" — he gestured toward his two companions, who'd removed their hands from their pistol butts and now sat their saddles negligently, dull-eyed — "you think we were *following* you?"

Yakima bent his knees slowly, squatting and resting his shotgun across his knees. He poked his hat brim off his forehead and stared down at the three Mexicans, his eyes slitted against the sun's glare.

Hook-Nose turned to his companions and

told them in broken English that Yakima thought they were following him to kill him in his sleep.

The man directly beside him cocked a brow and dropped his jaw with phony exasperation while the third man, who had a nasty scar in the shape of barbed wire just over his left brow, maintained his dull-eyed expression, jerking his horse's head up from a tuft of grama grass.

Hook-Nose chuckled, leaning back in his saddle. "Senor, we are innocent pilgrims. If I thought it any of your business, I would tell you our destination and our business, but since it is not . . ."

Staring up the grade at Yakima's hard eyes, the man let his voice trail off. After a time, his eyes shifting back and forth in their sockets, he lifted his mouth corners and spread his mustache with another grin.

"Amigo," he said sadly, lifting his narrow shoulders under his wash-worn underwear shirt with a shrug, "Senor Lopez is in a very bad way this morning. His wrist is broken, his shoulder . . . *oh!* . . . and I won't even talk about his head. It is not known how long he will be in bed. . . ."

"But more importantly," said the man to Hook-Nose's right, "is that he is very dishonored. For such an indignity to happen in such a place, to a man who holds himself so high above others, is a very bad thing."

"So he paid you boys to follow me out from town and bushwack me." And if Yakima had not spied them first, they might very well have bushwacked the five other riders in his charge. His idiotic performance last night might very well have gotten Faith killed.

The three Mexicans stared up the grade without saying anything. Slowly, the smile faded from Hook-Nose's lips, and his eyes grew dark as he studied Yakima's expression as well as the rifle resting across his thighs. The others were doing the same, though not with quite Hook-Nose's enervation. He knew what they were thinking: How fast could Yakima raise that long gun and aim?

By the well-oiled revolvers on their hips, they fancied themselves pistoleros. Now each man was taking a bald look at his own abilities, silently comparing them to the unknown ability of the man before him.

Yakima just hunkered atop the ridge, his hands resting lightly across the Yellowboy.

At length, doubt played across their faces. Yakima said, "Turn your horses around and ride back to Nogales. I see you on my trail again, I won't warn you before I drill you."

The trio sat there for another half minute before Hook-Nose, scowling, glanced at his two companions. Keeping his eyes on Yakima, he reined his horse around sharply. "Keep your life this day, amigo. I suggest, however, that if you ever pass through this country again, that you swing wide of Nogales." He put the iron to his steeldust, barking as the horse lunged off through the chaparral, "Or your *indio* scalp will be hanging in the central plaza!"

The other two riders, glancing over their shoulders at Yakima, followed Hook-Nose off through the scrub, their dust rising behind them, hoof clomps dwindling into the distance.

When the three were out of sight, Yakima moved down the other side of the hill and over to where Wolf waited, neck craned to peer behind him, thrashing his tail. Yakima slid the Yellowboy into its boot, grabbed Wolf's reins, and climbed into the saddle.

"Come on, fella," Yakima said, booting the horse back along the crease between the hills. "Let's make sure we shook the lice off our blanket, huh?" He genuinely hoped he had. He didn't want to have to kill those men. Killing left a trail.

He climbed the rise where he'd squatted and followed the Mexicans' fresh tracks for half a mile before he reined up suddenly, frowning. Ahead sounded a low murmur of voices and the muffled thud of hooves.

"Goddamnit."

Yakima reined Wolf sharply right and booted him into a shallow gulley. He dropped out of the saddle and shucked the Winchester from the boot.

"Stay, boy."

Walking back up out of the gulley, he crouched behind a buggy-sized boulder, pressing his back to the uneven rock. On the other side of the boulder, the three riders were approaching at a shambling jog, muttering angrily amongst themselves, their dry saddle leather creaking like hinges.

When he figured, judging by the sound, that the trio was twenty yards away and closing, Yakima straightened. Turning, he stepped out beside the rock and rested the Winchester barrel on his right shoulder, the maw aimed behind him.

All three riders saw him at the same time, eyes flashing surprise and fear as they jerked their reins back toward their chests. Their deeply tanned, unshaven faces flushed with fury.

The horses stomped, their eyes white-ringed with apprehension.

Yakima waited, one hip cocked, his index finger curled through the Winchester's trigger guard. "Goddamn, you stupid sons of bitches!" he raked out, scolding himself as much as them.

Hook-Nose's eyes crossed with rage as, jerking the steeldust's reins against his chest once more, he screamed, *"Bastardo!"* and slapped his free hand to the worn walnut grips of the Schofield positioned for the cross-draw on his left hip.

Yakima swung the Yellowboy down, the forestock slapping into his gloved left hand as he drew the rear stock against his shoulder, planting a bead on Hook-Nose's chest. The Winchester roared, slamming a round through the man's heart a half second before he triggered his revolver into the ground midway between his prancing steeldust's hooves and Yakima's boots. Hook-Nose tumbled, screaming, off the lunging horse's rump.

Yakima ejected the smoking cartridge, seated fresh, and slid the Winchester left where both of the other two Mexicans fought to maintain control of their horses while lifting six-shooters.

Standing with his feet spread, face as calm as though he were only taking target practice with coffee cans, Yakima aimed and fired, aimed and fired again. Powder smoke wafted against his face, foul and peppery. The hot cartridges winked in the sunlight as they arced back over his shoulder, shrilling against rocks.

Less than three seconds after the first man had hit the brush, the other two followed suit, tumbling, grunting, and yelling as blood geysered from the ragged holes in their chests. Their horses screamed, wheeled, and ran back in the direction from which they'd come, stirrups flapping, reins bouncing along the ground.

"Dios mío!" one of the dying men cried as he climbed to his hands and knees.

Somehow, he'd managed to hold on to his .44. His hat hung by a thong down his back, and blood spurted from his upper-left chest, bibbing his pin-striped shirt and vest. He rose to his knees and twisted around toward Yakima.

Moving with savage deliberation, Yakima took one step forward as he rammed a fresh shell into the rifle's breech. The man's Remington swung around and up, but before he could squeeze the trigger, Yakima's Yellowboy roared.

Plunging through the Mexican's forehead, just above the bridge of his nose, the soft-nosed .44/40 whipped the man's head back on his shoulders as though someone had collared him from behind. The rest of him followed, tumbling straight back into the galetta grass beneath a paloverde tree, which the blood and brains jetting out the back of his head had already soaked with viscera.

"Goddamnit," Yakima barked again, staring down at the carnage as he plucked fresh shells from his cartridge belt and slipped them through the Yellowboy's loading gate.

When the Yellowboy was loaded, he spat gunpowder from his lips, retrieved Wolf, and galloped back toward Faith and the others.

CHAPTER 12

At the same time but a good fifteen miles northwest of the ruined casa to which Yakima was headed, Captain Luis Ramon Lazaro gigged his high-stepping cream barb through a fold in the sandy hills and into a hollow in which brush corrals and stock pens huddled with a sprawling, brush-roofed shanty. As Lazaro reined the barb to a halt with one hand, he held up the other, and the seven rurales in the captain's charge checked their own mounts down behind and to either side of him.

The tall, angular Lazaro poked the brim of his palm-frond sombrero up slightly and tossed his braided hair over his shoulder. As per his habit, he pensively rolled the liver-colored, thimble-sized mole beside his nose between his thumb and index finger as he studied the hard-packed, dung-littered yard before him.

Smoke curled from the shack's stone

chimney, rising above the straw and iron-wood branches that, woven in a herringbone pattern, composed the hovel's roof. Hogs snorted and knocked about a pen across the rutted trail from the shack, as an old man in a frayed straw sombrero tossed slop over the pen's slatted fence.

A shirtless, barefoot boy — maybe ten years old and wearing baggy white slacks — was winching a bucket up from the covered well that stood in the middle of the dun brown yard. The winch squawked like an unoiled wheel hub with each turn of the boy's slender, coffee-colored arm.

"Time for a drink and a little chat with Senor Estevez," said Lazaro lazily, still fingering the mole beside his nose. "And then a well-deserved siesta —"

He stopped when the well winch suddenly began squealing like a rabbit in a coyote's jaws, and cast his gaze back to the well. The wooden handle of the well winch spun like a windmill in a heavy gale. It stopped suddenly, and then the report of the bucket hitting the water rose from the stone well coping — a hollow, cannonading splash.

"*Papá!*" the boy cried. He wheeled and, putting his head down and scissoring his arms, bare feet kicking up little puffs of dust and finely ground dung, sprinted toward the shanty. He ran between the two horses tied to one of the two dilapidated hitch rails and was promptly swallowed by the velvet shade beneath the brush arbor, his screams for *"Papá"* receding inside the shack.

Rapid footsteps sounded to the right. Lazaro turned to see the old man running down the hill behind the hog pen, his empty feed bucket nudging his denim-clad thigh as he split-ass for a tiny, straw-roofed hovel, which sent up a thin, gray smoke plume from a shallow ravine.

Lazaro chuckled delightedly and gigged the barb forward. "Our reputation precedes us, amigos."

The other rurales — lean, jug-eared privates, mostly, and big, lantern-jawed lieutenant Montana — followed his lead, chuckling and spurring their horses across the yard, past the well, and up to the shack. As Lazaro stepped down from his saddle, the Apache scalps jostled down from the red sash encircling his lean waist above his cartridge belt.

The longest one brushed his left knee. It was one of the finest scalps Lazaro had ever taken. He'd been considering whether he should turn it in for the ten-peso bounty that the hacendados were currently offering for Apache scalps, or turn it into a bridle, maybe weaving some silver conchos into the hair. Such a bridle would look very sharp indeed on the barb's sleek, cream head.

As the other rurales dismounted around the captain, a short hombre with unruly hair and a pug nose stepped through the cantina's main, doorless entrance. Stopping under the brush arbor, the man nervously rubbed his dirty, blood-encrusted hands on his flour-sack apron and offered an unctuous grin. "Captain Lazaro, what an honor to see you again, *mi amigo!* What brings you to this neck of the woods so soon after your last visit?"

Looping his reins over the three mesquite branches that formed one of the two spindly hitch rails, Lazaro glanced at the big, broad-shouldered Montana who was helping himself to a dipperful of water from an *oja* hanging from an arbor beam. Montana returned the glance briefly as water streamed from the long, scraggly mustache hanging down both corners of his puffy-lipped mouth.

"Your wonderful accommodations, of course, Senor Estevez," Lazaro said with a grin that did not reach his eyes. "But I was also wondering if you've seen the vermin horde of revolutionaries led by that *puta mestizo* Leonora Domingo and her mongrel amigo, Christos Arvada. I have been searching everywhere for that gang, and so help me I've found nothing but *indios!*"

Estevez smiled wanly. "Not in several months, *Capitán.* I apologize. But I think you have finally run the senorita and Christos Arvada deep into the Sierra Olivadas."

"Like rabbits to their lairs, *sì,*" said Lazaro, sharing a dark glance with Montana. "That bitch has become a bigger thorn in my ass than all the Apaches and Yaquis in Sonora!"

"I apologize, *Capitán,*" Estevez said again.

"No need for you to apologize, senor," said Lazaro, waving a hand in front of his face as if to shoo a fly. Planting his high-topped, scarred leather boots on the sun-blistered boards of the porch, he added, "How about a cup of your delightful pulque to ease my frustration?"

"Sí, sí, Capitan!"

Nervously running his splayed hands up and down his full-body apron, Estevez stepped aside as Lazaro moved through the door and into the roadhouse. Lazaro was followed by the six rurale privates and Montana. Bringing up the rear, the six-foot-six-inch lieutenant removed his steeple-crowned sombrero as he ducked under the door frame, and ran a big, brown paw over the grisly scalping scars marring his big, pink, hairless pate.

Lazaro sauntered across the shack's dirt floor, swinging his head from side to side, noting the three whores playing a dice game at a rough-hewn table to his right, and two vaqueros gambling at another table to his left. Two whores — obscenely fat and double-chinned — glanced up at the rurales, smiling tensely. Their small eyes bulged fearfully in their doughy sockets.

The third whore, a pretty half-breed who wore a loose, low-cut cotton shift through which her nipples and broad aureoles shone, and whose thick, black hair hung in her eyes, gave the newcomers a semibored, queenly glance. Then she plucked a cornhusk cigarette from an ashtray and took a long, distracted drag. Her face was oval-shaped, her lips full, her cheeks smooth as polished oak.

On the left side of the room, neither of the two vaqueros looked up from their poker game. They kept their heads down, sombrero brims tipped over their eyes. Near their table, a large kangaroo rat was trying to pull a half-eaten tortilla through a small hole at the base of the mud-brick wall.

"Senores, I apologize again that I cannot help you in your pursuit of Senorita Domingo, but I *can* offer you not only the best pulque in the province, but the most wonderful tacos, as well!" Estevez intoned, hustling across the room to the plank bar at the rear, where a fire snapped and cracked in a broad hearth. A pot of beans bubbled over the low flames, sending its contents boiling over the sides. On a table near the hearth, a darkly roasted hog shank rested, still steaming in its own thick grease pool. A black iron skillet flanked it, piled high with brown tortillas nearly opaque with the lard they'd been fried in.

"The pork smells heavenly," said Lazaro, turning and resting his elbows on the bar planks, and studying the dim, smoky room through slitted lids, the single ornament of hand-tooled silver dangling from his right ear. He settled his gaze on the pretty half-breed, who held her cigarette in one hand and shook the dice with the other, keeping her smoky eyes on the table.

Fingering the thimble-sized mole once again, Lazaro said, "We enjoyed a large breakfast and *other* refinements in Nogales just this morning. My men and I are not as hungry as thirsty. You still can't find a good glass of spirits in that border perdition."

"The *putas,* on the other hand," muttered

Montana, dragging out a chair not far from the whores and sitting down heavily, "make the *putas* anywhere else look like hogs crossed with monkeys."

"Not all *putas*," Lazaro said, eyeing the half-breed who did not lift her distracted gaze from the table. He canted his head toward Estevez, who was dipping pulque from a wooden bucket at the end of the bar, near the whores, and handing the tin cups to the eagerly waiting rurale privates. "How is the new senorita working out?"

Estevez paused to glance at the pretty whore, revealed a mouthful of brown, chipped teeth through a grin, and resumed filling the cup in his hand with the colorless alcohol that smelled like unshucked corn left too long in the sun. The potent stench mixed with the smell of the roasted pork and boiling beans to permeate the entire room.

"That one!" Estevez said, slitting his eyes greedily and chuckling. "She's the best moneymaker I've ever had. The border boys with extra *dinero,* they don't mind spending it on her, and they spread it around. What a bewitching time they had!"

As Estevez chuckled, the half-breed shook her thick hair back from her eyes, tipped her head to one side, and took a deep drag off the corn-husk cigarette. Regally, she exhaled the smoke plume toward the far rafters and muttered something to the fat whore beside her, as though oblivious of the men's attention.

"I will have to give her a try sometime," Lazaro mused, dropping his eyes to the half-breed's deep, coffee-colored cleavage.

Estevez, who'd finished serving the privates and Montana, now set a brimming cup in front of the captain, bowing and chuckling with an air of great servitude. "For you, Captain, your time with the whore will be free, of course. It is my small payment for the invaluable work you do, holding the Apaches and the banditos at bay. Where would *Méjico* be without men like you? It would still be the dark, savage ages, would it not?"

Unmoved by the compliment, Lazaro turned slowly, like a cat rising from a long nap. He wrapped his fingers around the tin cup filled with pulque, and lifted it to his nose.

He inhaled the astringent aroma, half closing his eyes. "Speaking of banditos," he said with a desultory air, then closing his upper lip over the rim of the cup and sucking the liquor into his mouth through his shaggy mustache, "I was told recently — just this morning in Nogales, in fact — that you sold a couple of rifles to men riding with One-Eyed Hector Eusebio."

Lazaro lifted his head away from the cup, the pulque dripping off his mustache and onto the stained bar planks, and raised his snakelike gaze to the barman. The bridge of his nose creased deeply, as though his feelings had been suddenly, badly hurt. "Tell me that is not true, Pico."

Estevez leaned back slowly, his ruddy, sweaty face blanching, as though he'd just been slapped. He stared at the captain, in shock for several seconds, eyes dancing, a whole range of various expressions washing through them like vapor clouds wafting across a lake in the early morning, as though he were trying them on to find out which one best suited the occasion.

He chose befuddled exasperation. Turning his hands inward to indicate his chest, he said, "Me, *Capitán?* You mean, *me?* Selling arms to banditos?"

Leaning forward on his arms, Lazaro stared at him while Estevez stood, shifting his weight from one foot to the other and tracing a slow circle on his apron with his left hand. Sweat trickled through the dust on his cheeks, his chest rising and falling heavily.

Keeping his gaze on the barman, Lazaro lifted his cup to his lips and tipped his head back, his Adam's apple bobbing like a plum in a water barrel as he quaffed a good half of the pulque. His eyes teared up and his cheeks flushed as, making a sour expression, he set the cup back down on the bar. "I congratulate you, Eduardo," he rasped, sucking a ragged breath as the liquor dripped from his soaked mustache. "That's some of your best panther piss yet."

"Gracias, amigo."

"Now, tell me," Lazaro said, smiling with false affability, "doesn't your brother-in-law, Tomás, ride with Eusebio's bunch?"

The barman glanced at the whores flanking the captain. The room had fallen so silent, the only other sounds being those of the bubbling bean pot, that the barman's enervated breaths resonated like a small, gathering rainstorm within the roadhouse's close quarters. Estevez licked his slightly trembling lower lip. "I have told Tomás many times, *Capitán,* that he should not. . . ."

Lazaro abruptly slammed his open palm down on the bar planks with a sound like a single-bore shotgun being triggered inside a cave. The planks leaped, as did Lazaro's pulque cup, a good bit of the remaining liquid splashing over the sides and onto the bar.

"You are evading the question, my friend!" Lazaro shrieked at the tops of his lungs, his face turning brick red, the thimblelike mole turning one shade even darker. "Did you or did you not sell Winchester rifles to three banditos riding with One-Eyed Hector Eusebio?"

Estevez gasped and winced as though beset by a sharp pain somewhere behind his eyes. His lips moved but no sounds issued. Several streams of sweat cut through the dust on his ashen cheeks.

With a grunt of strained patience, Lazaro turned to Montana, who had pulled one of the fat whores onto his knee and had shoved a big hand down the girl's baggy blouse, kneading a breast. The round-faced puta wore a tense smile, a single tear rolling down her cheek as she stared at Lazaro. "Lieutenant, round up the boy. Bring him to me pronto!"

"*No, Capitán!*" Estevez cried, bolting forward and holding out his hands beseechingly. "*Por favor!* He is but a child — my only grandson!"

"If you want him to grow to manhood, I suggest you answer my question truthfully, senor!"

"*Sí, sí, Capitán!*" Estevez swallowed loudly but spoke softly. "*Sí* . . . I sold three Winchesters to the gang of Hector Eusebio." Then he hung his head and balled his cheeks like a chastised youngster.

Lazaro glanced at Montana. The lieutenant grinned as his hand continued working over the fat *puta*'s heavy breast. Tears now rolled down both the girl's cheeks. The other fat whore sat frozen in her chair, her back to the bar, while the pretty half-breed continued smoking and playing a leisurely game of dice by herself, still seeming oblivious of what was happening around her.

Lazaro turned his flat, bemused eyes back to Estevez. Leaning forward on both elbows, he raised the cup to his lips, took another long swallow of the pulque, made another sour expression as his eyes watered and his face flushed slightly, then cleared his throat and set the cup once more upon the bar planks. "Where did you get the rifles, Pico?"

Estevez spoke softly to the floor. "*Norteamericanos,* senor. Army deserters. They were heading for the Sierra Madre and they needed money, so they sold me their rifles." He sighed fatefully, and his voice notched up an octave. "I sold them to the men of Hector Eusebio for a very small profit, *Capitán.* A very small profit."

"But you know the penalty for selling contraband, don't you, Pico?"

Estevez raised his dread-pinched eyes to Lazaro. *"Por favor, Capitán.* I beg you. It was only . . ."

"It was only what? A small thing because you made a small profit?" Lazaro threw back the last of his liquor, straightened, and ran a sleeve of his dove gray tunic across his mustache. "What if all the sellers of illegal contraband in northern Méjico saw selling only a few rifles for a small profit to banditos as a *small thing,* Pico?"

Lazaro swaggered along the bar, turned toward the whores' table, and brushed his hands across the shoulders of the fat whore sitting with her back to the bar. The girl squealed and tensed. Lazaro lifted her hair in his right hand, let it fall back against her thick, pale neck as he continued sashaying around the table to stand to the right of the pretty half-breed.

The girl had stopped playing dice. She leaned forward, elbows on the table, her cigarette stub smoldering between two fingers of her right hand. She held her head forward but rolled her eyes to the side as she gazed up at Lazaro through two heavy wings of coal black hair.

Her lips were pursed slightly, long nose

wrinkled, as though against a foul odor. Her dark eyes were smoky with obvious hate and defiance.

"Do you know what would happen then, amigo?" Lazaro barked at Estevez, still standing behind the bar, ashen-faced with dread. "Men like me and these youngsters you see before you" — he swung an arm to indicate the young rurales sitting at a table beyond Montana, bleary-eyed from drink and watching their captain with delight and expectation — "men who risk their lives every day and night to bring law and order to the Sonoran countryside, and to scour this great land of the fetid Apache, will have to do battle with half-human vermin like your brother-in-law and Hector Eusebio *armed with lever-action repeating rifles!*"

Lazaro's shouts echoed off the walls. The beans bubbled and the fire snapped. The fat whore sitting with her back to the bar, hands in her lap, held her head down, sobbing. Somewhere outside, a goat bleated.

The pretty half-breed stared sidelong up at Lazaro, the cigarette smoldering between her fingers. Her eyes were as hard as black volcanic rock.

Lazaro kept his eyes on the barman. "You know that I have every right to burn your hovel to the ground and to hang you and your boy and your fat whores from the nearest tree, no?"

"Sí, sí, sí, Capitán," Estevez said, steepling his hands in front of his chin. "Please . . . I beg you. . . ."

"You will *thank* me when I only take out my frustration on this insolent bitch of a rock-worshipping Apache *whore!*"

As he shouted that last, he grabbed the pretty half-breed's arm and jerked her to her feet. The chair flew out behind her and tumbled backward against the floor. Gritting her teeth, the whore whipped toward him, her hair flying back from her smooth, penny-colored features, and slapped the captain's left cheek. Cursing shrilly, she bounded up on her toes and thrust her head forward, spitting a gob of saliva onto the man's scraggly mustache.

Lazaro laughed, whipped his hand up, grabbed the whore's blouse, and thrust his fist back sharply, ripping the blouse off the girl's slender frame with a single screech of torn cotton. As he tossed the blouse into the shadows behind him, the girl jerked back, naked and startled — the blouse was all she'd been wearing — and raised her hands to her breasts.

She stopped abruptly, the defiant coldness returning to her gaze. Her hands fell slowly to her flaring hips. She lifted her chin and stared back at the captain with barely contained rage, throwing her shoulders back defiantly, thrusting out her full, clay-colored, brown-nippled breasts.

A low murmur of appreciation rose up from the young rurales sitting within view of the naked girl's profile.

"Madre," grunted Montana, who'd stopped massaging the breast of the fat whore to scrutinize those of the pretty half-breed, his black brows mantling his deep-set eyes.

"Ahhh!" said Lazaro, his own eyes roving across the girl's heaving bosom, then canting and turning his head to inspect her legs and naked bottom. "As pretty in the body as she is in the face. I bet she is quite the moneymaker for you, huh, Pico?"

The barman's voice trembled. *"Sí, Capitán.* The best moneymaker I have ever had." He paused to lick his lips, then continued slowly, softly, beseechingly, while gesturing with his outstretched hands. "And she is my wife's cousin, senor. In the name of all the saints, *por favor* . . . if you wish to have her, *have* her . . . but please do not *kill* her."

"Kill her?"

In a blur of motion, Lazaro brought his right hand back behind his shoulder, then swung it savagely forward. The bulging knuckles connected with the girl's left cheek with a resounding smack. The half-breed gave a shrill, enraged cry as she spun and fell in a heap, knocking over a chair.

"I won't kill her, Pico." Lazaro dropped his right hand to his side and unshucked one of the two bone-handled, wide-bladed bowies sheathed side by side with his cartridge belt. "But by the time I'm done with her, you'll wish I had."

As Lazaro dropped to a knee beside the girl and jerked her head up by her hair, Estevez gave a feeble cry and stepped back away from the plank bar, muttering a cry as he crossed himself. Wincing, eyes slitted, he watched the rurale captain tip the girl's head back by her hair and raise the big, razor-edged bowie up to her face.

The madman let the girl get a good look at the wickedly curved steel blade. The half-breed's hard eyes dropped to the weapon and twitched only slightly. As they turned even harder than before, she spat again into the captain's face and grunted a string of epithets in both Apache and Spanish.

"Puta bitch!" Lazaro bellowed.

Again, Estevez winced and crossed himself as Lazaro lowered the point of the knife to the girl's marble-smooth left cheek. His gut turning to jelly, unable to stare straight-on at what the madman was doing to his prized *puta*'s face with that horrible blade, Estevez turned sideways to the bar.

In the periphery of his vision he saw the captain's hand moving the knife slowly, purposefully. With each turn of the man's wrist, Estevez winced and groaned.

To his astonishment, the girl did not move while the captain worked on her face. She lay with her back arched, breasts thrust toward the ceiling, her bare, brown legs stretched nearly straight out in front of her. She gave not a single cry, made no sound whatsoever.

As the captain carved the girl's face, the room seemingly became even more silent than before. No one except Lazaro himself seemed to breathe. The captain rasped quietly and grunted softly as he worked with the adeptness of a practiced surgeon or a master wood-carver.

"There you are, Estevez!" Lazaro bellowed suddenly.

Estevez turned his head forward and gasped.

The captain held the girl's head up by her hair, showing off his handiwork. The *puta*'s face was a bleeding mass of long, deep, intersecting lines — like a map of the Sierra Madre drawn in red ink. She blinked as the captain jerked her head up and down, and then she winced slightly, blood oozing thickly from the cuts traversing the length of her full lips.

"I'll wager those two fat sows will earn more in a week than this bitch will ever make again in a whole year!"

Guffawing, Lazaro tossed the girl away from him. As she slumped to the floor, blinking dully as blood pooled on the hard-packed dirt beneath her naked body, Lazaro climbed to his feet. He extended the bloody bowie to the fat whore sitting on Montana's knee.

The *puta* shrieked and jerked away, then sat, tense and sobbing, as Montana cleaned the blade on her broad upper arm before slipping the knife back into its sheath.

"I would have taken her scalp, rich and black as it is," Lazaro said, staring down at the half-breed who lay nearly motionless on her side, slightly trembling knees drawn toward her belly, "but a good artist knows when the painting is finished."

With that, the captain wheeled on a heel and headed toward the stairs in the shadows at the right side of the room. The Apache scalps danced across his thighs.

"Siesta time, amigos! Estevez, I want a plate delivered to my cot in two hours!"

Chapter 13

When Yakima returned to the ruined casa moldering under the giant basalt obelisk, he found the others all sprawled in the shade within the casa's ruined walls. He turned and headed back down to the horses. Not far from where Wolf cropped the sparse green grass, he threw down his saddle and dropped down beside it, laying his rifle nearby and tipping his hat over his eyes.

He slept for several hours, roused by the screech of a hunting eagle, when the sun was halfway down the western sky and the shade of the obelisk had engulfed the ruined house. When he'd rousted the others, and cleaned out a fire pit in the purple shadows on the south side of the house, he cooked a meal of salt pork, beans, and coffee, and they all ate hungrily before saddling the horses.

They mounted up and headed out as the sun sank over the low western hills. Soon the sun was gone and the moon rose, shedding an eerie, pearl light across the desert, bizarrely silhouetting the ocotillo and greasewood and dappling the slender mesquite leaves with silver. The air turned cool enough that Faith donned a poncho, but there was no breeze, and the desert silence was like that at the bottom of a deep cave; a coyote howling from a crag ten miles away sounded nearly close enough to throw a rock at.

They rested the horses every couple of miles, then resumed their clomping trek through the chaparral and occasional stretches of sand dunes in which only small tufts of Spanish bayonet grew. When the sun vaulted like a huge lemon wafer above the horizon, shedding heat like a raging wildfire, they rode slouched and silent and sweating in their creaking saddles, a silver foam rising from the horses' dusty coats.

Around noon, Yakima led the bedraggled, sunburned group up a box-canyon shaped like a dog leg, and drew rein in a *bosquecillo* of paloverde, mesquite, and juniper, where the canyon walls formed a cool, shading overhang. He remembered that, at least during part of the year, an underground river formed a falls just north of the canyon. When he'd tended Wolf and laid out his gear, he hiked up through the rocks and junipers and found the river — which wasn't much more than a narrow stream — tumbling down the side of a razor-backed ridge in which, over the centuries, the water had formed a narrow trough. He scouted the area to make sure no one else was here, then filled his canteens from the tepid black pool churning at the base of the falls, and returned to the canyon.

"A falls about a quarter mile north," he told the others milling about the shaded defile, tending their gear and getting ready to sleep. "It's too rocky for the horses, but you can wash up and fill your canteens."

"There enough water for a bath?" Faith asked. She'd plopped down on a flat rock in the overhang's shade, looking exhausted, elbows on her knees.

"More than enough." Yakima slid his Winchester from its sheath. "I'm gonna scout around."

"I know I'd feel safer if you did," Cavanaugh said, sitting on the rock beside Faith and pulling off a boot. He gave Lou Brahma a surreptitious glance, and the large, dark man chuckled as he dropped his cartridge belt in the dirt beside his saddle.

Yakima hoofed it off down the canyon, spying some old Apache sign — scuffed moccasin prints and dry horse apples — but nothing recent. A bobcat had been through the canyon yesterday, no doubt heading to or from the falls, but desert bobcats tended to stalk a broad area.

When he'd scouted around for about a half hour, he returned to the canyon and dropped down in front of his saddle, which he'd purposely placed around a bend in the canyon from the others. He liked his privacy. Moreover, he had a hard time stomaching Cavanaugh, and he didn't think it was only because Faith had shown such bad judgment in marrying the cardsharp.

After a deep but short sleep, he got up feeling refreshed, and turned his boots upside down to dislodge any spiders or scorpions that might have crawled inside. He stomped into them, donned his hat, picked up his rifle, and climbed the canyon wall.

Near the razor-backed ridge, which vaulted about a hundred feet against the northeast horizon, with the falls making a sparkling silver line down its own carved trough, he stopped with a lurch, a surprised grunt dying in his throat.

Faith knelt along the pool's edge, facing the falls. She'd taken off her shirt and camisole, and both lay with her tan felt hat atop a rock beside her. Naked from the waist up, she leaned out over the shallow pool, cupping water to her chest. She'd loosened her hair and let it fall free down her pale, slender back, her hips flaring into her black denims and dusty chaps. She was turned at a slight angle, so that Yakima could see the side of her full left breast sloping toward the pool, jostling slightly as she brought the water to her chest.

Blood surged in his loins. He wanted to march over there, pick her up in his arms, lay her down, and rip the rest of her clothes off — make love the way they'd made love on the trail to Gold Cache, and then for the month they'd spent together in the Gold Cache brothel that had become her own.

He felt a sharp, searing stab of regret that he had no claim on her, that he'd relinquished all rights to her when he'd left her in Colorado.

He pulled back behind the boulder, turned, and heeled it back down the rocky slope toward the canyon. He was within a few yards of the canyon's brush-sheathed lip when Cavanaugh ducked through the shrubs and started walking toward him. The gambler wore only his long underwear, boots, and hat. His gun belt was draped over his right shoulder. He had a towel draped over the other, and a cigar between his lips.

Yakima opened his mouth to tell the man the falls were occupied, but stopped himself.

"What's that?" the gambler said, frowning, squinting his good eye against the sun.

"Nothin'," Yakima said, and continued on past him to the canyon.

Yakima took another, longer siesta, which was interrupted once when he heard Faith's and Cavanaugh's voices as they returned to the canyon from the falls.

When he felt the air cool and the shadows in the canyon thickening, he rose, built his own fire, and cooked some beans and corn cakes, which he washed down with the green tea he preferred over coffee. He scrubbed his utensils with the loose sand of the defile's floor, topped his canteen at the falls, then saddled Wolf and rode around the bend to where the others were saddling the broncs and Faith's claybank.

"The country gets rougher from here on," Yakima said. "And the Indians and banditos get thicker."

"That's nice to know," Pop Longley grunted, puffing on a cigar. Having saddled his horse, he was running an oily rag up and down his Henry carbine. "I just hope the water's hot and the senoritas are soft in

Tocando."

"Hey, breed," Cavanaugh said, strapping one of his saddlebags closed, "what're the senoritas like in Tocando? Pop's too damn stove-up and old, but Willie and Brahma are *right* interested. Ain't you, boys? Hell, I'd be interested myself, if I hadn't had the good sense to pack my own whore!"

Cavanaugh slapped his thigh and laughed. Brahma and Willie Stiles chuckled, cutting their glances between Cavanaugh and Faith.

Swinging into the saddle of his buckskin, Pop Longley cursed under his breath. "Ah, Jesus . . ."

Faith stood facing her claybank, adjusting the right stirrup. She turned her head slightly, glancing at Yakima over her left shoulder, then at her husband, and Yakima saw that her cheek had turned red.

Yakima stared at Cavanaugh, resisting the urge to pluck his Arkansas toothpick from the sheath between his shoulder blades, and bury the seven inches of razor-edged steel in the man's neck.

Faith mounted the clay and rode up beside him, facing the opposite direction.

"Let it go," she said quietly, smiling, her blue eyes flashing beneath her hat brim. "He's just talking."

Yakima raked his heels against Wolf's ribs,

brushed past a flood-ravaged sycamore, and put the horse up an eroded notch in the canyon wall. "Move out."

He walked Wolf back along the rim of the canyon until the others had all climbed up out of the cleft behind him, their wafting dust showing like copper in the dying light, then urged the black into a lurching trot through the desert scrub. For the sake of Faith and her brother, he put Cavanaugh out of his mind as much as he could. He'd never liked the professional gambling breed, and he liked Cavanaugh even less than most. But if all went well in Tocando, he'd be free of the man in a week or so. He'd be free of his wife, as well, and he wouldn't think about her anymore.

Yakima had a brief, remembered image of his mentor, Ralph, drunk on tequila one night in a Kansas end-of-track hell-town, and staring at the sashaying backside of a passing woman. "That," he told Yakima, wagging his head, his dark, slanted eyes glistening in the light of a sparking torch, "is very bad. It looks good, yes?" He shook his head gravely. "Will turn a man's brain to pudding, turn his stomach inside out."

Like so many other things, Ralph had been right, and the half-breed wished now, with his guts churning, that he had followed the old Chinaman's sage advice and never fallen in love.

The group snaked through the moonlit desert throughout the night, stopping twice to rest the horses and build low, well-sheltered coffee fires from the near-smokeless branches of the curl-leaf shrub. Just after sunup they stopped again to eat a quick meal of beans and side pork, then mounted again and continued south between high, shelving mesas, the Sierra Olivadas growing larger and darker through the gaps in the formations straight ahead.

By late morning they were climbing a rise sheathed in scrub pinion and spotted with boulders fallen from the surrounding ridges, when Wolf stopped suddenly and shook his head so sharply that he nearly threw off his bit and bridle.

"Easy, boy," Yakima cajoled, patting the black's foamy neck with his gloved hand and looking around warily.

Wolf skitter-stepped and nickered. Yakima held the reins taut, casting his gaze toward the granite walls looming around him — cracked and fissured and gapped with wind caves. The hot wind wheezed over the parapetted peaks.

"What the hell's the matter with him?" Lou Brahma said, riding directly behind. "I thought the rest of *us* were riding the rough-string."

Yakima looked around carefully, his brows ridged. Swinging his head from right to left and back again, he turned Wolf around and rode back past Brahma, Faith, and the others, the black arching his neck and snorting loudly.

The others had stopped to watch him, befuddled.

"Well?" Cavanaugh said, scowling. He'd just had a skirmish with his own mount, which had spooked at a sidewinder coiled along the trail, nearly throwing its rider against a pipestem cactus, and he was growing impatient with the temperamental broncs. "He got a goat head under his blanket, or *what?*"

Behind Willie Stiles, who was riding drag, Yakima reined Wolf around once more, and checked the stallion down to a dead stop. The horse rippled its withers, sighed, and tossed his head. Reaching down to unshuck his Yellowboy and cocking it one-handed, Yakima stared down at him, brows hooding his eyes.

"The only thing Wolf hates worse than skunks and barn rats is Apaches."

"So?" Stiles said. "I don't see no Apaches. Haven't even seen no tracks, no smoke talk, noth—"

He stopped as a shrill, windy whistle sounded to the left of the trail. It was followed by a soft thump, like that of a rock landing in deep mud. Pop Longley, riding just ahead of Willie Stiles, suddenly lowered his head to his saddle horn, dropped his left hand to his left thigh, and scrunched up his face, loosing a raucous, *"Ahhh!"*

Yakima jerked his gaze left of the trail. At the same time that his eyes picked out the Apache kneeling between a couple of scrub pinions, the brave threw his head back and loosed an ear-rattling scream while reaching behind to draw another fletched arrow from the quiver hanging down his back.

"Apaches!" Yakima shouted. *"Ride!"*

The order hadn't died on his lips before he aimed the Yellowboy one-handed at the screaming Apache. He fired at the same time the brave drew the nocked arrow behind his right ear, the Winchester slug drilling a hole through the brave's forehead. As the brave flew straight back off his heels, his loosed arrow skimmed a half inch over Yakima's right shoulder with a swish of displaced air before clattering on the rocks behind him.

Wolf whinnied shrilly, and when Yakima got the black aimed up trail, he saw the others galloping on up the rise, heads down, dust rising from their broncs' hooves as arrows careened from the shrubs and rocks to the left of the trail to cleave the air around them.

Firing and cocking his Winchester one-handed, trying to pick out the braves hunkered down about thirty yards from the trail, Yakima booted the black stallion up the rise, into the billowing dust of the others. Arrows slashed around him, clattering on the rocks on the other side of the trail, one blurring past his nose, another nicking Wolf's right ear.

The horse lifted its head and whinnied as though the devil's hounds were nipping at his heels.

When the arrows dwindled to nothing and he was nearing the ridge crest behind the other riders, his heart lightened. But then Cavanaugh suddenly checked his own bronc down and turned the roan sideways in the trail, his mouth forming a large oval.

"Ah, Christ!" the gambler bellowed, holding his reins taut as the roan pitched, clawing at the air with its hooves. *"They're all around us!"*

CHAPTER 14

Yakima checked Wolf down with a curse. Beyond Cavanaugh, a dozen or so war-painted, half-naked braves were galloping down the rise, their short-legged ponies lurching around shrubs and boulders. Wielding bows or rifles or feathered lances, stone-headed war hatchets flapping along their sides, the warriors screamed like banshees.

Yakima quickly scanned the area and, spying no Apaches in the scrub on the trail's right side, shouted, "West!"

Faith turned her clay that way, and ground her spurs against its flanks, the wide-eyed horse flattening out over the caliche. Cavanaugh, Brahma, and Willie Stiles had all shucked their own repeating rifles and were throwing lead at the Apaches riding in from the southeast. Cavanaugh dislodged one brave from his paint pony, but most of their lead was nudged wide by their own lunging mounts. Pop Longley, wincing against the arrow bristling out from his left thigh, fumbled his Spencer from its boot and triggered a single shot before Stiles reined his dun around and yelled, "Come on, Pop!"

Holding Wolf as steady as possible with one hand, Yakima triggered his Yellowboy at a brave angling toward him from the north, leaping rocks and whooping like a coyote as two of Yakima's slugs kicked up dust around the brave's moccasins. The brave paused and raised his nocked arrow, but Yakima's third slug slammed through his lower-right chest and twirled him, shrieking, around and back down a shallow ravine.

The men's return fire had slowed the horseback warriors, but now that Cavanaugh and Brahma were hustling after Faith, Longley, and Stiles, the Indians were moving toward the trail once more, screaming, triggering saddle guns, and loosing arrows.

Yakima flinched as a slug buzzed past his ear, squeezed off one more round, then neck-reined Wolf in a tight one-eighty, and gave the horse its head. The stallion lurched forward so quickly that Yakima had to grab the horn to keep from being thrown straight back off the horse's ass. Then he had to duck under mesquite and pinion branches, and keep his knees squeezed tight against the stirrups, for the black lurched around the shrubs and rocks, leaping others, as though he were trying out for the Fourth of July rodeo in Tucson.

Aboard the frightened beast, Yakima drew within sight of the others of his party, spread out ahead and lurching around obstacles while slowly climbing toward a pinion-stippled saddle looming about a mile ahead.

He had thought he'd outdistanced the Indians, but as hoof falls rose on his right flank, he turned to see a brave on a spry Appaloosa angling toward him on a collision course. The brave was wiry — no more than a hundred and twenty pounds — with a narrow face and wide-set eyes ringed with red paint, and with white, lightninglike slashes on his pocked cheeks. His hair flew around his head like a black tumbleweed caught in a desert twister. He ground his moccasins against the Appaloosa's flanks and raised the willow-shafted spear he carried in his left hand.

Christ, Yakima thought. Here we are in Mexico, having one hell of a stomping good time!

As the brave closed on him, Yakima awkwardly extended his Winchester barrel out behind him and to the right, and triggered a shot. The brave ducked, closing quickly, riding his blanket saddle so lightly that he looked as though he'd fly off his galloping mount at any second.

Yakima cocked the Yellowboy one-handed as the young brave batted his heels wildly against the Appaloosa's flanks, drawing within ten yards — so close that Yakima could hear the horse's breath roaring up from its pounding lungs, see the phlegm stringing from its nostrils.

Yakima extended the cocked Winchester once more, but before he could level the barrel, the brave tightened his face savagely, and flung the lance. Yakima ducked and whipped his rifle up, deflecting the lance just enough that the serrated stone blade flew wide to impale an ironwood tree ten yards to Yakima's left.

Yakima aimed the Winchester once more as the brave reached for the tomahawk thonged on his waist, and fired. The brave's throat turned tomato red; his head snapped up and sideways, a grimace stretching his lips. Without a sound, the brave tumbled down the horse's right side, hit the ground, and bounced several times, rolling and dwindling into the dusty distance. The Appaloosa followed the black stallion for several more yards before it veered off and disappeared behind a boulder snag.

Jacking a fresh round into the Winchester's breech, Yakima turned forward. In his skirmish with the lance-wielding brave, he'd gotten a little off course. The others in his party were slightly ahead and to the left, climbing the steep slope rising toward the saddleback ridge. Forming a ragged wedge, with Longley and Stiles in the lead and Cavanaugh and Faith bringing up the rear, they had a half dozen Apaches on their tails.

As Yakima reined left to flank them and throw some lead down on the galloping Apaches, Faith's claybank screamed suddenly and dropped to its knees. Faith gave a startled cry and tumbled over the horse's right shoulder, hitting the ground and rolling in a dust cloud, the horse rolling behind her.

Just ahead of her, Ace Cavanaugh reined in his own pony and swung around toward her. As an arrow clipped the air to his left and a bullet tore through the crown of his hat, turning the hat askew, he winced and scowled, then turned the roan back uphill, batting his boots against its ribs.

Yakima jerked back on Wolf's reins. "Whoa, boy!"

The last thing the horse wanted to do was head back *toward* the Apaches, but Yakima put the steel to him and, giving a buck-kick in protest, the black stallion galloped off across the hillside. Downhill on the left, the Apaches were within fifty yards and closing. Yakima fired several rounds as he headed toward Faith, shooting the horse out from under one brave and searing the shoulder of another, slowing the other half dozen, some of whom leaped off their ponies and dove for cover.

He was about thirty yards from Faith when a slug burned a slit across his right forearm while, at the same time, an arrow plowed through his boot top and into his left shin. The two searing burns made him lose concentration for a second, and, when another bullet sparked off a rock in front of Wolf and caused him to scream and jerk sideways, Yakima found himself pinwheeling through open air.

He landed hard on his right hip and shoulder, sucking air through his teeth and cursing the whole business. Blinking against the dust flying against his face, he turned to see Wolf galloping on up the ridge where the other men had taken cover and were shooting back down the slope at the whooping, howling Apaches.

"Thanks a ton, you miserable cayuse," Yakima rasped as Wolf crested the ridge and disappeared down the other side.

The half-breed turned to peer across the rocky, pinion-studded slope. A stocky Apache in a lemon yellow tunic, hide breechclout, and knee-length moccasins ran up the incline toward Faith. Grinning, he shouldered his rifle and leaned toward the young woman.

Faith was on her back near the fallen, broken-legged clay, staring up in horror as the Indian approached. She brushed her right hand against her empty holster, and then her face crumpled as she kicked herself up the slope on her butt and shouted, *"No!"*

As rifles clamored up and down the slope, Cavanaugh and Brahma shouting unintelligibly atop the ridge, Yakima grabbed his rifle from between two large rocks and took quick aim at the Indian. At the same time, the stocky, grinning brave reached down and pulled Faith over his left shoulder, shielding himself with her body.

Yakima pulled his cheek away from the Yellowboy's stock.

Faith screamed and kicked and pummeled the man's neck and shoulders with her fists, but she was too addled from the tumble from the clay to put up much of a fight.

The Indian turned and, holding Faith over his left shoulder, began hoofing it back down the slope. Yakima snapped his cheek back to the Winchester's stock, lowered the barrel toward the man's scissoring lower legs, and triggered three quick rounds. The slugs tore up rock shards and gravel and clipped a couple of pinion branches. One tore into the man's left calf, and he went down howling, dragging Faith down into the rocks and shrubs.

Quickly, Yakima reached down, pulled the arrow out of his left boot top — it had gone only a half inch or so into the bone — and threw it away. Gaining his knees, still hearing the men shouting and triggering their rifles from the ridge, he raised the Winchester once more. His face etched with pain and fury, the Apache rose up from behind the rocks and lifted his own rifle to his shoulder.

Before the brave could level the carbine, Yakima drilled him twice, throwing him back into the brush with two blood fountains spewing from his chest, the rifle sailing high over the man's head and breaking against the rocks.

Yakima cocked the Winchester, off-cocked the hammer, and, limping slightly on his left calf, ran over to where Faith was clambering up from the rocks and brush near the dead Indian. A couple of shots, fired by

Apaches holed up behind boulders down slope, ricocheted off the rocks. Yakima squatted on a flat-topped boulder, grabbed Faith's right hand, and pulled her to her feet. She was blinking, dazed, her hair in her eyes, blood dribbling from a cut near the corner of her right eye.

"Are you all right?" Yakima said as the men on the ridge held the Apache's fire down to a couple of hastily squeezed-off rifle shots.

Faith nodded dully. "I'm all right."

Yakima turned her around, leaped off the rock, and began pulling her up slope around the thrashing claybank. "Let's go."

"The clay!" she yelled as she ran awkwardly behind him.

"He's finished!"

Yakima stopped and grabbed her rifle from the horse's saddle boot, leaning away from the clay's thrashing hooves. Handing the carbine to Faith, he put the horse out of its misery with his Yellowboy, then grabbed Faith's wrist once more.

"No, wait!" she shouted, ripping free of his grasp and darting toward the dead mount. "Money in the saddlebags!"

Cavanaugh's and the other men's covering fire whistled over their heads as Faith grabbed at the saddlebags, unable to free the right pouch, which the horse had fallen on. Yakima nudged her aside, grabbed the right bag, gave it a hard jerk while ramming his boot beneath the horse's hip, and tugged the left pouch free in a spray of rocks and gravel.

Draping the heavy bags over his left shoulder, Yakima pulled Faith up over the clay-colored boulders spilling across the ridge's lip. The half-breed glanced over his right shoulder to spy three Indians darting from boulder to boulder, heading up slope. The nearest one paused to trigger a pistol hanging from a leather thong around his neck. The .45-caliber slug barked off a rock near Faith's right leg.

"Oh!" she cried.

Lou Brahma snaked his Winchester around a boulder and fired. Twenty yards behind Yakima, the pistol-wielding Apache groaned and fell with a heavy thud.

Near the ridge crest, Yakima stopped and pushed Faith up in front of him. Cavanaugh half rose from behind a boulder, grabbed Faith's arm, and pulled her down beside him as Yakima leaped behind a rock near Pop Longley, who'd leaned back against the rock to thumb cartridges from his belt and into his Henry repeater. He'd broken the end off the arrow embedded in his left thigh, but a good six inches of the cotton-wood shaft still protruded; nearly the entire thigh of his faded denims was soaked with glistening red blood.

Faith dropped down beside her husband as he triggered a shot down slope. Scuttling onto her butt, Faith thumbed blood from her cheek and scowled, angry-eyed, at Cavanaugh. "Thanks for your help down there!"

"They were about to *perforate* my hide!" Cavanaugh said, ejecting a spent round from his Winchester's breech. "I was gonna climb on up here, pink a couple of those red savages, then scramble back down the slope for you."

"Too late now."

Cavanaugh glanced at Yakima, snorted, and aimed once more down his Winchester's smoking barrel. "I see that!"

On the other side of Faith, Yakima loaded his Winchester and edged a look around his covering boulder. The Apaches were no longer climbing the slope, but moving off to both sides. As the other men continued firing down the hill, Yakima looked down the other side of the ridge, where the horses, including Wolf, milled amidst more rocks and grama grass. The slope eased down to a broad, rocky valley.

"Cavanaugh!" he shouted. "The Indians

are trying to move around behind us. Take Faith, mount your horse, and ride west to the valley bottom yonder. Me and the other men will try to hold the Apaches off. Watch for us. We'll be along."

Cavanaugh fired one more shot at several Indians continuing to throw lead from farther down slope, nearly out of rifle range. Then he rose and, keeping his head low, helped Faith to her feet.

"Come along, darlin'," the gambler said, faintly mocking.

As she gathered her saddlebags and followed her husband down the back slope toward the horses milling below, Faith cut a look at Yakima. He turned away from her and peered along the ridgeline to both sides. No sign of the Indians trying to flank him yet.

He glanced at Willie Stiles wedged between a rock and a spindly mesquite, and stared down slope over his rifle's barrel. "Kid, help Longley down to the horses." He glanced at Brahma who'd fired another shot in spite of the fact he was only wasting lead. "Brahma, scout the ridgeline to your left. We'll hold the Indians off until the others have ridden out."

The big man's rifle barked and slammed back against his shoulder. He glanced, red-faced, at Yakima. A bullet or a rock shard had laid a cut across his forehead, blood dribbling into his heavy brows. "Anything else you want me to do?"

"That'll do for now," Yakima said tightly, thumbing another cartridge through his rifle's loading gate. As Stiles grabbed one of Longley's arms, Yakima moved south along the ridge, just below the crest, holding the rifle in both hands across his chest.

He paused behind a couple of boulders, watching and listening for the braves he knew were coming. They'd try to get around Yakima's party to keep them from getting away.

He'd just stepped out around a boulder about fifteen yards from the ridge crest when an arrow slammed past his right ear and smashed against the side of the boulder. Straight ahead, a dusky figure scrambled out of the shrubs and dove behind a large, cracked, mushroom-shaped hunk of granite.

More movement on Yakima's left, and he turned to see a brave with a bloody gash across his upper right arm kneeling beside a stout root curling up out of the gravel, and raising a Springfield trapdoor carbine to his shoulder.

CHAPTER 15

Yakima threw himself backward, hitting the ground on his butt as the bullet cut the air where his head had just been. Bounding up to a sitting position, he swung the Yellow-boy around and triggered a shot through the Apache's belly. Dropping the rifle and slapping both hands to the wound, the brave cried hoarsely, head jerking forward.

Yakima bounded up as the brave dropped to his knees. Jacking a fresh round, he sprinted up to the mushroom-shaped rock, tracing its crenellated, curving wall to the other side, holding the rifle straight out from his right hip. The only sign of the first brave was moccasin tracks in the tan, powdery dirt, which the wind had whipped up against the boulder's base.

Moving along the boulder's south side, pricking his ears to listen, Yakima stopped. A shadow had flicked along the ground behind him and to his right. He whipped around too late.

The brave — tall for an Apache, wild-eyed, and with sweat matting the hair behind his red headband and streaking the dust on his cheeks — gave a shrill, victorious screech and bolted toward the half-breed, raising a feathered war lance crossways in both hands in front of his face. On Yakima before Yakima could use the Winchester, the brave slammed the wooden shaft up under Yakima's chin and gritted his stubby teeth. He smelled like raw horse meat, sweat, and camp smoke.

Yakima fell back, hitting the dirt hard, dropping the Yellowboy, and grabbing the shaft with both hands before the brave could pinch his windpipe closed.

He bucked up hard, shoving the lance straight up from his chest. The brave, already celebrating the bare-handed kill, hadn't expected the wicked force that not only lifted the lance and his own body up off the half-breed's chest, but that turned him in a complete somersault over his quarry's head.

Yakima gave a savage grunt as he rolled off his right shoulder, the war lance now in his hands as the brave rolled several yards down the hill in a cloud of wafting red dust. Head ringing and his leg aching, a hundred scrapes and bruises nettling him, Yakima watched the brave pile up at the base of a broad mesquite. Grunting furiously, the Apache spat grit from his lips, then lurched up off his heels, blazing eyes and white teeth materializing from the dust as he lunged uphill toward Yakima.

Yakima swung the lance back behind his shoulder and flung it forward.

The brave stopped instantly and stumbled straight back, as the fire-hardened steel tip cleanly plundered his breastbone and spine before thumping into the tree trunk behind him. Pinned to the tree by the five feet of dyed cottonwood and steel, the brave, unblinking, stared up the slope at Yakima.

He moved both his hands to the shaft, just above his chest, and gave the shaft a half-hearted jerk as though to see how well it was set. Then he gave a liquid sigh. The lids closed heavily over his eyes. His hands fell away from the lance to drop straight down by his sides, and his chin dropped to his chest. He stood against the tree, like a giant bug on a pin, blood welling up from his chest to drip in stringy, thick webs to the ground.

Hearing three quick rifle reports echo back in the direction from which he'd come, Yakima scooped his Yellowboy off the ground, brushed it off with his gloved hand, and looked around quickly.

Spying no more Indians in the immediate area, he jogged back along the steeply angling slope to the saddle. A rifle barked in a clump of pinions just beyond the saddle. Then boots clomped and spurs chinged, and Lou Brahma ran out of the rocks and shrubs, carrying his smoking Spencer straight up and down in one hand.

"A couple were trying to make it up that steep slope yonder, and I *think* I changed their minds." The big man's voice quaked as he ran, leaping large rocks. "But it looks like they got more comin'."

Yakima cursed as he and Brahma jogged down the slope toward their horses waiting in the grass and boulders sixty yards away. There must have been several small raiding parties in the area, and the others, having heard the gunfire, decided to join the dance.

While Brahma grabbed the reins of his wide-eyed, nickering dun, which one of the others had tied to a shrub, Yakima ran Wolf down and leaped into the saddle. He cast a glance back up the slope.

Seeing no Apaches but hearing a horse whinny down the slope's other side, he said, "Let's move!" and gigged Wolf farther down the rocky grade, twisting around rocks and dwarf Mexican pinions, Brahma spurring the bronc behind him.

"A fine goddamn mess," the big man cajoled. "A fine mess sure as a blue-eyed hell awaitin'!"

Yakima descended a broad draw, which cut along the slope's base, and found the others waiting under a high stone wall, all mounted except for Cavanaugh who stood holding his blue roan's reins while Faith sat on the horse's back, behind the cantle, staring anxiously toward Yakima and Brahma. Her saddlebags were draped over her shoulder. Willie Stiles sat his own steeldust beside Pop Longley, who slouched atop his buckskin, one gloved hand wrapped around the broken arrow shaft, his teeth gritted, sweat streaming down his gray-bearded face.

They all looked harried, scared, peeved. Yakima resisted the urge to welcome them all to Mexico.

"They comin'?" Cavanaugh asked.

"They will be." Yakima checked his mount down before the group, Brahma following suit beside him. The half-breed glanced at Longley. "You fit to ride?"

"His leg needs tending," Faith said. "I checked the arrow — I think it's lodged in the bone."

"I can ride," Longley grouched, then bit

off a hunk of chaw from the braid in his fist. Chewing, shifting the tobacco around in his mouth, he said, "I'd rather bleed to death ridin' than let those savages hack off my eyelids and bury me up to my neck in an anthill."

"Chili chompers and howlin' savages — helluva damn country!" Brahma chuffed, holding the reins of the prancing dun taut against his chest. "Last time I was down here, I vowed I'd never come again — but, no, I couldn't say no to a woman!" Grimacing, he rammed his left fist against the mount's sweat-silvered neck. "Simmer down, you fiery-tailed demon!"

Yakima glanced over his shoulder, then heeled Wolf around Cavanaugh and into a three-pointed trot, heading off down the draw. "Move out. Stay close."

Yakima riding point, the group snaked through the deep canyon, pulled into the left tine of a fork, and watched the cracked, fluted walls around them rise even higher than before. The sandy, alluvial wash was gilded by a thin stream of noon sunlight, with cliff swallows darting and peeping high against the purple-shaded walls, their frantically beating wings dislodging occasional stones from crevices or clumps of dirt from their mud hovels.

Yakima had no idea where he was going; for the moment, he was simply trying to shake the Apaches off his trail. Later, after sundown, he'd try to get his bearings again and get them all back on the trail for Tocando.

They rode for over a half hour, down one canyon and through another, pausing occasionally to look around and listen. At the end of the scraggly line of riders, Pop Longley chewed his tobacco as though chewing back the pain in his wounded leg.

Yakima rounded a curve in the narrow canyon and pulled Wolf to a stop before a gap in the right wall. The gap was sheathed in fragrant cedars and junipers, cactus, and red stone rubble fallen from the walls above.

Yakima peered through the brush and into the jagged gap. At first he'd thought it was just a cave, but it seemed to open out into more sunlight at the other end. If it had only one entrance, it could be a nasty trap. On the other hand, it might also be the hiding place he'd been looking for.

He might as well chance it.

Dismounting, he turned to the others sitting their mounts in a semicircle around him. "We'll walk the horses in. Stiles, lead Longley's mount."

"I don't know," Brahma grumbled, turning his head this way and that to peer through brush and into the gap. "Don't look good to me. Them Apaches catch us in a cleft that narrow . . ."

"Shut up, Lou," Faith said wearily, sliding off the back of Cavanaugh's roan.

Taking Wolf's reins in his right hand, Yakima climbed over the rocks, pushing through the brush, staying clear of the long spikes jutting from the glove-shaped cactus pods. The stallion balked at the prospect of traversing such a tight enclosure — the walls were probably only about a foot wider than the horse itself — but after a few hard pulls, he got the stallion past the rubble and into the dim defile.

He continued forward, hearing the others cursing, their mounts shaking their heads, rattling their bits. A couple nickered and whinnied.

When Yakima had tramped a good forty yards into the corridor, which smelled of minerals and bat guano, he peered behind. All the others had made it, Longley's horse tied to the tail of Stiles's steeldust. The gangly, gray-bearded man slumped forward in his saddle, both hands on the horn, bearded chin brushing his chest.

Cavanaugh led his roan directly behind Wolf, scowling up at the walls, squinting his scarred eye, one hand on his pistol grips.

Faith moved along behind him, between the roan and Stiles's steeldust, staring straight ahead toward Yakima, her hazel eyes wary. Her hair hung in tattered curls beside her flushed, dust-streaked cheeks, her hat thong swinging across her chest.

The horses' shod hooves rang off stones like cracked bells. The tack squawked loudly in the close quarters. The only other sounds were those of strained breathing and the wind howling through the top of the corridor three hundred feet above.

As eager anticipation nibbled his belly, Yakima watched the golden sunlight ahead of him intensify. Patches of blue sky widened. More sunlight and more blue sky appeared the farther he walked, gravel crunching beneath his boots.

And then the high walls slipped back behind his shoulders, Wolf's hoof clomps ceased echoing, and sunlight washed over Yakima's hat like a gilded ocean wave, dry and hot, cicadas whining. Several yards out from the end of the corridor, he stood in front of Wolf, looking around at the bowl-shaped canyon yawning around him.

It was an oasis of sorts, alive with green plants and brush sprouting amongst the ocotillo, dwarf pinion, and mesquite. The canyon appeared to be large enough to hold a town, and it was ringed with high, craggy peaks, except in the east, where the mountain wall leaned back gradually, gentling the slope. It was pocked here and there with small, black, round-mouthed caves with one large one — egg-shaped and long as two train cars.

Heat waves shimmered and danced above the lime green shrubs, and birds flitted.

As the others moved up behind Yakima, leading their horses, silent as children in church and bewilderedly stretching their gazes across the gorge, the half-breed climbed into the saddle. He glanced over his shoulder at the others, silently commanding them to do likewise.

They'd ride over to the shade slowly engulfing the eastern wall, and hole up there where they could keep an eye on the defile for Apaches. While Faith and the others tended Longley, Yakima would hoof it back through the defile and wipe out their tracks with branches, picking up any horse apples.

Urging the stallion forward along a narrow trail that continued from the defile, he slowed when he heard the sound of running water. Continuing forward, the other horses clomping along behind him, no one saying anything, he spied a jagged cleft in the wall to his right. At the base of the cleft, black water rumbled out from beneath the wall, churning over black rocks, then spilling and widening placidly out into the canyon, and glistening in the midday light.

Faith and Cavanaugh rode up to either side of him, staring down at the faintly spraying stream gushing out from the earth beneath the mountain wall.

"Underground river," Yakima said, his voice shaking slightly as Wolf tossed his head, eager to get at the water, so cold that it freshened the hot air around it.

They allowed the horses only quick, light drinks at the stream before pushing them on across, and continued heading for the opposite wall, from which the westering sun slowly drew a broad wedge of purple shade. Catching a brief whiff of smoke, Yakima drew Wolf to an abrupt halt.

"What is it?" Cavanaugh said.

Yakima's eyes jerked to a pile of hardened lava jutting from the wall to his right. Something about the brush capping the rock didn't look natural.

The thought had no sooner crossed his mind than the cottonwood branch was suddenly thrust back behind the ledge to reveal the glistening, brass maw of a Gatling gun. A sombrero-clad figure was peering over the six-barreled canister, grinning under his broad hat brim, one brown hand wrapped around the gun's crank handle.

Yakima's heart thudded, but before he could reach for his rifle, the hand swung the crank up and around. The barrel dropped and began spewing smoke and fire, the *rat-tat-tat* of the Gatling's reports rising on the still air like sudden, unexpected thunder.

Ka-boom-boom-boom-boom-boom!

Sand and gravel blasted up around the horses' hooves. The green-broke broncs danced and whinnied. Brahma's dun buckkicked sharply, then rose up on its back legs, lifting a shrill scream. As the bullets continued spanking the ground in a broad semicircle around the group, Brahma fell heavily off the dun's right hip, hitting the ground with a thud that was drowned by the Gatling's shrill explosions.

"God*damnit!*" Brahma said, rolling off his shoulder and peering around through his own rising dust, just as the weapon's thunder died.

The Gatling's smoking canister lifted suddenly, bearing down on the group, swinging slowly from left to right as if assuring Yakima and the others that there wasn't one of them not in the line of its deadly fire.

Yakima held Wolf's reins taut in his hands and bit his cheek to keep from chuckling at the absurdity of the past few hours.

If he ever got out of Mexico alive — which looked like a very slim possibility — it was going to take a hell of a lot more than a pretty woman to bring him back.

CHAPTER 16

The dust from the Gatling slugs hadn't settled before brush snapped and thrashed behind Yakima. Holding his frightened mount's reins tightly in one fist, he turned to see a good seven or eight sombrero-wearing Mexicans — clad either in buckskin or cream canvas pantaloons and calico shirts, with cartridge belts crisscrossed on their chests — run out from the chaparral, wielding everything from Colt Patterson pistols to modern Winchester carbines.

A voice of indeterminate sex shouted from the scarp upon which the Gatling gun perched. "Reach for the sky, amigos, or die in a hail of hot lead!"

A figure rose up from behind the man still crouched over the deadly machine gun — a tall, shapely woman dressed in a bull-hide vest with nothing beneath it, and black leather *charro* pants with small, white horses sewn down the front and with the wide seams down the outside legs loosely tied with rawhide, revealing a good inch of bare skin. The tight vest was cut low and trimmed with small silver buttons, revealing deep, russet cleavage.

She wore a black, silver-stitched sombrero with a small stag-horn cross sewn into the horsehair thong drooping beneath her chin. Long, thick, black hair dropped to her narrow, naked shoulders. She was dark enough that Yakima figured she had a good dose of Mexican *indio* blood; she was oval faced and straight-nosed, with a firm jaw and a flat, dark brown mole off the left corner of her full-lipped mouth. A singularly beautiful, wild-looking woman, she appeared completely at home in her comely body, with flashing black eyes and shoulders thrown back, breasts out.

The sexy young woman swaggered up to the edge of the scarp, the large-rowled Mexican spurs adorning her hand-tooled black boots shrilling softly. She set her gloved fists on her hips and slitted her cunning eyes at the interlopers spread out before her on snorting, fiddle-footing mounts. "The Apaches call this the Devil's Canyon for a reason, gringos. Those who enter rarely get out alive. Those who do wish they hadn't!"

Yakima glanced at the still-smoking Gatling gun and gave a wry smile. "I wish I woulda known. I would have made other arrangements."

Still on the ground, legs curled beneath him, his horse having run off buck-kicking, Lou Brahma said, " 'Paches chased us in here!"

"Shut up!" the woman barked, scowling hatefully down at the big man. Sweeping her eyes across the group, she said, "Throw your weapons down, and be quick about it. Alejandro here" — she canted her head toward the square-faced man staring over the Gatling gun's barrel — "loves his new toy, and he needs the target practice!"

Cavanaugh, holding his reins in both hands against his chest, cast an enraged look up at the girl and the glistening brass weapon seated on a wooden tripod beside her. "Listen, senorita — !"

A pistol popped. Cavanaugh's hat flew off his blond head and tumbled into the brush on his right.

Yakima glanced to another, lower ledge to the right of the woman and the Gatling gun and where a tall, whipstock-thin man, dressed like the others but hatless and wearing a frayed serape, red and white checked neckerchief, and two black, hand-tooled

240

holsters on his lean hips, stood holding a smoking Remington .45 in his right hand. He had long, black hair and a narrow, cadaverous face, one side of which wore a large, pink burn in the form of a cattle brand.

The woman laughed. "I suggest you do as you've been ordered, senor. Christos rarely misses."

Yakima scowled up at the whipstock hombre holding the cocked, smoking pistol. "Christos Arvada?"

The woman slid her gaze back to Yakima, cocked a brow, and quirked her upper lip. "*Sí*. You've heard of him?"

Few people living along the border hadn't heard of the notorious Mexican gunman and bandito, the bane of large cattle ranchers on both sides of the international line. Story had it the man had been branded in his youth by the hacendado he'd worked for, when the rancher had caught him stealing horses, and he'd been on the warpath against the wealthy ever since.

Yakima glanced back the way they'd come. "We got Apaches behind us. . . ."

"You let me worry about the Apaches, amigo," the woman said.

Yakima cursed, unbuckled his gun belt, leaned down, and dropped it into the dust beneath his horse. Then he shucked the Yellowboy, leaned even lower, and dropped the prized rifle into a thick tuft of curly red mesquite grass, padding its fall.

He glanced at Cavanaugh, who stared back at him, incredulous, before he, too, unbuckled his cartridge belt and dropped it into the brush beneath his horse. The others behind him, including Faith and Longley, who looked a little more alert after the Gatling fire, followed suit. Shuttling their wary gazes back and forth between the beautiful Mexican woman and the thin gunman who, showing two fanglike eyeteeth, still held his cocked Remington and grinned.

A couple of Mexicans from Yakima's left scurried in and retrieved the weapons, draping the cartridge belts over their shoulders. Then, obviously awaiting the senorita's next orders, they stepped back to aim their pistols and rifles at the mounted interlopers.

Yakima wondered when the banditos would look in the saddlebags and find the money Faith intended to use in buying her brother out of jail. If the Mexicans stole the money — and they were bandits, after all — the trip would be over. But then, having seen the Gatling gun and knowing Arvada's reputation, Yakima figured their lives would be soon over, as well.

Out of the frying pan and into the fire. He wished like hell his four broncs hadn't been stolen out of his ranch corral. If not, he'd be home right now, probably chasing that big roan mare he'd set his sights on through Salt Creek Canyon.

But, then, Faith would be down here without him. . . .

"Off your horses," ordered the senorita, shifting her weight from one round hip to the other and hooking her thumbs behind her cartridge belt. "The wounded gringo, as well."

Faith said with strained tolerance, "If we don't tend to his leg, he's going to bleed to death."

"You will all be bleeding to death shortly if you don't follow my orders." The woman's eyes blazed like black rocks in the sunlight. *"Vamos!"*

Several of the horses started at the woman's shout. As the others swung down from their saddles, Yakima glanced up at the Gatling gun, which was aimed directly at his chest by the square-faced man grinning challengingly over the top of the broad barrel. Christos Arvada was grinning at him, too, flashing those sharp teeth, the barrel of his well-oiled revolver glistening brightly.

Yakima swung a leg over Wolf's rump and dropped to the ground. Taking the horse's reins in his right hand, he moved around in front of the horse and stopped, swinging his gaze up to the senorita, then back along his own group.

Faith and Stiles were helping the cursing Longley off his own horse while Brahma and Cavanaugh stood, dusty and sweaty and glancing warily around at the bandits.

The senorita muttered something to the man called Alejandro crouched behind the Gatling gun. As he tightened his grip on the wooden handle and hunkered low over the barrel, she turned and leaped several step-like rocks to the canyon floor.

She looked around at the ragtag group gathered before her, smiling with her customary cunning, slitting one eye, then sauntered up in front of Yakima. She stopped about two feet in front of him, so close he could smell her aroma of sage and horses with a slight hint of berries and greasewood. She gave him the up and down, letting her gaze rake across his broad shoulders; then, throwing her shoulders back and sticking out her well-formed breasts, she leveled her hard, bemused eyes at him.

"What are you called, hombre?"

"Yakima Henry." He gave her the same brash appraisal, keeping his own eyes hard and defiant. Putting a faint sneer into his voice, he said, "What are you called, senorita?"

"Leonora Domingo."

From the stone ledge flanking her, Christos Arvada chuckled. "People in these parts — especially the rurales — know her by her outlaw name, *Gato Salvaje de Sonora*."

"Is that so?" Brahma said, lifting his chin to the pistolero. "Well, what the hell does *that* mean?"

Keeping her eyes on Yakima, the senorita said, "It means . . ."

"Wild Cat of Sonora," Yakima finished for her, holding her gaze with his own.

"*Sí,*" she said huskily, smiling up at him.

Stepping sideways, she moved down the short line of *americanos*, scowling at the men, before stopping in front of Faith. The blonde stood beside Pop Longley, whose right shoulder was draped over the neck of Willie Stiles. The tall, bearded man appeared only half-conscious. The blood from the arrow wound had extended down to well below his left knee.

"Please let us tend this man," Faith said tightly, her dusty face flushed with anger. "We need to cut the arrow out of his thigh before he *bleeds* to death."

Leonora Domingo was nonplussed. When she'd given Faith the thrice-over, she glanced at Yakima, a conniving expression in her eyes. "Your woman?"

Yakima glanced at Faith. She glanced back at him tensely. Before either could respond, Cavanaugh growled, "She's *my* woman. And she's right — our friend needs tending. If you don't want us tending him here, we'll just say pardon the intrusion, and try to find some other canyon where we can build a fire and sterilize a blade."

"In due time, senor. First — and I hate to be rude — but I must ask your business here in *Méjico.* At first, I thought you were banditos. Horse thieves, perhaps, or some of those *muy bad* hombres who prey on the mining camps or smuggling caravans."

The Wild Cat of Sonora turned back to Faith, raked her eyes across the blonde's well-filled blouse, then lifted her gaze once more to her face. "But *norteamericanos* so seldom travel with beautiful women." Now she looked at Yakima. "And your half-breed leader — while he looks like the *toros* they breed for the bull ring — has a look of honesty in those strange, green eyes."

"He ain't our leader," Cavanaugh said as Brahma chuffed his disdain. "He hired on as our *guide.*"

Leonora Domingo turned to him sharply. "Guide to where?"

"Tocando," Faith said. "We've business there."

"What kind of business?"

"None of yours, lady," Brahma said.

Yakima ran a placating hand down Wolf's neck while he canted his head toward Faith but spoke to the comely, wild-eyed senorita. He saw no reason to keep their business from her and her men. "The girl's brother's in a rurale jail. We're heading down there to spring him."

Both senorita Domingo and Christos Arvada turned to Yakima sharply, eyes narrowed with interest. Neither said anything, however; just stared at him pensively until someone whistled back near the end of the line of horses, and a man intoned in Spanish, "Senorita, look here — we have hit the mother lode!"

There was a sudden, shrill rattle, and Yakima looked back to see one of the Mexicans standing beside Cavanaugh's mount and grappling with a burlap pouch he'd taken from Faith's saddlebags. From the pouch's neck, gold coins spilled onto the ground around the Mexican's rope-soled sandals.

"No!" Faith yelled swinging around and lunging back toward Cavanaugh's roan.

The wild-eyed senorita grabbed Faith's arm and gave it a jerk, spinning the blonde around sharply. As Faith lost her balance and fell to her butt with a startled yelp, Leonora Domingo strode quickly back toward the roan.

"Tequila!" she raged, grabbing the small man with the coin pouch by one arm, swinging him toward her, then slapping him across his long-nosed face, first with the back of her hand, then with the palm.

The slaps resounded, and the small man groaned and stumbled back, dropping the pouch, which hit the ground with a rattling thump. "How many times do I have to tell you, *pendajo* — we are not banditos! We are revolutionaries far along the road of turning *Méjico* back to the peons, and making peace with our brothers the Apache. If you wish to go back to your petty thievery, do so, but don't try it in front of me, you worthless coyote! Try it again, and I'll have you whipped down to bone and gristle!"

The little man, who had the dull-eyed look of the peon, staggered back, cowering, rubbing his cheek, and setting his ragged, straw sombrero back squarely on his head. Meanwhile, the senorita stared down at the gold coins spilled at her feet. As Christos Arvada skipped down from his pedestal to view the loot, she swung toward Faith.

She said skeptically, "Gold coins minted in America . . ." Then she smiled her incredulous smile again, her eyes flicking up and down Faith's delectable frame. "How do you earn your money, senorita?"

"Honestly," Faith snapped as Cavanaugh helped her back to her feet.

The senorita's knowing grin widened, dimpling her cheeks. "You hope to buy him out, huh?"

"If I have to." Faith brushed past the senorita, dropped to a knee, and began shoving the coins back into the bag.

"You may need more than money."

Senorita Domingo laughed huskily, then told her men to step down. Adjusting her double holsters on her full, round hips, she sauntered past Stiles, Longley, Brahma, and Cavanaugh who regarded her edgily, like unwashed boys in a strange church, and gave Yakima another bold, raking look as she brushed past him, heading toward the far, cave-mottled ridge.

"Follow me," she said. "For the time being, you may tend your friend. Then we will eat, drink, and" — she glanced over her left shoulder at Yakima — "sleep."

CHAPTER 17

Captain Luis Ramon Lazaro booted his cream barb into the foothills of the Sierra Olivadas, where the wind whined caustically down from the higher, bleaker peaks to rustle through the pipestem cactus and raise a shifting veil of alkali dust against the ghostly illumination of the full moon.

Crossing a saddleback ridge upon which the Mexican pinions wavered like clawing bear paws, he began to sniff the heavy stench of the prison — dead bodies, over-filled latrines, and the sweat of more than fifty suffering souls, Apaches as well as banditos, would-be revolutionaries, and their sympathizers — and knew he was almost home.

Lieutenant Montana, half-asleep in his saddle, rode his pinto off the captain's left stirrup — a large, hulking figure who, snoring softly, leaned precariously out over the side of his horse. The lieutenant often fell asleep in the saddle after a long, tiring campaign, though Lazaro had never seen him fall from the hurricane deck.

The six privates rode behind in fatigued silence, their horses clomping and snorting as they, too, smelled the stench of home. Amidst the privates rode the three banditos Lazaro had found camping in an eroded cut just below the ancient village of Coyotana — all three still packing money they'd stolen from a bank in Hermosillo, though the three hadn't confessed their transgressions until Lazaro had turned his bullwhip over to the more powerful and brutal Montana.

Beaten to bloody pulps, one of the men would occasionally lift an anguished groan or call out for *Madre Maria.*

"Miguel," the captain said.

Montana's eyes flickered in the moonlight and he muttered dreamily, just loudly enough for Lazaro to hear above the wind and their horses' clomping hooves and rattling bridles, "I know you can spread your legs farther than that, you lazy whore. . . ."

"Miguel," Lazaro repeated, louder this time.

The lieutenant's head shot up, back stiffening, one hand touching the grips of one of his big Remington revolvers. "Ambush?"

"No, idiot, we are almost home. Look

sharp. How would it look to the peons — a rurale patrol riding home half-asleep in their saddles and muttering to imaginary whores? Another patrol returning without that *puta* bitch, senorita Domingo . . ."

"*Sí,*" Montana growled, sheepish. "I am sorry, *Capitán.*"

"I will overlook it, Miguel. In fact, as a reward for how adeptly you extracted the confessions from the filthy coyotes riding behind us, I will buy the first drink as well as the second, and, if you let me win at cards, I will even buy you an hour with your favorite *puta.*"

Montana looked over at Lazaro, a wide grin on his broad, ugly face with its salt-and-pepper beard and the jagged scars running down from beneath the brim of his steeple-crowned sombrero.

"Phillipina, *Capitán?*"

"That fat sow?"

"Ah, yes, *Capitán.* Her ass is broad as a hay wagon." He cupped his big right hand to his chest. "But with big teats like a mother cow with twins!" Montana laughed. "And you should hear her squeal. It is very exciting, *Capitán!*"

Lazaro chuckled, threw his braid back over his shoulder, then gigged the barb up over the last hill. As he rode down the other side, he saw the lights of Tocando — torch lights and lamplit windows glistening up and down the rocky, cactus-studded hills, across which the town of timeworn adobes was strewn like dice.

The highest lights of all were the torches sparking from their wooden brackets embedded in the stout-walled, turreted prison, which stood in dark, Moorish splendor, like the figment of a deranged child's fantasy, on a high, flat ledge on the town's opposite side.

Moonlight silvered the red-tiled towers, glistening faintly off the Gatling guns protruding from each and aimed at the campfires of those who'd gathered in vigil outside the walls for those friends or family members imprisoned within — those who might decide, in their haste and bereavement, to storm the guards or try climbing the thirty-foot walls.

Lazaro grinned as the shacks and pens and privies pushed up on both sides of the trail, and then the more elaborate whorehouses with their arched doors and windows and wrought-iron balconies. The captain wondered what the families of his prisoners had brought him this week in payment for their loved ones' freedom. He'd seen everything from cartloads of hay to clucking chickens, from sides of pork to firewood. Even gold ingots or, more than a few times, a pretty, virginal daughter.

When he finally captured senorita Domingo, he wouldn't need another woman for quite some time. Until he grew tired of her — which would take many weeks, no doubt — he'd tie the curvaceous young woman naked to his bed, enslaving her, and have his servants feed her from pans, like the mongrel bitch she was, however lovely.

The rurales passed through the milling mob of drunken whores, vaqueros, and campesinos forming a dark, loose knot at the center of the narrow, twisting main street. They continued up a hill, where the street broadened as it climbed into the boulder-strewn mountain slopes, and pulled up before the Palacio Federal built into the hillside about fifty yards below the prison.

A red-tiled, two-story barrack, the palacio had once housed several official offices but, when he'd been transferred to this backwater privy pit, Lazaro had taken it over for himself and his men, and expanded his position from mere captain of the local rurale troupe to an unofficial governor of sorts, backed by several hacendados in the area, who paid handsome bounties not only for Apaches but for banditos and peons with revolutionary leanings, as well.

For a former peasant himself, the bastard son of a syphilitic *puta* servicing a mountain village on the other side of the Sierra Olivadas, Lazaro had done well for himself. And this was just the beginning. . . .

Lazaro ordered the privates to take their horses to the stables and then to head for bed in the barracks. He and Montana would deliver the half-dead banditos to the prison on the mesa flanking the Palacio Federal, for after a long patrol, Lazaro liked to see how badly his second-in-command, Lieutenant Frederico Pedro San Miguel de la Rodriguez, whom Lazaro knew simply as "the Worm," had let things go to pot.

He also wanted to see what gifts the country people had brought him.

He ordered Montana to stay with the prisoners, then dismounted the barb and threw the reins over the hitch rail. As he mounted the palace's broad front porch, a dark, hunched figure lurched out from the shadows near the front door, screeching like a hoarse zopilote, "*Capitán! Capitán! Por favor,* I beseech you, please see to the release of my boy." The old woman, dressed in her customary black shawl, wrapped long, skeletal fingers around his forearms. Her breath was fetid with sour pulque and marijuana. "My Cojo did not rob that mine, I assure you. It was that gang he got in with, drunken *pedajas* to a man. They robbed the mine and said it was him for a joke!"

"Goddamnit, woman!"

"*Capitán,* please set him free," the crone screeched, fingers digging into his arm. "He is my youngest child, and I can't go on living without him!"

One of the two rurales who'd been standing guard on either side of the palace's broad, wooden doors stepped forward and set his hand on the old woman's shoulder, regarding Lazaro apologetically. "I am most sorry, *Capitán.* She has been moping around here for the past two days waiting for you."

"Well, get her the hell away from me, for the love of Christ!" Lazaro jerked his arm free. As the rurale guard, holding his old trapdoor Springfield in one hand, began pulling the crone back away from the captain, the old woman screamed like a buzzard fighting with another over a viscera scrap.

"No, *Capitán!* I beg you in the name of all the saints in heaven . . . I can't live without him anymore!"

"Well, you just have to, you crazy bitch!" Lazaro shouted as the other rurale guard threw the doors open for him. "Your dear

Cojo has been moldering in his grave for the past two years!"

The second guard made a crazy motion with his fingers as Lazaro stepped past him and into the main room of the building. The guard drew the door closed, muffling the crazed crone's screeches. Lazaro looked around the lantern-lit chairs and desks arranged haphazardly in the cavelike, stone-floored room, and a few, half-uniformed men sitting around languidly, writing up reports or playing cards, all relieved in swaying shadows.

A lieutenant with a walrus mustache and long, gray-brown hair stood suddenly. *"Atención!"*

The others, looking up and spying Lazaro at the head of the room, scrambled to their feet, saluting, knocking ashtrays, court books, and other papers to the floor, one grunting as ash from his cigar burned through his pants.

"Welcome back, *Capitán!*" shouted Sergeant Raphael Jiminez, wincing as he pulled his uniform jacket across his incredible paunch.

Lazaro returned the salute halfheartedly, his own face and uniform caked with dust, then pushed through the gate in the low railing that partitioned the desk from the foyer, and plucked a black cigar off the sergeant's desk. Looking frantically around his cluttered desk, Concepción scratched a match to life on the rawhide blotter. Lazaro held the cigar in front of his mouth, and growled, "Where the hell is Rodriguez?"

"Here, *Capitán*."

Lazaro lifted his gaze to the plank loft suspended over the office area. The on-duty officers slept in the loft, and part of the red and gold curtain shielding this makeshift officers' quarters from the main office below had been swept back.

Lieutenant Frederico Pedro San Miguel de la Rodriguez stood in the opening with two whores — all three heavy-eyed and swaying drunkenly. Rodriguez held a cigar in his right hand, which was draped over the shoulder of one of the whores — the one who wore sandals and pink, fancily stitched pantaloons and nothing else, except for a few feathers in her hair and a string of colored, wooden beads hanging over her large, sagging, heavy-nippled breasts. The other — shorter and chubbier, but very wide-eyed and pretty — wore a thin, brown, red-striped serape, which hung halfway down her smooth, dark brown thighs.

Lazaro recognized both whores — two of the most prized *putas* in Tocando. None of the other lieutenants, Lazaro knew, could afford such pricey companionship. Rodriguez could afford them only because his father, Don Rodriguez, whose fifty-thousand-acre hacienda sprawled across the southern foothills of the Sierra Olivadas, supplemented his income with gold sent once every six weeks by special courier.

When the sergeant took the match away from Lazaro's cigar, the captain scowled through the thickening smoke cloud at the lieutenant grinning down at him, obviously three sheets to the wind — a handsome young man with thick, rumpled brown hair, long eyelashes, and two-days' growth of beard on his clean-lined jaws. Bold-eyed and arrogant, he wore uniform pants and suspenders over his underwear shirt, and unpolished stovepipe boots. He didn't seem at all self-conscious about his rumpled attire, nor about the two whores, though whores were forbidden within the rurale offices.

"Get down here, fool," Lazaro grumbled, veins forking above the bridge of his long, beaked nose.

The other officers and sergeants and two corporals stood before their desks and chairs and map tables, edgy expressions on their flushed faces as Rodriguez said, as though speaking to some peon who'd merely asked if he needed his shaving gear, "One minute, *Capitán*. As you can see, I have been otherwise disposed after a rather hectic week. Pardon me as I, with the aid of these two pretties, negotiate the stairs."

Lazaro stood, patiently puffing his cigar as the lieutenant awkwardly descended the wooden stairs at the right side of the room, sucking his own cheroot while draping his arms over the whores' slender shoulders. Holding their heads toward Lazaro, the other men in the room cut their eyes toward the inebriated young lieutenant, strained looks on their faces. The sergeant tensely buttoned his tunic while others tucked their shirttails into their trousers or quickly, nonchalantly disposed of tequila bottles and drink glasses.

The lieutenant stumbled on the steps a couple of times, but the whores, laughing and stumbling themselves but maintaining their balance, quickly caught him and hauled him upright. Finally the lieutenant crossed the room, sauntering and swaggering, sending a couple of surreptitious looks to the other officers and the sergeant.

Leaning over to kiss the cheek of the bare-breasted girl, Rodriguez stopped before the captain, managing a half salute, his broad grin showing off his perfect, large, white teeth. His watery, insolent eyes scuttled about their sockets, as if looking behind Lazaro.

Then the skin above the bridge of his nose wrinkled. "Oh, no, *Capitán!*" he said with mock sadness. "Don't tell me that bitch and Arvada have eluded you once again. . . ."

Lazaro tensed slightly, and his eyes receded into their sockets. Then a bemused smile lifted the corners of his broad mouth, and he said softly, mildly, "Lieutenant Rodriguez, you know my policy about whores and on-duty drunkenness, don't you?"

When the lieutenant merely dropped his chin and shook his head like an incorrigible but charming schoolboy, Lazaro said, "Don't you realize what a bad example this sets for the men whom I left in your charge?"

Rodriguez lifted his drunken, rheumy-eyed gaze to Lazaro, and again he shook his head charmingly. "*Sí, Capitán.* I apologize. It is just that it has been a busy week — two patrols rounded up nearly twenty banditos, fresh horses came in from Don Francisco — and the paperwork has been grueling. And then, of course, my father's allowance arrived, and, it being Saturday, I treated all the officers to a meal, and someone ordered a bottle, and . . ."

The handsome lieutenant laughed again and chucked the whore's bare breast, making it jiggle. "And these two beauties sauntered by the palace. . . ." The whores giggled, balancing themselves against the lieutenant as much as holding him up. "Forgive me, *por favor, Capitán.*"

Lazaro lifted the cigar to his lips, took a puff, and blew a smoke ring at the lieutenant's nose. Staring up at him, the young man's winning smile tensed slightly, and he blinked as the smoke dissipated against his cheeks.

Lazaro said softly, "You think, my dear young lieutenant, that just because your old man owns much land and has, in the past, supported my endeavors against the Yaqui and Apaches, that you can do whatever you want around here. Act however you like." Lazaro blew another smoke ring at the lieutenant's face. "Isn't that so?"

Blinking against the smoke, the lieutenant's eyes grew more tentative while his grin remained fixed. *"Capitán,"* he chuckled, glancing over his shoulder at the other men standing frozen like statues, sweat streaking their bearded cheeks, "I certainly am not one to remind anyone — least of all *you* —

262

who my family is. . . ."

"How noble of you, Frederico," Lazaro said, holding his cigar to his lips with his left hand while, with his right, he slipped his big Colt from its black leather cross-draw holster, nudging aside one of the Apache scalps hanging from his belts.

The lieutenant's jaw dropped and his eyes widened when he saw the seven-inches of cold, glistening steel swing toward him and hold on his belly. Both whores frowned, staring at the rock-steady gun as though they'd stumbled on something puzzling but regrettable lying in the street before them.

Rodriguez, apparently deciding the captain was making a joke, had just begun lifting his gaze back up to Lazaro's eyes, his mouth corners rising slightly, when the revolver barked and leaped in the captain's hand.

"Ach-hah!" the young lieutenant screamed, as flabbergasted as he was horrified.

His head snapped up and back, thick hair flying, and his body flew straight back between two large desks as though he'd been horse-collared from behind, and the lariat had been pulled tighter than a drumhead. He hit the floor on his right shoulder, rolled once, then piled up against a third desk, ankles crossed, arms thrown wide, head tipped to one side, open eyes staring from behind a sheen of tears back up through the wafting powder smoke at the man who'd killed him.

The whores, who'd been half-supported by Rodriguez, had fallen in opposite directions with shocked, horrified cries. Now, in sobbing, crumpled heaps on the floor, they stared back at the young lieutenant, whose life was gushing out onto the ancient, cracked flagstones. None of the other men in the room had moved except to twitch with a start when the captain's gun had exploded, and turn their heads to stare down at the young, dead lieutenant who'd come from more money than any of the others could even imagine.

Lazaro sheathed his revolver and broke the tense silence. "Raphael, throw this pile of overripe dog shit in that new pauper's trench behind the prison. Learn from this — *all* of you. And no word to anyone." He smiled down at the two sobbing whores. "Send these two lovely *putas* over to my quarters. Have Sergio clean them up and tuck them into my bed. I'll be there shortly."

With that, he turned from the room still heavy with stunned silence, and went out, stepping between the two guards, who regarded him with grave, wary curiosity.

Still mounted, Montana stared down at him, frowning, with one hand on a pistol butt.

"Nothing to worry about, Miguel." Lazaro grabbed his reins off the hitch rail. "You've just been promoted, that's all."

Swinging into the saddle, the captain urged the horse ahead to the trail climbing toward the torch-lit prison rearing up above the town, ringed with campfires and fetid with the smell of human waste. "Let's go see what kind of an overcrowded mess Rodriguez has left the prison in. I think it might be a good time for a firing squad, don't you? Just to cull the herd and liven things up around here?"

Lazaro laughed as he put the barb up the rocky incline.

CHAPTER 18

Earlier that same day, in the late afternoon, Yakima woke from his siesta in the oasislike canyon, opening his eyes and poking his hat brim up off his forehead. He and the rest of his group lay sprawled against their saddles, in the shade of creosote and mesquite shrubs. A coffee fire smoldered in a rock ring, orange late-afternoon light sliding across the gray coals sending up a single wisp of white smoke.

After Faith had dug the arrow out of Longley's thigh — the arrow had missed the bone by a hairbreadth — she and the men had thrown their gear down along another creek bubbling out of the rock wall from an underground river, at the base of the canyon's sloping northern wall.

On various shelves along the wall, the men of Leonora Domingo had built Apache-like brush jacales, with here and there a rack from which meat or skins dried. About halfway up the slope, the largest of the several caves opened. Yakima couldn't see inside the cave from this sharp angle, but he could see smoke billowing from a fire on the ledge just outside the opening and smell the stomach-warming aroma of roasting javelina.

Glancing around the canyon walls, he spied the slender silhouettes of two rifle-wielding lookouts. There were no doubt more. Senorita Leonora was a cunning woman, and it was obvious she didn't want her hideout discovered by anyone; it was also obvious she was miffed that Yakima had happened onto it. He wondered if, to preserve its secrecy, she and her men would let Yakima's group leave, or would they have to fight their way out.

Automatically, with an instant pang of regret, he glanced at his revolver rig snugged beside his saddle, the belt wrapped snake-like around it. His Colt was gone, as was his Yellowboy. All he had for weapons was his Arkansas toothpick, which wouldn't do much good against the twenty or so men the senorita obviously commanded in the canyon, nor against the Gatling gun.

He glanced to his left. Faith lay on one side, both hands wedged between her cheek and her saddle, legs curled. Her blouse hung partially open, revealing a good portion of a well-filled, lace-edged chemise. Yakima remembered how those breasts looked — full, pale, and pear-shaped — without their concealing garments . . . and how she'd felt struggling beneath him, in his passionate, lovemaking embrace.

In her sleep, she gave her head a jerk at an annoying fly, and groaned softly. As if in response, Cavanaugh lifted a snore just beyond her, asleep on his back, hat tipped low, one knee in the air, his beard-bristled cheeks expanding slightly with each exhalation.

Someone snorted, and Yakima stretched his gaze to where Lou Brahma, propped on one elbow, lay beneath a mesquite. The big man stared insinuatingly across the smoldering coals, a half smile on his thick, chapped lips. He gave another snort and glanced at Faith, then lay back down and rolled onto his opposite shoulder, drawing his knees up toward his chest.

Yakima rose, shook a brown recluse spider out of his right boot, donned it and then the left, and walked out away from the camp, passing Pop Longley who slept sitting upright against a sprawling mesquite tree, his thigh wrapped with white cloth, and a half-empty tequila bottle clenched in his fist — and walked west along the base of the canyon wall.

He figured he'd have a look around, see if there was another way out of here besides the one effectively covered by the Gatling gun. Glancing up the ridge on his right, he spied several Mexicans lounging around their jacales and in the shade of cabin-sized boulders, a couple shaking dice or playing poker. While they eyed him skeptically, none of the Mexicans made any moves to prevent Yakima from prowling around, so he continued strolling along the ridge base, noting ancient pictographs in the red sandstone layered with granite, and several large dinosaur teeth.

When he'd walked a hundred yards, muffled barks and chortles rose on the breeze, seemingly coming from a large break in the canyon wall filled with stone rubble and cacti. The barking and mewling continued, sounding like a complaining pack of half-dead coyotes.

The sweet, cloying smell of death thickened. Puzzled, wishing he had his guns, Yakima followed the hair-prickling sounds and the fetor over the rubble and into a cool, shaded cleft that opened gradually until he stood at the narrow end of a funnel-shaped canyon.

A chill swept him as his gaze found a makeshift rack formed from stout logs — four standing upright to support two square-hewn, vertical beams spanning a good fifty feet about ten feet off the ground. From the vertical beams, hanging either head-down or -up, ropes tied around their necks or ankles, then wrapped around the beams, a dozen or so men dangled like dead deer in a hunting camp.

Big, black, bald-headed and hook-nosed buzzards clung to the rack and the hanging bodies like flies to a slice of jelly-slathered bread. Feeding and fighting over the scraps of viscera that they plucked from the rotting cadavers, they lifted a screeching, scolding din that made Yakima stretch his lips back from his teeth as the sounds battered his eardrums.

One frazzled, ungainly old *zopilote,* perched atop the rack, a scrap of meat clinging to his bloody beak, regarded Yakima with proprietary disdain in its snakelike eyes, and barked like an enraged cur with a bone between its paws. Then it bent forward to poke its beak into an already empty eye socket.

Yakima nearly retched as the breeze shifted and sent the heavy, rotten fetor up his nostrils, making his eyes water and his stomach muscles contract. Fishing a necker-chief from his pocket, he held it over his nose as he studied the grisly visage before him.

The dozen cadavers were in various stages of decomposition, some with their clothes stripped nearly entirely away to reveal bloody bone and stringy, torn muscles and tendons. Most of the faces were so badly ruined by rot and the feeding buzzards that it was hard to tell, but a couple looked like Americans. Most appeared Mexican. Some still wore cartridge bandoliers, what was left of calico or burlap shirts, buckskin or white canvas breeches, and leather boots.

Two hanging from the front beam and one from the back, turning slowly as the buz-zards prodded them, wore the unmistakable dove gray tunics of the Mexican rurale, with covered holsters strapped to their hips and uniform slacks with the customary red stripe running down the sides.

Yakima was about to turn away when a mournful, beseeching rasp rose amongst the hanging bodies. He peered into the mass of torn, rotting flesh and flapping, black wings. An eye from the back row peered out at him, sunlight gleaming off the brown iris. The man was hanging upside down, twist-ing slowly back and forth in the breeze. He was round-faced, and one eye was gone. He was the most intact of all of the bodies. The lips beneath the single, squinted eye and bloody nose moved.

"Help me," he wheezed in Spanish, barely audible above the din.

Yakima's eyes raked him up and down. He'd been shot in both shoulders and a thigh, and it didn't appear that the buzzards had gotten to him yet, though one clinging to the dead man beside him gave him several appraising, inquiring glances.

The man's mouth moved again, though this time the plea was drowned by the birds.

Yakima's gut recoiled. Holding the neckerchief across his mouth and nose, fighting back a violent retch, he looked around for a tree branch or a rock — anything with which to put the man out of his misery. A hoof-sized, jagged-edged rock lay near a shriveled sage. He moved toward it.

There was the loud raking rasp of a bullet being rammed into a rifle breech.

Yakima stopped.

"What do you think you are doing, big man?" Leonora's mocking voice called from the ridge behind him. "Trying to spoil a girl's fun, when she gets so little of it out here?" She was squatting on a low shelf along the ridge, a Henry repeater laid across her thighs. Now she rose and descended the ridge, the vest drawing taut against her breasts, which bulged out from beneath — heavenly tan semicircles in the softening light.

As she drew up beside Yakima, coquettishly rubbing her bare arm against his, she glanced at the grisly rack around which the *zopilotes* squabbled and the fetor hung thick as sewage. "Don't feel sorry for them. Scalp hunters, to a man. The last one, the one still alive in spite of having been hanging there for three days, we caught just west of the canyon. He wore the scalps of three Apache children on his belt."

Removing the neckerchief from his face, Yakima glanced down at her and said in a skeptical tone, "Is that what you do out here — right the wrongs done to the Apaches?"

Leonora looked up at him, smiling, dark eyes flashing. She ran her hand around his bicep, squeezing and leaning into him, brashly flirtatious. Then she gave his arm a tug before strolling wide of the rack to move deeper into the feeder canyon. "You have questions, big man. Follow me, and I will try to answer them where it is" — she grimaced as she glanced once more at the rack — "not so smelly."

Yakima stared after her, incredulous, unable to keep his eyes off her round, swinging butt inside the tight leather pants. Beyond the rack, she stopped and glanced back over her left shoulder. "Come." She smiled that smile again, giving him an enticing profile shot of her left breast bulging out from beneath the vest. "You're not afraid of me, are you?"

She laughed and continued walking. With a last look at the rack — the lone, beseeching eye of the still-alive man following him — Yakima tramped wide of the hanging carnage and headed after the woman, taking long strides between the shelving slopes of red, boulder-strewn walls.

He followed her over a pile of logs stretched, gatelike, before a narrow gap, and into a greener fork of the canyon. The ground was marked with shod hoofprints and horse apples, and the smell of horses was welcome after the sickly sweet stench of human decay.

"This is where we keep our horses," she called without looking behind, from about ten feet ahead, still walking briskly. "The water is good and fresh, and the grass is green."

Catching glimpses of several mustangs grazing and swishing their tails farther back in the jagged-walled canyon, Yakima followed Leonora Domingo through a thick maze of shrubs toward the left wall, where the air cooled and became humid, tinged with the coppery smell of minerals and the verdant aroma of lush growth. Pushing through mesquite branches, she disappeared for a moment. He ducked through the growth himself, and when the last branch fell back behind him, he found her kneeling beside a spring bubbling up in a dug-out bowl ringed with red stones.

She doffed her hat and shook her hair out from her neck. "Hunting scalp-hunters is only a hobby."

As her thick, black hair fell back against her neck, she leaned out over the pool and slowly cupped water to her face. "The Apaches and the people of this province once had a truce, but the rurales and the rich hacendados couldn't stand the peace and quiet. Or maybe they fought the Apache so long they didn't know what to do with themselves without war."

She fingered the water through her hair and massaged it into the back of her neck, grunting softly and tilting her head from side to side. "So they broke the truce. The hacendados put bounties on the Apaches' heads — two pesos per scalp for civilians, five for the rurales. That's a lot of money around here. So now the rurales are in the business of scalp-hunting and taking, shall we say, subsidies from the dons to keep their land free of the red vermin."

Leonora Domingo blew water from her lips and tipped her head back, shaking her damp hair back behind her shoulders. "Why do I care? I am half Apache. If there are no Apaches around, the scalp-hunters are not above killing a mestizo or a peon with black hair, and turning the scalps in for the bounty."

"I saw it up north," Yakima said, doffing his hat, leaning out over the pool, and cupping the cool water to his face. "Some braided captain led a crew of rurales against women and children. Not a buck in the pack."

"A braid, you said?"

The hard tone of her voice made him look up, water streaming down his cheeks and off the tip of his nose. "That's right."

Her chin up, she stared down at him over the flat planes of her sculpted cheeks. "Lazaro. Captain Luis Ramon Lazaro. Murdering son of a bitch. He runs the prison in Tocando. That's why you travel there in vain, my friend."

Yakima sat back on his heels. Casually, Leonora unfastened the top button of her leather vest. He watched as her hands dropped to the next button and unfastened it, as well. When she got to the last button, he thought that she would leave it there, keeping her breasts partially covered as she cupped water to her chest.

Instead, as if she were undressing alone in her own boudoir, she threw her head back once more, pulled both flaps of the vest away from her chest, and let the leather garment drop down her arms to the ground behind her. She cupped the round, tan, exquisite orbs in her hands, squeezing and kneading and lifting, then leaned over the pool and cupped water to them quickly, as though they were on fire.

Yakima suppressed his rising desire and sank back on a hip, lifting one knee and resting an arm on it. "Tell me about this Lazaro."

"What is there to say?" Leonora continued cupping water to her breasts, rubbing it into her belly. "He kills at will. Those he doesn't kill, he imprisons. He's killed several of my men, imprisoned others." She looked up sharply, darkly. "He imprisoned my man, suspecting he was a *revolucionario*. He had no proof, but he held him for over a year until he finally shot him by firing squad."

She sat back on her heels and looked off pensively, hands on her thighs, water streaming down her breasts and through her cleavage. "Lazaro is the self-serving bastard who started the war with the Apaches. Seven years ago, when I was still a girl — an innocent child — he wiped out a village of Apache women and children. My father was a farmer, with some cornfields on the western slopes of the Sierra Olivadas. He took in several of the survivors of this massacre, members of my dead mother's own family. Lazaro found out, for he has spies everywhere.

"Lazaro came, killed them all. He and three of his officers raped me and were about to scalp me when Apache warriors rode in." An evil smile twisted Leonora's mouth, rerouting the tears streaming down her cheeks at the memory. "The fork-tailed bastard ran screaming with his men into the hills."

She turned to Yakima, her narrowed eyes hard as flint. "Since then, he has acquired many men, many guns. And he runs the prison, which he holds over the heads of the peons and the Apaches like a guillotine. Go up against him, you either die or get thrown into his prison, which is only a slower death. Meanwhile, he grows fat off the bounties paid to him by the hacendados, who are deathly afraid of the Apaches and the revolution that smolders in these sierras and barrancas, threatening to pit the Apaches and the peons against the fat, greedy hogs and their henchmen."

"Your man was a *revolucionario,* I take it."

She gave him a cockeyed glance, and her lips twisted again with a cunning smile. "*Sí.* Of course."

"How did you get your hands on the Gatling gun?"

"We stole it off a company Lazaro sent toward the Rio Rojo. A few more Gatlings, a few more repeating rifles . . . and once I've butchered Lazaro, slowly" — she held her hands up in front of her face as if to inspect the palms — "with my own hands . . . who knows what will happen around here?"

She lowered her hands, cupped her breasts, and squeezed them together, lifting until the nipples were pointed at her chin. She looked down at them and gazed up at Yakima from beneath her brows, puckering her lips out speculatively. "You will help me, huh?"

Yakima shook his head and lifted his eyes from the pinched breasts to the girl's face. "I'm no revolutionary. Besides, I told you my business down here."

She dropped her hands suddenly, scowling. "Don't be a fool. The blonde needs to write off her brother. He is dead, no doubt shot by firing squad a long time ago . . . or worse."

"I reckon we'll find out." Yakima dropped to both knees and leaned forward, soaking his head in the pool. He pulled it out and shook out his hair, blowing water through his lips. Holding his head low over the pool, he glanced up to see the girl kneeling beside him, shoulders back, breasts thrust out, smiling down at him.

She reached out and slid a lock of wet hair back from his cheek, running her thumb slowly across his jaw. He glanced at the irresistible breasts jutting toward him, full and round and smooth as varnished ironwood, the nipples pebbling slightly with desire. Then he glanced down at the ivory-handled .45's positioned for the cross-draw on her round hips.

Yakima's heart hammered. If he grabbed a gun and held her hostage, he might be able to retrieve his and his group's weapons as well as their freedom. On the other hand, he might only get them killed.

"Go on, make your choice," Leonora said, grinning at him knowingly. "Which do you want more, *mi amor?* Me — or my weapons?"

"You play a mean hand," he growled, grabbing her breasts in his hands, pulling her slowly down toward him, her dark eyes growing larger. "But I have a feelin' you have plenty of weapons."

"Give the big man a cigar," she breathed, sliding his damp hair back from his cheeks with both hands, relaxing her muscles, surrendering herself. "Stay with me here, be my man, and I will introduce you to some of them, uh?"

As he rolled her nipples under his thumbs, she gritted her teeth and groaned, gooseflesh rising on her arms and across her shoulders, and her breasts grew hard as cantaloupes. He closed his mouth over hers, kissed her for a time, then, twisting around, pulled her down beside him and rolled on top of her, spreading her legs wide with his own.

CHAPTER 19

Later, Yakima crawled naked to the pool within the red rocks and dunked his head. He pulled it out, shook himself like a dog, then turned to look back at Leonora Domingo lounging naked on their strewn clothes on the lee side of a domino-shaped boulder, next to a crack from which a gnarled ironwood tree protruded.

The sun had dropped behind the ridges, and the canyon was quickly filling with darkness.

Despite the chill, Leonora lay spread-eagled and sweating, breasts rising and falling as she breathed, wisps of black hair pasted to her cheeks. *"Madre Maria!"* She whistled. "You've done that before!"

"I got a feelin' you weren't exactly chaste," Yakima said, sucking air through his teeth, sweeping another handful of water off the pool, and splashing it across his face. He put his back to the rocks and stretched his long, muscle-corded legs out before him. "You gonna give us our guns, let us ride out of here tomorrow, or we gonna have to fight for 'em?"

"Giving you back your guns is not possible, *mi amor*," she said with a fatigued air, lifting up on her elbows, dipping her chin to her chest. "At least, not yet. I haven't decided if I should let you go." She brushed gravel from her naked thigh. "No one knows of my hideout but you and the beautiful blonde and the other gringos. I doubt even Lazaro could extract my whereabouts from your thick hide, but what about the girl and her manservants, huh?"

"As far as anyone knows outside this canyon, we don't know shit about you." Yakima reached for his buckskins. "You got no reason to keep us here . . . or turn that Gatling on us."

"I don't need reasons." Leonora clamped her heels down on top of the pants. Yakima gave them a jerk, and they slid out from beneath her, pulling her legs sideways. She grunted with excitement and anger, and stared at him with a hard smile etching her lips.

Yakima stood and dressed as she watched. It took him a while, because he had to fight for each piece of clothing, but he finally stomped into his boots and looked around for his hat. She was wearing it, staring up at him defiantly, her dark eyes holding the last rays of the dying light beneath the flat, black brim.

He reached for the hat, but she swiped it off her head and held it behind her back, thrusting her breasts toward him once more, mouth corners edging up. Yakima grabbed her shoulders and rolled her over. She cursed hotly as he pried her fingers open to remove the hat. Stepping back, he donned it. She grabbed one of her pretty .45's, whipped around, and pressed the barrel against the underside of his chin.

Yakima froze and dropped his eyes to stare down the five-inch barrel.

Leonora gave a steely smile as she said softly, "Sure you won't stay, *mi amor?* We could lift some dust around here, tie the rurales' shorts in a real knot. In a few years, we could have run out Lazaro and set up our own government on one of these wretched haciendas smelling up the Sierra Olivadas."

Yakima opened his mouth to speak, but she poked the barrel more firmly against his jaw, and added, "Think hard, half-breed. I do not take rejection well."

A gun hammer clicked behind her. She

jerked slightly with a start, and her eyes narrowed. Yakima looked beyond her and left.

Faith stood behind the boulder from which the twisted ironwood grew. She had a small, .36-caliber, pearl-gripped S&W in her right fist, aimed at Leonora's head.

"Neither do I," Faith said tightly, curling her nose and upper lip, showing her white, even teeth. "And I would feel mighty rejected if you shot my guide."

Leonora laughed, unperturbed. "Don't worry, blondie. I wasn't going to shoot your *guide*." She depressed the hammer and pulled the gun away from Yakima's jaw, keeping her gaze on the half-breed. "I was just going to see if I could make him squirm a little. I'd forgotten that there are men in the world who don't squirm even under threat of a .45 slug. How rare." She tossed the Colt aside and glanced at Faith still holding the .36 on her. "You are lucky to have him for a *guide*."

Leonora laughed. Faith flushed, eyes darting to Yakima, as she depressed her .36's hammer with a soft click, and lowered the gun to her side.

Making no move to cover herself, Leonora leaned back against the tree, stretched out her legs, and crossed her ankles. "Had that peashooter tucked away in your bodice, eh?

I must remind my men to be more careful with the next blonde who stumbles into our canyon."

Faith moved forward and looked down at the *revolucionaria* reclining, as naked as the day she was born, an expression of supreme insouciance on her wildly regal face.

"Are you gonna let us go?"

Leonora looked at Yakima. "Take her away, will you, big man? I wish to doze here in the last light before I return to my cave." She stretched and closed her eyes, yawning luxuriously, her breasts drawing up and flattening slightly against her chest.

Yakima glanced at Faith, canted his head toward the other side of the canyon, then turned and pushed through the brush. Faith caught up to him as he left the brush and began retracing his and Leonora's steps toward the main part of the canyon.

"I wasn't going to interrupt," she said, matching her strides to Yakima's. "But I thought she was about to let you have it. You really ought to choose your lovers more carefully."

"I take what I can get." Yakima stopped suddenly and turned to her. His face was warm with embarrassment. "How long had you been there before you showed yourself?"

"I didn't see you two *together,* if that's

what you mean."

"What're you doing out here?"

"Strolling around, looking for a way out of the canyon. Isn't that what you were doing, or had you *planned* your little tryst with senorita Domingo? Just killing time until she decided to hang us up for the buzzards from that neat little rack of hers?"

"Why not?" Yakima turned and continued walking.

Faith grabbed his arm, and he turned to face her once again. Her eyes were sharp, cheeks flushed with fury. "Hold on, Yakima. I wanna know what's going on. Are you with her now, or with me? I have to know if I can depend on you. If not, let's cut the ties right here and now, go our own separate ways."

Yakima chuckled. "Don't get your panties in a twist. It takes a hell of a lot more than one roll in the hay to turn me into a sucker. I'll get your brother out of jail — if he's still alive. From what Leonora tells me, he's probably not, and we're all down here running from Apaches and getting chased into Gatling guns for nothing. But I told you I'd help. Now, let's get the hell out of here before it's too dark to see where we're goin'."

He turned and walked past the rack from

which the dozen scalp-hunters hung — a vague, inky blotch in the gathering darkness but recognizable by its smell and from the sounds of the quarreling birds. There was another sound as well — the deep-throated snarls of coyotes with occasional snaps and yips bespeaking a fight over the carrion.

Yakima was well into the main part of the canyon when he realized he'd taken Faith's hand and was pulling her along behind him. She'd said nothing. Suddenly self-conscious, keeping his head forward, he released her hand and continued tramping through the chaparral, smelling the supper fires that flickered up the sloping canyon wall on his left.

He realized Faith was saying something, almost too softly for him to hear. ". . . make you my sucker?"

Yakima stopped once more. She drew up to him, and the last light shone in her sad eyes.

He frowned. "What?"

"Is that what you were afraid of back in Gold Cache?" she asked, shaking her hair out of her eyes. "That you'd become some sucker for me? Working *for* me in the brothel? Did you think it would be like it was at Thornton's?" She paused, staring up at him. "That isn't how I saw it, Yakima.

You and me, we —"

Suddenly, he reached out and grabbed her by the shoulders, pulled her to him brusquely, and kissed her. She returned the kiss, leaning into him, wrapping her hands around his arms, pressing her lips against his. He ran his hands down her back and through her hair. Despite having had Leonora Domingo less than an hour ago, his fire for Faith still raged.

She groaned as she rose up on her toes. She wrapped her arms around his neck, pressing her heaving breasts against his chest, running her hands brusquely up and down his cheeks and through his hair.

As he held her, squeezing her, reveling in her touch and smell and the familiar, passionate sighs issuing from her throat, his heart thudded heavily. Voices spoke to him half consciously. He'd been a fool to leave her. There was no denying his love for her. If he ever got her out of this canyon, this country, he'd never let her out of his sight again. What he'd do about Cavanaugh he had no idea.

But once this trouble was behind them, Faith was his. Cavanaugh would pay for any interference with his own blood.

To Yakima's right, voices rose from the chaparral. There was the distant thump of a boot kicking a stone.

"Faith?" Cavanaugh's voice echoed in the silent night, filling Yakima's gut with sour bile. Instinctively, the half-breed tightened his grip on the girl in his arms. At the same time, Faith gave a startled grunt and, pressing her palms against his heaving chest, wriggled out of his grasp.

As the footsteps grew louder, brush rustling and men breathing hard, Faith stepped back away from Yakima and turned. Yakima dropped his hands to his sides, anger and frustration burning inside him, and turned to see two silhouetted figures — the slender Cavanaugh and the bulky, round-shouldered Lou Brahma — approach through the chaparral.

"Faith, is that you?"

Faith drew a calming breath. Yakima heard the strain in her voice. "It's me, Ace."

"What the hell?" Cavanaugh said, his voice pitched with irritation as he and Brahma broke through the brush to stand before her and Yakima. "Me and Lou've been stumbling around out here for the past half hour."

"We thought them bean eaters got you and took you up to their cave or something," Brahma added, tipping his hat brim toward the ridge on which the cook fires grew brighter. His voice owned a liquor-laced drawl. "Damn near marched up there and demanded a reckonin' — didn't we, Ace?"

"I woke up and decided to kill time looking for a way out of the canyon," Faith said.

Brahma sneered at Yakima. "And look who you ran into."

"Something you wanna add to that, Brahma?" the half-breed said.

Frustration over the whole damn situation — the Apaches, the canyon trap, Faith, and Cavanaugh — had set his rage to boiling like a stew pot on a hot fire, and he found himself staring at the big man's wedge-shaped nose, wanting to flatten it out across his belligerent, pockmarked face. One word was all he needed.

Brahma seemed to sense it. The big man kept his lips pinched together, silently holding Yakima's hard gaze, his good eye slitted more than the other, an antagonizing half smile fixed on his face.

"Knock it off!" Faith said, keeping her voice low. "We have enough to think about without you two going head-to-head like a couple of lamebrained schoolboys. Has anyone considered how we're going to get our weapons back and make a break from this hellhole?"

The men stared at each other, faintly incredulous.

"Maybe we'd better get back to camp and talk it over," Faith said, striding off toward the fire winking about fifty yards ahead.

A coyote yammered on the purple-green ridge on the far side of the canyon.

Brahma glanced at Cavanaugh, shrugged, chuffed, and strode off toward the camp.

Cavanaugh turned to Yakima and glanced after Faith. "Nice piece of work, ain't she?"

"Few nicer."

"I don't know what you and her had goin' in the past." Scowling, the gambler quickly ran his flinty gaze up and down Yakima. "Don't care to think about it. But she's mine now. Bought and paid for. And she *ain't* for sale. You remember that. Understand, Henry? Cause when it comes to cards and women, I rarely lose."

CHAPTER 20

Over a tense supper of beans, tortillas, and coffee, Yakima's group decided they couldn't rely on Leonora Domingo to return their weapons out of the goodness of her heart, and to give them safe passage back out of the canyon.

They'd sleep a few hours, then, an hour or so before dawn, quietly saddle their horses and try to ride undetected across the canyon, staying as far from the walls and Leonora's pickets as they could, and slip back out the corridor through which they'd come. If they were spotted, they'd storm their way out, overrunning any pickets who stood in their way.

It was a sketchy plan, and it wouldn't work without a good dose of luck, but they all agreed it was the only hope they had. Yakima was glad when, during a final patrol of their camp's perimeter before turning in, he found that Leonora had posted no men nearby to keep a close watch on his group.

Aside from pickets on the canyon rim and no doubt behind the Gatling gun trained on the chasm's only entrance, the entire ragtag band seemed to be huddled by the cook fires on the shelving slope around the caves. Occasional fiddle strains and muffled laughter floated down the incline, mingling with the night wind harassing the shrubs.

Yakima slept lightly a good twenty feet from the fire, not far from where he'd tied Wolf. Though the horse gave no warnings, the half-breed woke a half-dozen times to lift his head and look around cautiously before the positions of the stars indicated it was about an hour before dawn.

He rose, donned his boots and hat, and whistled at Lou Brahma lying about ten feet away, under a willow branch bowing out from the bank behind him. The big man lifted his head with a start, reaching for the empty holster beside him. He froze, staring at Yakima shrewdly, then grumbled and threw his blankets back.

Brahma rousted the others, who quietly but frenetically clamored up out of their blankets. Yakima threw his own bedroll together, tied it with rawhide, then grabbed his saddle and headed toward Wolf, who eyed him tensely from between two mesquite trees, as though trying to judge the situation, anticipate what lay ahead.

"Easy, boy."

Yakima dropped the saddle beside the horse and reached down to grab the bridle. Wolf lifted his head suddenly, gave a low nicker, and swished his tail.

Leaving the bridle hanging around the saddle horn, Yakima straightened, the muscles bunching in his back. He cursed as he unconsciously reached for his holster and found it agonizingly empty — they had to get their hands on some guns somewhere soon — then looked around, pricking his ears.

There were only the scuffs of the others still packing their gear around the cold fire, and the other horses stomping nervously. Yakima placed a calming hand on Wolf's back as he walked around the horse's hindquarters, eyes drilling into the inky blotches of the chaparral limned with starlight.

From ahead about thirty yards rose the soft ching of a spur. Yakima walked toward it. Sensing something behind him, he stopped in time to catch the wink of starlight on brass.

He bent his knees in a sudden crouch.

Behind him, someone sucked air through his teeth as a rifle butt swept over Yakima's head, knocking his hat off. The half-breed wheeled, squeezing his hands together and swinging both arms around like a single club, connecting soundly with a shoulder.

The man behind him grunted as he rose about a foot in the air and flew sideways, turning an awkward cartwheel before piling up in a dark cloud of sifting sand and crunching gravel.

Hatless, the silver discs on his buckskin *chivarras* flashing in the starlight, Christos Arvada lifted his head and cursed sharply in Spanish. His hand moved in the darkness, and the starlight glistened off a gun barrel. Yakima leaped forward and swung his left leg back and up.

"Mierda!" the pistolero cried as the gun, knocked from his hand, flipped into the air, turning end over end into the shrubs behind him.

Running footsteps and labored breaths sounded to Yakima's right. A rifle flashed and roared, the bullet cutting the air near his right temple and thumping into a mesquite with an angry whine and a rain of shredded bark. Yakima turned to face the three shadows jouncing toward him, spurs chinging and rifles rattling, their steeple-peaked sombreros silhouetted against the stars.

To Yakima's left, a horse whinnied. Faith called his name as several pairs of boots thumped toward him from the camp. Before him, the three Mexicans stopped, one raising a trapdoor Springfield to his shoulder and snugging his bearded cheek up to the stock as he aimed.

"Hold on, morons!" senorita Domingo called in Spanish behind him.

The man held fire and lowered the rifle slightly as hoof thumps sounded. Over the three Mexicans' heads, Yakima watched the senorita ride toward him on a rangy, ewe-necked steeldust, her sensual, well-curved body moving with the horse's sway. By a lead line she trailed a handsome, saddled calico mare. In her hand, a gun flashed and popped. Her horse jerked its head up as the bullet tore into the ground behind the rifle-wielding Mexican's right foot.

"Ach!" the man cried, dropping the rifle as he fell to his knees, then reached around to grab his bullet-grazed heel, cursing loudly in Spanish. "Senorita, Christos gave the order!"

"Christos doesn't give the orders around here, you horn-headed son of a she-goat!"

She walked the steeldust and the calico up past the injured man, who continued to rub his heel and suck air through his teeth, and drew rein before Yakima. Behind him, the brush crackled, and he glanced back to see Christos Arvada bull his way through a mesquite thicket, aiming his revolver straight out from his belly.

The senorita's gun roared again, flames flashing in the dark predawn. Sand and gravel sprayed up two feet before the hatless, skeleton-thin pistolero who was breathing hard and cursing under his breath, the silver conchos on his leggings twinkling with starlight.

"Christos, I gave you my decision on the matter!"

"They know of the canyon, Leonora," Christos fired back, wagging his revolver up high around his shoulder. "Are you willing to endanger the whole group because the big *indio* lit a fire between your *legs?*"

Silence. The steeldust rippled a wither. It was too dark for Yakima to see the expression on Leonora's face, but something told him she wore her customarily steely, bemused smile.

Finally, Christos Arvada released the tension with a low chuckle. There was a rasp of iron against leather as he holstered his revolver and turned away, playfully kicking a rock.

"I was making a joke, senorita," he said as he walked back into the shrubs. "Just having a little fun with your half-breed, uh?"

He barked orders for the other three to mount their horses as planned, then, with the others sauntering after him, casting wary looks over their shoulders at the still-mounted senorita, disappeared with Christos Arvada in the darkness.

Senorita Domingo looked down at Yakima, then glanced at Faith and the others, except for Pop Longley, who'd come up to flank him, edgily silent. The senorita had two burlap bags hanging from her saddle horn, one on each side of her saddle. From one, several rifle butts jutted. This one she loosed from the horn and let drop, and it hit the ground with a heavy clatter. She released the second one, and it clattered more quietly onto the sand and sage.

"You'll need your weapons in Tocando." She tossed the calico's reins onto the ground before Faith. "And a horse."

Yakima's shoulders loosened with relief. "Much obliged."

"Get your people mounted and follow me. I'll show you the way to Tocando." She reined her horse sideways. "But don't blame

299

me when you wish I hadn't."

She spurred the steeldust back in the direction from which she'd come, trotting away and fading under the stars.

Yakima and the others grabbed their guns, made sure they were loaded, then quickly saddled their horses and rode off after senorita Domingo. Pop Longley was still in considerable pain, and he rode with one gnarled hand on the reins, the other wrapped around a tequila bottle, chuckling and cursing ironically. Willie Stiles rode behind him in case he fell off his buckskin. They all hoped to find him a doctor in Tocando.

Heading south across the canyon, Yakima reined up when he saw Leonora, Christos Arvada, and about five other riders lined out across the narrow entrance to the corridor leading back to the main part of the canyon. The Mexicans faced Yakima's group. Arvada's deep-set eyes — it was still too dark to see the expression in them — were fixed on the half-breed as he held a Sharps rifle across his saddle bows. Yakima held the man's gaze and spread his fingers across his left thigh, within a fast grab of his Colt .44.

Leonora held fast to the reins of her

fiddle-footing steeldust, then wheeled the horse suddenly, ground her spurred heels against the mount's flanks, and headed into the narrow, black mouth of the corridor. Two of the other Mexicans booted their mounts after the beautiful *revolucionaria,* the hollow clomps of their shod hooves echoing inside the chasm.

Arvada sat his horse to one side of the corridor's opening, grinning, his silver teeth shining in the pearl light slowly bleeding over the canyon walls.

He held out a hand to Yakima. "After you, amigo."

"You're one well-mannered bastard, Arvada." Yakima glanced behind at the others, then booted Wolf into the chasm's cavelike darkness, the hoof clacks echoing off the walls and growing to a near din as the others rode in behind him.

The dark gray light at the other end of the chasm grew, swelling around him until Wolf turned at the far end, following the other horses east down the main canyon. Given the still-dim light and treacherous footing, senorita Domingo kept up a pace too fast for Yakima's liking. But he held Wolf to a ball-busting jog-trot through one canyon fork and into another, until the granite and sandstone walls gradually slipped back behind him and he found himself tracing a curving cart trail into high, blue-green mountain reaches, with the thin, dry air warming quickly as the sun blossomed like a giant rose.

They passed a couple of crumbling, stone shrines bedecked with dead flowers, and the remains of a mission church surrounded by a broken, vine-covered adobe wall.

An hour after sunup the senorita pulled to a halt atop a breezy saddle. The huge sky and many shadowy ridgelines swept out around her in all directions. When Yakima, followed by his group who were in turn followed by Christos Arvada and another Mexican with a double-barreled shotgun, pulled up beside the senorita, she lifted her chin to the southwest.

"Over that second rise you will find Tocando." She sniffed the air, wrinkling her nose. "I can almost smell the stench from here. Many *indios* and *revolucionarios* have died in Lazaro's prison. A very bad place." Turning to Yakima, she reached over and set her hand on his broad, flat cheek. "Be careful such a fate is not yours, *mi indio amigo*. Perhaps our paths will cross again."

She reined around and gigged the steeldust back along the group and down the twisting trail, her men wheeling their own mounts and following close behind. Yakima watched the group dwindle down the rocky, brush-sheathed switchbacks, the *revolucionaria* at the head of the pack, rich hair dancing down the back of her doeskin vest.

"You musta made quite an impression," said Cavanaugh, grinning beside Faith.

He cut his eyes toward his wife, flipping the ends of his reins from one side of his saddle to the other. Faith dropped her gaze to the calico's neck.

Cavanaugh continued in his sneering, mocking tone, "But now that we've wasted a good day, you think we might be able to pull on into Tocando and get the whippersnapper out of jail? I haven't had near as much fun down here as you obviously have, and I'm gettin' right homesick."

CHAPTER 21

An hour later, Yakima lay atop a rocky ridge crest, training his spyglass on the castlelike adobe prison on the other side of the village of Tocando. The town was scattered across several chalky, cactus-studded hills in the canyon below, while the prison loomed on a broad, sandy bench above.

Its shadow angled over a corner of the village, blue and menacing.

The prison had four parapetted towers with either a Gatling or two armed guards in each tower. Two guards stood at the large, arched wooden doors recessed in the front wall overlooking the town. Spilling down the slope to the right of the prison were several cook fires, brush jacales, and canvas tents, with here and there a rack from which meat had been hung to dry. Peasants clad in straw sombreros milled about this makeshift village, several hauling wooden water buckets up a switchbacking trail from the town below.

"It's hotter'n hell on a hot day up here," complained Lou Brahma, sitting halfway down the slope behind Yakima, and squinting up slope against the sunlight. The horses and Pop Longley remained below, in a shady grove of pin-oaks and sycamores. "We ain't *bustin'* the kid out of the hoosegow. We're *buyin'* him out. Let's get the hell down there and go to it."

"It doesn't hurt givin' the town a gander," Yakima said, keeping the glass trained on the village and picking out the Palacio Federal, over which the Mexican flag ruffled in a slight breeze. The government building, which probably housed the rurales, sat nearly directly below the prison, built into the side of a rocky hill. "Just in case we need a way out fast . . . maybe in the dark. . . ."

"Like I *said*," Brahma complained again with frustration, "we ain't *bustin'* . . ."

Propped on her elbows beside Yakima, Faith whipped her head around and rasped, "Shut up, Lou! Just shut up or go home. Decide now."

Yakima turned to look at Brahma staring up at Faith with a sheepish but contentious expression.

"He's with me," Cavanaugh said on the other side of Faith. "And he's here to help

305

you, my sweet. And I think he has a point. It's goddamn hot up here, and we're only wasting time." Cavanaugh pushed to his feet and brushed off his corduroys and the front of his vest, over which his long, silk neckerchief drooped from around his sunburned neck.

The gambler nodded toward Yakima, his scarred eye looking milky in the sharp light. "You hired *him* to keep us out of trouble. Well, we've already had plenty of that. If we have any more trouble down there, it's gonna take a hell of a lot more than a layout of the town to get us out."

He cursed and stomped off down the slope. Brahma got up and followed him down to where the horses cropped galetta grass and Pop Longley was rewrapping his leg.

Yakima glanced to his left. The kid, Willie Stiles, rested on his elbows, staring into the village.

"What about you?" Yakima said.

Stiles hiked his shoulders. "My old man was a bank robber. He taught me to always get the lay of the land. Said it was embarrassing as hell when making a run from a town with filled saddlebags to get trapped in a box canyon." He shrugged again as he squinted his young, blue eyes up at the prison. "*Pee-yew!* You can smell that place from here."

"Kelly's been in there for nearly three months now," Faith said. "I got his letter a whole month after he'd been jailed."

"I'm surprised the rurales let him get a letter out."

"They didn't. A friend he worked with in Arizona got it from him when he came down to visit, and smuggled it out. Posted it in Tucson." Faith, her gloved hand to her cheek, rubbed away a tear. "I know he's likely dead. But I have to know."

She glanced at the half-breed, another tear spilling down from her eye to draw a muddy trough through the dust on her smooth, suntanned cheek. "If he's alive, I've got to get him out of there, Yakima."

"If he's alive, we will."

Yakima lifted the spyglass once more and swept the village, memorizing the main trails while picking out livery barns and hotels. He crawled back away from the ridge, stood with a sigh, took Faith's hand, and helped her to her feet.

"Thanks." She looked up at him, her eyes darkly serious. "I'll never ask anything of you again."

Then she walked down the slope where the others had already mounted up and

307

were gigging their horses back toward the trail. Yakima followed, letting the spyglass hang from the rawhide cord around his neck, and watched Faith, willowy and long-legged in her tight black denims, kicking up dust as she descended the slope.

He had no intention of holding her to her promise. When this was over, they'd be together whether Cavanaugh liked it or not.

At the bottom of the slope, Yakima grabbed Wolf's reins off a sycamore branch, and swung into the saddle. Not long after, he and Faith, riding side by side, followed the others down the last switchback before the village shacks began pushing up beside the trail — some built of stone, some of brown or yellow adobe, mostly cracked and discolored, no doubt built a good hundred years ago or more.

The group clomped across the dry, shit-littered planks of a dry arroyo and bottomed out in the canyon. Flies whined around the carcass of a dead dog. Yakima and Faith were walking their horses between two long, white blocks of adobe housing a good twenty or so homes and businesses, including a general store, a town jail, and a cantina, when the frenetic rattle of a Gatling gun cut the early afternoon silence.

It was a short spurt, lasting less than five

seconds, but the echoes chased themselves around the canyon and set several horses tied to hitch rails pitching and whinnying. Dogs around the village howled and barked. Holding a tight rein on Wolf, Yakima peered up at the prison on the other side of the town, appearing to float in the bright sunlight on its high, clay-colored bench. The reports had originated from there, but he couldn't see much except the top of the walls and the tower from this angle.

"What the hell was that?" Cavanaugh said, riding at the head of the pack and checking down his prancing roan.

As if in reply, a muffled din rose from the bench near the prison. Women wailed and children bawled. Someone shouted epithets in Spanish, and then there was another short burst of Gatling fire, setting the horses to nickering once more.

Yakima, Faith, and the others held their horses in check and looked around as several shop owners crept out of dark doorways on both sides of the street to stare up at the prison. Several muttered prayers and crossed themselves. A black and yellow cur came running toward Yakima from up-street, tail between its legs, tongue drooping over its jaws, eyes showing a coppery fear and dread. It fled back the way Yakima's group had come, and disappeared behind a rocky knoll.

At the same time, a bell in a nearby church tower clanged, each toll rolling out across the canyon and setting even more dogs to barking and howling and babies to crying. When the bell had tolled five times, the last one reverberating for what seemed an eternity, a heavy silence settled back over the village, tumbleweeds leaping in a sudden, chill breeze.

"Firing squad."

Yakima hipped around in his saddle, sweeping his gaze back past his own group sitting their own mounts tensely and looking around as though awaiting a slow-moving storm. A man stood on a balcony protruding from the white adobe wall on the south side of the street. A young, naked whore, holding an uncorked bottle down low in her right hand, clung to the man's arm, her black hair partially obscuring her sleepy eyes. The man was an American with light brown hair, a sweeping dark-red mustache, and broad sunburned cheeks.

He wore a dark-red shirt beneath a fancily stitched, alpaca vest, and brown leather chaps over buckskin breeches, with two old-model Colts in cross-draw rigs set high on both hips. Holding a tin cup, he cocked his head toward the prison. "That hotbox yonder must've been getting too crowded, or not enough bale was bein' shelled out to the head turnkey."

As wails and shrieks emanated from the bench around the prison, and a couple of dogs continued yipping, the American smiled down at his cup. "They'll be howlin' like that all night, till Lazaro runs 'em off. Don't let it bother you none. First time I was down here sellin' hosses to the rurales, it got under my skin so's I couldn't sleep even with two *putas* in my bed. Now, I don't even hear it anymore."

The man glanced at Faith and the others, then lifted his cup in salute. "Whatever your business is, have a good time here in To-cando." Chuckling, he draped an arm around the whore's shoulders, turned them both around, and ducked through the open door behind him.

"Jesus Christ," said Pop Longley, glaring up at the prison. "What kind of a hellhole is this, anyway?"

"I wonder how often they decide to cull the herd," said Cavanaugh.

Faith glanced at Yakima, eyes pinched and horrified. As she began to swing her horse up the street, Yakima booted Wolf up beside her and grabbed her arm. "Don't get in a hurry. You storming up to the rurales de-manding your brother's release will get you nothing but laughs."

"What do you suppose I do? Wait for the next firing squad?"

Yakima glanced at a big, sandstone build-ing half a block away, on the left side of the street. The shingle above the pillared col-umns over its front porch announced HO-TEL MEDINA. "We'll head yonder, get cleaned up, have a drink, cool down, and talk it over."

Faith glanced up at the prison once more. Several mourners were still wailing, though not as loudly as before. She nodded. Yakima reined Wolf past her and the others and drew up in the shade before one of the three hitch rails fronting the big cantina, and swung down. As the others drew up behind him, Yakima loosened the black's saddle cinch, slipped his bit, shucked his Yellowboy from its boot, and sauntered up to the boardwalk under the tiled roof. Two *ojas* hung from viga poles protruding from the adobe facade, with gourd dippers hanging nearby.

Yakima stepped up to the *oja* right of the swinging doors, nodded at the man sitting in a hide-bottom, rope-backed chair near the front door — a thin hombre in a cheap suit, holding a beer bottle on one thigh, a straw sombrero on the other knee. He dipped his chin, slowly, the corners of his thin-lipped mouth twisting upward.

"Welcome to Tocando, senor."

Yakima dipped up some water and sipped the tepid but refreshing liquid. He drank half the dipper, doffed his hat, and poured the rest of the water over his head.

He nodded at the gent by the door, who wore a faintly unctuous expression on his patch-bearded face. *"Por favor.* Are you in Tocando for business or pleasure?"

Yakima let the dipper hang down against the pitted adobe wall from its frayed rope. "Whatever it is, it's none of *your* business, amigo."

The man merely smiled and turned away from Yakima, his eyes sliding up and down in their red-rimmed sockets as Faith mounted the porch, slapping dust from her chaps with her hat.

Yakima pushed through the batwings into the cool shadows of the cantina — a large room with a surprisingly elaborate, mahogany bar and back bar with a scrolled, gold leaf–edged mirror against the rear wall. The shelves boasted a good array of tanglefoot that, judging from the fancy labels, hadn't been brewed in some tub out back. There were a good twenty hardwood tables positioned along the flagstone floor, with four or five occupied by afternoon drinkers conversing in desultory tones or not at all — a few vaqueros, a couple of men in rurale uniforms and private's stripes, and two pudgy gents in cheap suits similar to the one on the nosey porch-loafer outside.

Yakima, flanked by Faith and the others, including the limping Pop Longley, crossed the room, boots scuffing along the stone flags, spurs trilling softly, and spread out along the bar. The apron was a tall, beefy gent, glistening with sweat, with long, coal black, silver-streaked hair framing his flat-planed, long-nosed face. He had a wandering eye, with a drooping mustache and a tuft of hair growing under his bottom lip. Pure Yaqui.

The pretty, sullen-looking girl sitting on the back bar in a sheer, ratty, flour-sack dress appeared Yaqui, as well, with facial features bearing a familial resemblance to the man's.

Faith wasted no time ordering a room and fresh water and, when she'd taken her key, saddlebags, and rifle, and headed up the stairs right of the bar, Longley ordered a room, as well. Willie Stiles asked the big barman if there were any sawbones hereabouts, and, while the man was frowning and trying to translate the kid's too-quick English to Spanish, Longley grumbled that he didn't need a damn sawbones. All he needed was tequila, mescal, and a little peace and quiet.

In barely understandable English, the big Yaqui, canting his head to the girl flanking him, asked Longley if he wanted a girl to wrap his leg and to make him feel better.

"How much?" the gray-bearded mossyhorn grumbled, swiping a key off the bar.

"Fife Ameree-can dollars," the girl said with slow awkwardness, holding up five fingers while pulling the arm of her dress down to reveal a brick red, pear-shaped, brown-nippled breast.

Stiles laughed caustically at the price, but Longley sniffed and said, "Ready yourself for a special treat, senorita!"; then he tossed the money on the bar, grabbed the bottles, and limped to the bottom of the stairs. The girl leaped off the back bar, nudged the big barman aside with her little, willowy body, and swiped up the five gold pieces.

The big man cursed at her, annoyed. Undeterred, and with a self-satisfied expression on her coarse-featured but not unattractive face, jiggled the coins in her hand as she jogged around the bar. Long dress swishing around her brown, shapely calves, she padded up the stairs to wrap an arm around Longley's waist and help him climb to the second story.

Yakima bought a warm beer, took it over to a table, and dropped into a chair. He was bringing the glass to his lips when he saw the two rurales — both middle-aged though sporting private's stripes — cast sneering glances at him and whisper amongst themselves. A medium-long Apache scalp dangled from the belt of one while the other wore a necklace of black hair adorned with two red-brown chunks of desiccated skin that Yakima recognized as dried human ears.

Yakima raised his beer glass to the men, his green eyes hard and challenging, and drank.

CHAPTER 22

Yakima watched the two rurale privates out of the corner of his right eye as he catnapped between sips of his warm but flavorful beer. The rurales eyed him belligerently out of the corners of their own eyes, and spoke across the table to each other, their voices growing slightly louder the more mescal they downed from the clear bottle between them.

Faith drifted downstairs only about fifteen minutes after she'd gone up, minus the dust, with her hair brushed out damp and secured in a ponytail. She'd also donned a long, leather skirt and a powder blue blouse with red piping around the shoulders. She still wore her man's boots, however, but they only added a quirky, sensual flair to her otherwise more female-looking attire.

She owned a strained, worried look in her hazel eyes. She was about to find out if her only living brother was still alive and, if so, what condition he was in. Then she'd worry about getting him out of the Gothic prison spreading its death stench across the village.

"Drink?" Ace asked as she approached the table.

"One." She sat down between Cavanaugh and Willie Stiles. Brahma sat near Yakima, the big man facing the room with his rifle laid across the table before him and obsessively laying out cards for solitaire.

Cavanaugh poured out a shot of tequila, causing the white worm at the bottom of the bottle to curl its tail. Faith tipped back half the shot, making only a slight face as the raw Mexican busthead hit her stomach, then drew a breath and threw back the rest.

She set the glass on the table and slid back her chair. "Okay."

"Hold on," Cavanaugh said, frowning and grabbing her arm. "You think you're going over there?"

"Of course I'm going over there," she said with edgy exasperation but keeping her voice a couple of notches above a whisper. "That's what we came down here for. I'm gonna get my brother the hell out of there!"

"Your husband better go alone." Yakima sleeved beer foam from his lip and set his glass on the table. "This is Mexico. A pretty blond woman goes over there, we're liable

318

to never see you again. More than one of us goes, they're liable to think we're trying to make a show of force."

"Yeah, the breed's right," Brahma said, nervously shuffling the card deck in his big, brown, rope-scarred hands. "Ace should go, see how Kelly's doin', then make an offer to get him out."

Faith shook her head vehemently and set her hands on her thighs. "No. I'm going. I'll concede to Ace going with me. They'd expect me to be with a man . . . my husband."

Cavanaugh turned to Yakima. "What happens if they don't speak English?"

"You better hope one of them has rustled horses across the border a few times, or we're shit out of luck."

Brahma and Stiles chuckled nervously.

Yakima's guts were knotted, and the muscles in the backs of his legs were taut with tension. He wished he could accompany Faith to the rurale's lair — no telling what she would run into over there — but her showing up with a half-breed would give the Mexicans too much to think about, and they might not take her seriously.

Faith smoothed stray wisps of hair back from her eyes, adjusted her hat, glanced at Yakima, and stood. "Let's do what we came here for."

As she made for the door, Cavanaugh threw back a tequila shot. He glanced fatefully at Brahma and Stiles, took a deep breath, and followed his wife to the door and outside.

When they'd gone, Lou Brahma shook his head and set a card down with a sharp tick. Willie Stiles sipped his tequila, coughed, eyes watering, then leaned back in his chair and shoved his hands in his pockets.

Spying movement across the room to his right, Yakima turned toward the two rurales sitting at a table against the fall wall. They were muttering to each other in Spanish. Yakima recognized a couple of curse words and parts of a few phrases. They were talking about the arrogant breed who obviously had some Apache blood.

The one on the right side of the table, glaring at Yakima, began to stand while the other man chuckled with devilish delight into his beer glass. Yakima slid his chair back abruptly, reached up and back for the hide-wrapped handle of his Arkansas toothpick sheathed behind his neck, quickly picked out a target, and flicked the weapon out in front of him. He'd moved so quickly that anyone watching might have thought he'd merely been swiping a fly away from his ear.

The seven inches of razor-edged, fire-tempered steel plowed past the rurale's own right ear and into the stout window shutter behind him with a loud, wooden bark. The rurale who had come within six inches of losing his ear jerked with a start and loosed a horrified cry. Bounding backward, glancing at the vibrating knife handle, he got his feet tangled up. He twisted around and fell forward over his table, knocking over the bottle and his own beer glass before plopping back down in his chair, his butt hanging halfway to the floor.

He froze, one arm draped across a corner of the table, as Yakima stood quickly and palmed his .44. The rurale on the left side of the table sat stiffly in his chair, lower jaw hanging, back against the wall, as Yakima, taking long strides, crossed the room. The private who half lay and half sat in his own chair stayed in that same awkward position, dark eyes wide and growing wider as Yakima grew before him, cocked Colt half-extended straight out from his belly.

"Mierda!" the rurale sitting hang-jawed against the wall murmured. He had one hand on his pistol butt, but it rested there like a dead fish hanging from a stringer.

Yakima stopped before the other man — whose face was shaped like the side of an ax handle, with jug ears, pug nose with a black wart on the side, and straight, dust-flecked hair hanging to his single black eyebrow. He stared straight up at Yakima, like a man waiting at the bottom of a deep pit for a rope he wasn't sure would come. Yakima's shadow angled across him. The rurale tensed, one eyelid quivering, as Yakima took his revolver in his left hand, leaned forward, reached up with his right hand, and pulled the blade out of the shutter with a slight grunt and a squawk of grinding wood slivers.

He lowered the blade to the man's face, so the man could see the furry, black tarantula impaled at the end. "You're damn lucky I seen that when I did," Yakima said, scraping the dead spider off on the man's dust-caked, sky blue uniform slacks. "He might've bit you."

Yakima nodded affably to the other hombre. Sheathing the toothpick but holding his cocked Colt straight out from his belly, he walked backward toward his table where Lou Brahma and Willie Stiles were looking toward the rurales, grinning.

When Faith and Cavanaugh had pushed through the batwings, Faith paused for a moment and glanced up the street, toward where the Mexican flag buffeted in the wind above the tile-roofed rurale headquarters — or what she figured to be the headquarters since it was the only building in town, other than the prison, boasting a flag. A couple of men in rurale uniforms were meandering in that direction, on the other side of the street.

Standing beside her, Cavanaugh sighed loudly and hooked his arm, smiling down at her. "Stow it, Ace," Faith said, and, ignoring the offered arm, stepped off the hotel's porch. She and Cavanaugh, walking side by side, had taken two steps toward the other side of the street, when someone cleared his throat loudly behind them.

"Senor! Senorita!"

Faith and Cavanaugh wheeled, the gambler dropping his hand to his Colt's pearl grips. The thin man in the drab serge suit sitting in the chair near the hotel's front door glanced up and down the street, as if making sure they were alone, then beckoned quickly with the hand holding his straw sombrero.

Faith and Cavanaugh exchanged wary glances.

"Por favor," the man rasped. "Only a moment of your precious time. *Es el más importante!"*

Faith narrowed an eye at the man, sizing

him up as he rose from his creaky chair. Smiling like a dog begging for a little beef liver, he had a gawky, hangdog look, and, judging by his red-rimmed eyes, he'd been drinking beer for several hours, or maybe he hadn't stopped since last night. She glanced at Cavanaugh, then moved back up onto the porch, the gambler flanking her, looking around as though for a possible trap, his right hand closed over his pearl pistol grips.

Keeping his voice down, the man said, blowing his sour beer breath, "Pardon the intrusion, but it is my suspicion — and forgive me if I am wrong — that you are here to visit the prison, no?"

"So what if we are?" Cavanaugh said, bunching his cheek skeptically.

The man glanced around once more, studied the batwings flanking him closely, then moved several yards left of the doors, beckoning for Faith and Cavanaugh to follow suit. When they did, both stepping lightly as though they were moving through a field littered with unexploded grapeshot canisters, the Mex said, "One does not want others to learn one's private business in Tocando, if it can be helped." He smiled sheepishly. "Unless, of course, others like *myself* may be of humble service."

"What the hell are you getting at?" Faith said. "It's too hot to stand out here bullshitting with you, mister."

The man frowned, a little taken aback by the girl's brashness. Then he smiled. "*Sí, senorita*. I apologize for taking up your time. My name is senor Mateo Chavez. If you are, indeed, here to secure the release of a prisoner, perhaps I may be of help. You see, I know the rurale officers, including *Capitán* Lazaro himself, personally, and I am quite accustomed to working as — how you say? — liaison between the prison and those wishing to visit or to beseech the officials for the release of their friends or loved ones."

"Why can't we do that ourselves?" Cavanaugh asked.

Chavez shook his head quickly. "You see, the rurales are . . . how can I put this to make it clear? They are not quite as *lawful* as they should be. Let me just say, there are many *secrets* here in Tocando, and *Capitán* Lazaro never deals with americanos directly. If you were to personally ask to visit your loved one, perhaps to seek the *release* of your loved one, the *capitán* might very well deny such a person even exists. He might very well have you imprisoned as American spies or *revolucionarios*."

325

Chavez spread his lips with a wan smile. "You see, *Capitán* Lazaro is very much king of his castle. And he rules that castle — and this village — with an iron fist. That being so, he is very suspicious of strangers."

Faith and Cavanaugh exchanged another dark, skeptical glance before Faith said, "I fail to see the difference between you talking to him and us talking to him."

"If I act as liaison, you have no story to tell, senorita. Except merely that you came down here to see your friend or your loved one, you saw him, and, if all goes well" — Chavez shrugged his bony shoulders inside his shabby suit coat — "he will be released." He smiled unctuously, dropping his eyes, his cheeks coloring slightly. "And I will be able to assure him that you are not spies. *Capitán* Lazaro, to be sure, is most deathly afraid of spies. And when a man such as the captain is afraid, it makes him *muy* dangerous!"

"I see what's going on here, mister," Faith scoffed. "You play both ends against the middle for a percentage of the take."

"Got it all worked out with Lazaro," Cavanaugh put in, smiling coldly. "So, how much is this gonna cost us — you runnin' up there and arranging for us to see the senorita's brother?"

"A mere fifty dollars in gold. That is a buy, I assure you." When Faith and Cavanaugh just stared at the gawky Mexican, Chavez smiled again, shrugging, and said, "Honestly, senorita, this way saves *so* much time."

Faith turned and grabbed the gourd dipper from the wall. With a pensive cast to her gaze, she dippered water from the *oja* hanging near the door. She drank half the water, then looked up at the Mexican from beneath her thin, blond brows. "How do we know we can trust you?"

The man spread his hands and gave the *americanos* a sad, helpless look, as though the situation was beyond his control. "You don't, senorita. You have only my assurance that this is the only way you will be able to see your loved one."

Faith bit her upper lip, then, glancing at Cavanaugh, returned the dipper to her mouth to continue drinking. The gambler stared, slit-eyed, up at the smiling Chavez as he dug in his trouser pocket for a small hide sack from which he shook fifty dollars worth of gold coins into the smiling Mexican's open palm.

Later, when Faith had given the Mexican her brother's name and then watched him shuffle up the street, whistling and lighting a cigar, she and Cavanaugh returned to the saloon. She could hear Pop Longley chuckling somewhere upstairs while Brahma and Stiles played a game of five-card-stud. Yakima sat back in his chair, snoring softly, boots crossed on the chair before him, his hat tipped over his eyes.

"That was fast," Lou Brahma said through the smoke of the quirley smoldering between his teeth.

Yakima poked his hat brim up off his head and frowned at Faith who poured out a shot of tequila and threw it back. She had a pale, gaunt look. "Lazaro doesn't entertain *americanos.*"

"So we sent some greaser over who fleeced us for fifty gold pieces," Cavanaugh said a little too loudly.

He glanced sheepishly around the room. The half-dozen Mexicans sitting around the room in desultory silence — including the two rurales whom Yakima had successfully quieted — stared at him grimly.

"Whoops," Cavanaugh said with a tense grin, raising his shot glass to the room. "Sorry."

He sat down and was dealt into Brahma's and Stiles's stud game. Faith sank into her own chair directly across from Yakima. She sat parallel to the table, and hiked a boot onto her knee. She threw her hat down her back and tossed out her hair. Her eyes were understandably tense. She caught Yakima's glance, and her full lips shaped an ironic smile. She lifted her shot glass in salute, and threw it back.

Yakima sipped his own beer and slumped back in his chair, which was shoved against the pitted and fractured wall from where he had a good view of the room and the outside door. He dug in his tunic pocket for his makings sack, and busied himself with slowly, methodically rolling a smoke.

Another thing Ralph had taught him was, during tense, anxious times, to pay attention to the smallest details — objects as well as sounds — to keep himself steady and prepared.

Yakima didn't know what to make of the liaison. He was probably a relative of Lazaro's, a man too lazy or inept to make a living any other way except in taking advantage of prison visitors — especially Americans who didn't have an official leg to stand on in Mexico.

Well, he'd see what happened. He didn't know how many rurales Lazaro had in his stable, but probably too many to make having to shoot his way out of town a very lucrative proposition.

He glanced at Faith sitting with her right shoulder facing him, staring pensively across the room, one hand wrapped around her empty shot glass, anxiously wagging the boot propped on her knee. He could imagine a hundred better scenarios for his and her reunion, and this was far from one of them. But these were the cards they'd drawn. They'd play them. If he died down here, at least he'd die having seen her, smelled her, kissed her one last time, even if she was another man's wife.

An hour passed. The two pie-eyed rurales got up, grumbling drunkenly but not making eye contact with Yakima, and staggered heavy-footed out the doors. Other customers came and went. Flies buzzed, and the town quieted down for siesta.

After an hour and a half, just as Yakima took his last sip of the tepid beer, the clomp of a good dozen horses rose quickly from the street. He could feel the vibration in the floor beneath his boots. His gut tightening, he turned to the window to the right of the door. His gut tightened another notch as a dozen men clad in powder blue, gold-buttoned tunics and blue slacks with the traditional red stripes galloped in from the direction of the rurale office, reining their horses up sharply in front of the hotel.

"Oh . . . *shit* . . . ," Lou Brahma muttered in Yakima's left ear.

In a cloud of adobe-colored dust, the rurales dropped out of their saddles, tossed their reins over the hitch rail, and scurried onto the porch. Two by two, and breathing hard, eyes wide and expressions stony, they burst through the batwings and into the saloon.

No one else said anything as the sombrero-clad Mexican rural police jogged up to Yakima's table and raised their Spencers, Springfields, and Winchesters to their shoulders, the rasps of the cocking mechanisms echoing loudly above the clatter of leather heels on the flagstones, and the raking chings of large-roweled spurs.

The rifle barrels slid this way and that as the darkly twinkling eyes behind the cocked hammers skirmished for targets.

CHAPTER 23

Yakima found himself, like the others around his table, slowly raising his open hands as the rurales stared down their aimed rifle barrels, chests rising and falling as they breathed. They were mostly privates with a couple of corporals and a young sergeant who was only slightly taller than a midget and with a paunch bulging through the buttons of his ratty tunic.

The dwarflike sergeant, in the middle of the semicircle, had his square, yellow teeth clamped down on a fat stogie. Extending a .36 Colt Navy Conversion revolver in his small, brown fist, he grinned but didn't say anything, as they all just stood there, aiming their rifles at the seated group before them.

A moment later, Yakima saw what — or whom — they were waiting for when two more men appeared out the windows on either side of the batwings. One was the man in the cheap suit who'd been sitting outside the saloon when Yakima's group had arrived in Tocando. The liaison rode a frayed-eared, rope-haltered mule bareback beside a man in a rurale captain's uniform — a lean hombre with a long salt-and-pepper braid, wolf's-head earring, and a pocked, pitted face. It was the man Yakima had watched scalp the pretty Apache girl across the border in Arizona.

Yakima's pulse quickened and his throat turned dry as Captain Lazaro and the cheap-suited, hangdog liaison drew up before the saloon and the dozen other horses milling at the hitch rail. The savage-looking rurale captain leaned forward on his silver-trimmed, dinner-plate saddle horn, hesitated, swaying slightly as though half-drunk, then swung slowly and heavily down from the elaborately stitched, silver-trimmed, hand-tooled saddle. The tail of his gaudy red sash buffeted about his thighs, as did the two scalps dangling from his cartridge belt; two ivory-gripped Smith & Wessons jutted from cross-draw holsters on both hips, in front of two wide, bone-handled bowie knives in gold-studded sheaths.

The liaison swung down from the mule with the same drunken deliberation as the captain, and followed Lazaro onto the porch and through the batwings. The liaison remained about three feet behind Lazaro, doffing his straw sombrero as though entering a church. The captain moved slowly into the room, kicking each stovepipe boot out with a show of elaborate self-assurance and grandiosity, the scalps and sash sliding to and fro across his thighs.

As he drew within a few feet of his men, half the enlisted men shuffled right, the other half left, to open a gap while they all continued aiming their rifles at Yakima, Brahma, Stiles, Faith, and Cavanaugh. The captain sidled up to the little, mean-faced sergeant, who, smoke curling from his cornhusk cigarette, kept his revolver sliding back and forth between Yakima and Lou Brahma, as though daring either man to make a move.

"Hola, amigos," Lazaro said, resting his gloved hands on his cartridge belt. He nodded formally at Faith, the lids half closing over his snakelike eyes. *"Amiga."*

"What's this all about?" Lou Brahma said tensely, holding his hands, fingers curled toward his palms, on both sides of his head. "Our horses kick a dog or somethin'?"

Stiles chuckled nervously, a death's-head smile forming on his young, bearded face as he twisted around to regard the rifle-wielding rurales flanking him.

Cavanaugh said through gritted teeth, "Plug it, Lou."

"No, no, senor," said Lazaro, chuckling, his shoulders shaking and making the silver wolf's head dance below his elongated left earlobe. "I enjoy a joke." He continued chuckling while the other rurales, except the dwarfish sergeant, stared darkly down their rifle barrels. The sergeant continued grinning around his quirley, large, green-brown eyes unblinking over the hammer of his cocked revolver.

"But if I could be serious for one moment."

The captain glanced to where the liaison stood, about fifteen feet behind him, silhouetted against the batwings, holding his straw sombrero before him in both hands, as though he were about to deliver a eulogy.

"Senor Chavez, who has the distinction of being our 'welcoming committee' here in Tocando, has brought to my attention that five gunmen and a pretty *gringa* rode into Tocando with the intention of visiting a bandito I have the grave misfortune of housing in my crowded prison. A depraved weapons merchant whom we caught — what is the Yanqui expression?" — he snapped his thumb and forefinger in the ear

335

of the little, square-faced, lantern-jawed sergeant.

"Red-handed, jefe," the little man said slowly, in a surprisingly deep, gravelly voice for one so small.

"Red-handed!" Lazaro cackled, poking his tongue through his large, yellow teeth and blowing breath reeking of raw liquor and beer. "That is one of my favorites, though I have no idea what it means."

Faith lowered her hands to the table and stared angrily up at the captain, darting a quick, enraged glance at the liaison standing in the shadows. "I paid your *welcoming committee* over there fifty dollars because he said —"

"*Silence gringa!*" Lazaro's booming voice filled the room like a sudden thunderclap, making even a couple of the rifle-wielding privates jerk with starts. "Now you are in my country, and in my country women do not speak unless they are spoken to. Even one as pretty as yourself. Do I make myself clear?"

Faith's cheeks colored as though she'd been slapped, and her enraged expression was replaced by shock and fear. On the other side of the table, Yakima felt his hands edging down from his shoulders, closer to his pistol, though he knew he'd never be

336

able to reach the grips before a rifle slug ripped through his heart. If the captain made a threatening move toward Faith, however, Yakima would snatch his revolver up and drill a hole through his head.

A satisfying last act.

"No one insults senor Chavez," Lazaro said, lowering his voice and glancing over his shoulder at the liaison. "He performs an invaluable duty here in Tocando, reporting the comings and goings of undesirables to our fair town. The prison, you see, filled as it is with banditos and revolutionaries and *indio* vermin, attracts the accomplices of such undesirables. If it were not for senor Chavez, I might very well be overrun!" Lazaro paused and rocked back on his heels, letting his eyes stray across Faith's well-filled blouse before letting his gaze rake the others in her party, stopping on Yakima.

"Indio?" Lazaro asked the half-breed, lifting his chin and pursing his lips.

Holding his hands to his shoulders, Yakima shrugged.

"But one who makes an effort at being a civilized man," Lazaro said, glancing at the big Yaqui standing with his arms crossed behind the bar. "Like Rocco."

The Yaqui's dark, flat face beneath his straight-cut bangs remained expressionless as he glowered back at Lazaro.

"I shoot at it with both barrels," Yakima drawled, his sheepish smile in place. "Sometimes I hit it only with one, though. You mind if we lower our hands? These civilized arms are getting tired."

"Certainly." Lazaro's eyes swept the group around Yakima. "But keep them on the table where I can see them. You are obviously self-respecting gringos. Otherwise, you would not be in the company of a senorita of such obvious beauty and charm." He smiled at Faith, then glanced again at Yakima. "Your one failing is what brings you here in the first place. It is an impossibility you see — the release of this . . . this . . ." He glanced at Chavez for help.

"Kelly Larsen," said the liaison, lifting his chin and enunciating the name carefully.

"This Kelly Larsen has been sentenced to two years hard labor for running rifles to the Apaches across the International Boundary. The release of such a bandit —"

"That's a lie," Faith said, setting her jaws and regarding the captain with outrage. "Kelly was cowboying north of the line, in Arizona, and drifted down after herd-quitting cattle."

Yakima braced himself as Lazaro swung his head toward her sharply, but felt a twinge of relief as the captain only ran his gaze across her blouse once more, and smiled appreciatively. "You are beautiful and spirited. The two complement the other. It is a shame I will give you only until sundown this evening to leave Tocando or find yourself and your friends locked up with your brother. My prison is notorious for being harsh on the men. For the women" — Lazaro clucked and shook his head — "it is another thing altogether."

With that, Lazaro bowed again formally, turned awkwardly on his half-drunk heels, called to his men, and began marching toward the doors.

"Hold on, Captain!" Cavanaugh called, sliding his chair back. The rurales had started lowering their rifles and turning, but now all barrels swerved toward the gambler, as did the .36 held by the dwarf. Cavanaugh raised his hands again as he rose from his chair and turned to regard Lazaro. "Por favor," the gambler said, grinning and shrugging. "Just one moment, huh? Man to man."

"Man to man." Lazaro threw out his hands and let them flop back against his sides. "Sure. Why not? Man to man."

As he began sauntering back toward the table, Cavanaugh stepped out around it. He winked his good eye and canted his head toward the back of the room. With a shrewd, amused expression, Lazaro followed the gambler up to the bar.

Cavanaugh rested an elbow atop the mahogany and ordered two shots of tequila. The big Yaqui plucked two glasses off a pyramid, filled them from a clear bottle, and slid one in front of the gambler, the other before Lazaro who stood facing the bar from a foot away, one eye slitted skeptically, a bemused little smile twisting his savage mouth. Stepping straight back against the back bar, the Indian folded his heavy arms, cocked a hip, and continued staring into space without interest.

Cavanaugh lifted his glass in salute. "Cheers." He sipped the tequila, then held the glass in front of his chin. His smile widening slightly, Lazaro blinked slowly, then lifted his own tequila shot, and threw back half.

Satisfied, Cavanaugh set his glass onto the bar near his left elbow, and pitched his voice confidentially as he said, "It's time we got down to brass tacks, Captain. You see, we came down here to free my wife's brother, and it was one long, hot, dangerous ride. One of my boys took an arrow. I'd hate to think we did all that for nothing."

Cavanaugh sighed, then reached down to twirl his shot glass between his fingers. "Now, let's not trouble ourselves over the issue of innocence or guilt, shall we? You know as well as I, that ain't the real issue. My lovely wife and I are prepared to offer you a thousand dollars in American-minted gold coins for the release of her brother."

Cavanaugh nodded as if to emphasize his sincerity.

Lazaro sipped his tequila, stared into the glass, and puckered his lips. "A thousand American dollars . . ."

"That's a hell of a lot of tacos and tequila, Captain," Cavanaugh said. "With that, you can probably have a different senorita every day for the next —"

Cavanaugh screamed suddenly as he doubled over the tequila bottle, which the rurale captain had rammed into his gut, bottom first. Arm thrust forward and up, Lazaro held the bottle there for a moment, suspending the gambler, hunched over and on the toes of his boots, for a good five seconds. Cavanaugh grunted, groaned, and sighed like a horse in labor. Lazaro stepped back and withdrew the bottle. Cavanaugh dropped to his knees with the wooden thump of bone on rock.

He retched as his forehead hit the floor.

He continued retching until yellow alcohol bile seeped across the flagstones around his face.

The captain's subordinates, rifles now only half-raised toward Yakima and the others, shifted their gazes between the table and the man writhing and retching on the floor in front of the bar. The big Yaqui leaned forward, braced on his arms, to peer over the bar at Cavanaugh. The little sergeant chuckled around his quirley, his shoulders and potato-sack belly quivering, jiggling the gold buttons on his coat. He'd dropped the cocked .36 to his stubby thigh.

"Jesus Christ!" Ignoring the rifles, Faith bolted up from her chair. She crossed to Lazaro and Cavanaugh and, shoving the tall captain back with one arm, dropped to a knee beside the gambler who continued to cough, wheeze, and suck at the air for a complete breath. "That wasn't necessary."

Lazaro glared down at Cavanaugh. "You come down here to my country and insult me with your petty bribes?" He spit onto the back of the gambler's bare head. "When you come down here, gringos, and insult us with your bribes," he raged, red-faced and round-eyed and glancing toward Yakima, Brahma, and Stiles while reaching down to curl his long, talonlike fingers around

Faith's arm, "you better be prepared to throw *everything* into the pot."

He jerked Faith to her feet. She grunted as his fingers bit into her arm, and, cursing loudly, swung her free hand up toward his face. Lazaro laughed and ducked the blow. Holding Faith with one hand before him, he slapped her quickly, first with the back of his left hand, then with the palm. The cracks sounded like pistol shots.

Yakima bolted half out of his chair, then saw two rifle barrels aimed at his face. He sagged back down, jaws hard, fists clenched.

Faith screamed and slumped backward, lids closing down over her eyes, gold hair tumbling around her shoulders.

Lazaro laughed as he swung her violently around him and onto a table before him. He crouched to pull both revolvers from Cavanaugh's holsters, then tossed them across the room. Turning to the woman sprawled supine across the table, shaking her head from side to side as if to clear it, he dropped his hands to the buckle of his cartridge belt.

"And I mean *everything,* amigos." Laughing maniacally, Lazaro let the belt drop to the floor, then the sash. He reached down, took Faith's blouse in both hands, and ripped it off her body, exposing her full breasts pushing up from beneath a thin, cream negligee as buttons clattered to the flagstones like rain.

"Even your women!"

CHAPTER 24

Yakima's pulse throbbed hotly in his temples as, through the eleven rurales standing before him, he watched Lazaro step between Faith's spread legs hanging down over the table edge, her boots swinging about a foot above the floor. Despite the rifles in his face, Yakima slid his hand slowly toward his holstered Colt.

Wait, he told himself. The right time would show itself. If he wasn't patient, he'd merely get himself splattered against the wall behind him, doing Faith no good at all.

Near the bar, Cavanaugh continued to retch and groan, holding both arms across his belly while driving his forehead into the flagstones.

Holding their fisted hands on the table, both Brahma and Stiles glanced at Yakima, their faces bleached, eyes hard with fear and fury. His own face expressionless, jaws taut, Yakima peered again between the two rurales directly before him, and the rifles aimed at his head. All six subordinates shuttled their lusty, grinning stares between his group and the raging captain's fevered work behind them. One nudged the man beside him and said something in Spanish while lifting a hand to his chest, hefting an imaginary breast.

The little sergeant had turned full around and was chuckling through his teeth, his entire torso rocking on his skinny hips as his cocked Colt slapped against his thigh.

Lazaro crouched over Faith once more and, with a single violent thrust, ripped the chemise off her shoulders, exposing her full, round breasts, which rose and fell as she writhed and groaned, trying to regain her senses. He tossed the frilly garment back over his shoulder, and it fell over Cavanaugh's jerking head like a burial shroud.

"Now, that's a set of tits, eh, boys?" the captain roared, speaking English for the benefit of the gringos.

Guffawing and swaying drunkenly, Lazaro dropped his hands and began unbuckling Faith's wide leather belt. He was breathing hard and grunting with a lusty, animal fury, gritting his teeth and cursing in Spanish as he let the belt fall to the floor and began jerking her skirt up her thighs.

Yakima leaned slightly toward Lou Brahma and nudged the man with his left elbow. Brahma turned to him, the big man's broad face mottled red, sweat streaking his cheeks, soaking his brows. Yakima nodded. Brahma nodded back. His shoulders jerked slightly as he kicked Stiles beneath the table. The kid turned toward him and Yakima, his eyes wide, his own jaws set like wedges.

Yakima gave him a surreptitious glance, silently ordering him to follow Yakima's lead.

The half-breed raked his eyes across the six rurales standing before his table, half turned toward Faith, grinning and chuckling, rifles sagging in their arms. Faith, eyes slitted with fury, lifted her head slightly, still dazed but gritting her teeth at Lazaro. The captain had stepped back to drop his trousers, ordering his men to keep a sharp eye on their "guests" and to enjoy the ecstatic screams of the *gringa* as she was finally taken by a *real* man.

Cursing, Faith kicked at Lazaro, one boot toe narrowly missing his exposed groin as he dropped his outer and underpants to his knees.

"Bitch!" the captain shouted, his voice cracking shrilly as he whipped his right arm behind his left shoulder and flung it forward, the back of that hand smacking Faith's cheek with another pistollike crack.

Faith screamed as her head hit the table with a loud thud. Lazaro laughed and began wrestling her long skirt up her legs.

Despite Lazaro's orders, over half his men were partly turned to watch the festivities. One more turned in that direction, and the little sergeant backed toward the bar, casting his gaze back and forth between Yakima's table and Lazaro, his revolver half-raised in his small, plump fist. Meanwhile Cavanaugh lay in the fetal position on the floor, sucking air like a fish out of water as Lazaro lifted Faith's skirts up to her waist while snatching at her underpants.

Yakima slipped his right hand off the table suddenly, moving little more than that arm, and wrapped his fingers around his pistol's bone grips. A quarter second later, before any of the rurales had time to react, the Colt leaped and roared in his hand, and the rurale standing directly before his table jerked suddenly as the .44 slug plowed through his cheek between his right ear and his nose.

As the man's head whipped back on his shoulders, Yakima thumbed the Colt's hammer back, slid the barrel slightly left, and drilled the next man, who'd only started to jerk his head toward Yakima, through his right eye. The explosions echoed around the room as Lou Brahma and Willie Stiles both grabbed iron, sliding back or twisting around in their chairs.

Yakima drilled one more rurale, then threw himself right, hitting the floor on his shoulder as two more rurales, shouting in Spanish, jerked their rifles up and around and triggered lead into the wall behind him.

Yakima ground his elbow into the floor and angled his smoking Colt upward. Two more blasts, and he'd emptied the cylinder into one more rurale. The other uniformed men screamed in shock or horror and twisted around or were punched backward by Brahma's and Stiles's lead, the kid screaming beneath the cacophony of exploding rifles and pistols, "Take *that* pill, you bean-eatin' son of a *bitch!*"

Thumbing his Colt's loading gate open, Yakima glanced to his left. Brahma had shoved the table over and, from one knee, was firing his two pistols over the top and into the group of scrambling, tumbling rurales. Stiles crouched behind a chair to the big man's left, his revolver smoking and leaping in one hand while he jerked one of his bowies up to his ear, and snapped it forward. Arcing through the hazy, smoky air, the blade thumped into the chest of the little sergeant, who'd been firing his .36 from one knee and shrieking Spanish epithets.

"Ay-*yaaaahhhhh!*" the little man squealed, grabbing at the still-quivering handle with one hand while falling straight back and triggering two more shots toward the ceiling.

Knocking spent casings from his Colt's cylinder, Yakima leaped to his feet and, flinching at a ricochet from the stone floor, shouldered up to a broad adobe floor joist. He plucked a shell from his cartridge belt and glanced around the joist toward the table where Lazaro had been assaulting Faith.

Lazaro was crawling toward the far wall, stopping frequently to pull up his pants. Faith lay prone on the floor near the table on which the rurale captain had thrown her, covering her head with her arms, one knee bent, a shoulder exposed by her torn blouse.

Yakima quickly finished filling his Colt with fresh brass as the gunfire on the other side of the joist became sporadic while the screams and curses grew louder amidst the crash of breaking chairs and tables. Lazaro was shouting shrilly, "Kill them, you stupid bastards! *Kill them!*"

Yakima flicked the loading gate closed and

stepped out from around the joist, Colt extended straight out from his shoulder, hammer cocked. The smoke was so thick he couldn't see much but the uncertain shapes of bodies strewn in the middle of the room, before the bar, several lying over spilled tables and chairs.

Lou Brahma fired one more shot over his table, his gun flashing and popping. Someone grunted, and a shadow fell back from an overturned chair ahead and to Yakima's right.

Two rurales groaned. One called out in a rasping voice for *Madre Maria.* Outside, a dog barked hysterically, and the horses pitched and nickered at the hitch rail. Inside, the wounded rurales slumped into unconsciousness or death, and silence fell like a shroud. Yakima dropped slowly to a knee, keeping his revolver aimed straight out before him, sweeping the room from left to right and behind, wary of sudden movement or a pistol jerked toward him.

Apparently, the other customers had slipped out the front door when the shooting had started. The room beyond the field of fire appeared deserted, only bottles and glasses and some playing cards remaining atop a few of the abandoned tables. Brahma and Stiles peered out from behind the table and a bullet-riddled chair respectively, their revolvers glowing in the wan light angling through the windows.

Straight ahead of Yakima, Ace Cavanaugh sat with his back against the bar, knees raised to his chest, head in his hands. In front of Cavanaugh, the little sergeant lay on his back, raising his butt off the floor by his heels and struggling to pull the big bowie from his blood-bibbed chest while snarling like a leg-trapped fox.

Lowering his hands from his pain-racked face, Cavanaugh looked around dully before dropping his eyes to the sergeant. He kicked his legs out, crawled forward, and grabbed the sergeant's .36 popper from the floor. Gritting his teeth and squinting his scarred eye, the gambler extended the pistol at the little man's head and fired.

Ka-pop!

The little man jerked as the bullet plowed through his cheek and out the top of his head before burying itself in an overturned table, which it sprayed with blood and brain matter.

Someone groaned to Yakima's right. He turned. Faith lay peering toward this side of the room over her bare right shoulder, one eye slitted with pain. To her left, near the cold, stone fireplace in the far wall, something moved.

"Die, you gringo sons of bitches!"

Lazaro's shout echoed shrilly as two pistols flashed over the top of a stout plank box heaped with split cordwood. The revolver pops filled the room like a cannonade.

Yakima drew back behind the joist, wincing as two bullets pounded into it, spraying adobe shards onto the tiles. He could hear the other slugs hammering the wall to his right and the furniture that Brahma and Stiles were crouched behind.

Amidst the pops and spangs, Yakima peered out around the joist, extended his pistol toward the flashing, smoke-belching revolvers, and fired three quick shots, fanning his hammer.

"Ach!" Lazaro screamed, one pistol clattering onto the floor while he flew back against the wall. A hand slapped the adobe, and then the captain dropped behind the wood box, groaning.

Brahma's head shot up above his table, and he triggered two quick shots into the wall over Lazaro.

"Hold it!" Yakima shouted, holding up his hand as he moved out from behind the joist.

He continued holding up his left hand while he swept the room with his gaze.

Brahma and Stiles rose slowly from behind their cover, the kid quickly reloading one of his Smith & Wessons while casting enervated glances around the room. He took short, nervous breaths. Yakima looked over the rurales strewn and twisted before him.

None moved or made a peep. Dead eyes and brass buttons glistened dully. Gunsmoke sifted over the bloody bodies like dust.

Outside, voices rose. Yakima ordered Stiles to watch the door, and Brahma to keep an eye on the dead men. As Yakima began moving toward Lazaro, a man shouted from somewhere above the bar, "Behind you, breed!"

A pistol flashed and barked on the second-story balcony above the bar, and Yakima ducked as he heard a groan behind him. He swung around to see the liaison, Chavez, stagger back out the batwing doors with two blood-pumping holes in his chest. As the batwings shuddered on their spring hinges, Chavez stumbled back off the boardwalk and into the dung-littered, cobbled street, setting the horses to pitching even more than before.

Yakima turned to stare up at the balcony above the bar. Pop Longley stood behind the scrolled wood railing, clad in only his balbriggans and hat, a fat stogie smoldering in a corner of his mouth. He or the whore had cut off the left leg of his underwear bottoms, and beneath the fresh bandage wrapped around his thigh, his long, thin leg was fish-belly white.

The long-barreled Schofield he held out over the railing was still smoking. The little whore's round face peered out from around the tall man, eyes wide and dark. Slowly, Longley lowered the gun to the railing and looked around before removing the stogie from his teeth, making a sour face. "You boys are bound and determined to keep me from my nap, ain't ye?"

Again, Yakima started across the room, kicking chairs out of his way, meandering around tables, extending his cocked Colt. He stopped in front of the wood box and peered behind it.

Lazaro lay wedged up between the floor and the wall, one knee raised, his left hand clamped over the bloody hole in his shoulder. He was breathing hard, wincing, pinching up his flat, snakelike eyes at Yakima, blood streaming down from the graze in his left temple. His long braid snaked around his neck like a whip, a gray tuft splayed at the end beneath the last wrap of rawhide.

The man's eyes rolled toward the cocked,

pearl-gripped revolver lying beside him. Yakima narrowed an eye as he aimed down the Colt's barrel, then lifted a leg over the wood box and kicked the pistol against the back wall.

He stepped back, keeping the Colt aimed at Lazaro's head. "Get up."

Lazaro glared up at him, nostrils flaring as he breathed. Blood oozed out from beneath the hand spread across the shoulder wound.

Staring down the Colt's barrel, Yakima canted his head slightly. "I won't tell you again."

Lazaro winced and pushed himself to a sitting position. He climbed to a knee and, breathing hard and grunting painfully, pushed off the knee, getting both feet under him. When he stood before Yakima, the half-breed stepped aside and wagged the gun. His unbuckled belt and pants sagging low on his waist, the rurale captain stepped awkwardly over the wood box and into the room.

Chuckling nervously, Lou Brahma got up from behind his table and, moving toward Yakima, swept the dead rurales with his two still-smoking pistols, his dark face glistening with sweat.

Yakima glanced at Willie Stiles standing just to the right of the front door, swinging his head to peer up and down the street. "What's it look like out there?"

Stiles glanced toward Yakima. "Quiet as Easter mornin'."

Yakima looked around the room once more and saw the big Yaqui standing behind the bar again, big fists on the bar top. He had the same expression as before the lead swap. Yakima aimed the Colt at him.

"Since I'm not sure what side you're on, come on out here and have a seat, where I can keep an eye on you."

The big man stared at him, blinking dully, then turned and moved out from around the bar, moving heavily and limping slightly on one hip. Beneath his cotton smock and apron, he wore burlap slacks that came down only to midcalf, and rope-soled sandals. He took a seat at one of the tables the other customers had abandoned, and filled a shot glass from an uncorked bottle.

Yakima moved behind Lazaro and shoved him toward the middle of the room, toward where Brahma stood. The big man's eyes were still bright, an incredulous, nervous look on his face. "What're we gonna do with him?"

"Kill him." Faith had climbed to her feet. Holding her blouse closed with one hand, she stooped, scooped one of the rurale's pistols off the floor, cocked it, and extended the gun at Lazaro.

CHAPTER 25

"Faith, wait," Yakima said, holding his cocked .44 against Lazaro's back, as Faith extended a Colt Navy at the man's left temple. Her face was bruised from Lazaro's knuckles, and three or four small cuts trickled blood. "I'd like nothing better than to blow out this murderin' bastard's wick — send him to the devil on a hot shovel in little bitty pieces — but, how are we gonna get your brother out of jail without the head turnkey?"

Lou Brahma narrowed a nerve-shiny eye at Yakima. "What in the hell you plannin' to do?"

Boots clomped, and Yakima glanced toward the staircase rising above the bar. Pop Longley had dressed and was coming down, not limping quite as badly as before. The young whore stood at the top of the stairs, swinging her head from side to side as she studied the dead rurales who were already starting to attract flies.

"Hey," Stiles called from the door. "Better put on a pot of coffee. Company's comin'."

Yakima glanced at Faith. She returned her hard gaze to Lazaro who stood before Yakima, breathing harshly and wincing as he pressed his hand against his bullet-torn shoulder. Keeping her eyes on the captain, she depressed the Colt's hammer and dropped it to her side.

"You should have taken the money," Faith told the man.

Yakima pushed Lazaro brusquely forward, told Brahma to watch him, then strode toward the front of the saloon. He sidled up to Stiles and followed the kid's gaze into the street and to the left, over the backs of the still-jittery horses tied to the hitch rails.

He saw nothing but shuttered windows and the breeze stirring the dust along the cobbles. Except for a few barking dogs and bleating goats, it was as if the town had suddenly become abandoned. The prison hulked on its bluff, silent and salmon-colored in the angling afternoon sunshine. It laid a long wedge of purple shadow down the rocky slope toward the red-roofed rurale headquarters.

"Three uniformed men were movin' along the far side of the street, just beyond that hill," Stiles said quietly, edging the right batwing open with his gun hand. "Seen 'em just a minute ago."

The street climbed a low rise to the left of the saloon. Yakima studied the rise, the adobe shacks on either side of the trace. Suddenly, a man, moving slowly, stepped onto a gallery in front of a barbershop, shoulders hunched, rifle held low in one hand. Two more stepped out from behind the building and mounted the gallery behind the first — all three dressed in the red-striped slacks of the rurale, with steeple-crowned sombreros, black belts, and pistols on their hips.

Yakima pushed Stiles back against the front wall right of the doors. He stepped to the other side, pressed his back to the wall, and stared into the saloon's shadows beyond the big Yaqui who sat drinking casually by himself.

Cavanaugh was sitting in a chair, his revolver on the table before him, breathing raspily as he popped the cork on a tequila bottle. In front of the bar, Brahma stood with one hand hidden behind Lazaro. Longley stood to his left, holding his Henry across his chest. Faith stood on Brahma's other side. She, too, held a rifle in her hands, her blouse hanging open, both flaps only partly concealing her breasts. Worried, she gazed toward Yakima.

"Keep that son of a bitch quiet," Yakima said, nodding at the captain. "He so much as clears his throat, drill him."

Yakima glanced once more over the batwings, then turned to the big Yaqui staring glumly into his tequila glass. "There a back door?"

The Yaqui lifted a hand to indicate the beaded curtain behind the back bar.

Yakima glanced at Stiles. "Stay here."

As he walked toward the bar, he told Brahma to help him keep an eye on the door and ordered Cavanaugh, who still winced and wheezed as he held an arm across his gut, still in agony, to help Faith keep an eye on Lazaro.

"What should Pop do?" Brahma said ironically as he sauntered toward the front of the room.

"He can give his leg a rest," Yakima said. "He'll no doubt be using it to run like hell real soon."

Then he moved behind the bar, ducked through the beaded curtain and into a large storeroom, part of which had been partitioned off with ropes and blankets and furnished with a cot, dilapidated dresser, washstand, and an overstuffed leather chair with steer-horn arms.

He crossed the large main room to a back door, opened the door slowly, and stepped into a trash- and firewood-littered back alley, with several small adobe casas hunkered back in the brush. Cicadas whined and the breeze rustled sycamore leaves.

Turning right, Yakima moved along the rear of the saloon, then stole around the corner and up along the saloon's north wall, through a gap between the saloon and a low, crumbling brick wall that was part of a livery setup. A couple of mules and a horse stared at him from the other side, nickering nervously.

Crouching, holding the Winchester in both hands, he stopped at the front of the saloon, to the left of the porch and the horses tied to the hitch rails, and knelt behind a rain barrel.

He stared into the narrow, sunlit trace before him. The three rurales he'd seen from the saloon door suddenly jogged out from a gap between two buildings on the other side of the street. While one hunkered down behind a narrow porch post beneath a sagging brush arbor, the other two scurried toward a stock trough in front of the porch.

Yakima snaked his Winchester around the

rain barrel, aimed quickly, and fired. The Yellowboy roared in the gap between buildings, immediately setting his ears to ringing. As one of the men behind the stock trough screamed, dropped his rifle, and clapped both hands to his face, Yakima ejected the smoking shell and quickly fired five more rounds, one after the other, sliding the Winchester's barrel this way and that as he aimed.

The slugs tore into the stock trough, into the adobe wall behind it, and blew the other rurale out from behind the trough, sending him sprawling back against the wall behind him. The other man, hit twice in the torso, was thrown into the gap between the buildings — pirouetting backward on his boot heels before falling facedown and kicking, spurs flashing, as he died.

As the last casing clinked onto the ground behind him, Yakima raised the Winchester to his cheek once more and slid it left to right, surveying the street. Spying no movement, he turned his attention to a wagon sitting on the other side of the street, about fifty yards south of the saloon. A beefy mule stood in the traces, staring straight ahead, ears twitching, occasionally lifting and lowering a front hoof with a muffled clack.

Lowering the rifle, the half-breed rose and

stepped onto the saloon's front porch. Brahma and Stiles were staring warily over the batwings.

"I'll be right back," Yakima said, then, glancing up the hilly street over his left shoulder, jogged across the street to the wagon.

He patted the mule and ran his hand re-assuringly down its dusty neck, soothing the jittery beast as he looked around once more at the mostly shuttered windows around him. Spying a barrel of mining tools in the wagon's shallow box, and a couple bundles of parched corn, he kicked the supplies out the open back end, then crawled into the driver's seat.

The mule glanced behind, an obstinate look in its eyes. Yakima said, "Easy," then unwrapped the rope reins from around the brake handle, released the break, and shook the ribbons over the mule's broad, patch-haired back, around which flies swirled, buzzing.

The mule hee-hawed, shook its head, rippled its withers, and set off up the street. The mule wanted to keep going, but Yakima drew hard on the left ribbon, coaxing the mule over to the saloon, drawing up at the near end of the tied horses. Brahma and Stiles were still peering over the batwings, skeptical looks on their faces.

Yakima set the brake, leaped down from the wagon, then moved around to the hitch rail and began untying the rurale's dozen or so mounts, including the liaison's mule. He hazed the horses off down the street, the mule braying and causing the wagon mule to bray, as well.

When they'd disappeared over the low rise just beyond the saloon, Yakima pushed through the batwings between Brahma and Stiles, and strode inside. He blinked against the thickening shadows, smelling the heavy copper odor of the blood and hearing the flies buzz around the bodies.

In front of the bar, Lazaro was down on his knees, head lowered nearly to the floor, raking draughts of air into his lungs with a raucous effort, his hatless head bobbing on his shoulders. The hide-wrapped ponytail hanging over his wounded shoulder was blood-soaked.

Cavanaugh sat at a table beside the captain, a self-satisfied look on his face as he sipped a tequila shot. Longley sat across from him. Faith stood on the other side of Lazaro, holding a pistol on the man but looking perturbed.

"What the hell happened?" Yakima said.

Faith scowled at her husband. "Ace."

Cavanaugh set his shot glass on the table and smacked his lips with satisfaction. "Gave the bastard a taste of his own medicine." He glanced at Lazaro gasping for breath on the floor. "How you feelin' now, you chili-chompin' son of a bitch?"

Faith glanced at Yakima. "You really think we can exchange him for Kelly?"

"I don't know," the half-breed said with a shrug. "You wanna find out or go home?"

She gazed back at him hard, rivulets of blood streaking her smooth, bruised cheeks. "I wanna find out."

Pop Longley said from the table, "I for one am all funned out and ready to head home just any old time."

"If you pulled foot, I'd understand, Pop," Faith told him.

Longley cursed and took a pull from the bottle in his fist. "Hell . . ."

Yakima glanced toward Stiles and Brahma. "How's it look out there?"

"A dog just hiked his leg on one o' them rurale stiffs," Stiles said. "Otherwise, clear."

Yakima prodded Lazaro's good shoulder with his boot toe, then tapped his rifle barrel against the man's head. "Get your pants off, Captain. *Rápido!*"

Lazaro lifted his head to glower skeptically up at Yakima, as though he weren't sure he'd understood correctly.

"That's right," Yakima said. "Get out of your pants, boots, and underwear. I got a feelin' you'll be a little more cooperative if your miserable ass is exposed to the whole town."

Lazaro stared up at him, eyes bright with rage, quivering lips stretched back from his large, yellow teeth. "Go to hell!"

"What's the matter?" Yakima said. "You seemed willing a few minutes ago." He poked his rifle barrel hard against the man's temple. "Get to it!"

Lazaro grunted and cursed in Spanish, then, still glaring up at Yakima, turned onto his butt and began kicking out of his boots. Brahma and Cavanaugh laughed.

Longley smoked a quirley and sipped his tequila, smiling bemusedly down at the rurale captain.

As Lazaro undressed, in Spanish calling Yakima's mother a whore and his father a dog, the half-breed removed a leather lanyard from one of the dead men's rifles, and quickly fashioned a noose at one end, leaving a small, open tongue about the size of a rifle barrel. When Lazaro had removed his underwear and tossed it aside with disgust, Yakima moved around behind him and dropped the leather noose around the man's neck, positioning the open tongue at the back.

Still sitting on the floor, his shirttails half covering his naked crotch, his pale, veined legs covered with long, curly black hair, Lazaro looked up again with his eyes flashing fury. He lifted a bloody hand to the noose.

"Uh-uh," Yakima said, tapping the rifle barrel against his head.

When Lazaro settled down, breathing heavily as he sat on his bare ass on the cold tiles, bent legs extended before him, Yakima stepped back and told him to stand. Lazaro cursed again, planted one hand, and heaved himself to his feet. He was holding a neckerchief against the shoulder wound.

"Ready to pay your brother a visit?" Yakima asked Faith, who'd stood nearby, staring coolly down at the captain.

"Let's go," she said.

"The lady's ready," Yakima told Cavanaugh and Longley. "Let's take a ride."

Yakima moved around behind Lazaro and prodded the man with his rifle barrel. Seething, bare feet slapping on the stone tiles, the captain moved toward the front of the saloon, staring straight ahead, his shirttails dancing around the tops of his thighs.

When he got to the batwings, Brahma and

Stiles stepped to each side. Brahma grinned as he gave the captain the up and down, then glanced at Yakima, his expression turning serious.

"We gonna just waltz on up to the prison, knock on the doors, tell 'em hidy-ho — look what *we* got?"

"I don't think we'll have to knock," Yakima said. "They'll know we're comin'."

Then he pushed the half-naked rurale captain through the batwings and onto the porch.

CHAPTER 26

Yakima looked up and down the street. A couple of shop owners peered at him from half-open doorways, and a few shadows appeared in dusty windows. Otherwise, the street was still clear. Only Wolf and the other broncs stood at the hitch rails, bits slipped beneath their snouts, latigos hanging loose beneath their bellies.

"Get up on the wagon," Yakima said, prodding Lazaro again with the Yellowboy.

"You are a fool," the captain said as, hands raised to his shoulders, he moved barefoot down the boardwalk, toward the wagon sitting behind the owly mule. "You are about to die a very painful death, amigo. And you are about to get your friends killed, as well."

"Shut up and climb up there. If anyone dies, you'll be the first to go."

Lazaro reached up to grab the seat, planting a bare foot on the wheel hub, and hauled himself into the driver's boot. The wagon lurched under the captain's weight. Lips stretched back from his teeth, he sat down, looking around at the red-tiled adobes on both sides of the street, his cheeks burning crimson, the silver wolf's head bouncing above his wounded shoulder.

"Amigos," he said, chuckling without mirth, "you are going to pay for this very severely, I assure you."

"I didn't tell you to sit down," Yakima said. He'd climbed into the box behind the seat, and rammed the rifle barrel several times against the back of Lazaro's neck. "Up!"

Lazaro snarled as he rose from the seat, clutching his shoulder with one hand. With the other he arranged his shirttails to cover his crotch.

The others had filed out of the saloon, glancing around warily, weapons raised. Yakima glanced at the men. "Tie the horses to the wagon. There's a couple of steel tongues on both sides. Then hop aboard."

When Brahma, Stiles, and Cavanaugh had tied the horses to the wagon, so that the wagon was surrounded by the jittery mounts on three sides, they all climbed into the shallow box and hunkered down on their haunches. Faith knelt directly behind Yakima, who stood behind Lazaro, poking the end of the Yellowboy's barrel through the extra loop at the back of the captain's neck.

When he'd tightened the small noose around the barrel, so that the Yellowboy was drawn taught to Lazaro's neck, he said, "Everybody ready?"

Only Brahma responded, chuckling dryly. "Shit, this is crazy!"

Keeping his head forward and the Yellowboy's barrel against the back of Lazaro's brown, unshaven neck, Yakima said, "Brahma, take the reins."

"Whatever you say, Major."

Brahma rose, stood beside Yakima, looking around warily, then leaned over the driver's boot to untie the reins from the brake handle.

Yakima said softly into Lazaro's ear, "Anybody shoots at us, I'm gonna blow your head off. You might want to inform any of your men we encounter along our route. *Comprende?*"

"You're a fool," Lazaro said.

Yakima pressed the Yellowboy hard against the man's neck. The captain's jaws tightened and his cheeks dimpled as he winced.

Yakima glanced around the wagon bed partly shielded on three sides by the horses. Wolf stood to his right, regarding him with wild eyes, as if to say, "Now, what the hell have you gotten us into?"

Faith sat with her back against the front of the box between Yakima and the horse. Stiles and Longley sat hanging their legs over the end of the box, holding rifles, while Cavanaugh sat near Faith, resting his own rifle over his shoulder, his back against the panel. The gambler wore a strange, incredulous smile, as though he'd found himself deep in a bet he couldn't back and was amusing himself, wondering how he was going to come out of it.

Brahma stood to Yakima's left, holding the reins in both hands. Yakima glanced at him. "Ease ahead."

As the mule pulled forward, the wagon jerked and rocked beneath Yakima's boots, and he grabbed the seat back with his left hand to steady himself. In front of the seat before him, Lazaro rocked, as well, spreading his bare feet and digging his toes into the gray, cracked floorboards.

As Brahma pulled the wagon forward, Yakima glanced around at the roofs and alleys on both sides of the street, spying a couple of faces pulling away from open windows. Ahead, on the street's right side, a fat woman in a shapeless, flowered shift sat on a second-story balcony, knitting and rocking, glancing toward the oncoming wagon with an expression of only vague interest on her round, flat face. A tabby cat nuzzled the wrought-iron rail before her, arching its back and curling its tail.

As the wagon crested the low rise north of the saloon, Yakima spied a couple of rurales lingering in alley mouths, holding rifles across their chests.

"Behind us," Stiles said.

Steadying himself on the seat back before him, Yakima glanced over his left shoulder. Two rurales, striding out from between buildings beyond the saloon, walked slowly toward the wagon. They were in no hurry to catch up to Yakima's group, which meant they were part of a larger faction intending to surround them.

"If they start shooting," Yakima said, "jump on a horse and ride the hell out of here."

Faith glanced up at him from his right knee. She'd tied her blouse closed with rawhide, though there was still a wide gap between the flaps, exposing a long curve of each breast. "And leave Kelly?"

Yakima sighed, shifting his weight from foot to foot as the wagon rocked and swayed, rattling and squawking. "It's either leave him or join him."

The wagon lurched around a rock in the

road. Yakima spied movement on his left —
two rurales crouched on a low roof, wincing
against the sun glare, trapdoor Springfield
rifles in their hands. As one began inching
his rifle toward his shoulder, Lazaro, glancing in that direction, shouted hoarsely,
"Stand down, idiots. No shooting!"

Yakima smiled.

Faith was still staring up at him, slitting
one eye doubtfully. "Why are you doing
this?"

Yakima glanced down at her, then lifted
his head to stare straight over the captain's
left shoulder. "You know."

They climbed several more rises as they
twisted through the hilly town, spying fewer
rurales than Yakima had expected. But then,
Lazaro probably had no more than thirty or
forty men total out here, including those
guarding the prison looming ever larger on
the hill northeast of the town. A good fifteen
had already given up their ghosts. If Yakima
figured right, there were probably only
about twenty more at the most, and the better part of those were probably up at the
prison.

The rurale headquarters grew before the
wagon, built into a hill on the right side of
the street, with the prison rising nearly
directly above. Salmon sunlight reflected off

the brass Gatling guns aimed at the wagon from two of the parapets.

"You better get those Gatling barrels turned up," Yakima warned Lazaro. "I'd hate to think what a .44/40 round would do to your neck at such close range."

As the wagon lurched onto level ground and approached the rurale headquarters, the Mexican flag on the roof buffeting and snapping, Yakima saw about five rurales gathered out front, on the broad wooden gallery flanked by the two big, oak doors and several viga poles from which masses of Apache scalps had been hung to dry.

Some stood behind posts while others knelt, ready for trouble. Most held rifles, while a big, bearded bear of a man with lieutenant's bars held a Colt Army in one hand, a Colt Navy jutting from a shoulder holster. Thick, black hair curled down from beneath his palm-leaf sombrero.

A couple more rurales — privates and corporals, judging by their ages — were hunkered behind stock troughs and a haystack on the other side of the street. They stared at their half-naked superior incredulously, though one moonfaced private grinned at the man beside him, who covered a chuckle with a throat clearing.

"Stand down, Montana," Lazaro called as

Brahma drew back on the mule's reins, bringing the wagon to a crawl as it pulled within a few yards of the headquarters.

Montana turned to mutter something to the men around him, and they let their weapons sag in their arms. He yelled for the others across the street to follow suit, then regarded Lazaro skeptically, dropping his eyes to the captain's bare legs.

"They're after a prisoner," the captain said in Spanish.

"Kelly Larsen," Faith said, kneeling beside Yakima, staying low in case someone decided to dare a shot in spite of Yakima's Yellowboy pressed against the captain's neck.

Montana's big, dull eyes flicked between Lazaro and the girl. They swept the wagon partially concealed by the horses, then returned to the man's superior officer. They were hard but befuddled, vaguely defiant while betraying embarrassment for Lazaro's compromising position.

"Ride up to the prison," Lazaro said. "Order the men in the towers to move away from the Gatlings, and release this . . . this" — Lazaro waved his arm with disgust — *"Kelly Larsen!"*

Montana hesitated a little, as though he wasn't quite sure the half-naked, blood-soaked man standing in the wagon's driver's box was really his captain. Then he lumbered off to the far end of the gallery, where a big mouse brown dun was tied, and swung into the saddle. He turned the horse into the street and, casting wary glances over his shoulder, rode up to the end of the cobbled street and began climbing the switchbacks rising toward the prison.

When he'd disappeared, though his hoofbeats continued clacking on the rocky incline, Yakima looked around at the rurales regarding him owlishly, their eyes as uncertain as Montana's. He elbowed Brahma. "Let's go."

The big man glanced at Yakima. "We ain't gonna wait here?"

"I don't trust that big bastard," Yakima growled. "Besides, I got an idea. . . ."

"Ah, shit," Brahma said, glancing at Cavanaugh before turning forward once more and shaking the ribbons over the mule's back.

Everyone grabbed for a handhold as the wagon lurched forward. Lazaro fell back against Yakima with a startled yelp. Yakima pushed the man upright, keeping the Winchester against his neck, and once more the captain dug his feet into the weathered floorboards.

Slowly, the rurale headquarters drifted off

behind them, and the uniformed men drifted into the street to stare toward the slow-plodding, bouncing wagon, turning their heads and moving their jaws as they talked amongst themselves.

When Brahma turned the mule onto the trail switchbacking up the side of the bluff, Yakima shoved Lazaro onto the seat, for the pitch was too steep to keep the man standing and, for the moment, there was nothing around them but brush and rocks and occasional sycamores and Mexican pinions. As they turned onto the second switchback, the mule balking and Brahma cursing and shaking the ribbons against its back, Yakima looked up at the two tile-roofed towers looming on the bluff above.

The Gatlings were angled low to track the wagon's progress, two silhouetted figures flanking each brass-chased weapon. When the wagon turned onto the last switchback, the men turned the Gatling barrel toward the tower ceilings, and fell back, until only their sombrero crowns were visible.

Still standing behind Lazaro, keeping the Winchester aimed at the captain's back, Yakima glanced down at Faith. She peered up the slope, both hands on the wagon box. The blood had dried on her cheeks, and the late, desert light played across her face, turning her skin and hair golden.

Looking up at Yakima, she smiled crook-edly. "We might be too late." Then she frowned, as if the thought pained her too much to keep considering it, and, eyes glistening, she turned away again to lift her gaze toward the ridge crest.

As the wagon approached the summit, the prison shouldered back atop the crest, about fifty yards from the edge. The front wall stretching between the two front towers grew up out of the ground, until the arched, iron-riveted and reinforced oak doors — three times the size of your average barn doors — appeared, as well, flanked by two Winchester-wielding rurales.

The sentries appeared the size of midgets beside the massive doors and against the fifty-foot wall. One was smoking. They watched the wagon warily, rifles held out before them in both hands, dark eyes bright with incredulity and fear.

"Put your weapons down," Lazaro said as Yakima prodded him back to his bare feet. His voice was growing weaker, most likely because of the loss of blood from his shoulder wound.

Yakima glanced up at the towers once more. The Gatlings were still tipped toward the peaked tower roofs. He said to the captain, "Tell 'em to open the doors. I wanna see what's goin' on in there."

Lazaro stood, shoulders moving as he breathed, as though thinking about it. Then he hiked his good shoulder and told the sentries, who'd leaned their rifles against the prison wall, to open the doors.

One man stared at the captain as though he'd been speaking Greek, then turned to the doors and rammed the right one with the back of his fist three times, tapping out some sort of code and muttering something through the wood. He stepped back. The doors rasped, bulging outward, paused, then continued opening slowly. Each rurale grabbed a wooden handle and pulled.

The doors separated, swinging out, and the breeze they created was rife with the smell of stone, sweat, overfilled latrines, and rot. Two other guards stood just inside, one holding a rifle, the other a shotgun, both staring out with looks of wary surprise. The mule shied at the smell, tossing its head and braying.

Yakima stared into the open yard beyond the doors and the guards, unable to make out much from this angle except the hard-packed dirt yard and wooden scaffolds rising to several tiers of cell blocks, with several visible stone stairways, a screechy windmill, and a barracklike building to the right. Guards milled, armed with rifles or shotguns, most glancing toward the open doors. Dark faces stared through several cell doors in the back wall, with here and there a glimpse of orange- and black-striped prison fatigues showing in the fading sunlight.

"Christ," Faith murmured, wrinkling her nose at the stench.

Montana's horse, reins drooping, stood in the middle of the yard, shaking its head as though bored.

For several minutes, as Lou Brahma and Willie Stiles strolled along the lip of the ridge, making sure they hadn't been followed, Yakima, Faith, Cavanaugh, and Lazaro waited in tense silence, staring at the four sentries who stared back at them, blinking and looking around uncomfortably. Yakima kept his rifle barrel pressed up tight against Lazaro's neck, looking around to make sure no sniper was drawing a bead on him.

Lazaro was breathing hard, as much from anger as pain. Yakima knew he'd have to kill the man when they had Faith's brother in hand — if he was still alive, that was. After the humiliation he'd been through here, Lazaro would track the half-breed to the end of the earth to exact his revenge. Yakima had never killed in cold blood, but having seen what the rurale captain had done to the pretty Apache girl and what he'd tried to do to Faith, Yakima wouldn't lose any sleep over it.

"What's taking so long?" Faith said edgily, standing in the wagon box to Yakima's right.

Yakima didn't say anything. It could be Kelly was dead and the men inside were just buying time, trying to figure a way to free their commander without getting him killed. Or maybe they were going to lie, just *tell* them Kelly was dead. Hell, they could say anything they wanted.

Yakima's group had neither the time nor the manpower to find out the facts of anything around here. But they did have Lazaro for leverage.

An iron door clanked, echoing. There was the rattle of a chain, and then three men appeared, moving from right to left on the prison's second tier. The big lieutenant Montana was in the lead, with a young, blond man in prison orange and black shuffling along behind, barefoot, ankles and wrists shackled. Behind the young blond, a guard strode, glancing over the balcony's peeled log rail toward the open doors below.

"That him?" Yakima asked Faith.

She didn't reply for a time. Then she licked her lips, and her voice rose, just above a whisper. "I think it is."

Yakima glanced over his shoulder at Brahma and Stiles. "Anyone coming up from the town?"

"Not yet," Brahma said.

When Yakima turned his head back toward the prison to watch Montana and the guards lead the young blond man down a set of wooden stairs to the right, he heard Willie Stiles mutter to Brahma, "I'm sweatin' like a damn butcher!"

Lazaro turned his head to one side and curled his upper lip in a grin. "You do know," he said to Yakima, "that you will never get away with this, don't you?"

"All I know is, you play by the rules, you got a chance," Yakima replied. "You give the guards any reason to turn their horns out, your head is gonna be rollin' around in the dust outside your own prison."

CHAPTER 27

Yakima's warning effectively silenced Lazaro, who turned forward as the big lieutenant Montana led the young blond man through the open prison doors, followed by the guard, who held one leathery hand on his holstered pistol grips. Behind him, there was some scrambling around inside the prison grounds, as word had gotten around about what was happening.

Small groups of guards, obviously agitated, stood conferring, pointing or looking toward the doors. Many of the prisoners stared through their cell doors, hands wrapped around the bars.

Montana's mouse brown dun plodded slowly toward the opening, head hanging, reins drooping, oblivious of the goings-on.

"Kelly!" Faith cried.

As she lurched to the right, about to leap over the wagon's sideboard, Yakima snapped, "Hold on!"

She stopped and glanced at him, then turned back to her brother who stood beside and slightly behind Montana. Yakima figured the boy wasn't much over twenty. He was slender and wiry, with a thick thatch of red-blond hair nearly the same shade as his sister's.

He stood stoop-shouldered, head tipped to one side, a wary, skeptical expression on his thin-bearded, peeling, sunburned face. His eyes were so slitted that Yakima couldn't tell if he'd yet discovered his sister in the wagon before him.

"You're sure it's him?" Yakima asked Faith.

"Yes!"

"Tell your boys to take his cuffs and shackles off," Yakima told Lazaro, pressing the rifle barrel firmly against the man's neck once again. "Any bullshit" — he glanced at the guard towers again, in which the Gatlings continued to be aimed at the roofs — "and you're gonna look mighty funny running around without your head."

Lazaro relayed the order to Montana in Spanish, who in turn relayed it to the guard who'd followed him out — a middle-aged man with an evil slash of a mouth beneath a gray, longhorn mustache, and shoulder-length salt-and-pepper hair trimmed with several small braids wrapped in deer hide. As he turned to Kelly, the young man's knees buckled suddenly, and he dropped to the dirt.

"Kelly!" Faith yelled and turned once more to leap out of the wagon.

Quickly, Yakima took his rifle in his left hand, keeping the barrel against Lazaro, and grabbed her arm brusquely with his right. "Hold on!" he rasped. "You go down there and they get their hands on you, you could blow the whole thing!"

"What have you done to him, goddamnit?" Faith snapped at Lazaro as she turned back toward Yakima, her eyes flashing fire.

While the guard crouched down with a key to remove Kelly's ankle cuffs, Lazaro's cheeks drew back with a grin. "He's part of the crew building a road for Don Sebastian. They work terribly hard, you see — sometimes eighteen hours a day — and do not get much sleep!"

Faith curled her upper lip at the man. "I hope you die a slow death, you son of a bitch!"

"For your sake, senorita," Lazaro said, watching the guard remove Kelly's handcuffs, "I'd better not."

When the cuffs had been removed and the young man knelt in the dung-littered dust between the open prison doors, his head lolling on his shoulders as though his neck were broken, Yakima had Lazaro tell the men to step back, hands raised high. Then he ordered Cavanaugh, Brahma, and Stiles to move forward and hold their guns on them.

"Okay," he told Faith, the tension beginning to draw his nerves tight as razor wire. It was just him and his group against maybe twenty or thirty rurales and four Gatling guns. All they had for chips was the commanding officer. Their luck would sour sooner or later; someone was bound to call their bluff. "Get him on your horse. Kid, help her. Make it fast!"

Faith had leaped out of the wagon in a half second. Tears running down her cheeks, she dropped to her knees beside her brother, throwing her arms around his neck and calling his name softly.

"Faith?" the young man said, frowning at his sister, eyelids fluttering.

"It's me," Faith sobbed, then cleared her throat and put some steel in her voice. "We're going to get you out of here."

When Stiles had brought her calico over between the doors, he held the reins while he and Faith, each taking an arm and wrapping their own arms around Kelly's waist, eased him to a standing position. Stiles set the young man's bare left foot in a stirrup; then he and Faith hoisted him up into the leather, where he sat, shaking his head as if to clear it and clinging to the saddle horn.

"Jesus H. Christ," he said, slurring his words as though drunk and staring down at Faith. "It is you, ain't it? You come for your kid brother, just like I knew you would."

"Hold on, Kelly."

She glanced at Cavanaugh. "Ace, mount up with Kelly, will you? You can keep him on the horse better than I can."

Cavanaugh grabbed the reins of his own mount. "He's your brother — you keep him seated!"

"You son of a bitch," she rasped as she toed the stirrup and swung up behind her brother.

"I don't know about you, boys!" Cavanaugh shouted at Longley, Brahma, and Stiles, "but this game's gotten too rich for my blood!"

"Reckon I'll pack it in, too," said Stiles, backing away from the guards and grabbing his own reins off the wagon.

"Ride out," Yakima told Faith.

She turned to him. "What about you?"

"I'll be along."

"You'd better." As her brother slumped

back against her, his head wobbling around like that of a rag doll, she neck-reined the calico around and booted him north along the prison's front wall, into the sifting dust of the men.

When the others were merely bobbing silhouettes heading north, their hoof clomps dwindling into the distance, it was just Yakima sitting there with Lazaro standing half naked before him, Montana and the three guards in front of the wagon.

"As you see, amigo," said Lazaro tightly, "I have kept my part of the bargain. Now, you turn me loose, yes?"

"Sure," Yakima said, "when we're about a mile away from the prison and I've seen all the other prisoners walking out these open doors."

Lazaro turned his head slightly, rolling one eye back to glance at Yakima. "Pardon?"

"Tell your men to turn the others loose. I want to see a good crowd of prisoners bursting out these doors in no less than ten minutes." He nudged the rurale captain hard once more. "Tell them."

"Don't be ridiculous. I don't have the authority to authorize such an order!"

"Bullshit. You run this prison the way you wanna run it. Turn all the others loose, or I'll blow your head off!"

"Amigo, you are not keeping your word!"

"No, but you're keeping your head. For now. You got to the count of three to tell them, or I'm gonna blow your brains out. You an' me'll be waiting on that rise yonder. When I've seen a good crowd move through those doors, and when they're far enough to not get cut down by your Gatling guns, I'll turn you loose."

Lazaro was breathing hard again, turning his head a little farther to the right, his jaw set hard. "You're bluffing. You know you're bluffing. If you don't turn me loose at *once* —"

Yakima rammed the barrel forward savagely, so that the beaded sight carved a gouge in the man's leathery skin from which bright red blood trickled.

"Ach!" the captain cried as his head fell sharply forward.

He sucked a sharp breath and lifted his chin slightly toward Montana. He snapped out a long string of Spanish. Yakima recognized enough of the words to know that the man had ordered the lieutenant and the guards to turn the other prisoners loose. When Montana and the other men only stood staring, mouths agape, at Lazaro, Yakima pressed the gun barrel into the bloody notch, and Lazaro gave the order again, with more vehemence this time. His shrill voice cracked, and he seemed to be sobbing with fury, his entire body shaking.

Montana glanced at the other men, muttered something, then, with the others following, turned and strode quickly back through the open doors and into the prison yard, where a half-dozen other guards had gathered, rifles raised, as though awaiting orders to use them.

Holding his Yellowboy in his right hand, Yakima grabbed the reins off the brake handle. To his left, Wolf stared at him dubiously. "Yeah, I know, horse," he said as he flicked the reins against the mule's back and turned the horse north. "I'm pushin' it again."

Driving the wagon with one hand while holding the Winchester against Lazaro's neck with the other, he moved along the prison's front wall, following a well-used trail through the scrub, angling beyond the north wall and into the boulder-studded chaparral beyond. A good hundred yards from the prison, he swung the mule up a low, flat-topped rise, and turned sideways to stare back at the prison.

He couldn't see the doors from this angle, but already a couple of men in black and orange striped uniforms were striding through the walls. Several more followed, and then more, some casting skeptical looks behind them, some rubbing their wrists.

Then several burst through the doors running, and that started the others to running. Within minutes a veritable horde of sprinting, shouting prisoners — Mexicans and Indians and everything in between, including women and a few white men — was bursting through the doors and wasting no time in spreading out. Hoofing in all directions, they fled the massive adobe walls, which were turning chocolate brown as the orange sun hovered over a western ridge, cut in half by a jutting monolith.

Most of the prisoners would probably be rounded up again. Some might even be killed for fleeing. But Yakima had felt compelled to give them a chance.

"Well, senor?" Lazaro turned. His face was drawn from blood loss, his shoulders hunched, his knees bent. "As you can see . . ."

Yakima looked at him, keeping the Winchester rammed against his neck. He reached over with his left hand and untied Wolf from the side of the wagon box, for the mule might take off with the wagon at the sound of the shot, and flung the reins over the stallion's neck. As he drew his finger back against the trigger, combating his reluctance at shooting an unarmed man — even one as vile as Lazaro — the captain swung around with surprising agility for a man in his condition.

He rammed his right forearm against the rifle at the same time Yakima tripped the trigger. The rifle barked, the slug careening past Lazaro and over the mule's head. As the mule bolted forward, braying, Lazaro leaped over the wagon's right front wheel, landed on bare feet, and fell forward, hitting the ground on his chest.

At the same time, Yakima threw himself out the back of the wagon. As the mule galloped off the rise in the direction of the darkening prison, the half-breed hit the ground on his left shoulder, rolled once, and rose to a knee. He snapped the rifle stock to his shoulder and swung the barrel to the right.

Grunting, crouching, and holding his hand over his ruined shoulder, Lazaro bounded off through the brush, leaping rocks and small boulders — a darting shadow in the gathering night.

Yakima fired three quick shots, triggering and levering the Yellowboy. The slugs tore up dirt and rocks around Lazaro's heels and clipped the greasewood and pinions around him. When the man leveled out at the bottom of the rise and began sprinting through a dense brush thicket, Yakima fired once more. Lazaro's shadow disappeared in the boulder-pocked scrub.

Cursing, ramming a fresh round into the Yellowboy's chamber, Yakima rose and began striding forward, intending to finish the son of a bitch. Shouts and thuds rose from the prison, and Yakima swung around.

Several horseback rurales were galloping out the open doors, the sun's last rays flashing off their rifles and their horses' tack. They turned their mounts in the half-breed's direction and ground their spurred heels into the horses' flanks.

Jaws hard, Yakima cast another glance into the brush where he'd last seen Lazaro. Nothing moved. Had he hit him?

He glanced again at the seven riders galloping toward him, heads low as they shouted in Spanish, rifles in their hands. Cursing and thumbing fresh cartridges into the Winchester's loading gate, wishing like hell he could make sure Lazaro was bleeding dry in that catclaw thicket — Yakima jogged back toward Wolf, who stood snorting and shaking his head. He grabbed the horse's reins, swung into the saddle, and, glancing over his shoulder at the seven rurales, who were within sixty yards and closing fast, ground his heels into the stallion's ribs.

Wolf lunged off his rear hooves and stretched out in an instant, rock-spitting gallop, and Yakima tipped his hat low and put his head down as the early-evening wind swept against him. Following a well-worn trace through the pine-studded chaparral, the horse and Yakima traversed the gradually descending mesa for two miles before dropping down the sloping side and into a rock-strewn wash.

As they climbed up the wash's far side, Yakima saw Faith and the others sitting their mounts before him. They were mere silhouettes, with the sun having disappeared behind them, leaving only a wash of fast-fading green light over the dark brown western ridges. Making wet, sucking sounds, Kelly was drinking from Faith's canteen.

"Anyone behind you?" Cavanaugh shouted.

Stopped before Faith, Yakima hipped around in his saddle and stared back the way he'd come. He couldn't see the rurales, but he could hear the thuds and rings of their hooves on the clear evening air.

He booted Wolf between Cavanaugh and Longley, continuing north. "Yep."

CHAPTER 28

Yakima led the group north through a boulder field, across a dry wash, and onto an ancient cart trail that wound through a field of milling goats getting ready to bed down for the night. They climbed northwest through the foothills of the Olivadas — or, not knowing the country, what Yakima assumed were the Forgotten Mountains. He and the group would try to lose the rurales in the rugged, timbered folds of the sierras, maybe holing up for a day or two, to help Faith's brother regain his strength. Then they'd find another horse for Kelly, and make a beeline north to the border.

When they'd ridden a couple of miles, they stopped briefly to rest the horses. Faith looked exhausted from the effort of holding her brother in the saddle, so Yakima pulled the young man onto Wolf's back and tied Kelly's hands around his waist. Tense and silent but no longer hearing the rurales behind them, the group continued climbing steadily through boulder-strewn canyons, up and across pine-clad slopes, with a cool breeze whispering down from the rocky heights.

Wolves called, and stars danced in the branches.

When the exhausted horses began stumbling and blowing, Yakima pulled into a broad, sandy-floored canyon. The walls were a sheer five hundred feet on the north side, two hundred on the other. A spring bubbled out from the side of the north wall, forming a shallow pool before running off over gravel and seeping into the sand.

He released the thong holding Kelly's arms around his waist, then swung out of the saddle and helped the kid, only about half conscious, down and into the shade of the wall, near the spring. Faith knelt down beside Kelly and, using her bandanna, dampened his forehead.

"We'll rest the horses here," Yakima told the other men, who stared up the ridges cautiously as they loosened their saddle cinches.

Yakima slipped his Winchester from its boot, then hoofed it back down the canyon, scrutinizing the south wall and the canyon floor itself. He hadn't detected a sign of anyone on their trail for several hours, but he'd take no chances.

When he was relatively certain they had this section of the Sierra Olivadas to themselves, he headed back toward camp. Skirting a small island of willows, he paused and sniffed the air, detecting the smell of burning wood smoke. He moved around a bend in the south canyon wall, staring back toward the makeshift camp they'd made near the spring, with the horses hobbled near the seep, grain sacks draped over their snouts.

Thick, white smoke rose from a small fire about ten feet out from the wall. While the other men, Faith, and Kelly lounged with their backs against the wall, and Cavanaugh and Stiles reclined with their hats tipped over their eyes, Brahma, head down, was down on all fours, blowing on the tinder to raise a flame.

Yakima strode up to the camp and kicked sand on the flames. Brahma looked up, eyes pinched with fury. "Goddamnit, I was fixin' to brew coffee!"

"No fires."

"I thought you said we lost 'em," Cavanaugh said, sneering as he tipped his hat back off his forehead.

"I *think* we lost 'em. But if they're around,

they could smell that green smoke within a mile."

"Listen, breed," Brahma said, "we been ridin' all night. We need a cup of coffee to get us through!"

Yakima glared at him, his nerves drawn taut as razor wire. "You tinhorns are gonna have to go without coffee for a day or two. Get used to it."

"Who the hell are you callin' a tinhorn, you half-breed son of a bitch?"

Brahma slapped leather and, crouching, started raising his revolver. Yakima swung toward him and kicked the pistol out of his hand. Brahma cursed, grabbing the injured wrist and staring up at Yakima, forked veins protruding from his forehead. When his dark eyes dropped to the cocked Colt in Yakima's fist, they stood out even farther.

"You're more trouble than you're worth, Brahma."

He squeezed the Colt in his fist until his knuckles turned white. Brama's mouth opened slightly as fear touched his eyes. In his face, Yakima saw the faces of all the others who'd regarded him as though he were nothing more than a three-legged cur running wild in civilized streets. Ralph had lectured him about patience and tolerance. Try as he might, he hadn't gotten that part.

He'd found it even more elusive after he'd found Ralph hanging from that cottonwood outside Wichita. That's why he usually tried to go his own way.

If it weren't for Faith, he'd shed this group as though a prairie twister were swirling around his heels.

His heart thudded. The pistol shook slightly in his big, red fist. Staring down at the Colt, Brahma's features slackened, and the blood drained from his cheeks.

The other men were silent, frozen and watching.

Faith said softly, "Yakima . . ."

Her voice was like a rope thrown to the bottom of a deep well. Reaching for it, he raised the Colt's barrel and depressed the trigger. He flipped the revolver into his holster, moved a ways off down canyon, dropped beneath a pine, and tipped his hat over his eyes.

He'd slept for about twenty minutes when something woke him. He opened his eyes and slowly poked the hat brim back off his forehead. His eyes darted from left to right then, drifting up the southern ridge shouldering up on the other side of the canyon, scrutinized the rocks, boulders, and shrub clumps. Warning bells tolled in his head.

Something flashed in the hazy, purple wedge of shade beside a triangular-shaped boulder. Yakima jerked upright and reached for his Winchester. At the same time, a rifle cracked, the report flatting out and echoing across the canyon.

To his left, someone groaned. He turned to see Ace Cavanaugh slump forward, away from the canyon wall, grabbing his upper-left chest.

As the others jerked out of their slumbers, Yakima returned his gaze to the ridge. A man in a dove gray tunic crouched beside the triangular-shaped boulder, raising his Winchester's barrel to jack another shell into the chamber. The rifle's brown leather lanyard swung to and fro, glinting in the sunlight. Smoke wafted around the Mexican's straw sombrero.

As Yakima pushed onto his knees and raised the Yellowboy to his shoulder, he spied several more rurales stealing down from the far ridge, moving like mountain goats amongst the rocks and boulders. Another rifle cracked, and once more a grunt rose to Yakima's left, followed by the thump of a body hitting the dirt.

Yakima aimed quickly at the first rurale and squeezed the Yellowboy's trigger. The man's yell rose a second after his mouth opened and he'd tumbled back behind the rock.

"Rurales!" Lou Brahma shouted as he and Longley grabbed their rifles, looking around wildly.

Several more shots sounded, the bullets kicking up dust along the canyon floor, setting the horses to skitter-stepping and screaming.

"Mount up!" Yakima shouted, glancing left to see Willie Stiles rolling around on the canyon floor while clutching his belly. Faith crouched beside Kelly, half covering the young man with her body as she stared in horror at the ridge on the other side of the canyon.

Swinging his rifle from right to left and back again, hearing hoofbeats rising on his right, Yakima loosed a flurry of lead at the ridge, halfway through which he paused to shout, "Mount up and get the hell out of here! Up canyon! *Vamoose!*"

He emptied his rifle, ran several yards forward, then dropped to a knee. As he plucked shells from his cartridge belt and pushed them through the rifle's loading gate, he glanced left again. Stiles was still down, flat on his back and breathing hard as blood gushed from his chest. Cavanaugh was up and running toward his horse, limping slightly, while Faith was helping her brother onto the calico.

Wolf stared toward Yakima, wide-eyed and jumping around, the only mount they hadn't hobbled.

"I'm comin'!" Yakima heard himself shout at the antsy horse.

He winced as a slug spanged off a stone to his right, spraying lead and rock slivers, the report following a half second later. He aimed at the smoke puff about halfway up the ridge, and fired two quick rounds, spying a sun flash off gun-steel as the rurale tumbled backward off the boulder he'd been perched upon, throwing his rifle into the air.

Yakima fired three more rounds, causing another rurale to scream and reach for his shin, then glanced up canyon to see riders moving toward him from around both sides of the island of willows. He snapped off two quick shots in their direction, then sprinted down canyon, toward where Wolf was side-stepping and fiddle-footing, giving occasional, anxious kicks.

The others had ridden out, their dust still sifting behind them. The kid, Willie Stiles, lay near the hole in which Brahma had been trying to start a fire, on his back, unmoving, one hand on his bloody chest, the other lying flat atop the sand. The kid's head was turned to the side, his dusty lids half covering his death-glazed eyes.

Yakima continued on past the kid and mounted Wolf on the run, grabbing the reins and dropping his head low as rifles cracked behind him, a couple of slugs plunking dust around him, a couple more zinging through the air above his head. Wolf stretched out, head down, hooves scissoring, laid-back ears twitching with fear and irritation.

As horse and rider rounded a bend in the sandy-floored canyon, Yakima spied the others dead ahead, with Willie Stiles's riderless horse bringing up the rear, loose reins bouncing as the pounding hooves clipped them. The group disappeared down a right-forking corridor, only to reappear a moment later, Brahma and Cavanaugh heading back toward Yakima, with Longley, Faith, and Kelly turning their horses around behind them. They all had looks of grim desperation on their dust-streaked faces.

Behind Kelly and Faith, someone shouted in Spanish. Rifles cracked and pistols popped. Hooves thundered.

Brahma and Cavanaugh reined their horses down the canyon's left fork, Cavanaugh shouting, "Thought you said we lost 'em!" He winced, crouching low, and, as he and Brahma galloped down the other forking corridor, turned his head to shout behind him. "Looks to me like we just picked up *more!*"

Yakima checked Wolf down, cursing under his breath. He'd figured most of the rurales would be out trying to round up their prisoners. He'd figured wrong, it appeared. He cursed again, mind reeling, as Faith pulled the calico up before him. Kelly now rode behind her, leaning against her, looking a little stronger than he did yesterday but still too weak to ride his own mount.

"It's Lazaro!" Faith shouted.

Then she reined the calico down the left-forking corridor, her brother turning his head to squint behind him, cheeks bunched with terror.

Skeptically, Yakima looked down the canyon's right fork, through the dust kicked up by Faith and the others. Faith had to be wrong. There was no way that Lazaro could have pursued him with that shredded shoulder, and not after the man had lost a good half gallon of blood.

Two riders appeared at the head of a dusty pack of rifle-wielding rurales. Yakima didn't wait to make sure Faith had been right; he lifted the Winchester to his shoulder and squeezed off four quick shots before reining

Wolf sharply to the left and following Faith and the others down the canyon's left fork.

Rifles cracked behind as Wolf leaned into a hard run. Yakima glanced over his shoulder to see several orange gun flashes through the heavy, sifting dust. Voices rose as men shouted and there were several more rifle cracks, a couple of slugs pounding into the rock wall to Yakima's left.

Faith and Kelly were dead ahead, the young man leaning over Faith's right shoulder. In spite of the weight of the two riders, however, the calico was keeping pace with Cavanaugh, Brahma, and Longley galloping about thirty yards beyond. One of them should have taken the kid, but they were obviously more concerned about saving their own asses than helping Faith. A real winning team she'd chosen for her excursion into Mexico.

As more rifles cracked behind him, Yakima urged Wolf up beside Faith. The riderless horse galloped to her right. Cavanaugh and his cohorts were about twenty yards beyond, riding spread out across the widening, jagged-walled canyon. The gambler rode low in the saddle, slumped forward, head bobbing weakly.

As the staccato clatter of hoofbeats grew louder behind him, Yakima glanced behind, and winced. Four lead riders were closing fast. Judging by the bobbing sombrero-clad heads and the cartridge bandoliers flashing in the sunlight behind them, at least a half dozen more followed. Yakima began snaking his rifle around his body to fire behind him, but then he remembered he had only one or two rounds left in the Winchester's breech. His stomach fell.

As he squeezed the Yellowboy's trigger, a rumble rose from up canyon — a din so great he thought the canyon wall was rolling down on top of him.

Only it wasn't boulders being flung at him. Bullets fired by a Gatling gun mounted on a nearby thumb of rock whipped around his head, humming like angry hornets.

Rat-a-tat-tat-tat-tat-tat-tat-tat!

CHAPTER 29

Yakima's bullet punched through the bandolier of one of the rurales galloping toward him. A wink later, as the Gatling gun roared somewhere over his right shoulder, the other three rurales flew backward, screaming, dropping their rifles and their horses' reins, dust puffing from the slugs pounding through their tunics and bandoliers, blood spraying out before them.

Rat-a-tat-tat-tat-tat-tat-tat-tat-tat!

Christ, what now? Yakima wondered.

The rurales' wide-eyed, riderless horses screamed to skidding halts, falling back behind Yakima and Faith. The half-breed crouched low beneath the flying bullets, expecting to catch a couple himself. As he and the others hauled back on their reins, their own horses skidding in the dry sand and gravel, Yakima glanced ahead and right, at the smoke- and fire-spitting Gatling perched on the rock thumb protruding from the canyon's right wall. As he did so, the Gatling fell suddenly silent, and behind the brass canister a sombrero rose. Beneath the sombrero dropped a thin, hawkish face with a drooping mustache and a row of gold teeth glistening between spread lips.

Christos Arvada.

Leonora Domingo bounded up the rocks beside Arvada, her angular, calico- and leather-clad frame looming over the canyon floor. She put two fingers to her lips and whistled, jerked a thumb to indicate up canyon, then turned and disappeared as Arvada, abandoning the Gatling gun, followed her.

"What the hell?" Pop Longley said, trying to check down his wild-eyed, pitching buckskin.

Yakima glanced at Faith, then looked behind where the five or six wounded rurales were screaming and rolling in the dirt while others, out of sight down canyon, shouted angrily and triggered a few angry shots. They'd no doubt be along soon.

Yakima booted Wolf ahead. "Let's go!"

As he passed the rock thumb and checked Wolf back to a trot, Leonora Domingo dropped down off a rocky ledge to his right and onto the back of one of the two horses waiting there in the shadows, tied to shrubs.

Christos Arvada, holding his arms out for balance, skipped down the rocks, then dropped smoothly off the wall and into his own saddle. Both gigged their horses toward Yakima.

"You two get around," he said as the girl kept pace off his right stirrup, her thick black hair bouncing on her shoulders.

"We were tracking federal soldiers, from whom we acquired that magnificent weapon to add to my collection, when we spied you and those vermin behind you." She gestured back toward the Gatling they'd left on the knob. "Unfortunately, it's out of ammunition."

"Damn the luck," Yakima said, glancing behind at the rurales rounding the bend behind Cavanaugh, Faith, and the others. "They're back on our trail."

Leonora swung her head around, then turned forward once more, grinding her spurs into her mustang's ribs. "Follow us!"

As Leonora and Christos Arvada galloped off down the canyon, Yakima and the others spurred their own mounts into ground-eating lopes. Behind, the rurales triggered pistols and rifles, but the canyon curved enough that most of the slugs slammed into the walls, though one drifted close enough to Cavanaugh's mount to evoke an exasperated whinny.

As he followed another broad curve, Yakima saw several men — some sitting horses, others standing holding their reins — on the canyon's left side, in the shade of an overhanging rock.

Leonora shouted at them in Spanish, and, while three scrambled onto their mounts, those already saddled reined their horses into the canyon. As Yakima passed the niche in which they'd been milling, he saw a bullet-riddled wagon and three men in the dark-blue uniforms of the Mexican *federales* hanging from a stout, gnarled oak growing out of the rocks.

"You've been busy, senorita!" Yakima shouted at Leonora as the rurales continued triggering lead behind them.

"I'm always busy!" she shouted back. "Do you expect me to take over this province by sitting on my thumbs?" Suddenly, as another corridor forked to the right, she drew back on her mare's reins, turning sharply. "This way!"

"Where the hell we goin'?" Pop Longley shouted.

"Shut up, old man, and I will show you!" Leonora returned as she swung into the corridor's dark mouth.

As the others followed, Yakima pulled over

toward Faith, her brother still riding behind her. "You all right?"

Faith turned her head sharply as a bullet plunked into a boulder beside her. The wind bent her hat brim back and dried the sweat on her dusty cheeks. "For now, but the calico can't keep up this pace much longer!"

Yakima glanced behind. He would have tried to draw Kelly onto his own mount, but the rurales were gaining ground. They were being pushed hard — if not by Lazaro, then by someone nearly as zealous.

Yakima rammed his rifle butt against the calico's hindquarters, then followed Faith and Kelly into the dark, narrow corridor. At the tail end of the pack, Yakima triggered several shots over his shoulder, and one of the rurale horses screamed.

Wolf galloped just off the calico's tail, the clack of his and the other horses' hooves resounding around the tunnel, which was so narrow that Yakima could have reached out with either hand and touched a knobby wall. As the rurales entered the tunnel behind, hooves cracking like pistol fire, the tunnel walls dropped suddenly back, and sunlight fell over Yakima once more.

Still galloping behind Faith, he found himself in a broad valley, sheer on the right but with a boulder-strewn slope rising toward a sandstone ridge on the left. Leonora Domingo and Christos Arvada were angling up the slope, twisting around boulders, the senorita looking behind, her mouth moving. She was shouting, but Yakima couldn't make out the words above the pounding hooves and the shots echoing around the corridor behind him.

She wanted him and his group to follow her up the ridge, toward a narrow, black gap sitting at the base of the long, sandstone block capping the ridge crest. It looked to Yakima like a good place to get trapped. But then, they weren't going to run much farther, anyway. Somewhere between here and Tocando, the rurales must have appropriated fresh horses. Even Wolf was beginning to blow and sag.

Faith glanced at Yakima, her eyes wary as she turned the calico up the slope behind Pop Longley, who was riding behind Cavanaugh and Brahma.

"Keep going," Yakima shouted, wincing as the rurales' hooves clattered loudly behind him and several rifles cracked. A bullet clipped a shrub to his right, making Wolf jerk to the left.

The black tore up the slope, overtaking Faith's mount. Ahead and left, Pop Longley screamed and jerked forward. His horse whinnied and fiddle-footed, lowering its head as though preparing to sunfish. A ragged hole showed in the back of Pop's threadbare suit coat. The man stretched his lips in agony, threw his head back on his shoulders, and screamed.

More rifles cracked down slope, and Pop's head jerked once more as a bullet slammed through its base and out his right temple in a shower of brains and blood. His horse screamed again, and Pop tumbled over his right stirrup, hitting the ground on his back, his heels digging into the dirt as though he were trying to run. Buck-kicking, the bronc wheeled and headed up the slope, angling left.

Knowing there was nothing he could do for the man, Yakima continued pushing Wolf up the slope behind Faith. The calico was slowing, dropping its head and blowing hard, its ribs expanding and contracting. With every inhalation, silver sweat bubbled around the stirrups and latigo. Yakima rode up off Faith's left stirrup and leaped out of his saddle. He hustled around Wolf and held his reins up to Kelly, who appeared more alert than he'd looked before, though his eyes were still glazed.

"Take my horse, kid!"

Kelly's eyes sharpened. He leaped off the

calico's back, one knee buckling as both feet hit the ground, then took the reins Yakima offered.

"What're you gonna do?" Faith said.

"I'll be along in a minute."

"That's what you always say."

"And I'm always along!"

When Kelly had clamored onto Wolf's back, Yakima slammed the Yellowboy's butt against the black's right hip. Wolf blew and nickered. Normally, he wouldn't carry someone besides the half-breed on his back, but the staccato hammering of rifles and pistols encouraged him. He lit out after the other horses. Yakima slapped the calico's rump, and then Faith was galloping off behind her brother, the calico digging its rear hooves into the soft gravel and blowing like a locomotive climbing a steep hill.

"Don't go getting yourself killed, damnit!" Faith called to Yakima, then ducked as a bullet barked into the ground nearby, blowing up gravel.

Thumbing fresh shells through his Winchester's loading gate, Yakima ducked behind a boulder and edged a look down slope.

The rurales — a good twenty or thirty men — were still galloping out of the corridor. Three were heading up slope into the sifting dust of Yakima's group while several more leaped from their saddles to drop to a knee and steady their rifles. A couple had hunkered down behind boulders at the slope's base and were triggering their own Henry and Winchester repeaters — no doubt stolen from U.S. Army outposts or patrols — toward their quarry.

A quick glance up slope told Yakima that Leonora and Christos Arvada were about halfway up the long, rubble- and shrub-pocked slope, heading toward that long, thin gap at the base of the bulging crown of sandstone. Faith and the others were spread out across the slope behind them, vague shapes in the adobe-colored dust, twisting and turning around boulders and stunt pinions and yucca snags. Several horses balked and had to be kicked hard.

Lead sizzled through the air around Yakima's head. He ducked down behind the boulder as a slug slammed into it, making the rock shudder against his shoulder.

He snaked his Winchester over the rock and fired three rounds, dropping down as a slug slammed into the dirt beside the rock and another crashed against the rock itself. He lifted his head once more and drew a bead on a rider angling toward him — a big man with a thick goatee, a gray sombrero,

418

and a large silver cross hanging from a leather thong around his neck.

Yakima triggered the Yellowboy. The man grunted, firing his Henry into the air, and sagged back in the saddle, clapping one hand to the wound in his shoulder. His horse whinnied and continued toward Yakima, who fired once more, this time blowing the man straight back off the horse's ass.

Behind him, a half-dozen rurales were galloping uphill. Some were on foot, arms scissoring, holding their rifles in one hand. Yakima caught no glimpse of Lazaro. If he was part of this group, he was hanging back. Too bad. Yakima would like nothing more — aside from getting Faith and her brother safely back to Arizona — than turning the demonic rurale toe-down once and for all.

He emptied his Winchester, slowing the rurales' progress up slope, then turned and, keeping the boulder between him and the canyon floor, scurried up the incline. Tracing a serpentine course around obstacles and breathing hard, wishing he were wearing his moccasins instead of the hard leather stockmen's boots better suited for riding, he slipped six more shells through the Winchester's loading gate.

He reached for another shell, but his

fingers found only empty belt loops.

He'd used up all the ammo on his shell belt. He had only the six cartridges he'd just slipped into the Yellowboy and the six in his revolver's cylinder.

Cursing, glancing behind to see the rurales climbing the slope through the dust, several whooping like banshees as they fired their rifles or pistols, Yakima ran hard, angling toward the gap growing at the top of the slope. Slugs sizzled around his ears. Several plunked into the rocks and gravel around him. One burned across his upper left shoulder; another ripped along the side of his right thigh, both grazes feeling like hot knives laid across his skin and making him suck air sharply through gritted teeth.

One of the Mexican's horses lay before him, dead. Yakima leaped the glassy-eyed mount and found the Mexican rider lying a few yards farther up slope with a hole in the back of his neck, one more in his right shoulder blade.

He squinted up slope through the sifting dust. Faith and Kelly were nearing the ridge crest. At least they'd be safe for a time in the cave . . . until the group's ammo ran out, which wouldn't be long. There were just too many rurales, and they were closing fast, with an almost religious fervor. Doubtless, whether Lazaro was here or licking his wounds back in Tocando, the captain had put a significant bounty on the heads of the gringos who'd humiliated him in front of his own men.

As a slug clipped his boot heel, Yakima leaped a flat-topped boulder and dropped behind it.

He glanced up slope. He was about thirty yards from the top. Leonora and three of her men, including Arvada, were on their knees in front of the cave, triggering lead down the ridge, smoke puffing around their heads. Yakima couldn't see any of his own group. As he swung his head forward, he glimpsed a figure in the corner of his eye, and turned back.

Cavanaugh lay slumped against a low, rocky shelf tufted with dry, brown grass, behind another boulder about twenty yards away. The gambler stared steely-eyed at Yakima, a revolver clenched in his right hand resting atop his thigh. With his other hand, he held a wadded neckerchief to the bloody wound in his upper-left chest. The cloth wasn't doing much to stem the blood flow. The thick, red liquid dribbled out around it, bubbling and glinting in the sunlight.

"How bad you hit?" Yakima asked, jerking

his head down as a slug blasted the top of the boulder before him, spraying rock shards.

"Bad enough," Cavanaugh grunted. He smiled crookedly. "Fortunate for you, eh?"

Yakima snaked his rifle over the boulder, snapped off a shot, and glanced at Cavanaugh once more. "Come again?"

"You've got your hat set for my wife, you red-skinned bastard."

Yakima fired another shot, clipping the thigh of a rurale scrambling for cover about thirty yards away. "It's not the time or the place for that bullshit." He triggered another round, taking the horse out from beneath a sergeant wielding a double-barreled shotgun.

As the horse screamed and rolled atop the sergeant, Cavanaugh chuckled dryly. "A half-breed horse-breaker and a beautiful, white whore. Now, how in the hell you think *that's* gonna work?"

Yakima said nothing, only triggered another shot downhill, counting his cartridges and aiming carefully.

There was the click of a gun hammer behind him and to his right. He glanced back to see Cavanaugh extending his cocked revolver at him. The man had a savage look on his sweat-streaked face, his scarred eye slitted, lips bunched. His good eye bored a hole through the half-breed, who stood frozen, holding his uncocked rifle in one hand.

Yakima's heart skipped a beat. The gambler had the drop on him.

"Don't be a fool, Cavanaugh. You won't get out of here without me."

The gambler curled his upper lip, the tail of his green neckerchief blowing around in the breeze. "I ain't gettin' out of here, anyway. But it sure comforts me to know you won't have her, either."

The man gritted his teeth. His knuckles turned white as he squeezed his revolver's grips.

Yakima steeled himself.

A rumble rose out of nowhere, and the ground began quivering. Cavanaugh let the revolver drop slightly as he looked around, puzzled.

The rumbling grew louder, and the ground jumped around beneath Yakima's boots as though a locomotive were approaching at a thunderous clip. Above, the clacks and cracks of tumbling rock added to the growing din, and Yakima looked up to see several large boulders rolling down from the crest of the sandstone ridge, tumbling and bouncing, the booming echoes chasing themselves around the canyon.

"Rock slide!" he shouted as small stones and gravel began raining off the ridge and the thunder of tumbling boulders grew louder.

As he bounded forward, crouching, he stopped and looked over at Cavanaugh. The gambler, lower jaw hanging, was on his knees, staring up at the ridge.

A shadow passed over the gambler. Yakima jerked a look upward once more. A wagon-sized boulder bounced off the side of the sandstone wall and plunged toward the slope, angling out from the ridge wall, twisting and turning so that Yakima could see the cracks, knobs, and ridges along its surface.

The boulder moved between the sun and Yakima and Cavanaugh, casting a shadow over them both as it plunged, its twenty-plus tons roaring as it tore through the air.

Yakima scrambled left and dove.

CHAPTER 30

As Yakima landed on his chest and belly, spraying gravel and skinning his elbows, the ground leaped violently beneath him.

There was a boom like an enormous thunderclap, instantly setting his ears to ringing, his head to aching, and the ground to lurching. A great wind lifted dust and gravel.

He pushed off one bloody elbow to glance behind at Cavanaugh — or where Cavanaugh had been. The shelf behind which Cavanaugh had been resting was pulverized, and all that remained of the gambler himself was his pancaked hat and a large patch of blood and viscera. The body itself had apparently been carried downhill by the still-rolling boulder.

More gravel, rocks, and boulders thundered down around Yakima. As the ground leaped beneath his boots and his eardrums rattled with the deafening cacophony, he lurched to his feet. Pushing off the ground with his hands and keeping his head down, he bolted straight up the slope. He figured he had no chance to make the cave, but he kept his feet moving and his arms scissoring, blowing with the effort, wincing as the sand and dirt stung his cheeks and eyes.

The dust was so thick that he couldn't see how far he was from the cave when his boot slipped off a rock, twisting his ankle, and he dropped to a knee. Suddenly, two hands wrapped around his left arm, and someone was pulling him forward.

"Rápido!" Leonora Domingo screamed.

He lurched to his feet once more. The cave yawned darkly before him, behind a thin curtain of sifting sand and falling rocks. At the same time, he and Leonora dove forward, becoming airborne. They hit the ground just inside the cave, and rolled. When Yakima lifted his head, choking on dust while trying to suck air down his throat, he was staring at the cave's opening six feet behind him. Beyond the gap, several large boulders plunged, hitting the slope with resounding booms, spraying dirt and gravel as they continued bounding on down the mountain.

Coughing, Leonora scrambled onto her knees. She'd lost her hat, and her black, dust-streaked hair hung loose about her face. Spitting grit from her lips, she grabbed Yakima's shoulder and straightened.

"Come!"

"Come where?"

Yakima glanced around the dark, sandy-floored cavern, his mind reeling. Christos Arvada, one knee raised, sat with his back against a wall, clutching his right hand to a bullet wound under his left arm. He was the only other person in sight. Yakima's brain clenched as he jerked a look back out the gap where the rocks were still raining.

Reading his mind, Leonora said, "She and your horse are safe . . . for now." Again she tugged on Yakima's arm. "Come!"

"Where the hell we going?"

"Quit asking questions, you stubborn gringo!" Leonora shouted as she reached down and tugged on Arvada's right elbow, trying to haul the man to his feet. "Christos, you lazy goat," she screamed in Spanish, "get up!"

As Arvada groaned and pushed away from the wall, Yakima looked around quickly. The front of the cave was fast building up with rocks and boulders, and chunks of the ceiling began to slide around like the scales on a moving snake, with several beginning to protrude and fall. With what little light remained in the cavern, he saw that there was no back wall, which meant the cave continued farther into the mountain.

As Leonora helped the cursing, groaning Arvada move back into the cave's stygian darkness, Yakima followed, running his left hand along the wall, holding the Yellowboy up and out with his right, shielding himself from unseen obstacles.

For a time, it was so dark he couldn't see anything but black, and he squinted and walked heavy-footed, expecting to run into something. To his right, he could hear Leonora's and Arvada's footfalls and breaths. The pistolero rasped frustrated curses.

The rumble of the rock slide grew faint behind them. The air of the cave smelled like mushrooms and bird shit.

The uneven floor dropped gradually. After a time, Yakima felt fresh, damp air caress his face. Suddenly, a horse whinnied shrilly, the din echoing, nearly drowning the low, constant rushing sound beneath it. Faith's voice rose, muffled with distance, the words distorted by echoes. Yakima increased his pace, continuing to run his left hand along the wall.

Lou Brahma's voice boomed, "I'll be damned if I'm jumpin' in there!"

Pale light appeared, casting Leonora's and Arvada's figures in shadow, and limning the jagged walls and low ceiling. As the floor began to even out and the ceiling rise, Yakima saw two figures and three horses about fifty yards ahead. One of the horses — Wolf, it appeared — was pitching, tail raised, tossing its head, while Faith clung to the reins. Yakima bolted forward. Faith turned to him sharply.

"I didn't think you made it!"

"So far . . ." Yakima grabbed Wolf's reins, and the horse, appeased by his master's presence, stopped pitching but continued to snort and prance in place. Yakima looked at Faith. "You all right?"

She nodded. "Ace?"

Yakima shook his head.

Her eyes held his for a moment, vaguely pensive, even regretful, and then she glanced at the river running through a ravine just ahead. It was fed by black water tumbling over a falls in the high-ceilinged, cathedral-like room. At the very top, the ceiling opened to sunlight. The underground river, gleaming in the sun shafts angling through the roof, snaked around to Yakima's right and dropped out of sight between narrowing walls sheathed in cracked, granite boulders of all shapes and sizes.

"How do you like my hideout?" Leonora said, grabbing the reins of the other two horses, both sporting silver-trimmed Mexican saddles. Apparently, Yakima's other broncs hadn't survived the rock slide.

"Right handy." Yakima's glance fell on Kelly sitting slumped against the wall. The young man sat with his knees up, a wry smile twisting his lips. Yakima read his mind: out of the frying pan and into the fire.

He turned to the senorita as she led both horses to the edge of the dark ravine through which the river swirled. Behind her, Christos Arvada stood, facing the direction from which they'd come, his silver-plated revolver in his right hand, held low against his leg. He held his thumb over the hammer.

"We gotta swim our way out of here?" Yakima asked the girl.

"You can walk, if you wish," she said, stepping back and slapping the hindquarters of one of the Mexican mounts. As the horse whinnied and lunged over the edge and into the stream with a splash resounding like a cannon blast, the senorita added, "But it's a good forty feet deep here in the cave!"

"I can't swim!" Lou Brahma shouted. He stood downstream, facing the ravine but staring over his shoulder at Yakima and the senorita, his dusty, bloody features slack with exasperation.

The senorita laughed and sent the other Mexican mount plunging over the ravine's edge and into the broiling stream. "There's no swimming, amigo — only praying. Pray that the river takes you out of the mountain without smashing you to pieces, and spits you safely into the valley below!"

A pistol cracked, sounding little louder than the snapping of a matchstick above the river's rush. Yakima turned toward Arvada. The pistolero held his revolver straight out and, aiming down the barrel, triggered another shot in the direction from which they'd come, smoke and orange flames stabbing from the silver-plated barrel.

He glanced over his shoulder, the man's narrow face pinched with pain, natural belligerence, and fear. "I saw something," he said in Spanish. "Shadows moved."

"Shadows moved in your head. No one could have survived the rock slide." The senorita glanced at Yakima. "Better get your people in the water, in the rare event that my soft-headed partner is right!"

Yakima slid his Yellowboy into the saddle boot, then took Wolf's reins in both hands. He pulled the horse's head down toward his and stared into his coffee black, white-ringed eyes. "Sorry, old buddy, but this is the only way. I'll see you wherever this river leaks out."

With that, he slipped the horse's bridle off, so it wouldn't snag and drag him under, then removed the lariat coiled at the side of the saddle. Stepping back quickly, not giving the horse time to turn around and run back through the cavern, he slapped his right hand hard against the stallion's hip, shouting, *"Go!"*

Wolf whinnied shrilly and jerked his tail high as he lurched forward, bounding over the lip of the bank and plunging into the water with a boom of displaced water. His heart clenching, silently praying Wolf made it — he didn't know what he'd do without the hammerheaded, shoulder-nipping cuss — Yakima watched as the stallion tore off downstream, twisting and turning and shaking his head frantically as he tried to make for one of the banks.

When the horse drifted off around a bend in the riverbed, the half-breed turned to Faith, who'd led Kelly out away from the wall.

The kid still wore that bemused, fateful expression, as though he were halfway thinking he'd rather have stayed in Lazaro's prison. Yakima looped the lariat around Kelly's waist, secured it with a slipknot, then dropped another loop over Faith's head. She glanced up at him curiously.

"This'll keep us together no matter what happens," Yakima told her as he formed one more loop, dropped it over his head, and fashioned a slipknot in front of his chest. When he glanced up, he saw Faith studying him with a half smile on her full lips.

"Thanks."

"Don't thank me until we've made it."

The smile on her lips grew, and she set a hand against Yakima's cheek. "We'll make it."

Leonora sidled up against Yakima, smiling seductively. "You're not going to include me? You hurt my feelings, wild man." She kissed his cheek and sneered at Faith. "But I'll forgive you if you buy me a drink on the other side."

She called to Arvada, moved to the edge of the bank, and stepped forward, plunging straight down into the water. She howled as the water hit her. Her head disappeared for a moment, then reappeared about ten yards down the roiling stream. She flopped her arms, threw up a hand in a hasty wave, grinning dementedly, then swung to and fro and disappeared around the bend.

Arvada moved to the bank, glanced back the way they'd come, and turned to Yakima.

"Better hurry, *indio*. I think we have company!"

He removed his hat, held it taut against his belly, and plunged into the river.

Yakima, Faith, and Kelly moved to the edge of the bank. "Just try to keep your heads above the water. Don't fight the current."

He thought he heard something behind him, and turned. Nothing but the mouth of the dark cavern leading back toward the opening, which was no doubt blocked now with rocks and boulders. He turned to Brahma. The big man stood staring down at the water.

"See you downstream," Yakima said.

Brahma didn't look at him, but kept his eyes on the churning, black water. "I'll be along when I'm good and goddamned ready!"

Yakima stepped to the edge of the riverbank. He doffed his hat, held it before him, and glanced at Faith and Kelly. "Wait," Faith said, staring wide-eyed at the water swirling about ten feet below. "I'm not ready."

"Let's go!" Yakima stepped off the bank. The four feet of rope connecting him to Faith jerked taut, and she screamed as she tumbled after him. The kid was next, but

434

Yakima didn't see Kelly leave the bank, because his head was about two feet beneath the swirling river.

When his head bobbed to the surface, he was facing downstream. Both banks slid past him in a rocky blur. He turned his head as Faith, wincing and choking, surfaced just behind him, hair plastered against her head and cheeks. She plunged after him. Behind her, her brother's head broke the surface, mouth drawn wide. The kid's yowl clipped off as the rope connecting him to his sister and Yakima jerked taut, and he tumbled downstream behind them.

The water, probably bubbling up from deep underground, was cold as snowmelt. Yakima's limbs numbed as the current jerked him this way and that while pulling him nearly straight downstream. The rope around his chest jerked taut, then slackened as Faith and Kelly moved toward him, then tightened again when side eddies and swirls pulled them in a different direction. The perpetual motion kept their heads above the surface, though they had to lift their chins up to keep from gulping water.

As the river plunged in a near waterfall, the banks drew back while the ceiling lowered sharply. Then, suddenly, the ceiling was gone. Yakima's gut leaped into his throat as the river dropped once again, even more sharply, and suddenly he was squinting against brassy sunlight reflecting off the water. Above him, a brassy blue sky yawned above serrated ridges.

Still, the river dropped, the rocky banks rushing past so quickly Yakima could just barely make out distinguishing features. All around, white water churned over barely submerged boulders. Yakima had to kick off a couple of rocks, but mostly the river pushed and pulled him through the gaps of clear-rushing troughs.

Then the river sped up even more, the stone walls climbing around him. The rope jerked taut, and he turned to see Faith and Kelly, caught in an alternate current, swing out toward his right flank. Ahead and to Yakima's right was a large boulder up against which a near-solid sheet of whitewater was dancing. On their current course, Faith would be slammed right up against it. At this speed, the impact would kill her.

She'd spotted the obstacle, and her eyes were wide. "Yakima!"

A smaller, half-submerged boulder lay between him and the big rock. "Hold on!" He kicked toward it, throwing his arms out and pulling the water back toward him, trying to steer against the iron-willed river. To his right, Faith and Kelly swung out slowly, both heading for the large, merciless boulder.

Yakima got himself positioned so that the smaller rock was fast growing before him, the river fountaining up around it. He steeled himself, throwing his arms and legs out before him, bracing himself for impact.

CHAPTER 31

The boulder hit Yakima straight on, brutally slamming against his chest and purging the air from his lungs in one throaty grunt.

He slumped against it, the water behind him pushing him forward against the slick surface. As it did, he used what remained of his strength to grab the semislack rope to his right. Lowering his head and puffing his cheeks out, he drew the rope back toward him. As he pulled, he slowly lifted his head, gritting his teeth, the veins in his forehead and neck standing out sharply.

He opened his eyes enough to see Faith swing up in front of him, then Kelly, the kid just barely grazing the large boulder before the current swept him downstream. The rope between Yakima and Faith jerked slack and, with the help of the river pushing behind him, Yakima was lifted up and over the top of the smaller rock. The knobby crest gouged his belly, ribs, and chest, tearing his skin, as the river pulled him brusquely over. He turned a half somersault, hitting the river on the rock's other side, going under for a moment before the river continued pulling him on downstream.

When he raised his aching head, choking on the lungful of water he'd inhaled, his ribs and gut burning and aching, he saw the large boulder dance off to his right and behind him. He slipped through the trough like a leaf caught in a millrace.

The rock had pummeled him nearly senseless for a time, and he had to struggle to keep his head above water. Several times he heard Faith call his name and saw her and Kelly swirling around him. He nodded, gritting his teeth against the pain of his raked belly and aching gut.

Suddenly, the canyon walls pulled gradually back as the river became calmer and slower. Yakima's left boot kicked a rock, then his right, and he began skidding over the tops of several as the river slowed even more as it widened and flattened out and the level dropped. Large, sprawling oaks, pecans, cottonwoods, and sycamores pushed up to both sides of the broad, gurgling stream, all thrusting their leafy branches up from a meadow carpeted in deep, green grass. Beyond, the canyon walls were little more than low, saddleback hills.

When the water dropped to three feet, Yakima got his water-logged boots beneath him, and stood, looking around. Faith knelt in the shallows to his right, Kelly just beside her, the kid scrubbing water from his face and turning his head from left to right, blinking.

Ahead, the gently rippling river flowed straight on through the trees and grassy meadow, disappearing against a backdrop of distant sierras dominated by what appeared, from at least sixty miles away, an ancient volcano painted saffron and blue by the westering Mexican sun.

"I'll be damned," Yakima said.

"Jesus, you're a mess." Faith climbed to her feet, her eyes on his midsection.

Following the young woman's gaze, he saw that his buckskin shirt was shredded, his chest and belly red with blood thinned by river water. Though it burned and ached like hell, it looked worse than it was.

Someone whistled. Yakima looked around until he spotted two figures sitting side by side under a sprawling cottonwood on the river's left shore. Lounging beside Christos Arvada, senorita Domingo lifted an arm above her head and waved. She and the pistolero had shucked out of their wet outer garments and were lounging around like a couple of Sunday afternoon picnickers, in their underwear, while their two horses grazed behind them.

As he began looking around for his own mount, a brassy whinny rose to his right. He whipped his head around. Staring at Yakima, Wolf, half-concealed by saw grass and river willows, stood in the shallows, his saddle hanging down over his ribs. His wet, black coat glistened in the sunlight.

The horse snorted and shook his head, as if reprimanding his owner for transgressions beyond the norm, then turned away haughtily and began tearing at the willow leaves.

"I'll be double-damned." Yakima turned toward Faith and Kelly. As he shucked his Arkansas toothpick from the sheath behind his neck and cut their ropes free, tossing the frayed lengths into the stream, he said, "You two all right?"

Faith ran her hand through Kelly's hair, nearly the same shade of blond as her own. "What do you think, Kel? Can I break a brother out of prison, or can I?"

Kelly draped an arm around Faith's shoulders and shook his head. "I don't know, but for a while there I was thinkin' I'd rather be breaking rock for ole Lazaro!"

"Come on," Faith said, wrapping her free

arm around Yakima's waist. "Let's get ourselves dried out" — she glanced up at Yakima — "and our wounds tended."

"You two go on. Get out of those wet clothes. I'll tend Wolf here and be back directly."

As Yakima led the horse up the low bank through the cattails, he glanced upstream, looking for Lou Brahma, the only other survivor of their Mexican jailbreak party. Seeing nothing but sun-glinting water running back toward the mountains from which they'd come, Yakima continued leading the horse through the brush.

Back in the breeze-rustled trees' deep shade, he ran his hand down Wolf's neck and scratched the mount's ears. "That wasn't so bad, now, was it, old pard?"

The horse blew, stared at him skeptically, and shook his head.

"We'll be heading home soon," he told the tired, wary stallion. "After a good night's sleep."

He didn't know how he was going to get himself, Faith, and Kelly back to Arizona with only one horse — Faith had likely lost all her money with the broncs in the landslide — but he'd worry about that later. For now, he was just glad she, Kelly, and Wolf had made it down that river alive.

When Yakima had the saddle and saddle boot off and had examined Wolf's hide thoroughly for deep bruises and wounds, finding nothing more than a couple of small scrapes and scratches, he headed back toward the river.

Under a tree near Leonora and Christos Arvada, Kelly and Faith had stripped down to their underwear and were lying supine in patches of sunlight filtering through the arching, creaking branches. Their drying hair slid around in the breeze.

Yakima stepped into the shallows and peered upstream, squinting his eyes against the west-angling sunlight winking off the river as off a snake's scales. After a time, his keen gaze picked out a dark shape lolling against a rock about fifty yards upstream, about twenty yards from Yakima's side of the river.

Brahma?

Yakima waded upstream, taking long strides against the current. The body lolled facedown, caught between two rocks in about two feet of water. Brahma's thick arms bobbed out around his bulky body, and his curly, black hair swirled around his head.

Yakima sighed. He reached down, grabbed the man's right arm, and turned him onto

443

his back. He froze, staring down at the dead man whose half-open eyes gazed past him at the sky, and a bizarre smile lifted Brahma's thin-lipped mouth corners.

Two quarter-sized holes appeared in his chest, one just beneath his right shoulder, the other through his breastbone. Watery blood seeped like black ink from the wounds.

Yakima let Brahma flop back in the shallows, and straightened, jerking his gaze around, his eyes sharp, apprehension stabbing at his spine.

"Lazaro," he muttered, turning his head this way and that, inspecting the river and then both shores.

Spying nothing but water and breeze-rustled brush and grass, Yakima made for shore and strode quickly back toward Faith and Kelly. Only Kelly lay beneath the cottonwood, flat on his back as though he'd been dropped from the ground. His chest rose and fell slowly as he breathed, sound asleep.

Leonora Domingo and Christos Arvada slept, as well, under a tree just beyond Kelly's, their clothes strewn about the grass around them, cartridge belts coiled near their heads.

Yakima grabbed his Colt from its holster,

hoping the cylinder held a few dry cartridges, and looked around. His heart sputtered as he began moving back toward the shore, not saying anything to alarm the others.

If Lazaro was out here, and if he had Faith, it might be best to make as little commotion as possible.

He stopped near the water, pricking his ears to listen as his eyes swept the ground around him. To his left, the tall grass had been freshly bent, forming a faint, silvery path downstream along the gurgling river.

Yakima followed the trail, moving slowly, hesitating as his wet boots squawked softly. He'd moved fifteen yards when he stopped and glanced at the upthrust branch of a sun-bleached deadfall.

A thin ribbon of white cotton cloth clung to the sharp branch tip, waving gently in the afternoon breeze.

Yakima plucked the cloth from the branch and held it before his face. He was no expert in the area of women's underwear, but unless he missed his guess, the cotton strip had been recently torn from a camisole.

Yakima dropped the cloth and continued moving along the faint path through the grass, which appeared to have been trampled by only one person. A few yards farther on, he stopped once more. Another faint trail branched toward the first from the stream. The two joined just ahead, where the grass was badly trampled and torn, and a larger strip of torn cloth clung to a low shrub nearly buried in the bluestem.

A figure moved in the upper periphery of Yakima's vision. He snapped his head up and squeezed the Colt's butt in his right hand.

Lazaro stepped out from behind the forked trunk of a sycamore. He held Faith in front of him, one hand wrapped around her mouth, the other holding a razor-edged stiletto in front of her throat, the point nudging the soft skin beneath her chin.

Faith gazed in horror at Yakima, eyes wide, her smooth cheeks mottled red above the man's large, brown hand. One arm strap of her camisole hung down her slender arm, revealing her right breast. Her bare feet appeared pale and heart-breakingly fragile in front of the rurale's scuffed, high-topped boots.

Lazaro himself looked like a cadaver, his face drawn and bleached, speckled with blood from several scrapes and cuts. The wolf's head at the end of his earring was gone, leaving only the dangling wire, and the large mole beside his nose was dark blue. His uniform was still dripping wet, his shoulder bloodstained. He must have only a few minutes ago waded out of the river to intercept Faith on a nature call.

Christ, how had the man survived both the landslide and the river in his condition?

Yakima stared at the knife point pressed against the underside of Faith's chin. "All right. You can turn her loose." He depressed the Colt's trigger and tossed the revolver into the brush without hesitation, then raised both hands, palms out. "You got me."

"*Sí.*" Lazaro nodded wearily, but his dark eyes bored into Yakima's. His voice was low and gravelly. He rolled his gaze toward Yakima's revolver lying in the brush, and smiled faintly, showing the tips of his large, yellow teeth. "The *gringa* must mean a lot to you, uh, *indio?*"

Yakima swallowed. Despite the hammering of his heart, he kept his voice even. "You have me. Turn her loose."

Lazaro chuckled again, a crazy light entering his eyes. "Yes, I have you. Now, *indio* . . . watch me cut the *gringa's throat!*"

"*No!*" Yakima leaped forward.

At the same time, Lazaro snapped his head up sharply and dropped the hand holding the knife. The captain's lower jaw

447

hung as though broken, and his eyes flashed wide. He staggered forward, and Faith bolted toward Yakima, who grabbed her arm and pulled her so brusquely around and behind him that she tumbled into the grass with a groan.

Lazaro took another stumbling step forward, eyes still wide as his face hung slack, his back taut as stretched wire. The man half turned, revealing Leonora Domingo standing behind him, dressed in only a thin, damp blouse — unbuttoned to reveal half of each round, brown breast — and a pair of men's underwear cut off at her muscular thighs.

The senorita had a savage expression as she stared up at Lazaro. In her right hand she held a long-bladed, obsidian-handled stiletto. Blood coated the entire blade and dripped over the senorita's hand, sagging in thick webs to the ground around her bare feet.

When Lazaro turned to face her, dropping his own stiletto in the grass, Yakima saw the ragged, bloody hole down low in the man's back, over his right kidney.

"What's the matter, Captain?" Leonora said, smiling up at the man, brown eyes slanting with glee. "Do you have a backache?"

"Leonora . . . Domingo . . . !" Stiffly, Lazaro stumbled toward her, dropped to his knees, and clawed up at her feebly with his outstretched hands as if to wrap his fingers around her throat.

Staring down at him, Leonora laughed as she fluffed her thick, damp hair with her left hand, cocking one leg. "You've been hunting my beautiful scalp for many years, haven't you, Lazaro? Unfortunately, for you . . ."

She moved forward with the grace of a black panther, sidestepping the man's flailing arms, and got around behind him. Crouching over him and holding his chin taut in one hand, she used the other to draw a line across the top of his forehead with her bloody stiletto.

Lazaro grimaced, eyes snapping even wider than before.

". . . your scalp will be adorning my saddle horn, you son of a wild javelina *whore!*"

With that last utterance, she grabbed the front of the captain's scalp and jerked back sharply.

Lazaro's jaw dropped to his chest as he flung his head back and screamed like a warlock loosed from hell. He screamed for what seemed like a long time, flopping onto his back and rolling from side to side, both hands clutching his bloody head. Meanwhile, Leonora held up the man's scalp by the coarse, loosely woven braid.

"Of course, it's not nearly as lovely as the scalps you've worn, Captain." She twirled the bloody scalp by the braid and laughed down at the howling rurale. "But I will wear yours for a trophy, just the same, as you've worn so many of ours."

Her expression soured. She spit a wad of saliva against the man's cheek. "Die slow, bastard. Take your time. *El diablo* laughs as he waits."

With that, Leonora wheeled and, swinging the long braid like a whip beside her, stomped back toward the camp, disappearing amongst the waving grass and tree shadows.

As Lazaro's screams and wails slowly died, Yakima turned to Faith. She was standing just behind him, staring down at the dying demon. Yakima led her to the slowly darkening river, and wrapped her in his arms.

She slid her arms around his waist and pressed her cheek against his chest. He could feel the dampness of her tears through his torn tunic.

Faith drew a deep breath as her body relaxed against him. "When we get back to Arizona, you're gonna have a much tougher time getting away from me than you did last time you tried."

Yakima drew his arms around her even tighter, lifted her chin, and kissed her lips. "Yeah, I reckon I will."